Leon Saunders' writing career began with the publication of *Shadow People*, a photo/essay on Sydney's 'Skid Row'. He followed this with a long career as a television scriptwriter on shows such as *Home and Away*, *Carson's Law*, *Flying Doctors*, *A Country Practice* and the top rating mini-series *Cyclone Tracy*. He has won four Australian Writers Guild 'Awgie' awards, a 'Penguin' from the Television Society of Australia and a Media Peace Award from the United Nations Association. He scripted the feature-length documentary, *With Prejudice*, on the infamous 'Hilton bombing' trial.

In 1995 he won the 'Suspended Sentence' award through the James Joyce Foundation, earning him an eight-weeks residency at Trinity College, Dublin.

Trapper, the winning entry for the 'Sentence' award, was the catalyst for his shift from script writing to the prose fiction form. *The Gaze of Dogs* is his first novel.

THE GAZE OF DOGS

LEON SAUNDERS

Valentine Press

First published in 2019 by Valentine Press

Copyright © Leon Saunders 2019

ISBN 9780994515759 (paperback)

All rights reserved. No part of this book may be reproduced or transmitted in any form or by any means, electronic or mechanical, including photocopying, recording or by any information storage and retrieval system, without prior permission in writing from the publisher. The Australian Copyright Act 1968 allows a maximum of one chapter or 10 percent of this book, whichever is the greater, to be photocopied by any educational institution for its educational purposes.

Valentine Press
P.O. Box 527,
Bellingen NSW 2454
www.valentinepress.com.au

 A catalogue record for this book is available from the National Library of Australia

Front Cover design and artwork by Jim Anderson. Back Cover photograph of Queensland gem field by Blake Taylor.

Printed in Australia, U.K. and U.S. by Lightning Source.

For Penny. TFB, at last.

Acknowledgments

I have received encouragement and help from so many people since I started this book, they would make another story. I will have to make do by mentioning a few who stand out.

Herb, Gwen, Malveena and the Lawton mob from Emerald and surrounds were the inspiration for Jess and her family. Tom, Joe, Jimmy, Hank and many others from the gemfields live on in the characters.

Bob Sessions from Penguin could see the potential of the book and was never dismissive. So too my agent in London, Pat Kavanagh. Her faith kept me going. My good mate and blood relative Michael Thomas was the agent for the agent. In Australia Sally Bird pulled out all the stops, to no avail. Not forgotten. Matt Ainsworth's edit took the text to a new level.

My dear friend Peter Carey did his best to teach me how to keep it in the moment. My partner in crime from the soaps, Chris McCourt, helped me turn a rambling narrative into a cohesive whole.

Valentine Press principals Lyn Gain and April Pressler have demonstrated their faith in *Gaze* by putting the words between covers - first brought to your attention by Jim Anderson's wonderful artwork.

The gaze of dogs who don't understand and who don't know that they may be right not to understand.

        Italo Calvino, *The Baron in the Trees*

Contents

Prologue	1
Burning Dog	5
Capricorn	15
Dead Darby's	28
Hungry Joe	41
Eureka	51
Big Bessy	64
Jess	76
King Star	90
Jack and Joe	98
Tibrogargan	111
Midnight Butcher	123
Apricot Yellow	132
Deep Creek	140
Time Please!	151
Circle H	161
Taipan	173
Sparra	183
Bombs Away	195
Beneath Stars	210
Miserable Bastards	225
Partners in Crime	240
Payback	252
Last Camp	269
Kerracan Revisited	280
Epilogue	290

Prologue

Winter 1998, northern tablelands of New South Wales. Bundarra. Never thought I'd see this place again. Park the car at the top of the road running down to the show ground. Snot-drops of drizzle on the wire-strand fence surrounding the church. Not worth an umbrella you thought, then your hair starts dripping and you wish you'd worn a hat at least. *Perfect day for a funeral,* Jack said at Joe's, twenty years ago. Pissing down for weeks then. Queensland wet season dump that filled the hole we'd dug brimful and the coffin was floating. Jesus. Did I dream that? And Jessica? Joe and Sparra and the League of Nations out on the Scrub Lead? Hegarty and his pig dogs. Tex, the midnight butcher.

Walk up the path to the Anglican Church of St Mary the Virgin.

These
Stones Were
Placed
To The Honour And Glory Of
The Holy Eternal
And Undivided Trinity
On August XX
A:D
M:DCCLXXIV

Fading ciphers sinking into the stone they were chiselled from. A century of sullen resistance. After thirty-eight years, a sense of a dying town, its dwindling faith rising on unanswered prayers through the slate roof to a dull halt against a leaden sky.

Zip on my jacket's broken. Have to get it fixed before I fly out, or buy a new one in Singapore. Should've given myself another week, only I hadn't counted on this little detour. Better get inside before I freeze to bloody death. Who is that woman? Only other person here. Should I know her? 'Relatives and friends of the late…' Well, here we are. Both of us. Let her go in ahead of me.

Thank Christ it's not graveside like Joe's. Cold back then too. Middle of Queensland, middle of summer! Bloody thing floating. Had to drill holes in it to sink it. She's looking for something in her handbag now. Older than I thought… mid 60s? Swannish neck, Rampling eyes, looker in her time. She must've organised the flowers.

Poor old Jack. If I'd known I could've paid for a schmicker box for him. Well, at least we won't be drilling holes in this one. Unbelievable when you think about it. Not the only unbelievable thing about that place. Maybe I should finish the book… yeah, pigs'll fly. Stick to the Timor piece. Don't stuff up this deadline old son, you need the money. Crazy keeping that flat empty when I only spend half the year in it. Might have to sublet.

Bloody freezing in here, surely they could've turned a heater on! No heater, no priest. Maybe they thought nobody would turn up. Ah, here he is, about bloody time. Young, likes the swing of the cassock. Clerical catwalk. Hope he gets a bigger turnout on Sundays. Posted here as a punishment, or he loves the place. Hard to imagine; like a bloody ghost town now. Keep it short mate, Jack wasn't a believer.

Wonder where they found him? Some weekend shooter it said in the paper, by chance. How long had he been lying out there alone? The blowflies, the crows… same ones used to pick the eyes out of the old man's lambs. Jesus, Jack. Poor bastard. Should go out to Sentry Box while I'm here. Scene of the crime. Might never get another chance.

Wind it up sport, you've done a good job. Pastorally appropriate. Piped music conjures lilting waterfalls, lily infested gardens. Softly to sleep. Don't be so bloody cynical for Chrissakes, he's doing the best he can. Where were *you*, if it comes to that?

Head bowed for 'quiet reflection'. Skirt rustle, startling shimmer of ankle from the pew up ahead… flat-heeled shoe from the corner of my eye, moth-like, hurrying out while the Musak pipes.

Alone in the stone cocoon of the vestibule, hunched against spray from a wind that had got up driving the rain in scuds through the open castle-keep door with its iron studs and black bolts. Fumbling with the busted zip. Can't see her anywhere. Could've offered her a lift at least. Give up on the zipper and curl my shoulders to make a dash for the rented car, clutching the jacket, dodging puddles along the red-gravel path through the Cypress pines to the deserted street.

-oo0oo-

Never dreamed when I was a kid I'd be booking a room in the Commercial. Furniture '50s spartan, chipped varnish, cracked lino, chenille bedspread. One bentwood chair. Mattress little better than prison issue. (Wonder what happened to Taipan?) The old man used to drink in the bar downstairs… Friday nights roaring. Nearly empty these days. Did Jack ever shout him a Resch's, I wonder, when they came into town together? Don't go there… water under the bridge. Both gone now…

Buggered after the drive out to Sentry Box. Shouldn't have gone. Ashes to ashes… had to see it though. Nothing to see in the end. Not even the chimney left standing. Flattened toy tin truck… tragic relic. Might frame it one day. Little keepsake. Should sleep. Pour myself a finger of bad whisky from the only bottle available in the bar. Flip a fag out of the last pack of duty-free. Light up and lie down. Stub it out a minute later. Sink into a jumbled doze of flight schedules, dead zips and deadlines, stale lonely rooms, pudgy fingers, dusty toy floating coffins…

Dead dark, drifting off… come back to a tentative knock, persistent. Feel my way round the furniture… fumble for the light switch. Get the door open. It's her.

'I'm sorry if I woke you. You weren't here earlier.' Hatless, same recycled coat. Eyes sadder close-up. Needier.

'That's okay.'

'You're Ned, aren't you?'

'That's right.'

'My name's Ailsa.' The smile strained, apologetic. *Ailsa*. She offers a hand defiantly. I accept it without speaking, which she seems to mistake for hostility. 'Jack might not have mentioned me.'

'Of course he did. Do you want to come in? I'm not...'

'I'll be leaving early tomorrow. I wanted to give you this.'

From a pocket in the coat, a slip of paper. A name I don't recognise, a town I've never heard of. A phone number.

'It's your brother,' she says. 'I thought you might like to meet him.'

Burning Dog

A lot of people died in 1978. Among them: Australia's 12th prime minister, Robert Menzies; in Rome, Aldo Moro, plus two Popes; the Who's drummer; Australia's first rock star, Johnny O'Keefe; George Moscone and Harvey Milk in San Francisco; 909 men, women and children in Jonestown, Guyana; countless numbers in the Vietnamese offensive against the Khmer Rouge in Cambodia. A few million others. Not me, though I came close.

That September I was still clinging to the idea I could sort the whole mess out if only I could find Jack. I didn't know where he was, or what he would look like after so long. He was a fuzzy photograph, a ghost from a childhood peopled with ghosts. It was all I had to go on.

I might never have seen it if I'd had a proper breakfast. Not that I ever did. I was always starved by twelve o'clock, and Johnny's Fish & Chips was just around the corner from Terry Huxtable's rented terrace in Surry Hills. I had gone there to score an ounce of grass. Terry had been selling me dope for years, so I didn't feel the need to sample it. What I'm saying is, I wasn't stoned when I saw Jack's greasy face staring at me from the newspaper wrapped around Johnny's dollar fifty lunch-time special. I was almost certain it was him, standing stiff in the doorway of some bush shack, glaring at the photographer from under the brim of a chewed-up Akubra. The hat more familiar than the face. The beard didn't help.

Either way, it stirred up a lot of freaky shit I thought I had put away forever. A week or two after I saw the photo, it got to a point I was so strung out I had to do *something*. It was so intense and personal, so inexplicable, I couldn't tell Cathie about it. I felt like I was going crazy. I didn't want her to know that. I told her I was going away for a few days to look up some old school friends.

Armidale, education hub of the New England tablelands, boasted three state and four private schools, a teacher's college and a university. And St Andrew's Hostel for Boys. Run by the Anglicans, it provided boarding accommodation for country kids whose parents couldn't afford The Armidale School or De La Salle College; plus any other misfits or outcasts around the place. An orphan from a neighbouring town, for instance.

By the time I saw the chains strung across the gates at the bottom of the driveway, the coach had pulled back onto the bitumen. Through rust-pitted bars I could see sheep grazing the uncut grass on the playing field below the warden's quarters; smashed windows in the dormitory blocks left unrepaired. Not a soul in sight. It had never occurred to me to ring and check the place still existed. It had been there from when I was five years of age; God knows how long before that.

Through the rusting bars I could see myself walking up the drive on my way home from school; pass under the shadow of the Gothic, two-storied clinker-brick pile at the top of the drive; along the corridor entrance near Dorm 3, through the Dettol fumes of the sick-bay; out onto a Y-shaped concrete path.

The day I arrived I had stood on that same path, a big wooden post to my left, brass bell swinging on top; the smell of boiled mutton wafting through a fly-screen door in the building ahead of me. To my right, a brick portal like the entrance to a dungeon.

All memory began on that day.

'You go in there, alright? They're waiting for you.' He was crouched in front of me, grime-furrowed hands gripping my shoulders, holding me together. The creases at the corners of his eyes were like soft claws; his sweet tobacco breath puffed in my face as he talked. 'You go in there now. It'll be alright. Everything's going to be alright.'

He stood up and I clung to the leg of his trousers. The dark stains. Dried blood of a hundred rabbit pelts, pegged and steaming in the sun. His hands came down to prise mine loose. 'Don't be frightened. They'll take good care of you.'

He started walking away and I followed. He turned and pointed to the arch. 'Go in there now, you hear me?' Louder, like he did to the dog. He started walking again. I watched him until he disappeared around the corner of the building. He never looked back.

The chains across the gate were padlocked. I set off to walk the rest of the way into town, the string of poplars at the first bend in the highway offering little shade from a hostile sun. I stuck my thumb out for a passing car. It buzzed off over the rise without stopping.

'Oh yes, at least five years now.' The clerk at the Church's administration office in Beardy Street was as helpful as he felt his position allowed. 'Have you come far, Mr Sheridan?' A stationary ceiling fan above his balding head had died of the heat. His knuckles seemed glued to the varnished counter-top as he inclined himself towards me, establishing authority.

'Sydney,' I said.

'Oh dear. If you'd phoned…' He peered at me over the top of wire-rimmed spectacles clamped to the bridge of a snubby nose.

'You said there was a fire.'

'In the warden's office. It was the last straw I'm afraid. We'd been running at a loss for some time…'

'*All* the records were destroyed?'

'Any that would interest you, yes.' A finger strayed to the grease-stained clipping I'd spread out on the counter. 'The gentleman you're trying to trace, he was your… legal guardian, did you say?'

'I don't know.'

'If I'm to help you at all, you see, it's important to know exactly what relationship…'

'I said I don't know.' One of his eyebrows danced. I took a breath. 'I'm sorry. I was too young to know about stuff like that.'

'What I'm trying to tell you is, if you were initially registered by your parents…'

'They were both dead…'

'Yes, of course, the accident. Then perhaps an aunt, an uncle…?'

'There aren't any. My father was an only child. So was my mother.'

'I see.' Like he didn't believe it was true; and if it was, it was unnatural. The guy was giving me the shits. I sensed it was becoming mutual.

'I remember this man,' I tapped a finger on the photo, 'taking me there. That was the last time I saw him.'

'I understand. However, unless he was your legally-appointed guardian, there would have been no details filed about your Mr…' he glanced at the clipping, 'Wilson.'

'Raithall.'

He leaned closer. 'It says this man's name is "Wilson".'

'I think he might have changed it.'

The dancing eyebrow registered amusement. 'Whatever his name is, or was, the warden was very strict on such matters.' His lips thinned in a watery smile, like 'such matters' were part of some secret I wouldn't know anything about. His index finger nudged the clipping towards my side of the counter. I clamped a hand on it.

'Did you know the warden?'

'Mr Paterson?'

'Yeah, Porky Paterson.' I thought, *That'll wipe the smile off your face.*

'Reverend Paterson died earlier this year. I knew him well.'

Bugger. 'Did he ever mention me?'

'Mr Paterson was responsible for hundreds of boys during the time he was warden of St Andrews.'

'But he must've arranged for the church to pay for my keep. You'd think he might've…'

'I'm sure I would have remembered.' He removed the glasses and squidged an eye with the tip of a pudgy finger. 'I'm afraid there's nothing more I can do to help, Mr Sheridan. Perhaps you could try the Registrar General, in Sydney.'

I snatched the clipping off the counter and held it in front of him. 'Have you ever seen anyone who might be this man?'

He was looking at me, not the photo. 'If you haven't seen him since you were five years old, what makes you so sure this is the person you're looking for?'

'I didn't say I was sure about anything.'

I had run out of bullets. I pulled the clipping back, and looked at the 'Jack' in the photo. The expression on his face said, *'Fuck off and leave me alone'*. I didn't envy the journalist who had been sent by the *Courier Mail* to track down the person who had reportedly found a big yellow sapphire on some remote gemfield in Central Queensland. He never found him. He'd had to settle for second best, this 'Trapper' Wilson, who lived on a claim near the spot where the stone was said to have been found.

'I'm sorry,' the clerk was saying. 'I understand how important this is to you, but…' he shrugged.

No you don't, I thought. I folded the clipping along its creases and returned it to my pocket. *You've got no fucking idea.* I said, 'Thanks for your time.'

I stepped outside… into the past. The soles of my sneakers baked with the heat of the same concrete footpath we tramped on Saturday mornings, on our way to the Hoyts Odeon - Ray Quinlan, me and Acko - St Andrew's boys - for a rendezvous with Roy Rogers, the Three Stooges and Kit Carson. Loaded up with empty bottles pinched from the back of Logan's cordial factory, the refunds from which would give us the price of admission. Ninepence each to get in; enough left over to share an Icy Pole.

My anger forgotten, I took in the splintered telegraph pole outside the smeared-glass window of Abood's Hardware. The same sun simmered overhead, with its promise of a cicada-croaking, bitumen-melting Northern Tablelands summer. The gum-dust smell of the place, its verandahed pubs and grey fences, its sea of red tiled rooves riding the suburban swell below the marsupial hump of Mt Duval on the horizon, came riding back on a westerly breath of nostalgia, a childhood away.

That much was familiar, the child still in me. The fabric I could touch whenever proof was needed of who I was and where I came from. Beyond that were the dead threads I had convinced myself only Jack could help me stitch together. Some part of me knew it was the incomplete child who couldn't write the Book That Had to be Written; couldn't be honest with Cathie.

I had kept her in the dark about that, and she didn't deserve it. All I could think to do was get back to Sydney and square things up with her. Hold her. Sleep with her. Jack was what I needed; Cathie was all I had.

The coach depot was out on the old Glen Innes Road, on the way to the Blue Hole where we swam in summer. If I followed Beardy Street through the centre of town, I would be there in twenty minutes.

About to cross the street near the Rural Bank, I gave way to an old Bedford loaded with bricks. It rattled past and I saw a kid in grey school shorts sauntering out of the swing doors of Richardson's department store. *You've just nicked something*, I thought. He quickened his pace till he reached the boot maker's on the corner of Rusden Street. Took a squiz over his shoulder, and broke into a trot.

I thought of the things we went to so much trouble to pinch: Presley-purple neckties, Coca Cola yo-yos, lime-green nylon socks; our biggest heist, the ripple-soled brothel-creepers Acko got them to fit him up for, then walked out still wearing while Ray and I created a diversion.

As I crossed the street, the kid was skipping round a group of Aboriginal people making their way past Tattersall's Hotel. Flashest pub in town. *They won't be going in there*, I thought, even in their Sunday best – clean checked-rayon shirts for the boys, a floral print dress for Mum. Travelling clobber. The father's elastic-sided boots had been scrubbed, the kids were barefoot. Not likely any of them owned a pair of shoes.

Ray Quinlan did; given to him by the St Andrew's authorities, as part of its project to provide a needy Aboriginal kid with an education and a chance to find a place in civilised White Australian society. All of us at St Andrew's were needy in one way or another; most of us had parents who could afford to buy us shoes. Except Ray and myself. I didn't have parents. Ray did, but they didn't have any money.

By the time I reached the opposite kerb the family had passed Tatts and the IXL café next door. Headed for the other end of town, by the looks. *They might know the Quinlans*, I thought. If I could find Ray, he might remember hearing something about Jack from somebody else – something he hadn't wanted to tell me at the time, for whatever reason. It was the slenderest of straws, but I had travelled a long way and got nowhere. It might just mean the trip to Armidale hadn't been a total waste of time. I could get a bus in the morning, so I'd be travelling during the day; arrive in Sydney when Cathie was home from work. Good plan. I turned left instead of right.

A few days after they gave Ray the shoes, he started wearing them with the back of the heel pushed down so he could slip them on and off like sandals. 'It's the abo in him,' Acko explained. 'They aren't used to wearing anything on their feet.' It seemed a fair enough explanation at the time. Later, I realised it was because they were too small for him and he hadn't wanted to complain. He knew better than to bite the hand that fed him. Acko and I gave him the ripple-soled shoes we nicked from Richardson's. They fitted perfectly.

We had latched onto Ray within days of his arrival at St Andrews. He made us laugh, he didn't suck up to the teachers, he was a brilliant rugby inside-centre. A thirteen-year-old boy couldn't ask for more in a friend. Ray could snap Acko out of his moods and rages with a single comic gesture; cut me down to size when I got smart-arsed about my superior academic abilities. (I was the brainy one of the group, destined to win a scholarship to Sydney Uni.) All this he did with unassuming flair, and we loved him. Ray, Acko and I became an inseparable unit, dedicated to having as much fun as we could, at maximum risk, crammed into the shortest possible space of time. It was like we knew it couldn't last.

When we had to elect prefects for the coming year, Ray was at the top of everybody's list. We were yet to learn from our elders that Aborigines were dirty, lazy, socially-inferior people; that Ray, Aboriginal, was unfit to hold a position of responsibility over his White Australian peers. When the new prefects' names were read out at assembly, Ray Quinlan's wasn't amongst them.

The family was crossing the street, the oldest boy lagging. I noticed the brace on his leg for the first time. Polio? Probably still lingering as late as the 70's in places like the Reserve. Ray had never talked about the place; never discussed his family.

I followed them into Butler Street. A flat-top truck with a load of milled timber was pulling out of Reddet's sawmill. Headed for the railway station a couple of blocks away, most likely. We used to cross the tracks at the end of the platform on our way home from church on Sunday. I could see a taxi up there on the rank; Daylight Express must be due. There used to be a goods train straight after it. We'd stick a penny on the rail, and wait. Poor old George VI, flat as a maggot after the diesel had rolled by.

They were a block and a half away now, the kids skittering around the back of the truck as it laboured out onto the street; Mum yelling at them in a vain attempt to keep them from getting too far ahead. Approaching the next cross street, yelling and tugging at each other, making a helluva racket, they drew level with a dark-brick bungalow with fibro gables and a crumbling tiled roof. 'Loony Len's place. We used to lob goolies on its roof, in the hope of seeing old Len yank open the front door, shake his fist and shout 'Bugger off you liddle bastards, or I'll sool the dog onta youse!'

The dog was called 'Tess'. As in 'Skitch 'em, Tess, skitch the liddle bastards!' You could hear her claws raking the lino behind her, revving herself up before he stepped aside to let her loose – a gingered-up ball of cattle-dog-bitzer gelignite, streaking down the path, teeth blazing. We cacked ourselves when she crashed into the gate at the bottom of the path, jaws snapping like she'd tear it to pieces if she had wire-cutters for teeth. She was too old and fat to jump it. It crossed my mind to warn the kids, but I wasn't sure if old Len, or Tess, were still alive.

He was alive alright. He came crunching out, fist waving at the end of his bony arm like a sock-full of knuckle-bones. 'Bugger off outa here, you liddle boong bastards, or I'll sool the dog onta youse!' Like a re-run of an old black and white newsreel. I could've cheered.

I doubted Tess, eight years down the track, was capable of sooling anybody; but that wasn't an issue. I heard, 'Skitch 'em, Tiger!', and Tiger, son of Tess, leaner, musclier, rocketed down the path, cleared the gate with inches to spare, and latched on to the seat of the oldest kid's shorts. With the brace and all, he was slower than the others.

He yelled… and in that instant I could feel his fear. A deep terror out of all proportion to the comical scene being played out ahead of me. I saw the father running, racehorse legs pumping. Len, shirt tail flapping over his sunken old arse, shuffling down the path as fast as his arthritic feet allowed. Saw the father grab hold of the dog's tail: 'Gid ouda that, ya mongrel bloody thing!' while Len, the cords in his neck stretched taut, hollered, 'You keep your friggin' boong hands orf that dog, or I'll sool the cops onta youse!'

Their voices came from somewhere distant… I was conscious only of the dog. Everything around it had dissolved, leaving the solid form of its body - its brindled coat, smoking, its snap-white teeth - picked out in relief like a fresco on the wall of some bleak Plutonian cavern. I wasn't afraid of it. I was afraid of what was happening to it - convinced that at any second it would burst into flames. My nostrils filled with a stench so acrid, it burnt…

I must've sunk to my knees, because the next thing I knew I was staring at a crack in the footpath, inches from my nose. A century had passed.

'Y'alright, mate?' It was the father, his dusty breath fanning my ear as he crouched over me.

'He's had a friggin' seizure,' I heard Len say.

I looked up, to see Tiger sloping up the path to the house. Not burning. The kid was twisted around, checking a tear in his shorts.

'What happened?' said the father. There was concern in his furrowed brow; I could feel it in the gentle weight of his hand on my shoulder.

'He's a friggin' epileptic,' Len pronounced. There was worry in his voice too. I must've looked like shit.

It wasn't the first of the dogs. I had known them for years, lying in wait during the waking hours to emerge, burning, in the heightened reality of dreams; then hurl me back to the conscious world in a sweat. Now one of them had come into the daylight. I wondered how many would follow.

I had no idea why it should have happened just then, only that it was somehow connected to what had been stirred up by the sudden appearance of Jack's face on a greasy page of newsprint. I was shit scared. Hooking up with Ray didn't matter anymore. All I wanted to do was get back to Cathie.

I got to my feet. My rescuers retreated a pace, as if wary of what I might do next. I said, 'Thanks very much. I'm okay now. Must've been something I ate.' I could feel their eyes following me as I headed for the depot.

I bought a ticket on a McCafferty's overnighter departing at 6.00, going straight down the New England highway to Sydney.

Capricorn

Half past two in the afternoon. I waited for one, two, three cars, dodging fans of water pumped from their tyres as they rounded the bend in Edgecliff Road at the bottom of Trelawney Street. It had started raining ten minutes after I decided to hoof it from the coach terminal. Now it was pissing down. A typical Sydney black-as-a-bat's-arse southerly buster.

I dashed across the street, hooding my head uselessly with a sodden jacket, and squelched through a soggy mat of fruit from the Morton Bay fig out the front of No. 276. I yanked open the gate at the top of the path, splashed down it to the porch and fumbled for the key.

Thunder rumbled. It was darkening already. I threw the brass switch inside the door and the hallway light flickered like it'd been doing for weeks, half-clearing the gloom. I hung the drenched jacket on a hook amongst a platoon of other people's coats and shook my hair out like a hosed dog; found a towel in the bathroom and came back out drying myself off. The muffled drumming of the rain swelled then dimmed, swelled and dimmed as I pummelled my hair with the towel.

I had managed to sleep on the coach. The terror of the day before had retreated, but I still needed to see Cathie. Talk to her, try to get a handle on what the fuck was happening to me. If I had expected her to be home, I would have called her name. Would have gone to the bottom of the stairs as she appeared on the landing, rubbing her forehead to emphasise the pain that had forced her to leave work and come home early. I would have explained why I had decided to come back from Armidale sooner than planned.

I would have started filling her in on all that had happened; she would have commiserated, and steered me to the kitchen. The same drumming rain that had masked my arrival would have drowned out the creak of sagging stair timbers, the furtive click of the front door latch. I would never have known.

But I didn't call out. I went straight to the kitchen. I made my own coffee, and commiserated with myself. Not easy. Right then I wasn't someone I liked. I had been deceiving the woman who loved me more than anyone I could remember. It was Cathie who had signed the lease on the flat; who owned the car we drove around in. All I did was kick in for food and rent, from money I made taxi-trucking from time to time. My end of the deal was, I was supposed to be writing this terrific book that was going to make me famous, and her proud of me. I hadn't even started it. No. I'd started it a hundred times. The least I owed her was to come clean about that.

Lightning crackled. A white flash lit up the room for a second. The clap of thunder that followed rattled a stack of food-encrusted plates piled in the sink. I poured coffee from the saucepan and sat down at the table, trying to make sense of what had happened in Armidale. I never did get to see Ray Quinlan. I had found out nothing about Jack. I'd had a major freak-out concerning a dog, the cause of which was a mystery to me. I was back where I started, no idea where I was going next.

I finished the coffee and decided to change out of my travelling clothes before Cathie got home. As I climbed the stairs I heard a sheet of roof iron flapping somewhere, banging out a back-beat to the rhythm of the driving rain. A weirdly human moan rose above the monotonous throb of the storm. A branch of the fig tree out the front lashed against a window. For a second, I imagined the sound had somehow been wrung from it as it wrestled the wind. Then came another, followed by a long, drawn out wail. I stood, as they say, rooted to the spot.

In those few seconds, a whole relationship collapsed. I didn't need to see the intertwined bodies laid out on a sheet like Exhibit A, the frantic scramble, the initial shock of guilt in Cathie's eyes swiftly turning to anger. It was over long before Steve's defensively sarcastic, 'G'day Ned. Fancy seeing you here.'

He played it pretty cool for a guy who had just been sprung rooting the arse off his best friend's woman. Having pulled the sheet up, the first thing he did was reach across to the bedside table for his fags.

Cathie got quickly out of bed to retrieve a dressing gown from the floor. Standing arms crossed to keep it from slipping off her narrow shoulders, she said accusingly, 'I thought you weren't coming home till the end of the week.'

I said, 'Sorry to spoil your fun.'

Steve took a drag on his cigarette and crumpled the rest of it in the ashtray beside the bed. 'Ned…' he began.

'Forget it,' I said. 'It's alright.'

'Alright?' Cathie flung her arms wide. The dressing gown parted like the makeshift curtains of some cheap theatrical production, revealing the ripe swell of her breasts, the satin-skinned trunk of her pale torso, the crop of woolly brush at her crotch, before she gathered it round her again. 'It's alright! Is that the best you can do?' Her voice had become shrill, her eyes misted.

'This is the best *you* can do, is it?' I jerked a thumb at Steve. 'Is this what I should be doing? Fucking your best friend?'

Her arms dropped to her side, fists clenched in knots of frustration, neglectful of the gaping gown. 'No,' she said. 'You should be fucking me.'

A part of me wanted to hold and comfort her. Another part, the smart-arse, said, 'If it was fucking you were interested in, Cathie, why didn't you put an ad in the Trading Post?'

The flat of her hand smacked across my face like a rifle shot.

Before I saw Jack's photo wrapped around a buck fifty's worth of fish and chips, I had never heard of the Anakie gemfields. Two weeks later on the Pacific Highway north of Hornsby, I had my thumb stuck out, headed for Central Queensland, which is where they are. I had no choice. I had tried to pick up the trail from Armidale, and all I got for my trouble was some deadshit with chrome arm-bracelets telling me how sorry he was he couldn't help me locate the one person in the world who might keep me from going crazy. Then came the burning dog. Then the shit with Cathie.

I had lost a place to live and the love of my life; I felt like I was losing my mind.

I hitched rides in the daylight hours, and slept on the concrete aprons of truck stops. Grease-monkeys would turn up around seven, guaranteeing an early start on the road. I had an old rucksack with a few changes of clothes in it, whatever I was eating at the time, enough dope to last three weeks if I wasn't sharing; a copy of Peter Mathieson's *Far Tortuga*, and seventy-five bucks in a Commercial Bank savings account. The other book, the one I wasn't writing, was the heaviest part of my load. I never got a chance to make my confession to Cathie.

It was a relief to be on the road again. I felt protected by a kind of environmental intimacy I had never experienced in the city. I rode in rusted-out Holdens, souped-up Valiants, pokey little Fiats. I crossed the border into Queensland at Tweed Heads, rumbled through Coolangatta and Surfers in a clapped-out Chrysler with a leaky muffler, and made it to Brisbane an hour and a half later. I stayed a couple of days in Red Hill with a friend of a friend, and set off again, letting the road and the weather and the generosity of long-haul truckies write my itinerary. I travelled one of the most beautiful stretches of highway in the country, too absorbed in misery to notice it.

Rounding a bend in the road north of Beerburrum, I was startled to see, rising sharply from the surrounding plain, a massive outcrop of rock. On its eastern escarpment the cavernous eye and stony cheek-bone of an ancient face could be clearly seen, gazing out to sea.

'Glasshouse Mountains,' said my driver, a florid-faced stock-and-station agent in rolled up shirt sleeves. 'That's Tibrogargan, up ahead. The abos reckon he's the father of all the other mountains. That's Beerwah over there.' He hunched over the wheel to peer through the windscreen at a bigger mountain in the distance. 'She's pregnant, so she's the biggest. They say one day Beerwah saw the ocean rising, so he sent his eldest son Coonowrin to help his mother, while he got the kids to higher ground. When he looked around, he saw Coonowrin had bolted, to save himself. He whacked him over the shoulder with his nulla nulla, for being a coward. That's him over there.'

Between the two bigger mountains a smaller, more sharply defined plug rose into the sky, its crown sheared off at a painful angle. 'He begged his father for forgiveness, but Tibrogargan refused to even look at him. And there the old man sits to this day, weeping out of shame for his disgraced son.' He cocked his head to spit into the slipstream. 'Anyway, that's what the abos reckon.'

As we drew nearer, rivulets of rainwater streaming down Tibrogargan's craggy cheeks glistened in the sun. I tried to imagine coming upon the place for the first time through unmapped bush; the sensation of crushing power emanating from this sorrowful, monolithic old man.

The further I pushed into the tropics, the hotter and lusher it got. People spoke in a slow, easy drawl and squinted in the glare of the sun. Perched high over the onrushing bitumen in the cabin of an interstate semi, pushing all thought of Cathie and the Book and anything to do with Sydney down where it couldn't get at me, I gazed out the open window at hillsides quilted with a giant patchwork of squat pineapple bushes, stretching for mile upon mile, hour after hour. How, I wondered, could the entire population of the world ever eat that many fucking pineapples?

Everything about Queensland was excessive. Its sticky heat, its blue blazing skies, the energy-sapping distances between towns. The overwhelming spread of its landmass, that you could only ever know from a map, put its stamp on every forest, every road, every sprawling river system. It encrusted every coastal cut and gorge with its lush rainforests and rushing rivers; every acre of its vast inland with brigalow scrub too dense to see through; or saltbush plains that bled into an ever-receding mirage on the horizon. All this it whipped to pieces in shrieking cyclones, or baked to bleached-bone death in drought.

'It's a cunt of a state,' said my driver, who was from Victoria. It was beyond him why a kid like me from a reasonably decent city like Sydney, would want to cart his arse a thousand miles into banana-bender territory! 'You're not on the run from the cops or something, are you?' I assured him I wasn't. 'Then you must be fuckin' nuts.' I assured him I was, and we both laughed.

With a hissing of airbrakes he eased the big rig to a stop at a junction on the outskirts of Rockhampton, where the Capricorn Highway went west. 'Mind how you go,' he said.

'I will.'

He threw the idling diesel into gear, as I jumped to the ground. 'Watch them banana-benders, alright? They're mad as cut snakes, the fuckin' lot of 'em.'

I watched the square back of the rig grow smaller as it headed for Cairns. I picked up my rucksack and walked out onto the road west. I got to Emerald in two lifts. From there it was only 25 miles to the Anakie sapphire mining fields, a hundred and fifty miles due west of Rockhampton, smack on the Tropic of Capricorn.

Sapphire was the smallest of the three towns servicing the gemfields. After the towering forests and lush plantations of the coast, this place was a desert. What few trees there were gave their shade grudgingly. In place of an impenetrable underbrush of ferns and creepers was a sullen expanse of stony flats and ridges supporting occasional patches of stunted brown grass.

Off to my left an abandoned corrugated iron shack skirted with foot-high grass leaned at a stubborn angle, refusing to fall over. A hundred yards or so behind it, sections of bleached-grey post-and-rail fence poked up at intervals, seeming to form part of some ancient colonial Stonehenge.

'What's left of the old racecourse,' Gordon Archibald explained, as he slowed his flat-bed truck to a stop near the bridge at Retreat Creek. He had brought me all the way from Emerald. He had lived on the gemfields most of his life, and knew its history. In the early 1900s, he told me, the population had swelled to over 500, in response to the discovery of commercial quantities of gemstone. The town had boasted two hotels, a school and a community hall. They held dances and parties and fund-raisers.

They'd be having a dry old time of it these days, I thought. Not only for want of a pub. The 'creek' was a string of muddy holes splotched along an attenuated bed of crusty sand; the twenty-foot-deep channel it had carved out for itself the only clue that its waters, at times, ran deep.

A smattering of listless sheds and houses broke up a picture of palpable monotony across the other side of the creek. At the top of a sharp rise beyond the town, a stone-shingled ridge bristling with brigalow and rosewood stumbled into a rocky gully gouged out in the Wet season which, Gordon assured me, occurred even this far inland. For now, a mist of russet dust hung motionless in the heat. The silence was oppressive.

'That's the post office over there,' said Gordon, pointing. 'The one with the verandah. Ask Beryl, she'll show you where to find Jack.' His truck turned off the unsealed road that had rattled my arse for the last twenty minutes, to follow a barely discernible track through the scrub. I slung my rucksack over my shoulder and headed for the wooden trestle bridge spanning the creek.

I climbed the steps onto the verandah of the Sapphire post office, which doubled as a general store. The worst of the heat had gone out of the day; the temperature must have plummeted to 85 Fahrenheit. I stepped through the open door, to find the heat of the baking sun replaced by a cool, cavernous gloom. The scent of old sawmills rose from creaking floorboards. Stalactite formations of canned food and foil packaging spilled down walls overlooking an L-shaped counter with a hinged flap. A refrigerated cabinet to my right struggled noisily for breath.

As my eyes acclimatised, I saw a bank of pigeon-holes containing mail, on the wall furthest from the door. A woman was sitting on a stool under the soup packets, reading a newspaper. She put it away as she rose to come towards me, bringing a smile as tough as cracked boots along for the ride. The fabric of her floral-print shift, hanging loosely from her melon-shaped frame, riffled as she moved, creating an illusion of coolness in the stifling heat.

'What can I do you for?' she asked.

'I'm looking for a bloke called Trapper Wilson.'

'Is that right?' The smile didn't budge. 'Is that something he should be happy about?'

'I'm sorry…?'

'You don't exactly look like the man from the Golden Casket lottery office. There's a lot of people come out here, looking for lots of other people. If they've travelled all that distance, it's usually about something pretty important.'

'As a matter of fact it is.'

'To him or to you?'

I thought about it. 'To me, I guess.'

She nodded, like that was the right answer and it had been sensible of me not to try and pull the wool over her eyes. She studied me thoughtfully, like she was wondering if I was worth the effort. 'Alright,' she said abruptly. 'You're not a cop, you're not a debt collector, and I'm guessing you're not a bloody newspaper reporter.' I assured her I was none of those things. 'Only we had one o'them buggers here a few weeks back. Pain in the bloody arse. Mindin' everybody's business but his own.' I grimaced in sympathy, relieved that I hadn't produced the newspaper clipping to identify Jack with.

She took me back out onto the verandah and pointed to a two-wheel dirt track running past a creaking Comet windmill standing guard at the bottom of the slope. 'Follow your nose up that road,' she instructed. 'You'll see Jack's place about half a mile up. You can't miss it, it's the one with the green ute and the water trough out the front.' I thanked her. 'A word of advice,' she added, 'don't call him "Trapper". He doesn't like it.'

I could see the green ute parked outside. Then the trough, a thing of simple beauty. The trunk of an iron-bark had been carved out with an axe along its whole length, barring a foot or so at each end. Two poddy calves knelt on spindly legs to lap from the water it held. A wire-netting fence surrounded an area of half an acre around a corrugated-iron hut. I recognised its door from the photo in the clipping.

As I got closer, the calves bolted, trailing silvery slobber. Their sudden movement brought me to a dead halt, a few paces from the end of a journey that had begun with the abandonment of all that my life had amounted to, less than a week ago. I forced myself to walk on.

As I drew closer, the crunch of my shoes on the gravel road drew a canine welcoming committee of one, hurtling, barking, out of the hut. It was a blue heeler, like Tess and Tiger, and no less determined than its southern cousins to tear a leg off me if only it could get close enough. It was the first dog I had encountered since then. I was grateful for the fence.

'Gidout of it, Digger. Git back inside, you silly bloody animal.' While my attention was focused on the dog, its owner had emerged. Digger retreated sulkily. The man I had travelled twelve hundred miles to see thrust a bearded chin in my direction. 'How're you goin' there?' It was a challenge, wrapped up in a question.

My mouth had gone dry. 'Beryl at the post office said you might be able to help me,' I began.

It wasn't the truth, and he knew it. 'Is that right.' No pretence of a question this time.

I studied him closely, looking for something to get hold of. He seemed shorter than I remembered. Older, of course. His forehead was bare, where I could picture a mat of untidy hair. The shape of his jaw was obscured by the beard.

'I'm trying to find somebody.' More honest, but I wished I had rehearsed the thing better. 'Somebody I knew a long time ago.'

'What makes you think you're going to find him way out here?'

'I saw this story in the paper.' With little alternative now but to produce the clipping, I handed it to him. He held it at arm's length, adjusting his focus.

'Ah! That bastard,' he muttered. 'Lucky he didn't get his arse kicked.' He struggled to read the text accompanying the photograph, without the aid of the glasses he clearly needed. 'I suppose you're looking for the bloke that found the big yeller.'

'No,' I said. 'The man I'm looking for's name is Jack Raithall.'

If there was any reaction, I couldn't detect it. He took a long time getting to the end of the article.

He handed it back to me. 'What did you say your name was?'

'Ned. Ned Sheridan.'

'Well, Ned, I'm sorry to tell you, but I've never heard of the bloke you're looking for.'

I said, 'I've come all the way from Sydney to find him.'

I didn't move. Neither did he. His eyes narrowed, a network of tiny creases fanning out from their corners. He said, 'Well, it's a long way to come on a wild goose chase. The least I can do is offer you a cup of tea.' He held the wire gate in the fence open. I glanced at the dog. 'Don't worry about him,' he said. 'He's harmless, as long as he's on your side.'

Smoke drifted from burning cow dung in a cut-off kerosene tin in the middle of a bare concrete floor. He saw me looking at it. 'Best thing ever invented for keeping the mozzies away,' he explained. I thought of suggesting letting a bit of light in might be a better deterrent. But I didn't.

The hut's windows were squares of galvanised iron, hinged at the top, propped open at the bottom with a stick, allowing a flow of air and somewhere for the mosquito-repelling smoke to go. A solid iron stove with a picture of a kookaburra on its enamelled door squatted in a recess opposite the entrance. A chimney yawned above it. I watched him throw a handful of tea leaves into a billy bubbling away, trying to recall if I had seen him do it before.

There was a cast iron bed in one corner. A thin mattress and a grey blanket. Hooked over a nail in the darkest corner was a wide leather strap, two feet long, with an enormous buckle. A decrepit dresser with half a dozen drawers, some makeshift shelves fashioned out of packing cases, and a bush-timber table. An impressive-looking book lay closed on the dresser, the title on its cracked spine illegible. On the blanket, beside the hat which I also recognised from the photo, lay a neatly folded copy of the Brisbane *Courier Mail*; a headline: 'VIET PUSH INTO CAMBODIA' just visible. There was a stack of past copies a foot high on the floor.

Jack handed me a steaming mug of tea, and pulled up a second upturned oil drum for me to sit on. He put his own tea on the floor at his feet while he rolled a cigarette from a packet of Capstan ready-rubbed pulled from his shirt pocket. Yellowed fingers tamped the strands and caressed the little rice paper sheet with a feminine delicacy belying the leathery masculinity of his face, with its sharp, accusative nose. The absence of the hat revealed a thinned-out smattering of greying hair, flattened to the scalp with a pomade of sweat, at odds with the thick tangle of beard below.

He wedged the cigarette between his lips, struck a match and cupped his hands to light it. I sensed him examining me, through the stream of exhaled smoke.

'So what made you think this bloke was me?'

'It says in the newspaper article, you came from the New England area of New South Wales.'

'That'd be right.'

'So did the man I'm looking for. Jack Raithall came from a place called Bundarra, near Armidale. He was a rabbit trapper.'

'Is that a fact?' He picked up his mug of tea.

'It says your nickname was "Trapper". I thought he might be you, only you've changed your name.'

'And why would I want to do a thing like that?'

'I've got no idea. All I know is, I have to find him.'

'Owe you money or something, does he?'

'He doesn't owe me anything. I thought I might owe him something.'

He leant towards me. Tea slopped over the rim of his mug. 'You look like a nice kid,' he said. 'I wish I could help you. But maybe it isn't as important as you think, to find this bloke.' He was looking right into me, his voice soft. 'Sometimes it's better just to leave things the way they are.'

I drew strength from his quietness. I said, 'It was you who took me to St Andrew's, wasn't it?'

'I've already told you, I don't know what you're talking about.' If he was telling the truth, I was making an arse of myself by pushing it. If he was lying, why? I said nothing, letting him make the running. He sat up straight again, and said, 'Even if I did, what difference would it make now?'

'That's the first thing I can remember,' I said. 'Everything before that is... buried. If I don't get to the truth, it's going to kill me.' His brows knitted. The corners of his mouth twitched in disbelief. I felt a flush of embarrassment. 'My parents didn't die in a car crash, did they?'

Down on the hearth, the dog twitched in its dreams.

'You're a kid called Ned,' said Jack, 'that's all I know. A kid with his whole life ahead of him.' He breathed out evenly. 'But I'm not the bloke you're looking for. You understand what I'm saying?' His cigarette had gone out. He sipped from his tea. 'You need money?'

'No, I've got plenty.'

'Lucky you!' It was the first time I had seen him smile. It gave me no comfort, indicating as it seemed to, his belief that the matter had been settled and he could relax. As far as I was concerned nothing was settled and I was seriously pissed off.

'What do you do for a crust?' he asked.

'I'm a writer.'

Only anger could have made me say it. Perhaps he sensed that, because he flinched, I was sure of it, and it seemed like a strange reaction from the person who was in command of the situation.

'Is that right?' he said. 'What are you writing about?'

I said, 'What difference does it make to you?'

The dog stirred. Jack's lips puckered around the cigarette. He said, 'Maybe it's something you should think about.'

Something had sucked the air out of the room. I had spent five days getting to this shithole of a place, to find some prick who refused to tell me what I wanted to know, and now the bastard was taking the piss out of me!

I said, 'I don't need your advice. I just want to know the truth.'

His eyes drifted shut for a second. He exhaled noisily, like the whole business was becoming tiresome for him. He got to his feet. The dog became alert in an instant. He said, 'I think it might be time you were moving on.' I stayed put. Neither of us moved. He said, 'I hope you find what you're looking for.'

I could've hit him. But that would've been the end of it.

Dead Darby's

I didn't *want* to hang around the Anakie gemfields. I felt if I stayed there any longer, I might dry up and blow away in a gust of wind, or disappear down an abandoned bloody mine shaft. But I wasn't going to give up that easy. I made up my mind I wasn't going to leave until I was certain there was nothing to be gained by staying – however long that took.

It was too late in the day to start looking for somewhere to spend the night. Even though the Wet was officially a long way off, boiling packs of black cloud had started grumbling in from the east as the sun wound down. I headed for the empty shack I had passed on my arrival.

From the outside it had looked quaint, worth a photo. Inside, you wouldn't waste the shot. I came through an opening from which the door had been removed. A rusted-out section of one wall had been bridged with strips of cardboard packing crate, the legacy of some bygone drifter, I supposed. A mildewed kapok mattress had been dragged in and left to rot on the bare earth floor.

The thunder was getting louder. The mercury had dropped fifteen degrees in as many minutes, with a stiff wind stirring. I checked the mattress for redbacks, and decided to risk it. I scouted around for some wood for a fire. Half an hour later the night sky jerked to jagged slashes of lightning and cracks of thunder. Rain dumped in leaden sheets, quickening the dust to dancing mud. I watched the puny campfire sizzle to a lump of wet ash, and shrank into my tin cave to wait for the first leaks. One minute I'm baking my arse off in the devil's kitchen; next thing you knew I'd be using my sleeping bag for a fucking life raft.

The rain bucketed down. I was wondering if there might be a dry spot left for me to huddle in, when I realised not a drop was coming in. For the first time in days, I felt maybe something was going my way. I rolled a joint, took a few tokes and crimped it out. I curled up in the dark in a stoned fuzz, and tried not to think about Cathie.

I couldn't help thinking about Jack. All the evidence pointed to him being the person I was looking for. He was the right age, from the right part of the country, right occupation. His face, voice, the very smell of him fitted the blurred recollection I had of those details. And yet... how could I be sure? In the face of his denial, what proof could I offer that he was lying? More importantly, why would he *want* to lie about it? Maybe I was wrong, after all. Maybe... the reasoning started getting circular.

To blot it out, I started writing the first page of the Book. Again. It was brilliant. I fell into a deep sleep to the warm beat of the rain, and lost it forever.

I came out in the morning to a world washed clean. The sky seemed bigger, the air lucent. Trees spread their protective branches over muddy puddles winking in the sun. I was dry, I was healthy, the sun was shining. A feeling of well-being crept cautiously through me. Maybe I hadn't come all this way for nothing. Even if Jack turned out to be not who I thought he was, maybe the act of searching for him would open a door to the missing bit of me. I had to put my trust in something. I set off for the bridge, on my way to the shop across the other side of the creek. The fat lady might know somewhere I could stay.

For most of the year, according to Gordon, Retreat Creek was bone-dry, and you could fossick for gemstone in its sandy bed. That's what the kids had been doing, most likely, before they got bored with it and started fooling around in a puddle left by the storm. I stopped in the middle of the bridge when I caught sight of them a couple of hundred yards away, gangly black arms and legs all over the place as they pelted each other with handfuls of soggy sand, their playful yelps and giggles riding the heat haze to where I stood. I thought of the family in Armidale I never got to talk to. The kids with no shoes. Ray Quinlan.

A Murri man and a woman came into view, eyes darting, emuing their way along a curve in the bank. Every now and then a hand would reach down, then discard. Suddenly the woman's movements quickened. Something was held at arm's length to the sun. Her partner hurried over to look.

The kids, catching the buzz of excitement from their parents, came running over to check out the stone. Fingers snatched, a hand was slapped. There were tears, voices raised loud enough for me to pick out a word: 'Home.' A crow landed on the branch of a river redgum shading the bridge.

I watched the man and woman climb out of the creek up a defile in the steep bank, the mother turning every so often to yell and beckon to the kids. The littlest, nursing his slapped hand, hung back sulkily. One of his sisters grabbed his arm and yanked, but he broke free and ran back the way he had come, plonked himself down on the sand and howled.

'Leave him!' the mother shouted. The kid bawled louder. 'He'll come when he's good'n ready, just leave him.'

The crow dropped from its branch, swept upwards and got sucked into the heat. I leaned off the rail to move on. I stopped, puzzled by a sound like the rush of wind through leaves. I looked up. The redgum was still, the air all round quiet as a breath held in fear. The sun was blazing, but I felt cold. I spun around as I heard a shout: 'Get the fuck outa there!' Not in anger. A warning, hoarse and urgent from someone unseen.

I looked upstream and saw everything was as it had been, except for the curious band of jumbuck mist spreading from bank to bank at the last visible bend of the creek. A split second later, the rush of wind swelled to a roar and a ten-foot wall of boiling water burst into view - the juggernaut offspring of the previous night's deluge over some distant catchment.

The kids' mother screamed. A movement lower down caught my eye. The little boy had stopped rubbing his eyes to jerk his head in her direction, her terror transmitted. He got to his feet and stood bewildered, not knowing what was expected of him, the whole family yelling and screaming so he couldn't hear any of them. He couldn't work out which direction the terrible roaring sound was coming from.

'RUN!'

He heard that. He scrambled to his feet and ran, howling out of fear of the unknown, the most fearful thing of all, spindly little legs struggling against the pull of soft sand tugging at the soles of his feet. His brothers and sisters scrambled back down the bank to help him, the father yelling at them to get back up as he came pounding past in giant downhill strides, arms flailing, wild-eyed.

The kid battled gamely on, Dad hurtling to meet him. There was a louder scream from the mother as the wall of water came thundering round the bend, sweeping all in its path into its roiling maw. The kid stopped for a fateful second to stare, mesmerised. He turned back to face his father, eyes wide as a boobook owl, before his legs were taken from under him and he was swallowed by the monster.

'Pauleeee!!' The father's drawn-out, agonised wail.

I had never done anything heroic; I knew heroism was expected. A show of it, at least. I raced to the end of the bridge; slipped, dug-heeled for traction, down the steep bank beside it, nettles and burrs clawing at my arms and legs as I plunged on. I grabbed at a sapling, wrenching my arm half out of its socket as I slewed to a halt somewhere near what I guessed would be the high-water mark; hoping to Christ I wasn't below it. I scrambled back up the slope seconds before the crest of the flood-wave hit the bank at my feet. My arms flew up to protect my face from a stinging spray of water and sticks and bark as it roared past. I heard the bridge groan. When I lowered my arms the dry creek-bed had been transformed into a percolating sea of muddy treacle. Big logs floated by. A kerosene tin. The snapped-off branches of trees. A short-horn steer, legs up stiff like a quadrant mast.

I scanned the surface of the water as I moved up the slope. A log rolled by, travelling fast. Timber planks bobbed alongside sheets of plastic and a 44-gallon diesel fuel drum. A couple of packing crates; a fence post trailing yards of wire-netting; a kid's ball, burnt black by fire… no, not that. It was attached to something. Looked like… an arm? It was the kid. Must've got snagged somewhere and broke free. I looked around for something to poke into the water. There was nothing. He was coming fast, a few feet out.

I scrabbled down and took hold of the sapling. The little black head zipped along, face down, spidery arms and legs trawling behind. I slipped into waist-deep water and leaned out as far as I dared, fingers of one hand gripping the thin trunk of the sapling like talons. I stretched out with the other as he rushed past; felt my hand slide along his back and leg to clamp round his ankle; the shock of his weight with the might of the flood behind it, as he jerked to a halt. I felt my grip on the sapling slip, tighten like death… then release as the bank beneath my feet collapsed and we were cast into the muddy torrent along with the trees and the fence posts and the steer. Another bit of flotsam, joined at wrist and ankle.

I can't say why I didn't let go. I knew I was going to die, yet I hung on as we rushed to what I believed would be our final resting place, miles away. My hand would remain locked round his ankle, even in death. Proof of my heroism.

The tremendous force of the flood was so utter, so absolute, I felt strangely comforted. With resistance out of the question, nothing was left but submission. I was adrift and imprisoned at the same time; slowly, relentlessly turning in a dark universe rushing through and around me. There was none of the terror of the Armidale Dog. This Death had me cradled in its arms.

My life didn't flash before my eyes. Ask me if that's what happens when you know you're going to die, and I'll tell you it's bullshit. There isn't enough time. What I experienced in that instant was an electric burst of emotion – a sensation of profound euphoria connected to a single moment in time, a specific gesture: *Cathie's fingers touching my cheek, the day we moved into 276 Edgecliff Road… standing at the window of our new bedroom overlooking the jacaranda tree with its branches spread below us like a net, ready to catch us if we fell. The touch of her fingers made everything okay in that moment…*

A ball of white heat exploded between my ears. Something, a log, a fence-post had cracked the back of my skull just as my mouth broke the surface. With death no longer inevitable, panic rushed in.

I gulped for air, sucked in a mouthful of sludge, sank again. I still had hold of the kid. Something belted me in the back and I rolled under it. The two of us came together, and our forward motion suddenly came to a halt. I felt the force of a ton of water trying to impale me on whatever it was we had snagged on. I forced myself off it and started dragging us both towards the bank where the current was weaker. My foot touched something hard. My hand grappled for clumps of grass… latched onto the branch of an overhanging tree.

I tugged the kid towards me and inched him up the bank. When half his body was out of the water, I hauled myself after him. I knelt, gagging brown bile. I got round in front of him and pulled him clear. I tried to remember stuff from lifesaving classes at school. I leant on his chest with my palms. Not too hard. You could go right through him, he was that skinny. He looked like he was asleep, his mouth open the way kids do.

I took a breath and clamped my lips round his, like little marshmallows, and exhaled. My heart leapt as I felt a puff from his nose on my cheek. Forgot. I squeezed his nostrils shut between my fingers and breathed into him again; came up and sucked air and clasped his mouth and forced it in. Again… and again…

I bent over his sleeping face, still as a night pond. I knew I had been wasting my time before I saw the crimson flower blossom on the grass behind his head. My fingers came away sticky, tingling with the memory of the soft spot in the skull it had sprung from. *You'll never own a pair of shoes*, was all I could think.

My boots squelched. The kid's dangling arms jerked to the rhythm of my step. I saw them coming towards me along the road, running. The father reached me first. He took him from me, gently, as if afraid of waking him. His eyes were a passage to his grief, begging me to do something, because there was no one else to beg.

I said, 'He's gone. I'm sorry.'

The mother arrived, wailing. She reached out to touch her little boy as the man knelt by the side of the road to lay him on the ground. The three kids stood in a half circle, arms hung dead with disbelief. The man put his arm round the woman's shoulders as she rocked back and forth, moaning, clutching her boy, wrapping the last of him back into herself.

They didn't know I was there, so I turned and walked away. I was wet, exhausted, too fucked to think about travelling. I wanted to lie down. I found my rucksack where I'd dropped it near the bridge, and headed back to the shack I'd spent the night in.

I was woken by the sound of a vehicle pulling up outside. Spikes of orange stabbed the gloom through nail holes in the western wall. I heard a car door bang shut; seconds later, someone knocking tentatively on the iron wall. A backlit shape appeared in the doorway.

'Can I come in?'

'Sure.' I sat up, trying to focus. I was still wet, and my clothes stank.

Jack moved inside, leaving a rectangle of light in his place. He said, 'I see you've booked into the Hilton.'

'I told you I was loaded.'

He squatted on the floor at the end of the mattress. 'Hear there was a bit of excitement down at the creek this morning.' All one side of me ached, the taste of muddy water was still in my mouth. I was shivering. He said, 'We'd better get you somewhere a bit warmer.'

What the fuck do you care? I thought. I said, 'I've got dry clothes. I'll be alright here.' I didn't want him doing me any favours. If he wasn't who I wanted him to be, he might still be useful as someone to blame for everything that had gone wrong.

He persisted. 'There's an empty house up behind my place.'

'I'm okay.'

He put a hand on my shoulder. I let it rest there. He said, 'I'd feel better about it if you let me take you up to old Darby's place. You won't be going anywhere for a while.'

He was right, I was in no shape to travel. But I wasn't going to let him off the hook. I said, 'What difference does it make to you?'

He said, 'If you catch pneumonia and cark it, I'll have to take you all the way into Emerald. I reckon you've got a better chance of survival at Darby's.'

At least he had a sense of humour. I said, 'This Darby… will he mind me staying there?'

'I doubt it. He died six months ago.'

Dead Darby's hut was tucked in a hollow at the base of a ridge of brigalow scrub half a mile up the track from Jack's place. Made of corrugated iron nailed to a bush-timber frame, it looked like some crusty ruin exposed after the earth had eroded around it. A flat roof sloped back towards a shallow gully running behind, dry as a bone. The run-off from the storm had sunk through its parched bed as through a sieve.

We got out of Jack's ute and came through a sapling gate in a wire-netting fence enclosing the hut and the gully. There was an awning over the front door that Jack had opened, after removing his hat. He gave Digger a jab in the guts with his toe to let him know he wasn't welcome inside.

At one end of the room we came into was an open fireplace with a pot-hook rail and a chimney of wattle-and-daub. 'Draws like a beauty,' Jack assured me. He had helped Darby build it. There was an iron bed with a hard-looking mattress.

The second room had a table with barked rosewood saplings for legs; packing-case planks for its top. For seating there were oil drums with folded sugar bags for cushions, like the ones in Jack's place. There was a cast iron stove in one corner.

'Reckon you'll be right here?' he said.

'As soon as I get some dry clothes on. Yeah.'

He looked around the room again. 'I'll leave you to it then.' He paused at the door before he went out. 'That took some guts, what you did today.' A statement of fact, rather than an offer of praise.

He was wrong. If I'd known I was going to wind up in the fucking river I would never have done it. Accidental hero, at best. I didn't contradict him. It was something for nothing. I had a sense of having passed some kind of Outback initiation test.

He went out. A few seconds later I heard the ute rattle off down the track.

There was a bucket shower beside the rainwater tank at one corner of the hut. I washed the dried mud and blood off me, and changed into dry clothes. I unpacked the rucksack for the first time in weeks. Chucked out mouldy food that had wormed its way to the bottom, and turned it inside out to air. *Far Tortuga* was in bad shape. I separated the pages that had got stuck together, and spread it out to dry. I lit a fire in the stove and cooked a packet of soup.

As the last of the day faded, I realised I had nothing to light the place with. The night was breathless, so I left the door open for a flow of air, and what moonlight there was. I swallowed the Aspros Jack had given me. I lay on my back on the mattress, trying to ignore the malignant ache crawling through every bone that mattered; positioned my head so it didn't press against the melon sized bump on the back of my skull. I stared at the dim plane of corrugated iron separating me from the universe.

I woke early after a restless sleep. I stayed on the bed till it was too uncomfortable lying down; too hot to be inside. I got up and tested my legs. Took more Aspro. I decided to go for a walk. Something to do while I was trying to work out what to do next. I went out the front gate, and followed the road in the opposite direction to Jack's place.

Around the first bend, set back from the path and surrounded by sheltering ironbarks, was a hut similar to Jack's and Darby's, only different. It had rocks on its roof. Big boulders it must have taken two men to lift. Eight of them, set around its perimeter. I was on my way past it, when an eardrum-busting whistle stopped me in my tracks as surely as if I had walked into a wall.

I turned to see a little guy in khaki shorts and matching shirt, standing in the doorway of the hut. He removed the whistle producing fingers from between his teeth, and called out. 'If it's the bus you're looking for, I'm afraid you've missed the boat.' He came towards me, and introduced himself. His name was Jimmy Ryan. Nothing over five and a half wizened feet, with a spring in his step to compensate, he had a smile that wouldn't leave you alone.

After establishing I wasn't a stranded day-tripper, he went on to explain his interest in me. 'I like to keep my thumb on the pulse,' he confided, touching a finger to the side of a nose squashed into the space above the smile. 'If there's a face of a different hue in the vicinity, I want to be of insistence if it's needed.' Jimmy had turned the mangling of plain English into an art form. I would have found his invitation to 'come in and wag the old chin a bit', hard to resist; there was the added incentive that in doing so, I might learn something about Jack.

If Jack Wilson was the gemfield's unofficial real estate agent, Jimmy Ryan was clearly its self-appointed mayor. 'I like to keep abreast of the current of affairs,' he confided, leading me to a corner of the hut where two wooden orange crates sat one on top of the other, open sides out. He drew aside a calico curtain on a string, revealing all twenty-four volumes of the 1956 edition of *Encyclopaedia Britannica*, the serried pillars of their spines guarding the wealth of knowledge that was Jimmy's to plunder. A professor of geology from Adelaide had brought them up on one of his regular visits fossicking, I learned, after Jimmy had revealed his passion for keeping abreast of world events.

Evidently feeling no need of their wisdom right then, he veiled them with the curtain and declared it time for a drink. The stubbies came cold out of a clunking old Silent Knight fridge. Before its door closed I saw that slabs of Four X beer filled two thirds of it. There were a few eggs, some sliced bread and a container of margarine.

He quizzed me about where I was from, what I was doing on the gemfields and how long I intended staying. I told him I was on an extended holiday from a job in Sydney. I had read about Sapphire and it sounded like an interesting place. I said nothing about what had happened the day before. I was eager to find out what he might be able tell me about the man I had followed to this part of the world.

Jack had been resident on the gemfields, Jimmy told me, for several years before he himself arrived. 'He owned a horse, back then. He was a ringer, you understand. A stockman.'

'Did he ever trap rabbits for a living?' I asked.

'Well, you know, it's funny you mention that. I recollect some people used to call him "Trapper", in those days. But not anymore. He cocked his head, curious. 'Forgive me asking, Ned. Were you dissociated with him in some shape or form, before you came here?'

'No,' I said, too quickly. 'I met him yesterday, but he didn't tell me much about himself. I was just interested.'

Jimmy nodded. 'Jack's a man who keeps the best of his light under a bushel. Don't misrepresent me,' he raised a finger to stave off protest, 'he's the salt of the earth! But, you know what they say: Still waters run deep in a dark horse.' I got the drift. But it didn't teach me much about Jack.

We finished our beers. Impressed by how far I had travelled to experience his part of the world, Jimmy insisted on giving me a guided tour of the area.

As we walked along a narrow path through the trees, a sweep of his hand took in everything around us. 'Big Bessy,' he pronounced; then, pointing to a low hill obscuring Darby's hut, 'That's Little Bessy over there.' I had an address.

We came to a hole in the ground straddled by a windlass fashioned out of bush timber and fencing wire, its winding drum a barked brigalow trunk cut to size. He had started out mining the hard way, Jimmy told me; with pick-and-shovel and a partner, 'Sparra', whose prime source of energy, I gathered, derived from the cold room in the Anakie pub.

I looked down the gloomy throat of the shaft while Jimmy explained how they had driven off from the bottom, following a narrow band of sapphire-bearing wash further and further, until it became too difficult to shovel it all the way back to the shaft. They drove off in the opposite direction then, until the same thing happened. A second shaft would have been the next logical step, but they had a falling out.

'Don't misrepresent me,' Jimmy said. 'Sparra's a good bloke in the long and the short of it. It's just that when the drink takes over, he loses the run of the mill. Booze and gelignite make a dangerous cocktail.'

'You use gelignite?'

'Never touch the stuff! What's the point of shifting a ton of wash in a few seconds, if you shatter all your good stone in the proceeds? But Sparra swore black and blue by it. He refused to work without it, so we parted company.'

Jimmy went it alone for a bit, but it was a killer, he said, running up and down a twenty-five-foot ladder, winching buckets of wash to the surface. It was enough to drive a man to the dog pound.

He batted at a fly, as he eyed me shrewdly. 'All the way from the Big Smoke, eh? You must be very interested in this mining caper, Ned. How it's all done, that sort of paraphernalia?'

'That's right,' I lied.

He lowered his voice and leaned in closer like he was afraid someone might overhear. 'If you were planning on sticking around for a while, we might be able to tar two cats with the same brush. D'you get my meaning?'

Incredibly, I did. He was suggesting I should go into a mining partnership with him. Yeah, right. I would have laughed out loud, but for fear of offending him.

'There's no rush,' he added, assuming I was giving the matter serious thought. 'Come and see me in a day or so, when the dust has dried.'

'I will,' I promised, and we shook hands on it.

Back at his house, I asked him about the boulders on the roof. The iron was brand new, he explained. He hadn't wanted to spoil it by putting nail holes in it. It made sense. I didn't think to ask him how he got them up there.

Under Jimmy's direction, I took a different route back to Dead Darby's, via a landmark he identified as 'Bower Bird Hill'. The track wound up a slope through scrubby timber, to a plateau where a stand of stringybarks towered over the surrounding brigalow and acacia. Desert oak casuarinas stepped across the scree into rock-strewn gullies fanning off the spur like the ribs of some giant fossil reptile.

A wallaby sprang away at my approach, bounding effortlessly over the rocky ground, thick tail thumping the ground with every leap. A flock of Silvereyes flitted through the eucalypt canopy overhead. A skink on a rotting log blinked and dropped from sight with a brittle plop. She-oaks whispered in the hot breath of mid-morning. I could feel the bush wrapping itself round me, drawing me into its roaring silence. The territory of childhood. Unremembered, yet tangible.

As I climbed higher, a foreign sound intruded. Harsh, metallic. Cresting the ridge, I saw the road to Rubyvale meandering through the scrub below. What was left of it. Beyond a narrow band of trees lining the far side of the road, the landscape was lunar. Mountains of yellow-white overburden jagged skywards like teeth ripped from the bleeding gums of scores of dozer cuts. A series of painted claim-pegs, like the masts of sunken vessels, protruded from a heaving ocean of mullock heaps stretching to a shoreline of virgin scrub in the distance.

On a claim nearest the road, a clunking metal monster, a steel cable stretched taut over a wheel at the end of its cranelike arm, scooped soil and rock by the ton into its bucket mouth, to dump on a pile of clay and basalt tailings nearby. Bulldozers rattled along the bottom of the cuts, mechanical sharks tearing at the belly of the earth.

I turned and went back down the hill.

Hungry Joe

I woke next morning feeling like shit. Delayed shock, I guess. The nearest doctor was in Emerald, thirty miles away, and I had no way of getting there. I spent the day lying around the hut, too sick to even read. I wasn't too sick to brood over Jack and whether or not he was who I wanted him to be.

By the following day I had started to improve. Jack came up to see me. He'd brought cans of food, tea, sugar, a loaf of bread. It didn't soften the anger I felt towards him; anger born, not so much out of anything he had or hadn't said, as out of the intense frustration I felt from being powerless to take control of the situation.

'Thought you could do with some tucker,' he said, handing the stuff to me in a cardboard box. There was a copy of the *Courier Mail* as well. 'I've finished with the paper. Nothing much in it anyway.' He hovered, on the verge of leaving. 'Anything else you need?'

I said, 'Yes, I'll tell you what I need. I need the truth.'

He gave me a patronising smile, as though his kindness had earned him the privilege. 'The truth?' He rolled the word over like it was some novelty I had presented him with, that he knew all about. He handed it back to me, with suggestions for improvement. 'No, you don't want the truth. I'll tell you what you want. You want to do all the things a young bloke's supposed to do. You want to get on with life.'

'You know all about that, then? Life?'

'I've got this far.'

He was right. And he was more than a match for my sarcasm.

He said, 'It's Friday tomorrow. There's usually a bit of a shindig at the pub in Anakie, if you're looking for some social life.'

I said, 'Thanks. I'll shout you a beer.' I owed him that much for feeding me and finding me somewhere to stay. Besides which, a couple of drinks might loosen his tongue.

He might have been reading my thoughts. He said, 'I won't be going in, myself. But a mate of mine'll be there. His name's Joe. He'll be happy to have a drink with you.'

Anakie's one and only street was a bitumen extension of an unsealed road running off the Capricorn Highway, five miles from Sapphire, twenty-five west of Emerald. The township was essentially a rail siding servicing the gemfields and surrounding cattle stations. A mile or so beyond it, the road petered out along a track that died of boredom in a forest of harvested safflower stalks.

The pub, a general store, a garage and three or four houses straggled unenthusiastically along one side of the street; on the other, a steel-post fence with a token strand of barb along the top separated the road from the railway line. At its eastern end, the street dog-legged to the right across the line, just past the station. A dead tennis court and the police station were over that side.

Night was closing in as the miner I had got a lift with dropped me just short of the town. A blood-red sun blipped out over the tops of the trees. I could hear singing and a muted confusion of voices. I walked up the street and the singing got louder. A bunch of kids were chasing each other in the dark. Light spilled from wide open double doors under a tin-roofed porch. I stepped up onto the verandah, and walked into the Anakie Pub.

The babble of voices swelled as I entered, rocked on a tide of beer and smoke and laughter; the rackety scrape of chairs on a bare-board floor. The men amongst the drinkers were mostly miners, I guessed, wearing the mud-caked shorts, socks and boots they had been working in an hour earlier. Some had gone to the trouble to tog up in a pair of jeans and a clean T-shirt. There were mothers and fathers and their kids, darting in from outside every so often.

On a raised dais at the far end of the room, a man in a cowboy hat played guitar and sang. Two ringers in crimped Stetsons, Friday night jeans and checked shirts, looked like they were revving up for an end-of-week blowout. The rest I assumed to be tradesmen and shopkeepers. They milled and backslapped, growing hoarse with the effort to make themselves heard above the singer and his guitar. It was a long way from the Four in Hand near Edgecliff.

As I waited to be served, I spotted a group of people at a table near the far wall. A Murri girl was singing along with the guitar player, her eyes locked on his strumming fingers, sensing the notes before they reached her. It was a song about dust and sweat and the heartache of young love, and when the melody jumped an octave, the sinews in her neck tightened, chasing it. The eyes danced. Her hair shone. She stood out from the scrum of drinkers like a fire on a hill.

I might have succeeded in pushing Cathie somewhere she couldn't hurt, but there was an empty space where she had been. This girl rushed in to fill it. I wanted to touch that cinnamon skin, that tingle-silk neck so hard it hurt.

'What'll it be love?' The barmaid was the owner of a wild mane of ginger-coloured hair and sumptuous breasts. I ordered a beer. I didn't want to look poofy drinking anything with ice in it. She flicked the cap off a stubby of Four X and took my money in a single sweep.

'Do you know a bloke called Joe?' I had to shout to be heard.

'Who doesn't?'

'He's a mate of Jack Wilson's. I'm supposed to meet him here.'

'You will.' She turned away, straining to catch the next order. 'Spit it out, Sunshine, I haven't got all bloody night.'

When I turned back, a thin-boned man with lank hair was leaning over the Murri girl's shoulder, talking to her. There was a tetchiness in her response. The man spoke again, and she shook her head. She tossed back the rest of her drink and stood up. He was still talking to her as she moved towards the door.

The singer finished his song and paused for a drink. I found standing space against the wall and sipped my beer. The stringy-haired bloke came over to lean against the wall beside me, clutching a stubby in one hand. The other dropped to the pocket of his shorts, and came out holding a cigarette lighter. It was the size of half a matchbox, chrome, the top third of its casing hinged to protect the striker and wick. He flipped the top open, then shut. I expected him to pull out a packet of fags, but all he did was flip the lighter open and shut, time and again.

He caught me looking at him. 'Zippo,' he said. 'Best lighter ever made. The Yanks used 'em all through the second World War.' He thumbed the flint roller, and a flame shot up. He flicked the cover shut again.

I said, 'Is there someone here called Joe? He's a friend of Jack Wilson's.'

'Hungry Joe?'

'Is that what they call him?'

'Yeah, he's from Hungry. He'll be here, don't worry.' He put the lighter back in his pocket and thrust a hand at me. 'Cyril,' he said. 'Cyril Perkins. You'd better call me Sparra, everybody else does.' He glanced towards the door as we shook hands. He did it again from time to time while we talked. The girl never reappeared.

'I'm Ned Sheridan,' I said. 'I was talking to a friend of yours today. Jimmy Ryan?'

'That old bastard,' he laughed. 'Whatever he told you, it was all lies.' His hand dropped, and came up again with the lighter. He flipped its top back and forth while we talked, the way some people might use worry beads.

'He said you were a good bloke,' I said.

'There you go, see? Fulla shit.' He laughed louder, and tapped his forehead. 'Few roos loose in the top paddock, old Jimmy, but he's alright. Shoulda quit while he was ahead.' He sensed my puzzlement. 'Punch drunk. They're all the same those buggers, never want to stop till the damage's been done.'

'He was a boxer?'

'Yeah. The country tents, you know. Winton, Roma, Camooweal. Nothin' they like better out there, than watch two young bucks stripped to the waist, beltin' the shit out of each other. So what brings you to this neck of the woods?'

The change of topic caught me off guard. I said, 'I'm interested in gemstones.'

I was saved the embarrassment of having to justify a reckless answer, by a tremendous racket that had broken out behind me. 'Fuck me,' Sparra exclaimed, his eyes widening. I turned, to see...

...a bay horse had stepped through the double front doors. Skittish, eyes burning with fear, it came on reluctantly, driven forward by the insistent digging at its flanks from the yowie-sized bare feet of its rider. The place erupted. Chairs scraped and crashed. A table nearest the door slewed, spilling bottles and glasses in a spray of splintered foam. There were angry shouts and curses.

The owner of the feet straightened up after crouching to clear the lintel. 'Goot eveningk effryone!' he roared. His teeth gleamed out of a fierce grin topped by a bristling moustache. A cannonball head sat on shoulders looming like ramparts above a massive barrel chest. Ducking again to avoid a swinging lightshade, he slid across the unsaddled horse's shoulder, struggling to stay aboard.

'Voo-ah there Prinzess!' he commanded, reefing hard on the bit so the animal came round, bringing its hindquarters into contact with the table nearest to Sparra and me. It teetered and crashed, sending more bottles and glasses flying. Sparra went one way, I went the other, stumbling to my knees. I looked up to see the horse looming over me, its terrified eyes rolling in their sockets. Clambering to my feet, I pressed back against the wall. The Yowie, one arm raised like a victorious general, shouted, 'I'm been come to say goot eveningk vith you, you mizzerable bustards!' just as the horse's rear hoof skidded from under it. The sudden collapse of the animal's rump caught its rider by surprise, pitching him sideways. He let out a tremulous 'Whoo-oo-oop!' as he turned a hundred and eighty degrees and landed flat on his arse on the floor.

A ruddy-faced man in a striped shirt and bow tie came racing in from the public bar.

Sparra was by my side again. 'Missingham,' he muttered. 'This'll be interesting.'

Brushing beer from my jeans, I heard the Yowie say politely, 'Goot eveningk Gerald. I'm been like one stubby, pliz. And a bugget of vater for mine friendt here.'

'If that animal isn't out of here in the next thirty seconds,' the publican rasped, 'I'll call Gillespie down and have you charged with everything in the book he can throw at you.'

The two ringers came over to talk the horse down; coaxing it out the door, flanks aquiver, eyes all whites. The Yowie lumbered to his feet, favouring a leg. He dusted his pants with his hands. 'I'm been sorry aboud this, Gerald. Is nod my fault.'

'It never is,' Missingham fumed.

'This,' the big man protested, gesturing at the horse's retreating rump, 'voss for liddle bet only.'

'Then I hope you won a lot of money, because the damage you've caused is going to cost you plenty.'

'Voss yust a fun bet! Nod for money! I been pay for everythingk. I am sorry. Voss just a little joke.'

'You're banned from these premises until you pay,' said Missingham, 'And that's no joke.'

The banned party looked shocked. 'Nod efen one liddle drink before I goingk home?'

'Not even a glass of water. Maureen!' The publican snapped his fingers. 'Mop and bucket over here.'

He started picking up broken tables and chairs. Their destroyer looked on with the wounded innocence of a chastised child, the weight of his arms dragging his shoulders down.

I said, 'Is that him? Is that Hungry Joe?'

'It ain't Winston fuckin' Churchill,' said Sparra.

'A friendt of Jack's, eh!' Yellow-stained fingers were busy rolling a cigarette from the tin of Dr Pat tobacco Joe had plucked from his shirt pocket. 'Then must be you are friendt of mine!' He wedged the fag between fleshy lips. My hand got lost in his.

He released it and apologised for not being able to buy me a drink, due to the recent ban. I staggered from a friendly slap on the shoulder as he pointed out this didn't stop me buying him one. On second thoughts, he suggested, it might be better if we bought a whole carton. We could continue our drinking at his place.

If what I had seen so far was the 'bit of a shindig' recommended by Jack, I wondered what the rest of the night might hold in store. As I fumbled for the words for a polite refusal, Joe's eyes never left mine. Sparkling, it seemed, out of a well of sadness, at the same time they issued an appeal for some kind of roguish conspiracy; to join with him in the devilment he had in store for all those foolish enough to deny him the pleasures he demanded from life. I felt privileged. It was an invitation as irresistible as Jimmy's had been, to 'wag the old chin a bit'. It could be a chance, I reasoned, to find out more about Jack.

I forked out for a slab of Four X. It took most of the cash I had, but I figured I could get to the bank in Emerald during the week, to burrow into my seventy-five-dollar stockpile. Sparra tapped me on the shoulder. 'I've got mates waiting for me to bring grog back,' he said. 'Joe'll look after you.' He winked knowingly, and was gone.

Across the other side of the street, a car rattled to life and lurched off with bleary yellow eyes.

'This vay, Ned,' said Joe. The slab tucked under his arm like a briefcase, his free hand clutching the stubby I had bought him, he led the way to a vehicle that looked bad even in the dark. One of its headlights was smashed, a mudguard missing.

'Must I parkingk on this side off street, so Gillespie nod valkingk passed it on vay to pub,' he explained. 'Or vill book me for beingk nod register.' He reefed open the rear passenger door with his free hand, and placed the slab on the seat like a baby. 'Jump in!' he ordered.

I struggled with the door on my side, and got it open. I was about to climb in, when a shrill voice drifted out of the night.

'Piss off and leave me alone!'

In the darkness down the end of the street where the bitumen ended, shapes moved like puppets in a shadow play. One of the figures, skirted, was trying to wrench her outstretched hand from the grasp of someone wearing a hat. She pulled back violently; he wouldn't let go. A second hatted figure wrapped his arms around her from behind and she screamed again. 'Get your filthy friggin' hands off me!' There was the sound of throaty male laughter as her feet came up off the ground.

'Bedder ve haffingk a liddle look,' said Joe quietly. He downed the rest of his stubby and chucked the empty over the fence. He slammed the door shut on the beer and set off, me following. As we drew closer, I caught a glimpse of the girl's face in the semi-dark. It was the Murri girl from the pub.

'Vot been goingk on here?' Joe asked politely.

The ringers who had led the horse out spun round, startled. The girl slipped from their grasp. One of them spat on the ground. 'None a your fuckin' business.'

'Is thiz you, Jess?' said Joe, angling for a better look at the girl's face.

'Joe?' she said. She sounded relieved. 'I thought you was in Clermont.'

'Vot been happeningk here?'

'These mongrels are tryin'a rape me.'

'Rape, bullshit!' the taller one snorted. 'The little bitch was settin' herself up!'

The girl laughed. 'If I was goin' to sell meself mate, it wouldn't be to a streak of gubbah shit like you.'

'Watch your mouth, slag!'

'You watch your fucking mouth, arsehole.'

Four heads turned in my direction. I wished I was one of them. Wished I was Ned Sheridan, staring in astonishment at the blow-in with the big mouth.

'Who the fuck are you?' said the ringer closest to me.

'Him been friendt of mine,' said Joe.

'Can you take me home, Joe?' the girl said.

She took a step towards him. The short ringer made a grab for her, but Joe was in between them, fast for a big man. 'Vooa, vooa, vooa!' He wagged his finger in the other man's face. 'Vy you boys nod leafingk her alone now? I'm been thingk maybe is bedder you goingk home for this time.'

'I already told you, mate, it's none a your fuckin' business! Or yours.' He glared at me.

'Pliz nod swearingk before this girl.'

'What the fuck are you talkin' about?' They both laughed. 'She's not a girl, she's a fuckin' gin!'

'Pliz.'

'Pliz,' the tall one mocked. He squinted for a closer look at Joe. His eyes widened in recognition. 'This's the cunt rode the horse into the bar! He shacks up with the boongs out at Kerracan City!'

'The Polish gin-jockey,' sneered the other one. 'Mate, I reckon you're…' The rest was choked off with a wheezing sound as Joe's banana-sized fingers tightened around his neck. It was an effortless gesture, too quick to see. He seemed obliged to apologise for his dexterity, the way a superior chess player might defer to a novice. 'You nod listeningk from me,' he explained. 'I ask you nod swearingk, bud you doan stop. Now…'

The other one drew back a fist. Ned, the horrified onlooker, was powerless to prevent his alter ego, the big-mouthed blow-in, from lunging; an arm inexpertly swinging so its bunched fingers smacked the ringer behind the ear. He staggered. I hadn't thrown a punch since primary school. I had no idea what to do next. Luckily, it wasn't an issue. The ringer, regaining his balance, was evidently more concerned for his mate. He aimed a punch at Joe instead of me. Before the blow reached its target, I saw his head shoot back. He doubled over, clutching his nose with both hands, blood seeping between the fingers.

The short one gurgled. Joe eased the grip on his neck. 'You thingk is bedder you goingk home now?'

'Alright,' he croaked. Joe let him go and they picked up their hats and climbed into the Toyota. The vehicle's engine rumbled to life. Headlights stabbed the darkness, and they were gone.

Joe flexed his shoulders and grunted. 'Nobody callingk me Polish and geddingk away vith it!'

I was shaking. Ned the big-mouthed blow-in had given the practising coward a nasty fright. But there was something else. A thrill of satisfaction, a rush of adrenaline. No doubting it, I'd got a buzz out of hitting the fucker.

The girl came over and touched my arm. 'You alright, brother?'
'Yeah! I'm fine.'
'This been friendt of Jack,' said Joe. 'Him called Ned.'
'I'm Jess. Thanks for stickin' up for me, eh.' Light from the rising moon struck off the curve of her cheek and melted in the pools of her eyes.

I shrugged, like it was nothing. She turned to Joe again. She rubbed her forehead with the tips of her fingers. I saw she was crying. 'Can you take me home?'

Joe draped an arm, like a big hairy scarf, round her shoulders. 'Ve take you home now. Nod vorryingk for anythings now. Ve take you home.'

He removed his arm from her shoulders and linked it through one of hers. He signalled to me with a nod, and I latched onto her other arm. I felt like we were acting out a part in some western I had never seen. *The Magnificent Three*. We walked her back up the street to the Falcon, the stars raining down.

Eureka

Jess lived on the Aboriginal reserve out the other side of Emerald, a round trip from Anakie of fifty miles or so. She slept on the back seat of the Falcon for most of the trip.

It was past midnight as I followed Joe, the girl, and the slab of Four X along a path between junk-strewn humpies. There were some tents, mildewed and torn. Most of the houses were made of flattened kerosene tins for walls, with rusted gal-iron roofs. Where people were still awake, yellow slivers of light leaked into the night. Around us, star-splashed silence. The yipping howl of a mongrel pup. Kerracan City.

I might have been in another country, on another planet. I kept close to Joe and the girl. We came to a house different to the others. Raised up on stumps, with fibro walls and a pitched roof, it had a water tank squatting beside it, to catch the run-off from the roof. There were no lights on. Jess went up steps to the front door. A hinge groaned as she pushed it open.

A voice came from inside. 'Who's that?'

'It's me, Jess. Joe's with me.'

We went in. There was a creak of bedsprings, the scrape and flare of a match. A lamp wick bloomed and splashed dull colour over the room and its contents: The obligatory cast iron bed with grey blanket; up the other end of the room a cupboard, a Laminex-topped table, a Kelvinator fridge with a broken handle. A man came off the bed towards us, holding the lamp with a hand cupped round the flue. He said, 'I thought you was gunna stay with Bob?'

'Had a bit of trouble,' said Jess. 'I asked Joe to bring me home.'

'What sorta trouble?' He put the lamp on the table and turned the wick down to stop it smoking.

'This is Ned,' said Jess, leaving the question unanswered.

He looked up to shake my hand. There was a shock of recognition from both of us. 'Yeah,' he said, 'we've met.' We left it at that, his son's death too big a thing for either of us to deal with at short notice.

Reg, Joe and me - the men - sat around the table with stubbies while Joe elaborated on the 'bit of trouble'. Jess had gone off to bed in the next room with her mother and her younger sister.

'Fuckin' mongrels!' said Reg, when Joe had finished. He knew who the ringers were and where they worked, and was all for going over to beat the living shit out of them right there and then.

'Bedder forgeddingk it,' Joe advised. 'Been thingk these boys vill nod be makingk same mistake for two times. Only you mide stir op bloddy coppers from Emerald if you touchingk them.'

I spoke for the first time, telling Reg about the tall ringer's bloodied nose. This seemed to give him satisfaction, and he reluctantly conceded it might be better to call it quits. He thanked us both for keeping his daughter safe and bringing her home.

Joe asked how the kids were. Reg shot a look at me, as it dawned on both of us that Joe hadn't heard about Pauly. 'They're okay,' he said.

'That's good,' said Joe. He looked from one to the other of us, seeming to sense something was up. 'How you two bustards are meedingk?' he queried. Reg stared at the floor. I was wondering if he wanted me to tell the story, when he took a deep breath, and began...

Joe sat back in his chair and listened, the shock in his face intensifying as the story unfolded. Reg recalled his boy's last cry for help; my futile rescue attempt. He took us on the ride with his wife Val and the rest of the family in their Monaro, on the journey home.

'She couldn't stop cryin',' he said. He stared at the stubby wrapped in his hands like a dark memory. 'Still can't.' Her nightmares were keeping him awake. She had started drinking. He had taken to the bed in the front room, so he could sleep.

The sadness I had seen in Joe's eyes when I first met him seemed even deeper, as though Pauly's death had dredged up some personal tragedy he had been nursing. Silence closed round us. The lamp wick, starved of kero, glowed red and smoked. Reg drained his stubby and brought more out of the fridge. We drank by the light of a candle stub.

Joe rambled on, about nothing in particular. To avoid talking about Pauly, I guessed. Reg seemed happy to sit back and listen, Joe rolling fag after fag, Reg supplying the stubbies after mine had run out. They talked about the day they all went fishing. Val and the kids were there, and a dozen or so half-brothers and sisters and their husbands and wives and aunts and uncles. Joe's fist hit the table with a whack as he recalled the struggle to bring a big yellow-belly thrashing out of the water; the kids jumping in to grab it; the women yelling as they hooked fingers under its gills to haul it onto the bank.

The yellow-belly grew in size and importance until it became a symbol of all the good times they had shared. The banquet that followed, beer kept cool in a sugar bag dangling in the water, the fish grilled in its skin on smouldering coals alongside the T-bone steaks Joe had brought from the butcher in Emerald.

I could smell the juicy smoke spiralling into a cloudless sky, hear the kids shouting, feel the heat of the sun on Pauly's skinny arms and legs as he chased a goanna up a tree. All the rowdy laughter and tears and slaps and hugs, the unfathomable anguish at his passing, were distilled in this moment. A life re-created from fragments of memory, like snapshots pulled from a kitchen drawer, crinkled and stained, redolent with the flavour of the moment in time they captured.

The air was thick with the aroma of Joe's Dr Pat. My eyes wandered about the room, picking out details in its hazy recesses... dog-eared paperbacks in a pile on the floor, a travel clock ticking, a plastic jug on the sink, a gummy broom. It occurred to me that although I had been brought up in the bush, it was the first time I had been inside a black fella's house. I thought of Ray Quinlan and all the things we had never talked about.

Joe and Reg went quiet. Pauly, finally laid to rest, hovered in the deep space of their silence. They hadn't taken him to a doctor, or bothered telling the cops. He was buried by the bank of a creek, close to where he was conceived, a red-gum sapling marking the spot.

The beer was turning sour in my guts. A dog howled, somewhere close. My nostrils filled with the smell of something alien to the moment, yet familiar. Something rotten from the past. I fought down the urge to vomit.

In the morning, Joe and Becky walked ahead of me up the dusty street to the Falcon with the busted headlight. Becky had big, sea-swell hips. Joe leaned down to wrap his arm round them and she slapped at it and pushed him away, laughing. He said something that made her laugh even harder.

I heard a voice beside me. 'Thanks for what you done, eh.' It was Jessica.

Embarrassed, I said, 'I didn't do much.' I meant it. All I'd done was throw a lousy punch, then stand back and watch Joe do the rest.

But that wasn't what she was talking about. 'Dad told me it was you who tried to save Pauly.' She smiled, and I felt sadder than at any time during the boozy wake with Joe and her Dad.

I said, 'That didn't do much good, either.'

'You did your best, eh.' She touched my arm. 'Twice! You wanna watch out, you'll be gettin' a reputation.' The smile broadened in a flash of white and a crinkle of brown eyes.

She took the hand away from my arm to shade her brow, checking out something that had caught her attention in the distance. I could feel where her fingers had been.

The battery in the Falcon had gone flat. A bunch of kids pushed us along the track until the car lurched forward and its engine grumbled. The kids circled us like laughing grasshoppers, jumping up and down on the bumper bars and dropping off one by one to chuck clods of dirt as we picked up speed. Becky came hurrying out of a house up ahead, waving Joe's jumper in one hand as we cruised up the path between the shacks. He slowed down, and she poked it through the window. 'You was gunna come and say goodbye,' she accused.

'What for I want to say goodbye? I been come back for Sadurday.'

'Make sure you bloody do.' She pulled his ear.

He leaned out and slapped her on the arse with a beefy hand and gunned the Falcon before she had a chance to retaliate. I looked round to see her watching us, hands on hips, growing smaller as we sped away. Standing behind her was Jessica. She waved. For the next two days, her reflected image would be a comforting ache in my memory.

We stopped off at the Emerald branch of the Commercial Bank, where I drew out my life's savings. All seventy-five dollars of it. We turned left just out of town, and headed for Sapphire.

The Falcon's speed created a rush of hot air through the open windows, drying the sweat on my skin. Telegraph poles loomed and flashed by, marking off the miles. Not a tree broke the monotony of the clear-felled acres stretching to the horizon on all sides. The emptiness of it all – the lack of expectation from a featureless landscape, implying freedom from any kind of commitment to the future – felt strangely comforting. Maybe Jack was right, I thought hazily, maybe the past didn't matter as much as I imagined it did.

A band of heat shimmered over the bitumen ahead. A wedge-tailed eagle flapped away from the carcass of a roo I had noticed on the way in. I recognised the big shade tree left standing in the middle of a safflower crop. We would be taking the turnoff to Anakie soon, then the unsealed section winding over the ridge into Sapphire. After the bleak alienation of Kerracan City, Dead Darby's hut had taken on an aura of familiarity. A kind of 'home' – the only one I knew right then. I realised I was looking forward to getting there.

Joe remarked that I seemed a bit quiet. I said, 'I was thinking.' He reckoned that was a dangerous occupation. I said, 'I need money. I was thinking maybe I could get a job somewhere.'

Working was nearly as dangerous as thinking, he reckoned; but if I was serious about it, I should try Sylvester Hegarty. He was always looking for labourers on his machinery plant in the Scrub Lead. He could drop me off at the claim on the way to Rubyvale. I could make my own way back to Darby's hut, on foot.

He steered the Falcon off the main road, and we followed a track snaking through a man-made wilderness created by the dozers and draglines and loaders that had converged on the area at the beginning of the recent boom. This had begun earlier in the year, he told me, with the sudden appearance on the fields of a number of gem buyers from Thailand. The war in Cambodia had cut off their regular supply of the precious stone; they were hungry for what the Australian fields could offer, to keep their cutting industry alive.

Skirting a mountain of overburden, we dodged a dozer rattling up out of a cut, and arrived at Hegarty's plant. Joe pointed to a double-storeyed, corrugated iron shed. 'Him been here,' he shouted above the racket of the machinery. 'Op the stairs.' He roared off in the Falcon, leaving me to climb the steel staircase running to the top floor.

'Oliver Hegarty – that was my grandfather.' Sylvester Hegarty's blue eyes nailed me through the letter 'H' encircled in an 'O' wrought in iron. 'They reckon he branded everything he owned, including the men who worked for him, but that's bullshit. It didn't hurt to have a reputation as a hard man back in those days, though.' He returned the branding iron to its rack on the wall beside a framed photograph of a stud Angus bull, a blue sash draped over its pedigreed back.

Half an hour had elapsed since my arrival. An air-conditioning unit jutting into one corner of the room cranked cool air across a solid desk with a tooled-leather surface. There was a swivel chair behind it, nylon carpet tiles on the floor. A Chubb security safe squatted against the far wall, beneath glass-louvred windows. A swish little corporate cubby-hole in the midst of the mining turmoil surrounding it.

'What can I do for you?' was the first question he had asked, without looking up from the papers spread in front of him. The second, after I told him I was looking for work, 'What kind of work do you do?'

I said, 'I'm a writer.'

I know why I said it this time. I disliked the guy the minute I laid eyes on the stringy yellow hair scraped across the bowling ball scalp, which was all I could see of his head as he leant over the mahogany desk, scratching out something on a sheet of paper. No matter how desperate I was for a job, I couldn't bear the thought of answering to an arrogant arsehole who didn't see the need to raise his head when you walked in the door. I said it to put him off.

He looked up from whatever it was he was doing, those pale blue eyes set in slit trenches on either side of a parrot-beak nose. 'Bullshit,' he said. I couldn't have gained his attention better if I'd told him I was a child rapist.

'What sort of stuff do you write?'

I said, 'I'm writing a novel.'

'About this place?'

'Yes.' I wasn't consciously digging a hole for myself. I was stringing him along. Because I knew he was an arsehole.

'Jesus,' he snorted. He looked at me for a long time. 'What else have you written?'

The hole was getting deeper. I said, 'Nothing published. I'm researching.'

He rocked back in his chair. 'So you want to know what makes this place tick... What did you say your name was?'

'Ned. Sheridan.'

'Well, Ned Sheridan.' He stood up, affable arrogance lending stature to a stocky frame. 'You've come to the right place. Why do I say that?' I knew he was going to tell me. 'Because *I* make this place tick.' He came around from behind the desk, hand extended. 'Sylvester Hegarty,' he said. 'So you want a bit of a history of the area, do you?'

I saw the hole. I said, 'I don't want to take up your time...'

'Of course you do. You're a writer, aren't you? Like I said, you've come to the right place.'

Between then and the thrusting of the branding iron inches from my face, he had regaled me with the 'history of the area', for which read: How the Hegarty dynasty conquered Central Queensland.

His father, he told me, had been a grazier before him, and before that, his father's father. Oliver 'Boss' Hegarty had cleared the first five hundred acres on Upson Downs with horse and man-power alone, long before tractors or bulldozers were thought of. He felled whole forests of trees; dammed the water catchments; built cattle yards and grain sheds. He fenced off the ten thousand acres he had chosen to squat on. He personally drove the first hundred head of lean cattle along the wagon track from Rockhampton, a hundred and fifty miles to the east.

The Boss's eldest son, Percy, inherited the spread and began clear-felling with dozers and drag-chains. Grain and feed crops replaced the blackbutt forests and brigalow scrub that had stood for eons. Fences ran from horizon to horizon. Tractors and harvesters roared where kangaroo and emu once roamed. When Percy died, Sylvester took over.

The family history out of the way, the branding iron returned to its rack, he clamped a hat on his head and led the way to the door. 'Let me show you around the place,' he commanded.

With a guy like Hegarty, a guy like me did as he was told, even if I thought he was an arsehole. He clamped a broad-brimmed Stetson on his head, and I followed him out the door.

The heat belted us as I clattered down the stairs behind him. He put two fingers between his teeth and whistled up the next dog in my life. A rangy mutt hauled itself out of the shade of a tractor wheel and loped over to have its ears cuffed in a display of Hegarty-style affection. When the animal yelped, he cuffed it harder for being such a bloody sook. It looked like some sort of cross-bred bloodhound, strangely out of place in that part of the world.

Thrusting his hand into a hessian sugar bag lying at the bottom of the stairs, Hegarty hauled out a fleshless shinbone from a recently slaughtered beast and chucked it on the ground. 'There you go, Boof,' he laughed. 'Wrap your guts around that.'

The dog clamped its jaws around the bone. It didn't seem to know what to do next. Its mournful eyes appealed to its master, who shook his head and laughed again. 'You're a waste of bloody space, you know that?' He picked up the sugar bag of bloodied bones.

Though my legs were longer than his, I struggled to match his stride as we headed for the processing plant. The dog tagged along behind, the bone protruding from either side of its mouth like grotesque carbuncles. 'Great dog for sniffin' out pigs, old Boofhead,' Hegarty explained. 'Bloody useless for runnin' 'em down, but I've got a pack of good piggers for that.'

We stopped beside a cut and he pointed to a bulldozer twenty feet below us. After stripping the overburden and piling it up one end, he explained, the dozer would turn and push the sapphire-bearing wash up the other. This would be loaded onto trucks and brought back to the plant for processing. He hooked a thumb at a pile of gravelly dirt a short distance away. 'This is the Scrub Lead. Richest patch on the gemfields and the best quality stone, too. No sapphire in the world matches a Scrub blue with a white cross-table.'

I risked a bit of local knowledge I'd picked up from Jimmy. 'Hasn't the best of it already been taken?'

Hegarty nodded in agreement. 'That's right, back in the twenties. Those poor buggers had to burrow through the ground like a pack of randy wombats. They only had picks and shovels. If the wash got too skinny to follow, they'd just drive off in another direction! They stowed overburden with good stone in it! If they hit a big pocket, they'd work it until it was a dirty great ballroom. They had to leave pillars chock-a-block full of stone, though, or the whole lot'd come crashing down on top of 'em!' He grimaced at the misfortune of the poor souls who were making him a wealthy man today.

A front-end loader scooped a bucketful of wash out of the pile, and dumped it into a mechanical contraption resembling a giant horizontal suction pump. A continuous lava-flow of slurry spewed from an outlet at its downhill end.

'Pulsator,' Hegarty shouted above its racket. 'Made the bastard myself.' He patted its throbbing side like a man showing off a prize stallion from his stable of thoroughbreds. I guessed it was making him more money than any racehorse would have.

We jumped the slurry channel and came to an open-sided bough shelter made from cut-off tree branches. Half a dozen women sitting along either side of a mirror-topped table were sorting buckets of 'heavy' wash - the dark brown ironstone I had seen trapped in the pulsator's baskets. Nimble fingers plucked out the blackish-looking stones, which were added to piles graded according to size. A roving supervisor kept a watchful eye on the women.

An overly tall man, his stooped posture must have been a help in his current occupation. This, Hegarty explained, consisted chiefly of keeping a sharp eye out for sly fingers slipping the odd valuable stone off the table, into a waiting pocket. At regular intervals, this man would scoop the piles of precious stone into plastic bags destined for the safe in Hegarty's office.

The women stopped talking as we drew closer. The ones with their backs to us turned to see who had arrived. One of them smiled cheekily at me. Recovered from the shock of seeing her there, I smiled back. Joe hadn't mentioned Jess was working for Hegarty.

'Alright girls,' Hegarty joked. 'Don't let me hold you up. Heads down, bums up. Grahame!' The supervisor's head jerked around. 'Star's here next week. I want everything sorted and graded before then, right?'

The supervisor nodded sullenly. Jess rolled her eyes for my benefit, and went back to work. Hegarty reached down to pick out a stone from one of the piles. Encircling it between thumb and forefinger, he aimed it at the sun and squinted. 'Not bad,' he grunted. 'Bit dark on the cross, but it'd cut five or six carats.' He passed it to me.

I took it and mimicked what he had done. I wasn't prepared for what I would see. It was as if the sun had released the stone's imprisoned heart in a burst of incandescent blue. I knew it would be cut and polished into a gem fit to grace the hand of some glossy socialite. To me, though, it would never look more beautiful than it did at that moment, in its raw state. I handed it back to Hegarty and he chucked it back on the pile. We moved on.

A row of hollowed-out logs served as kennels for Hegarty's pig dogs. Six of them, with great hairy heads and steel-trap jaws. They wallowed in the dusty hollows they had dug for themselves around the base of a red gum. One, its chain attached to a strand of fencing wire strung between the gum and another tree, scrambled to its feet as we approached. Barking throatily, it ran the length of the wire in both directions. It lunged forward as we got closer, until the chain jerked taut, lifting its feet off the ground. I got the feeling it would be happy to crack its own neck in the effort to get its teeth around mine.

It was a flesh and blood version of the Dog from Hell I'd caught a glimpse of in Armidale, yet it held nothing of that terror for me. I kept myself behind Hegarty, just the same, as the rest of the pack lumbered to its feet to an unholy chorus of barking. Hegarty raised a fist at them and they cowered. He held the sugar bag upside down, emptying its contents on the ground. The dogs fell on the bloody bones in a flurry of gnashing teeth, ripping at each other in their attempt to get the meatiest ones.

'Never give a pig dog too much to eat,' Hegarty advised. 'They lose the incentive to kill.'

'You must like dogs,' I said.

'Not really,' he replied, the irony lost on him. 'Half of 'em around here have gone feral. Had to lay down baits to keep 'em away from this lot.' He must have sensed my unease at the idea of laying a minefield of deadly baits in the open bush. He gave a crooked smile and added, 'It doesn't hurt to have a reputation as a hard man in this day and age, either.' He folded the empty sugar bag and we started walking back to the shed. 'So, looking for work, eh? And you say you're a writer.'

I was sensitive to the fact that there wouldn't have been a great demand for novelists on the gemfields. I said, 'I'll do anything. I need the money.'

He paused to shout instructions to someone walking towards the pulsator. He turned back to fix me with the blue eyes that seemed still ringed by the circle H of his branding iron. 'If you want my advice,' he said, 'stick to what you know best. Here, shove that in your kick.' I looked down. He was holding three twenty dollar notes in his hand.

'What's that for?'

'It's to buy food with. What'd you think it was, wallpaper?'

I said, 'I can't take that!'

'It'll get you started won't it? At least you won't have to worry about getting a job for a few weeks.' I didn't move. 'Jesus,' he laughed, 'I'm not going to send it to you registered post!' He stuffed the notes in the pocket of my shirt and patted me on the shoulder. 'Now go and write your bloody book.' He whistled up Boofhead, and set off again at a brisk pace.

I watched him walk away, feeling guilty for having misjudged him; and with a vague sense that I had somehow acquired a literary mentor.

Darby had left a camp oven and a billy in the fireplace. I lit a fire and cooked up a stew with meat and vegetables I'd bought at Beryl's shop courtesy of Hegarty's largesse. I boiled the billy, and drank tea out of a tin mug. I smoked half a joint and read *Far Tortuga* by firelight. I lay back on the bed, and watched flame shadows dance on the roof beams.

I still didn't have a job. I'd made no progress as far as unravelling the mystery of my past was concerned. But I was warm, and I wasn't hungry. And the presence of Hegarty's dogs hadn't triggered an Armidale-style panic attack (or whatever it was) as I half expected when I first saw them.

I recalled Boofhead with the bone poking out either side of his great slobbery mouth and I laughed. Not at the dog so much as the whole situation. I'd been in the place for less than a week. I'd almost drowned in a flash flood. I had befriended two men - a man-mountain who rode horses into crowded rooms for fun, and a punch-drunk ex-boxer training to be a genius. I had acquired a literary patron for a book I wasn't writing. You had to laugh.

I thought about Cathie. I wondered what she was doing. I wondered what *I* was going to do next. One thing I sure as hell *wasn't* going to do, was go back to Sydney with my tail between my legs.

If I was going to stay on the gemfields, though, I would need work. I might have gained a patron, but patrons throughout history have been notoriously fickle. I wasn't going to put too many eggs in Sylvester Hegarty's basket. Then I remembered I had already been offered a job.

Big Bessy

'Well if that doesn't take your cake and eat it too!'

Jimmy was delighted that I had decided to become a 'permanent fixture' on the gemfields, and join forces with him to mine Big Bessy.

'We'll start tomorrow!' he pronounced. He produced a couple of stubbies from the Silent Knight to celebrate our new venture.

We got an early start the next morning, to beat the heat. At the top of the shaft Jimmy put the tools and a carbide lamp in a windlass bucket and wound it to the bottom. 'I'll go first,' he said, standing at the top of the ladder. 'Not that I want to pull rank and file on you. Wait till I call out, alright?' Peering over the edge of the hole a few moments later, I could just make out his face looking up at me from the bottom of the shaft. 'Down you come,' he yelled.

Jimmy had taken the tools out of the bucket by the time I got to the bottom. He struck a match, and a brilliant blue flame shot from the nozzle of the carbide lamp with a gentle hiss, blasting a new world from the darkness. A loungeroom-sized cavern spread out from the base of the shaft, the dips and humps of its floor mapping the course of Jimmy's pick where it had followed the 'wash' he was chasing. A band of rocky gravel, this varied in width from a few inches to three or four feet, skirting the wall at floor level. Half way round the wall, the knobbled snout of a 'billy' boulder protruded.

I was impressed by how much work he must have done to hollow out the space we were standing in. I said, 'You've been busy, Jimmy.'

'This is only a little fella,' he laughed. 'The old-timers dug out ballrooms much bigger than this, oh my word yes. It would've taken half a dozen toms like that to hold the roof up in some of them!'

He raised the lamp, so its light fell on a barked post in the centre of the ballroom, capped with a flat board about eight inches square. It occurred to me that this spindly pole was the only thing supporting the unimaginable mass of earth and rock above us. Evidently sensing my unease, Jimmy assured me there was no danger of collapse. The tom had been cut from a young rosewood, noted for its strength. In any case, the curve of the roof formed an arch, which probably would have held on its own. Cave-ins were only a concern in 'slippery-back' areas, he explained. I didn't want to think about 'slippery-back', so I didn't ask.

The roof was just high enough for Jimmy to stand. I had to stoop. He handed me the shovel and I stumbled on the uneven floor as I followed him to the mouth of the drive, gaping blackly where the band of gravel was at its thickest, right beside the billy. This was the wash he had been following when Sparra called it quits.

'I don't want to misrepresent you,' Jimmy had confessed, in the process of cementing our partnership. 'There's not much colour showing down there at the moment. But you've got to take the good with the bad in the mining game. Mother Nature can be a cruel task-master. Then,' he added, with his trademark grin, 'just when you think the jig is up, it starts raining sunbeams!' I told him I was looking forward to the sunbeams. We shook hands on it, and a clink of stubbies had sealed the deal.

The drive was barely wide enough for one person. Its ceiling was lower than the ballroom, and I bumped my head on the dips as the two of us scuttled along it like a pair of the 'randy wombats' of the 1920s that Hegarty had been so disparaging about.

'This,' Jimmy explained over his shoulder, 'was the bed of your river in architectural times.' The billy boulders were a good sign, he told me, their presence an indication that gemstones were nearby; the theory being that because they were heavy, like sapphire, they were likely to have gravitated to the same resting place when the volcanic stream surged towards its primeval ocean, long before life began. The bigger the billies, Jimmy reckoned, the better.

About forty feet in from the shaft, we came to a halt at the face of the drive. He positioned the lamp and, kneeling down, set to work with the pick, driving its point into the wash with short, deft strokes that brought gravel and rocks tumbling to the ground at his knees. He attacked the face with relentless precision, an attitude that would have stood him in good stead in the boxing ring, it occurred to me. Every now and again he paused to let me take the loosened wash away.

The shovel baulked at every attempt to drive its cutting edge into the pile, jarring up the handle whenever it hit rock. Dirt rained down when my head hit the roof. Sweat running down my arms onto the handle turned it to slippery mud, making it impossible to hold. My shoulders barked the walls as I turned in the confined space to throw the wash as far as possible back up the drive. I came to hate mining in a very short space of time.

Jimmy watched, waiting patiently while I struggled to shift the dirt he had knocked down with ease. 'You'll get the jest of it,' he promised. I doubted it. Either way.

After an hour or so, a quarter of a yard of wash had accumulated twenty feet along the drive behind me. Jimmy announced it was time to get it to the top. That meant shovelling the whole lot again, to the bottom of the shaft. He offered to spell me on the shovel, and I gladly accepted.

I stood back and watched as he worked it this way and that, sliding it effortlessly into cracks and crannies that were felt rather than seen. It came away piled high every time, to be flung with a casual flick of his bony wrist to a spot several feet beyond my own meagre pile. Jimmy could make a shovel sing.

I had another go, but he could see I was flagging. 'Time for smoko,' he said tactfully, and we went back up the ladder.

I helped him build a fire in a circle of rocks. He filled a billy can with water, hooked it under a tripod of steel rods, and we sat in the shade of a big coolabah to watch it boil. The flames, paled by the sun, licked the blackened sides of the billy. A flock of rainbow lorikeets chattered rowdily overhead in a dazzle of blue, red and green, shifting and shimmering in leaves rustled by a warm breeze, swirling in a psychedelic soup of colour and sun. I leant against the trunk of the tree and dozed.

I had a dream involving Cathie and a loaded gun. I was back in the city, it was a hot day and the traffic was snarled coming off the

Bridge. We had met for a coffee near her ad agency's office. We had an argument, and she got so pissed off she pulled a gun on me. She said she was going to put me out of my misery. 'Let's go, Ned!' she said with a smirk. Her finger tightened on the trigger.

'Let's go, Ned!' It seemed like only seconds had passed. Jimmy's grin hovered as he shook me by the shoulder. 'We'd better get cracking,' he said, 'before the heat of the day gets the worst of us.'

The shade had moved. I wiped sweat from my face with a dirt-caked arm and clambered to my feet. It pissed me off to think Cathie could get into my head so easily, from so far away.

Jimmy showed me how to guide the rope across the windlass drum with one hand, while winding with the other. 'You've gotta watch this fella,' he warned, nodding at the handle, a Z-shaped section of metal rod protruding from the end of the drum. 'Never let it go with a full bucket on. It'll whip around so fast you won't know what hit you. A chap on Goanna Flat lost his eye like that last year.'

The bucket of wash came up, and he reached over to haul it across and unhook it. He emptied its contents onto a sloping chicken-wire screen that got rid of the sand and bigger rocks. He hooked the empty bucket on and let it drop, the windlass handle spinning crazily. The bucket hit the bottom and Jimmy sprang to the top of the ladder.

'Wait till I give the signal,' he instructed, as he followed the bucket down. A minute later his voice floated up, 'Righto Ned, anchors away!' and I started winding.

I hauled the fully-laden bucket over when it reached the top, replaced it with an empty one, and let it drop.

After an hour or so Jimmy called, 'Last one!' He followed the bucket up after I had pulled it clear, and we moved over to the willoughby. This was an eight-foot-long jig-pole contraption, pivoted in a forked post, hanging over a cut-off galvanised tank full of muddy water. A boxed-in stainless steel sieve dangled from the end of the pole.

Jimmy shovelled the screened wash into the sieve, released the pole from its cleat, and began bouncing it up and down just below the surface of the water. The lighter clay and basalt rose to the top. He locked the pole off, leaving the basket swinging over the water. Raking the dross off with a tin scraper, he flung it on a pile of tailings to his right, until a layer of brown ironstone was left covering the bottom of the sieve. He repeated the process until the ironstone was several inches deep. Any sapphires, heavier than the ironstone, would be lying at the bottom.

I leant forward with Jimmy as his fingers worked, carefully pushing the top layers aside, until the sieve began to show through. I saw a flash of blue. 'There! There's one!'

It was about the size of a pea. Jimmy checked it against the sun, the way Hegarty had done. 'Full of silk,' he pronounced, before depositing it in the Vegemite jar we had brought for the purpose. 'But it'll do for the terrorists. What you want to see,' he explained as he resumed searching, 'is an oily-black-looking stone. Like that!' He picked out another, smaller one and checked it out. He passed it to me to do likewise. It was deep blue, pure crystal.

'What's it worth, d'you reckon?' I was itching to get back down and start hauling out more riches.

He shrugged. 'Bit on the darkish side. Maybe two or three weights... not a good shape. You'd have to cut it on the cross to get a decent sized gem out of it. Still, it'd have to be worth...' He paused to make a mental calculation, 'Twenty dollars. Maybe twenty-five.'

Twenty-five bucks, split two ways, for half a morning's back-breaking work. Delivering pizzas was starting to look like a fulfilling occupation. But Jimmy's eyes were sparkling. 'Ned,' he said, 'I reckon you're my good luck omen.'

We washed the rest of the pile. A few more chips of crystal, some parti-colours and a dog's-tooth that wouldn't cut anything of size, joined the stones in the jar. Then we went below to do it all over again.

The second wash-up yielded even less than the first. By my reckoning we had been working our guts out all morning for two bucks an hour. My muscles ached, my hair was full of gravel, I was bruised and scratched in a dozen places, my hands were covered in blisters. By the time Jimmy called a halt, I was already working on how to break it to him that I had decided to call it quits.

It was mid-afternoon by the time we got back to his hut. He produced stubbies from the fridge. The first one didn't touch the sides. He went to fetch more, and my eyes lit on a pile of books I hadn't noticed before, stacked beside the curtained crates containing the *Britannica*. They were all the same size, staple-bound, suitable for folding in half and slipping in the hip pocket.

'Marshall Grover,' Jimmy replied in answer to my query, 'and Carter Brown. By jingies, they can spin a good yarn, those fellas!' He had always been a big reader, he told me, though he had focused on westerns and detective fiction prior to the arrival of the *Britannica*. Over several more stubbies we fell to discussing world matters. He trotted out specific volumes to reinforce points made, or to follow-up half-remembered facts.

He burrowed into them like a hungry bandicoot foraging for the succulent roots of information he had been denied until the miraculous appearance of this cornucopia of knowledge. He marvelled, in particular, at what he had learned about the origins of the universe.

The Four X worked its magic on aching muscle and strained sinew. I was happy to drift on the cadences of Jimmy's enthusiastic chatter, as he expounded his own special theory on the formation of gemstones and its relation to the presence of sapphires somewhere very close to where we were digging. I was glad of his company; grateful now, despite earlier misgivings, that he had seen fit to take me on as a mining partner. I decided I would stick it out for a few weeks and see what happened. There was nothing better on offer.

That night I scribbled a note to my old dope dealer, Terry Huxtable, asking him to go around to Cathie's and pick up any mail that had come for me. I gave him a forwarding address to the post office in Sapphire; and strict instructions not to tell Cathie where I was.

We were back in Jimmy's hut at the end of my third day's mining. Jimmy was about to knock the scabs off the second round of stubbies, when there was a knock at the door. A voice called, 'Are you there, Jimmy? I want to talk to you.' It was Hegarty.

Jimmy let him in. He frowned when he saw me. 'Sylvester, this is…' Jimmy began, before Hegarty waved him to silence.

'Save your breath, Jimmy,' he said affably. 'We've met.' He got down to business without bothering to elaborate. 'Can we talk in private? I've got an offer you might be interested in.'

The smile on Jimmy's face set into an amiable rictus that I would come to recognise as a danger signal. 'Anything you've got to say, you can say in front of Ned,' he said evenly. 'We're partners now, if you get the meaning of my drift.'

'Is that right?' said Hegarty, shifting his gaze between the two of us. It settled on me. 'Haven't you got a little project you're supposed to be working on?'

'Research,' I said, worried he might be about to request the return of his investment in my literary future. 'I need firsthand experience of mining if I'm going to write about it.'

'Dead right,' he said. 'I can see you're a dedicated writer.' I couldn't be sure if he was taking the piss or not. He turned his attention to his host. 'How long've you been on the gemfields, Jimmy?'

'Ooh, about eleven years I'd say, hit or miss.'

'You must be getting on. What are you, sixty-five, pushing seventy?'

'Somewhere along the order of that.'

'Can't be getting any easier, swinging a pick and shovel.'

'I've got news for you!' I laughed.

He didn't hear me. He was leaning towards Jimmy, his profile limned in the red of the dying sun, leaking the last of itself through a gap in a sheet of iron.

He said, 'I'll give you twelve thousand bucks for your claim.'

'Crikey!' Jimmy laughed hesitantly, like he was waiting for the punchline.

Hegarty was happy to supply it. He extracted a bundle from his shirt pocket and dumped it on the ground. A clutch of twenty-dollar bills sprang open at Jimmy's feet. 'There's a down-payment,' he said.

Jimmy stared at the money. He picked it up and fingered the notes. I imagined he could hear the hoarse shouts of the fight fans. Smell the sweat, feel the pain, wondering how many times he would've had to stagger to his feet and box on, to make that much money; how many buckets of wash he would have to dig. Hegarty waited, eyes never leaving his quarry.

Jimmy handed him back the money. 'Not interested,' he said.

'Alright, make it thirteen. I might've known you'd drive a hard bargain.'

'The price is beyond the point.'

'Fifteen then,' Hegarty laughed. 'We're talking about a lump of dirt three-hundred-foot square, Jimmy. Think what you could do with fifteen thousand dollars!'

'It's a lot of money, no doubting the question! But it's the principle I have to consider here.'

'What principle would that be?'

Jimmy, in contrast to the frustration I sensed mounting in Hegarty, had become increasingly affable. 'Me and Ned are partners in this adventure, see. If I sell the claim, where are we going to dig?'

'You won't have to dig, for Christ's sake. Ned, explain it to him, will you?'

I felt I should make an effort on behalf of my patron. Besides which, I could see his point. Fifteen thousand bucks was a shitload of money. It could've set Jimmy up for the rest of his life. 'I think what he's saying, Jimmy, is fifteen thousand dollars represents a lot of time spent down a hole in the ground.'

'Exactly! That's exactly what I'm saying. So what d'you reckon?'

Jimmy threw it back to me. 'You're my partner, Ned. Was it fair dinkum when we shook hands on the mining caper? Or is this a horse of a different colour?' His grin shone in the half-dark, inviting me to confirm something more than the mere fact that we were partners. He was a lonely, damaged old man, washed up in the last refuge of his life. It was trust he was after.

Hegarty's gaze too, was full on me, promising retribution if I got in the way of what he wanted. He had invested trust in me. It made sense not to make an enemy of him. But nothing was making sense lately.

I said, 'I reckon it was fair dinkum, Jimmy.'

Hegarty picked the money up and tucked it in his pocket with a shrug. 'There's plenty of other claims.'

Jimmy was pleased it had all been resolved. 'I'm glad you're not defended,' he said. 'Could I interest you in a stubby, Sylvester?'

Hegarty looked thoughtful as he steered his blood-red Range Rover through the dusk to Darby's hut. The recently-acquired vehicle, I learned, was his current pride and joy; a visible testament to the wealth he was amassing. Everything about it gleamed. The upholstery squeaked, it smelt like vanilla beans. Just sitting in the passenger seat gave you a sense of the seductive potency of Big Money.

He had insisted on dropping me home, and I hadn't argued. It was a gracious gesture, given that he had failed in his attempt to buy Jimmy's claim.

'So you and Jimmy are partners, eh?' He swung the wheel to guide the vehicle around a bog-rut in the track. 'How much d'you reckon you've pulled out of that hole, so far?'

'We've only just started,' I said. 'It's looking promising though. Jimmy reckons we're close to a big pocket.'

'Is that right? No wonder he doesn't want to sell!' I couldn't see his face properly in the half-light, but I could hear the smirk in his voice. 'You'll be laughing when you hit it. Couple of hundred bucks in his kick, Jimmy'll hit the piss and you'll have the bloody thing all to yourself!' He glanced sideways at me, and I saw the smirk. 'Blokes like Jimmy think this place is a big bank. They go down a hole every now and again and make a withdrawal. Spend it all on piss, and they've gotta go down again. Where's it going to get 'em in the end though, eh? Where will it get you, more to the point?'

'It's research,' I reminded him.

'Of course, research, I was forgetting. For a minute there I was confusing you with those daydreamers that buy their little tubes of sapphire chips off Jimmy. The ones that scratch around old mullock heaps with a rented sieve. They all think they're going to win the lottery. But you're different to that, aren't you?' *This is where my patron gets fickle*, I thought.

We had arrived at the gate to Dead Darby's. Hegarty slowed the Range Rover to a halt. He turned to me and said, 'You are different. You don't realise it yet, but you will when you write that book.'

The book thing I didn't get. A degree of stability had crept into my life over the past few days; I had no idea why the guy had taken a shine to me, but I didn't want it to go any further. I hadn't come clean with Cathie, but I had a chance to do it now with him. It wouldn't help her, but it might help me.

I said, 'Sylvester, I've got to tell you something. I'm not really a writer.'

'Of course you aren't. But you will be.'

'I really appreciate you giving me money to do it. Nobody's ever done that before. And I'll give it back, as soon as I can.'

'No you won't. You'll write the book, that's what you'll do. What else are you going to do with your life?'

'I don't know.'

His head jerked back. He frowned. I recalled the way he had looked at me when we first met. I guessed he was expecting something from me, because he was used to getting things out of people. With me he wasn't sure what was on offer. He said, 'Well you'd better find out quick smart son, or it'll run through your fingers like a handful of fuckin' sand.'

It was a piece of advice I would never forget. I owed him some sort of explanation. I said, 'This probably won't make any sense to you, but before I do anything, I've got to find out where I came from. That's why I'm here.'

The frown deepened. 'It doesn't matter where you came from, for Christ's sake. Where you are, and where you're going is all that matters in this life. Take my word for it.'

I knew he would never understand. I said, 'Anyway, I've got to make a living. That's why I teamed up with Jimmy.'

He laughed. 'A living? There's a dirt floor in that house of his! If you could call it a house. He lives on bread and bully-beef. He can't afford a packet of nails to bang his roof down!' He shifted position in his seat, signalling a change of tack in his argument. 'Look, I've got nothing against Jimmy, he's a harmless enough poor bastard. But the question you've got to ask yourself is: is that how you want to live *your* life?'

I shot a look at Darby's hut, waiting dark and silent. I said, 'I guess it'll do till something better comes along.' I opened the door of the Range Rover and stepped out.

'It just did,' said Hegarty. He leaned across the seat to prevent the door from closing. 'How would you like to make fifteen hundred bucks without lifting a finger, let alone a shovel?'

'You're kidding.'

'I'll be honest with you, I need that claim of Jimmy's. And you know and I know, he could do with fifteen grand. That's more money than he's ever seen in his life.'

'But he doesn't want to sell.'

'Not to me he doesn't. Look, I know what's eating him. A few months back, I bought a claim off a friend of his, and they got it in their heads I cheated him somehow. I didn't, but I know that's what they think.'

I said, 'I don't see what any of this has to do with me.'

'You and Jimmy get along alright, I can see that. He'll listen to you. All you've got to do is persuade him to sell me that claim, and you're on a ten percent commission.'

I said, 'I don't know if I'm morally in a position to do that.'

His teeth flashed greyly in the moonlight. 'You can buy a lot of morals with fifteen hundred bucks.' He peeled two twenties off the bundle of notes Jimmy had refused, and shoved them at me. 'Here's a down-payment.' I looked at the notes. 'Take it,' he insisted. 'You're a struggling writer, aren't you?' I took the money. 'Only trouble with morals is you can't eat 'em.'

He yanked the door shut, and drove off.

Jess

Things had turned out better than I could've expected over the past few days. I had a rent-free home, a job, and someone who occasionally threw money at me. But I was still no closer to finding out what I needed to know, than when I first stuck my thumb out on the highway north of Sydney.

There were no bad dreams, no more burning dogs; just a persistent voice that kept whispering *Who are you? Where do you come from?* And a deeper-down sense that if I didn't uncover that missing bit of me, my life amounted to nothing; had no origin, nothing to anchor it to. It was a story without a beginning; and if it had no beginning, how could it have an end? So why stick around, waiting for nothing?

It was that endless, circular argument going round and round in my head that was driving me nuts.

I got a lift into the Anakie pub one afternoon and bought a slab of Four X. I cut it in half with a kitchen knife when I got back to the hut, and paid Jack a visit. I hadn't spoken to him since he came to see me at Dead Darby's. Whether he'd been lying to me or not, I still owed him for setting me up with a roof over my head. The real reason for my visit, if I was honest, was the excuse it gave me to talk to him some more, maybe draw him out.

Digger hurtled out the door as I approached the hut, then quietened down when he heard my voice. Jack was right behind him. I held out the half-box of stubbies. 'Thought you might like something to settle the dust.'

'Thanks,' he said, 'I don't touch the stuff.' It had never crossed my mind there might be someone on the gemfields who didn't drink alcohol. It seemed to be the life-blood of the place.

We stood looking at each other until the silently ticking seconds forced the obligatory invitation. 'Would you like a cup of tea?'

Through a veil of smoke curling from his smouldering can of mozzie-repelling dung, I watched him make the brew.

'So, you and Jimmy, eh?' He handed me a steaming mug, and sat opposite me. 'Looks like you've decided to stick around for a while.'

I said, 'I'll stick around for as long as it takes.' He looked at me sharply. 'Is it okay if I stay on at Darby's?'

He shrugged. 'Stay as long as you like.'

There was a faint scar above his left eyebrow that I hadn't noticed before. I had developed a habit of looking for facial features, behavioural habits, when I watched him - little things that might stir some recollection from the past. The scar stirred nothing. I said, 'I don't think you understand what's going on for me, Jack.'

'I understand a lot more than you think I do.' He raised the mug of tea to his lips. Smooth, deliberate. He said, 'You could buy the place if you wanted. His daughter up in Cairns owns it. She came down when Darby died. I've got her address somewhere.'

I told him I wasn't in a position to buy anything at the moment. I was flat broke.

'I thought you said you had plenty of money?'

'It's the night life around here, you know? I blew half my life's savings in the Anakie pub.'

He put the mug of tea at his feet, and pulled the packet of tobacco from his pocket. Capstan ready-rubbed. I remembered that from long ago, but it could've been anywhere. It was a common brand; my father might have smoked it for all I knew. He started rolling a fag.

'You found Joe, then?'

'It wasn't hard.'

'I heard he managed to get up Missingham's nose again. Joe isn't happy unless he's making life difficult for some poor bastard.' He lit the fag and drew on it. 'How's it looking up there on Bessy? Any colour?'

'A lot of billies. Not much else.' I felt a twinge of pride in being able to discuss mining matters like an old pro. 'Few parti-colours that'd cut a couple of carats. Lot of corundum.' I knew I wasn't going to get anything out of him. It'd have to wait for another day. I said, 'What's the story on Sylvester Hegarty?'

'He been sniffin' around again, has he?'

'He offered Jimmy fifteen grand for his claim. Jimmy knocked it back.'

'Good for him.'

'He must think it's a pretty good claim if he's willing to pay that much for it.'

He snorted. 'Have you got any idea how much money those machinery miners can pull out of a three-hundred-foot claim?' I didn't. 'That wash on Eureka must be returning twenty dollars a yard. A D9 dozer can push up a hundred yards a day, no sweat. Work it out for yourself.'

It worked out to a lot of moolah. It had puzzled me why Hegarty, with his twenty thousand acres out on Upson Downs, and the fifteen hundred head of prime Aberdeen Angus he had boasted of, would have diverted his energies to a risky business like mining. At two thousand bucks a day, with a taxable income figure plucked out of the air, I could see there wasn't a lot of risk involved.

'Can't he just go out and peg a claim? Why does he have to buy Jimmy's?'

'Department of Minerals and Energy brought in a proclamation a couple of years back: no more three-hundred-foot claims outside the designated machinery area. Up till then you could peg a claim anywhere you liked, for twenty-five bucks a year.'

'That's when you and Jimmy and all the small miners pegged yours.'

'We dug by hand. Everybody was happy. When the boom started, everything changed. The big boys moved in with their dozers and pulsators. They had the machinery area pegged out in a few days. They'll have it stripped bare before the year's out.' He got up to poke another bit of wood into the firebox of the stove.

I said, 'So the only way they can keep going, is to buy all the small miners up.'

'That's about the size of it. You watch your back with that bastard.'

'Hegarty? He's been pretty generous to me.'

'Watch your back.'

'Why, what's he likely to do?'

He jabbed a lump of wood at me. 'Got everything you need up there? Alright for firewood, are you?'

I told him there was plenty of dead wood in the scrub behind the hut. I was okay for food.

'Good.' He sat down again. He shifted to an easier position on his seat and stared into the fire.

I got to my feet and picked up the unwanted stubbies of beer. If I stayed any longer I knew I'd start feeling pissed off with him again, and I didn't want that. Whether he was who I wanted him to be or not, there was something I liked about him – his directness, his apparent concern for my wellbeing, whatever the reason. Remote as I was from the only friends I had back in Sydney, I needed people to like. Better still if they liked me. 'I should be getting back,' I said. 'Early start tomorrow.'

Jimmy and I pushed ahead over the next few weeks. Hegarty's visit was never mentioned. I got the feeling Jimmy had forgotten it already. I hadn't. I couldn't help thinking of all the things I could do with fifteen hundred bucks; all the things Jimmy could do with fifteen grand. I would be doing him a favour, I reasoned, by persuading him to sell.

At smoko one morning, watching him chuck a handful of Bushell's tea in the billy, I asked him, 'Did you give any more thought to Hegarty's offer?'

'Nothing to think about. Why do you ask?'

'You might never get another chance like it. In a place like this, you could live on that much money for a long time.'

An eyebrow arched quizzically as he poured the steaming tea. 'How come you're so worried about me?' he asked.

'I don't know, Jimmy. I guess I just like you.' It was clumsily true, even if it wasn't the truthful answer to his question.

'Well, that makes two bites of the same cherry!' He returned the billy to the fire. 'You know, the very first time I laid eyes on you, I thought, "Now this young fella's the genuine sixpence."' He saluted me with his mug of tea. 'I can see now, I was barking up the right tree.'

I saluted him back. 'Here's to us.'

I woke up one morning and realised I had been on the Anakie gemfields for six weeks. I hadn't found what I went there to find. I was living in a tin shack with no running water and no electricity. But I was still there. And I didn't want to leave.

I was feeling less crazy in the head than I had for a long time. The dog thing, it seemed, had gone into remission. I had a roof over my head, and an income of sorts. If that ran dry, I had a patron, though I didn't really consider it an option going cap-in-hand to Hegarty. Although I had grown to like him after an initial, instinctive antipathy towards him, I still felt uneasy about his interest in me. I could see how it was in his interests to foster my friendship, if he thought he could get his hands on Jimmy's claim, through me. But it had started before that. What difference did it make to him, whether or not I wrote a bloody book?

That said, it was because of him that I *had* started writing again - in an effort to ease the guilt I felt about taking his money, I guess. I say writing, it was more in the nature of notes about the people I had met, and the things that had happened since my arrival on the gemfields. Writing, nonetheless.

Being at some sort of peace with myself, and being happy, however, were two different things. The difference could be summed up in one word. Loneliness. Which was why I took a trip out to Kerracan City one Friday afternoon.

Reg didn't know where his daughter was. 'She's usually home by now. But if she can't get a lift to Emerald, she sometimes stays at her uncle Bob's place.' As an afterthought he said, 'She might've told Val where she was going. She'll be in Emerald somewhere, probably the Railway. I wouldn't count on getting much sense out of her, though.'

Joe was at Kerracan, and he lent me the Falcon for the weekend. I drove into Emerald. I found Val easily enough, in the saloon bar of the Railway as Reg had suggested. She was drinking with two women I had never met, and an older man.

I could see she didn't recognise me. I said, 'G'day, Val. I'm Ned.' Before I could stop myself, I added, 'Reg told me I might find you here.'

She said, 'Well, he'd know, wouldn't he?' Her eyes narrowed, like they were trying to hold me still. 'Do I know you?'

'Yes.' I didn't know what to say next, without resurrecting the tragedy she was trying to blot out. I said, 'We weren't introduced.'

She shrugged. 'If you're going to stick around here, you'd better make yourself useful. Mine's a sweet sherry.' She pushed her empty glass across the table towards me.

When I brought the drinks back to the table, she introduced me to Pearl and Sandy from Clermont. And Gus, a retired ringer from Camooweal. I pulled up a chair while they resumed the conversation they'd been having when I came in.

Gus's body language told me he fancied his chances with Pearl. I got the idea Pearl didn't fancy him in the least, but the three women would be happy enough to let him buy them round after round of drinks, in the hope that she might come across. The sherry came in pony glasses. Val knocked hers back like they were going out of style.

She banged an empty on the table. 'I could do with another one o'them,' she said. 'Whadda ya reckon, Gus?'

'If you'd like, Val,' said Gus politely. He went over to the bar.

I said, 'I can't have another one, Val.' I knew if I had more, I'd get involved in a cycle of shouting. I would've wound up having to take her home, half tanked myself, and the family would think I had been encouraging her. I said, 'I was wondering if you knew where I could find Jessica.'

She went from friendly to spiteful in the blink of an eye. 'Too friggin' good to drink with us, are ya?' she snapped. The hate came pouring out of her on a tide of Penfolds Sweet Solero. 'You gubbahs're all the friggin' same, you think your shit don't stink. Whadda you sniffin' round my daughter for anyway, eh? Whadda ya want with us? We're jus' a mob a boongs livin' in tin huts. Whyn't ya just bugger off and leave us alone?'

She picked up Sandy's half-full glass. Quick thinking Pearl knocked it down so its contents went all over the table, instead of me. Sandy scraped her chair back to keep from getting splashed. 'Jesus, Val!' she yelled, 'What'd you do that for?'

Pearl leant closer to me, to pat my knee. 'Don't take no notice of her mate, she's pissed.'

'Yeah,' said Sandy, 'it's the drink talkin'.'

Val lurched sideways. She looked like she was going to be sick. Pearl got her to her feet and steered her out to the toilets.

'She's not normally like this,' Sandy apologised. 'She had a bitta bad luck a while back. Her little boy got drowned. Got caught in a flash-flood out on Retreat Creek. Somebody jumped in to try and save him, but it wasn't no use.'

'Yeah,' Gus piped in, 'I heard about that! They both drownded. They found the bloke that tried to save 'im, wedged in the fork of a big tree twenty-mile downstream after the water went down. The crows'd picked his friggin' eyes out!'

I got to my feet and said goodbye, while my carcass was still in one piece.

I felt like shit when I got outside. I had done nothing to deserve Val's attack on me. I could have put it down to the pain of her grief; that I'd just happened to wander into the firing line. But I was in a fragile state myself, and the hatred that had poured out of her found fertile ground in doubts that had been lurking since the first time I met Jess. Was I getting out of my depth, I wondered, becoming involved with someone from a culture I knew nothing about? You didn't have to be racist, to be ignorant. Maybe I was asking for trouble. Maybe I should forget all about her.

Jimmy had mentioned I should get a miner's right. Without it, he warned, any gemstone I dug out of the ground technically belonged to the Government, not me. On the way back to Sapphire, I took the turn-off to Anakie.

The Anakie police station, squatting on its high stumps on the other side of the railway, was a big old converted Queenslander. It had been the home of the headmaster, Sparra told me, during the first mining boom, when the place had a school.

Walking up the gravel path to a flight of steps leading to the verandah, I passed a car sitting in the front yard, grass growing high around it. An HD Holden stationwagon, a common enough vehicle around those parts, this one was distinguished by the square-shaped holes peppering its hood and the driver's side door. The short-handled miner's pick that had evidently done the damage was still embedded in its roof.

Sergeant Trevor Gillespie, despite the unconventional trappings of his office, appeared, on the surface, to be every inch your typical country cop. The fact that his present headquarters had once been somebody's private home did nothing to lessen the steely air of authority he affected. Seated behind a kitchen table that had become his desk, he looked up from a magazine he was reading to fix me with an unflinching gaze.

'How can I be of assistance?' His speech was peppered with words bigger than they needed to be.

I said, 'I was wondering if I could get a miner's right.'

'Miner's right, miner's right,' he muttered as he shifted his bulky frame to a filing cabinet in a corner of the room. Without turning he said, 'Indulging in a bit of fossicking, are we?'

I said, 'Yeah, thought I might scratch around a bit. Make a quick fortune and move on, you know?'

My little joke went through to the keeper. 'Fossicking. Anywhere in particular?'

'Big Bessie, actually.'

He half turned. 'That's Jimmy Ryan's patch, isn't it?'

'That's right. Jimmy and I are partners.'

'Is that a fact?' He extracted a manila folder from the cabinet drawer and brought it back to the counter-top. 'I thought he was teamed up with Sparra Perkins.'

'Sparra's... taking time off.'

'Bit of R&R, eh?' A corner of his mouth twitched. 'Well, that's good news for the publican, I suppose. As long as Sparra behaves himself.'

In an effort to distance myself from those who didn't behave themselves, I said, 'I suppose they keep you pretty busy around here.'

'Just run your eye over those questions at the bottom of the page there, will you Mr...'

'Sheridan. Ned Sheridan.'

'Busy isn't the word. You wouldn't believe some of the stunts they get up to. No convictions of any sort? Drugs? Tax evasion?'

'No.'

'Only joking about the tax evasion. I came back one night from a call I had to make out at Rubyvale, a few weeks back. The publican flags me down. Some bloody ratbag's gone and ridden a horse into the saloon bar. Can you believe it? A horse!'

'Get out.'

'I'm serious. Just sign it down there, if you would please Ned. Missingham said the offender left in the company of some bloke he'd never seen before.' He shook his head. 'People drift in and out of this place like blowflies around a dunny. You've acquainted yourself with the pub, I take it?'

'Yes. I've been there a few times.'

'And where are you domiciled these days, Ned?'

'I'm living in a house on Little Bessie. Darby Prentice's place. Used to be,' I added, in deference to Darby's departure.

'Ah!' Something had clicked. 'You would've arrived here around the time of that flash flood on Retreat Creek, right?'

I was feeling uneasy. A lot of questions had been coming my way; the guy was a cop, after all. 'Yes,' I said. 'I was there.'

He nodded, more things falling into place. 'You'd be the writer bloke,' he said at last.

I was beginning to realise just how small a community the gemfields was; how close-knit its web of communications. To be accepted as a member of that community, it was handy to have some kind of label you could be identified by. A tag that spelt out your dominant characteristic, so everyone would know what kind of person they were dealing with. Jimmy the Duck, Hungry Joe, Hegarty the Arsehole, Ned the Writer. 'Scribbles', probably, if I stayed there long enough.

'And what are you writing?' He hunted around for a rubber stamp and an ink pad.

'It's a novel,' I said. 'Set on a mining field.'

'That'll keep you busy!' He extracted a slip of paper from a pile in a pigeon hole and banged the rubber stamp onto it. 'There you go, Ned. That'll be a dollar fifty. Sorry I messed it up.'

'*Miner's Right No.39383*', the slip proclaimed. In the top left-hand corner the cop's thumb had left a smudged imprint; not, as I had thought, from ink off the stamp pad, but from a dark residue staining the first two digits of his right hand.

'Tripoli paste,' he apologised, as he attempted to wipe the stuff off with a handkerchief he had pulled from his pocket. 'Little hobby of mine, cutting and polishing.'

The image of a delicate gemstone dwarfed by Gillespie's meaty fingers was ludicrous. I didn't say as much. I gave him a two dollar note, and he fished in a petty cash box pulled from under the counter. He handed me the change. 'Anything you take out of the ground from now on is legally yours. Anything you've already taken, you can bring in and leave with me for safe keeping.' He winked. 'Just joking. Mind you,' he continued as he started putting things away, 'it was no joke…,' he leaned back to grab the magazine he had been reading, and slapped it on the counter, '…for this poor little bugger.'

The photograph on the cover was of a grinning teen-aged boy in a mud-spattered shirt. Pinched between the thumb and forefinger of his outstretched hand was a golden-yellow coloured stone the size of half a matchbox. Lit from behind by the sun, it glowed as if powered by some internal force. 'Holiday Bonanza on Eureka', the caption beneath the photograph announced. And in smaller type under that: 'Young Fossicker Specks a Corker.'

It crossed my mind that the *Courier Mail* journo who ran foul of Jack would be less than thrilled to know he had been scooped by the *Rockhound Gazette*.

'He thought he'd made his fortune, when they took that picture,' Gillespie continued. 'Then our friend Mr Hegarty stepped in.' He sucked in a breath, like he felt pain.

'Sylvester Hegarty?'

'That's the one. The kid specked the stone on his claim, and he was silly enough to tell that to the person who wrote this.' He tapped the magazine with a finger. 'Somebody showed the article to Hegarty, and he decided the stone belonged to him.'

'Because the kid didn't have a miner's right?'

'That didn't help. But even if he'd had one, there was still the matter of it being found on Hegarty's claim.'

'So now Hegarty owns it.'

'No. That's the funny thing. A few days later this other bloke appears out of the blue and says the kid didn't find it, he did. D'you want to know where?'

'Not on Hegarty's claim, I'm guessing.'

'Just across the boundary, on the miners' common. Says he let the kid borrow the stone, for the photo. When they get around to questioning the kid, he confirms the story. It wasn't his stone, he says, he just wanted his picture taken with it. Hegarty couldn't prove otherwise.'

'He must've been majorly pissed off.'

'I'd say so.' His big frame shook. 'The kid was his own friggin' son!' It had never occurred to me that my benefactor could be married with children. 'The word around the traps is, it was his mother cooked the whole thing up with this other bloke. She left the gemfields not long after.' He pushed the slip of paper across the counter. I folded it in half and put it in my pocket. He looked at the cover of the magazine again, and shook his head. 'Twenty-two pennyweights. What I wouldn't give to get my hands on a rock like that.'

The phone rang before I had a chance to find out more about the saga of the big yellow stone, and Hegarty's involvement in it.

'Good luck,' said the cop, moving over to the phone. 'It's not as easy as everyone thinks.'

'Thank you.'

'Good luck with the fossicking, too.' He picked up the phone. 'Anakie police station. How can I be of assistance?'

I stopped off for a pot at the pub before getting back to Sapphire. I walked into the bar feeling thirsty from the heat; still depressed about the incident in the Railway Hotel.

She was sitting alone at a table close to the singer - someone new. He had a hat bigger than his voice and she wasn't singing along with him. She smiled when she saw me walking towards her. I said, 'How're you going?'

She said, 'Where've you been?'

So much for her mother's grief-driven tirade against a whitey's unwanted attentions. So much for my misgivings about getting involved with an Aboriginal girl. She'd been waiting for me all along.

I brought two beers over and pulled up a chair. I said, 'I was up at the cop shop, getting a miner's right.'

'You're going to stick around then.'

'Thought I might.'

'Sucker for punishment, eh.' She smiled.

I could've eaten that smile. I said, 'Is it that bad?'

'It doesn't seem like the sort of place you'd want to stick around in.'

'What sort of place *would* I want to stick around?'

'I don't know, somewhere... faster, I suppose.'

'Do I look fast?'

'No. You look like you come from somewhere like that.'
'I suppose you could call Sydney fast.'
'Wouldn't know. Never been there.'
'You haven't missed much.'
'So what brings you to this neck of the woods?'
'People ask that question like they think I shouldn't be here.'
'Should you?'
'I didn't have any choice.' I had to be honest. I wanted to get off on the right foot. She had come out of nowhere, and I wasn't about to let her fly off again. I didn't want to mess things up in advance by lying to her. I said, 'I'm a bit fucked in the head, to tell you the truth.'

She shrugged, 'Who isn't? Did you come out here to get away from whatever it was fucking you up?'

'No.'

'You don't have to talk about it, if you don't want to.'

'I'd like to. Another time.'

'Wanna make an appointment?'

We both laughed.

I said, 'How are you getting home tonight?'

She looked serious as she sipped her beer. She said, 'Where's home?'

I stopped the Falcon outside the hut. Before she had a chance to move, I was on my way to the gate. I got back in and we drove through and I switched off the headlights. I got out again and went to close the gate. By the time I got back she was already out of the car. She said, 'I wasn't going to let you open the bloody door for me.'

'I'm sorry.'

She took a step closer to me. She said, 'I wasn't complaining about you being nice to me.'

A full moon floated over the tree-tops. A puff of wind stirred the leaves of a scented gum across the gulley. Her hair shifted. Her mouth was welcoming and hungry. I kissed her mouth and her face. Kissed the neck that had strained for the singer's high note the first time I saw her. Her breath in my ear was the rush of wind in the trees, rustling their leaves, stirring my prick, guiding my hand to the weight of her breasts.

I said, 'D'you want to go inside?'

'No,' she said, 'I like it out here.' She put a hand behind my head, pressing me closer, drawing me in to the heat of her. We went down to the ground. I said, 'I could get something to…'

She said, 'I don't want nothin'. I just want you to fuck me.'

Flesh on flesh against the hard earth, it seemed like we had come up out of it, clinging, thrusting for some centre that would prevent us spinning off into the darkness. She cried out so loud I thought I had hurt her. She laughed, pulling me back into her, gripping me with her arms and legs, biting my ear softly until we were still.

We lay coiled on the ground listening, her arm laid across me like a smooth sapling, to the two-note serenade of a mopoke.

In the morning, over breakfast, I asked her when she would like me to take her home. 'Not yet,' she said.

She knew Reg needed her there to help him keep the family together, but Val's drinking was out of control. It had got too much for her, she said, watching her mother wiping out the pain of loss in a relentless, ugly binge.

I said, 'Stay as long as you like.'

King Star

Jess sorted stone for Hegarty during the week, and went back to Kerracan on the weekends. If Reg was away on the railways she would stay there all week till he came home. If Val went on a bender, which was often, she couldn't be relied on to look after the kids properly.

For me, Dead Darby's hut became a place I was anxious to return to at the end of the day, rather than a shelter to crawl into. Up till then it had been a place where loneliness had been warded off with booze or dope till it was time to crash; then get up the next morning to do it all over again. Now, my daily routine had become a string of events I looked forward to with interest, rather than anticipated with dread.

If Jess got home from work before me, the door would be open. There might be something cooking, a Charley Pride tape playing. We'd have a beer, blow a joint, chew the fat. It was so different to living with Cathie. There was nothing competitive about Jess. What you saw was how she was. With Cath, you had to weigh everything she said to get at what she really meant. Even then you might get it wrong. Jess wasn't interested in keeping you guessing; she wanted you to know. Which was good for me, because it left no room for paranoia.

There were half-hearted storms in the afternoons, enough to settle the dust and take the sting out of the heat. The Wet was holding off. We would eat dinner before dark, read books by the light of the carbide lamp or play music on the reedy tape deck Jess had brought with her. Patsy Cline, Hank Williams, Johnny Cash. And Charley, her favourite. We were making enough money to get by. We made love every night.

We made home-brew too. You needed beer in the heat, and a slab of Four X cost a motza. The brew bubbled away in a poly carboy all week; then we bottled it. We sold some of it to friends and acquaintances, and used the extra money to buy food and dope.

In the euphoria of new-found love, Jack and the quest for the missing bit of my life took a back seat to the hedonistic pursuit of the joys of the immediate future, with Jess.

She walked in the door one Sunday afternoon; I wasn't expecting her till the following morning. I was propped against the end of the mattress on the floor, making notes in one of the exercise books I had been using to write in.

'What's it about?' she asked. I had no confidence in anything I had written. I'd been careful to write when she wasn't around, to avoid talking about it. But my reputation as the gemfields scribe must have leaked through to Kerracan City. 'You've never talked to me about it,' she complained.

'I didn't think you'd be all that interested.'

'Must be a pretty boring book then, eh.'

'You could be right.' I put the pad down, and she came over and kissed me hullo.

'I bet you're writin' about that girl you left behind. What was her name?'

'Cathie.'

'That's why you don't want to show it to me.'

I said, 'She's the last person I want to write about.'

'You should write about that dog thing. The stuff you can't remember, from when you were a kid.'

'How can I write about it, if I can't remember it?'

'It might bring it all back for you.'

'Where did you say you did your degree in psychology?'

'You don't have to be a psychologist to work out somethin' that friggin' simple.' She flicked a hand across the top of my head. It reminded me of the way Hegarty cuffed poor old Boofhead's ears.

I got up and followed her to the kitchen. I watched the cool sweep of her arms, the flash off her hair in the light from the window, while she made coffee.

I said, 'What happened to that big stone Hegarty's kid specked near Eureka?'

'The one that was in the paper? Didn't Jack tell you?'

'I never asked him. According to the newspaper article, he didn't know anything about it.'

She snorted. 'Jack knows nothin' about nothin', if you want to listen to Jack.'

I could see the irascible old bugger standing in his doorway, glaring at the *Mail* photographer. I remembered what Gillespie had told me about someone intervening to prevent Hegarty getting his hands on the stone.

'Was it Jack who came out and said the stone belonged to him?'

'Go to the top of the class, university boy.'

'Drop-out university boy,' I reminded her. 'It must've been worth a fortune. How come he's still living in a shack on the gemfields?'

'He gave it away.'

'Gave it away!'

'To Ailsa Hegarty.' She frowned. 'You didn't know about Jack and Ailsa?'

I didn't, but I was getting there. 'How long had they been…?'

'Carryin' on behind his back?' She shrugged. 'Coupla years. Best thing that ever happened to Jack.'

'Why's that?'

'He was in pretty bad shape when he first come here. It was Ailsa got him on the wagon. Said she didn't want nothin' to do with him unless he sobered up. He's never touched a drop since.' She smiled ruefully. 'Maybe I should get her back, to work on Mum.'

'So Ailsa sold the stone. And that's how she could afford to leave Hegarty.'

'And Jack. She's never been back since.'

'Did Hegarty know about them?'

'He must've. Everybody else did. I don't think it bothered him that much. I don't think it even worried him that she left. Takin' the boy with her was what hurt him.'

'He doesn't strike me as the kind of guy who loves children. Not even his own.'

'I don't know about "love". He thought the sun shone out of him, but. Jason was the one goin' to carry on the Hegarty dynasty, wasn't he?'

'But he tried to steal the kid's stone!'

'Hegarty wouldn't've seen it like that. He would've thought he was protectin' him from being ripped off.'

She handed me my coffee, and we went into the other room. I said, 'What did they call it? All these big stones've got a name – the Centenary Gem, Star of Queensland….'

'Most people call it the Golden Shower.' She giggled. 'The kid specked it when he went to take a leak behind a tree.'

'He pissed on it?'

'You can get lucky, eh?'

I said, 'We could do with a bit of that, right now.'

The last few days digging on Bessie had produced no saleable stone – not even tucker money. I had nothing in the bank. Jess would have lent me some if I had asked, but I knew she needed every cent she earned for the family. And I'd made up my mind that I didn't want to encourage Hegarty's patronage. The trouble with a place like the gemfields was, you couldn't just go out and get a job driving taxi trucks.

We were creeping round the back of a billy that got bigger and bigger the further we went in. Jimmy reckoned sapphires might have got trapped behind it. It was a good sign. It was the forty-eighth good sign I had heard over the past two weeks. The bumpy floor, the compacted gravel, the band of wash narrowing (or broadening), the presence of clay, etc., etc.: all indicators of a sudden and spectacular upturn in our fortunes, that never materialised.

We hauled what we had dug all morning to the surface. We took it in turns to fill buckets and wind up. Wash rattled down the screen. Big rocks bounced off the chicken-wire onto a pile that would be specked after the first rains, for gems that might have bounced with them.

I fantasised about specking a fifteen or twenty weight blue with a white cross-table that would cut a hundred carats. I would smuggle it overseas and flog it to the Smithsonian Institute to sit alongside the 'Star of Queensland' that Jimmy had shown me a picture of in the *Britannica*. Such dreams kept me going between pockets; carats I dangled for myself to relieve the tedium and physical hardship of hacking away at an ever-receding wall of gravel and earth that might, with the next blow, yield a stone that would pay for booze and tucker for the next few months, or weeks. Or a day. The odds were against anything better than that, but you had to dream. I started thinking again about Hegarty's offer.

We wound the last bucket up and moved to the willoughby. Jimmy filled the sieve, I jigged the pole on its pivot. The sieve bounced up and down in the yellow water, sending dross to the top. I locked off and Jimmy scraped the dross and put another shovelful in and I jigged again. My mind was working on ways to persuade him that selling up to Hegarty might not be such a bad option, even if the guy wasn't the 'genuine sixpence'.

I locked off the pole, and waited for Jimmy to scrape off. He made a sweep, and hunched over the sieve like he was casting a spell. He leaned closer, then straightened up and said he had to go for a leak. He handed me the scraper as he moved past me and headed for the nearest tree.

I hated this part of the job. I never had faith in the theory that all the gemstone would gravitate to the bottom of the sieve. What if one got caught in a bit of clay? Or bounced back up after it hit the bottom at precisely the moment you decided to lock off? The thought of being cheated out of a five-weight stone because of the inefficiency of this primitive method of recovery gnawed at me like an ulcer. I saw an image of some snotty-nosed kid on a holiday with his low-life parents from Caboolture, specking my stone. They would know nothing of the hardship that had gone into gouging the fucking thing from forty-foot down.

I raked the dross, and chucked it to one side. I stared at the tank of muddy water and the dripping sieveful of wash suspended above its surface. The mounting pile of clay became a metaphor for all that my life amounted to: a slag heap of discarded scraps of useless experience. Everything about mining was giving me the shits. I forced my mind back to the problem of how to deal with Jimmy.

Ironstone began to show. The round chocolate-brown nodules blanketing the bottom of the sieve reminded me of the upside-down pudding they used to give us at St Andrew's - all wet and knobbly on the top, with shiny, black raisins poking through... I paused, the scraper resting at the edge of the sieve. I stopped breathing. Shiny, black...

I reached for one of the glistening stones, the size of a marble. I showed it to the sun and it sprang to life in a burst of blue brilliance. Darkish, with a blue cross-table, about five pennyweights. Probably worth half of all the stone we had mined so far. I reached for another black lump, a little smaller than the first, and held it to the sun. White cross-table cut about four carats. I swept the scraper across the top layer of ironstone.

The bottom of the sieve was smothered with oily black stone, sparkling in the sun. I turned to yell to Jimmy. I had forgotten to start breathing again, and it came out as a strangled yelp.

He was standing behind me, grinning. 'I thought you might like to see it from your own prospective,' he said. He had the Vegemite jar ready.

We spent the next half hour picking the stones off the bottom of the sieve, examining them one by one, discussing the relative merits of each in terms of weight, shape, absence of flaws, cross-table colour etc., etc., before consigning it to the mounting pile in the jar. By the time we finished, it was half full. I was all for going back down and knocking out another yard or two. Jimmy reckoned there was no rush. Whatever else was down there had been there for a million years. It would still be there in the morning.

King Star operated out of a tin shed behind the petrol station, down the hill from Beryl Carmody's general store. It had once housed 44-gallon drums of fuel before the underground tank went in. Jimmy and I hunkered outside it under a tree. A tiny porch roof jutted over the door of the shed. The shade it provided was taken up by somebody else waiting to sell - a thin-faced, middle-aged woman in T-shirt and shorts, stroking the head of the little boy who had gone to sleep beside her. We had arrived before her, but Jimmy had graciously offered her the spot in the shade.

A man in mud-spattered boots came out of the shed, patting the pocket of his shirt as if to reassure himself that six weeks' hard yakka underground was worth the little bulge he could feel there. As he headed for a Land Cruiser parked nearby, Jimmy got to his feet.

The gem dealer had driven straight from the Emerald airstrip in a rented air-conditioned Fairlane; his only luggage a black vinyl attaché case, like you would expect any visiting Asian businessman to carry. A dapper, slickly-groomed man, his neatly-pressed shirt and trousers incongruous in the rustic surrounds of his temporary office, he was seated behind a table near its only window. It was rumoured he kept a gun under the table. In front of him lay a silver-backed mirror. He smiled politely as we entered, and with an upturned palm indicated two folding chairs facing him.

Jimmy produced our three plastic sandwich bags of stone. We had graded them ourselves, bathing them in acid overnight; washing and oiling them before parcelling them up in the morning, so they would be at their sparkling best. The buyer's hand reached unerringly for the top-grade parcel. They splashed out on the mirror like a cluster of black termites. Reflected sun struck up through the crystals, sparking blue.

Star's chubby fingers flicked through the stone like they were beads on an abacus, pushing the smaller ones aside, pausing now and then to pick up a bigger one and inspect it. He scooped up each of the piles he had made, and weighed them on a set of scales. He jabbed keys on a calculator.

I looked across at Jimmy. His customary grin was pasted to his face, as he looked at Star. We had agreed between ourselves on a bottom price. If Star wouldn't come at it, Jimmy reckoned, he could go and get a woolly bull up him. A plastic fan hummed on a corner of the bench, keeping the buyer cool. Jimmy and I sweated. The roof of the shed creaked in the heat. A fly buzzed.

Star's index finger stabbed the calculator keys with an air of finality. He looked up and said, 'I give you three thousand five hunnard dollar.'

Jimmy's grin remained fixed. 'We were thinking in the vicinity of a little bit more than that,' he said.

'Okay, okay,' said Star impatiently. 'Four thousand. Top price.' He hauled his attaché case onto the bench and flicked the catches. Neatly stacked bundles of twenty-dollar notes filled it from bottom to top, edge-to-edge on all four sides. He peeled off four of the bundles and looked up at us. 'Okay?'

We came out of the shed and I punched Jimmy on the arm and he ducked and weaved and pulled a couple of jabs short of my ribs. Our bottom price had been two thousand five hundred.

Jimmy gripped my arm tight. 'What did I tell you, Ned? You were my lucky omen, make no bones about it!' I returned the grip. We stood there, locked. I was conscious, for an instant, of the two of us forming some kind of Olympian tableau to the glory of outback mateship.

Over his shoulder I saw a red vehicle roll to a halt. Jimmy turned to see what I was looking at. We watched Hegarty step out of the Range Rover and lean back in to haul something across the passenger seat, grunting with the effort. He banged the door shut with his arse. Cradled in his arms were two pumpkin-sized plastic bags, full of oily black stone.

The woman with the kid was standing at the door of the shed, waiting to go in. King Star came out to personally greet Hegarty. He said something to the woman. Hegarty strode past her, and the door closed. The woman sat back down to wait.

Jack and Joe

It was a Friday. Jess had got a lift to Kerracan with Joe, earlier on. Jimmy and I had celebrated our good fortune with a good helping of Four X, but I felt the need to share the euphoria with someone else. I used it as an excuse to pay Jack another visit, late in the afternoon. I hadn't seen him around for a while. I knew he wasn't going to go out of his way to see me.

He put aside his copy of the *Courier Mail* to congratulate me on the strike. 'I suppose you'll be hiring a dozer next, to rip the guts out of Bessy so you can buy us all out.' I told him I wasn't interested in doing a Hegarty.

A celebratory beer was out of the question. I watched a copper stream of tea arc into Jack's chipped mugs.

I said, 'Do you think he will? Buy us all out, in the end?'

'If he wants to bad enough.'

'And if we let him.'

He snorted. 'What're you going to do to stop him?'

'Has he made you an offer?'

'He knows better than to do that.'

'What would you say, if he did?'

He squinted at me through the smoke curling off his rollie. 'Why do you want to know?'

'I was just curious.'

'He knows what I'd say. Sylvester and I've got a bit of a history.'

'I know. Jess told me…' I trailed off.

'Whatever she told you, it was none of her business.'

We sat in silence. He'd probably guessed the real reason for my visit; he was probably waiting for me to take offence and leave. I wasn't going to be put off that easy. The problem was, I couldn't force him to tell me what I needed to know. If indeed he knew it. All I could think to do was keep him talking. About anything.

I said, 'I'm sorry. I didn't mean to pry, I was just…'

'It's no secret,' he said. 'But it beats me why people can't let it alone. The past is the past.'

Here was a chance, I thought, to steer the conversation where I wanted it. I said, 'That's fine, as long as you're lucky enough to know what the past is.'

He dislodged a strand of tobacco from his tongue and flicked it to the floor. I thought he wasn't going to respond at all; then he said, 'Sometimes it's better not to know.'

'Is that why you won't tell me?'

'Tell you what?' His brow creased with impatience. I didn't push it. His voice sank to a different level, out of reach. 'I told you before, you've got the wrong person.'

I took a different tack. 'Jack, when I first came to this place, I was a mess. I still am, but it's been good for me, being here. It's made me feel better about myself.'

'I'm glad to hear it.'

'But I'm still fucked in the head.'

The corners of his eyes puckered in disbelief. 'There's nothing wrong with you. What're you talking about?'

'Are you kidding? My whole life is strung out back there somewhere I can't get to, and if I don't find it I'm going to go fucking crazy! I don't think you understand how serious this is.'

It was a mistake. I couldn't be absolutely certain he was Jack Raithall. At best I was operating on a powerful hunch; I probably thought my outburst might bluff him into coming clean. But this Jack, whoever he was, wasn't the type to be bluffed.

He threw his head back and laughed. 'Christ!' he said. 'You've been smoking too much of that bloody stagger weed!'

I was too furious to respond in any logical way. I got to my feet. 'Well fuck you very much,' I said. Brilliant. Get him right offside, and he might never talk to me again.

He grew serious again. 'You're not the only one with problems, son.'

Something in his tone of voice came closer to sympathy than I'd ever heard from him. The door to whatever was rattling around inside him seemed to have opened a crack. I gave it one more shot. I said, 'Look, I don't give a stuff what you and Ailsa Hegarty got up to. You're right, it's none of my business. But I've got a right to know about my own childhood. That's my life we're talking about. And if there's something you know about it, that I don't, you have to tell me.'

He got quickly to his feet. 'I don't have to tell you anything,' he snapped. 'What about my life? You come barging into the joint, expecting everybody to feel sorry for you because you had a bit of bad luck when you were a kid! Well it wasn't my fault! Alright?'

I let it hang for a second. 'What wasn't?'

Digger had come between us, barking like fury. 'For Christ's sake!' said Jack.

'*What* wasn't your fault?'

The dog kept barking. Jack snatched a piece of stove wood off the hearth. 'If you don't belt up, I'll whack you over the bloody ear with this, so help me!' He raised the lump of wood... the dog cowered...

My throat contracted... I could feel myself sinking. The dog's coat was smoking, like the one in Armidale. I closed my eyes...

Jack's hand was gripping my arm so tight I could feel the fingers digging in. It was all that was stopping me from going down. His voice came from somewhere distant. 'Are you alright?' The question had become a signal that I was in trouble.

I kept my eyes closed, to shut out the dog. Controlled breathing. At least it wasn't as intense this time as the Armidale episode, when I had blacked out completely. 'You'd better sit down,' I heard Jack say. I must've looked like shit. I let him help me to the bed and I sat on the edge of it.

I was coming out of it... I risked creeping an eye open. Digger was back in his spot on the hearth. Not burning. Blood pounded in my temples. The pounding swelled to an explosive crash, drowning out all other sound.

Jack's head shot round, so I knew he had heard it too. Digger raced out the door, Jack right behind him. Whatever had happened outside was too momentous to ignore. I got to my feet and stumbled after them.

The sun had gone. Jack's shadow was thrown right-angled up the outer wall of the hut in the Falcon's single headlight beam. Its chrome grill, crumpled against the gate post, spurted steam from a ruptured radiator.

'Bloody Joe,' Jack muttered.

We hurried to the driver's side door. He was slumped over the steering wheel. There was a wet red smear on the dash, a spatter of pink dots on the windscreen. One side of his face was a mask of blood. Jack wrenched the door open. 'Give us a hand here, Ned!'

The sight of Joe snapped me out of my own dazed condition. I said, 'Is he dead?'

'It'd take more than that to kill the ugly bastard,' Jack grunted.

We struggled to haul the big man's dead weight inside, a fence-post arm draped round each of our shoulders. We laid him on his side on the bed. Jack crouched beside him. 'You'll be right, mate,' he soothed.

He poured boiling water into a bowl and he began wiping away the blood with a tea towel. 'There's some first-aid stuff in the drawer over there, in the tin,' he said, pointing.

I found a biscuit tin in the drawer. I picked up the book lying on top of the dresser, to make space for the tin. I remembered it as the one I had glimpsed the day I first met Jack. Two words, *Gods* and *Graves*, were barely discernible from the title on its jacketless spine. It seemed apposite to the image of Joe, lying like a fallen Easter Island statue behind me.

I put the book aside and took the lid off the tin. I found bandages and sticking plaster and a bottle of Friar's balsam. I took them over to Jack, who was peeling away a wet ribbon of congealed blood from his patient's brow. Joe groaned. He muttered something thickly in Hungarian. One word, 'Konji', became recognisable through repetition.

I said, 'It's alright Joe. You're going to be alright,' with a reassurance I didn't feel. I dreaded what would be revealed when the wound that had shed all that blood was uncovered. I could see the raw flesh, the smashed bone and gristle. There was no ringing a doctor; we would have to do the best we could with what we had.

His eyes flickered, and focused on mine. 'Konji?' he said again.

I said, 'No, it's me, Ned. You had a bit of a prang.'

He struggled to sit up. 'Keep him lying down,' said Jack.

Easier said than done. 'Whad you bustards doing?' Joe slurred. He brushed us aside and forced himself to a sitting position. 'Jesus bloddy Christ!' he exclaimed, staring at the bowl of crimson water. 'Whad you been do to youselluf, Ned?'

I said, 'It's not me, it's you. You pranged the car.'

'Ah!' he exclaimed, as it all came back. 'Bloddy brakes been gone. Kapoot!'

I persuaded him to sit still long enough for Jack to continue cleaning away the congealed blood, revealing the wellspring it had come from - a shallow cut about an inch long over his left eyebrow. I felt cheated. Jack looked angry. 'Ged me bloddy beer you mizzerable bustards,' Joe ordered.

'You've had enough to drink,' said Jack. I watched him rip the protective paper off a plaster strip. He jammed it hard over the cut, more to punish than heal.

'Hey, watch you nod kill me, you bustard!' Joe yelped. He wasn't so pissed he couldn't feel pain.

In a barely coherent monologue, he proceeded to tell us how he had had a row with Becky soon after he arrived at her place, picked up a couple of bottles of Bundy on his way through Emerald, and went out to pay his League of Nations buddies a visit. Then he must have decided to come and see Jack. The last thing he remembered was the brakes failing. He laughed when we told him how he had crashed into the gate post.

Jack grew darker and stonier-faced as the story rambled on. When Joe had finished, he said, 'Well you've had your fun. Now you can piss off.'

Joe looked perplexed for a second or two, then grinned as he realised his old mate must be having him on. Jack glared back, and he knew he was serious. He said, 'Whad you talking aboud you silly bucker? Been I am only just geddingk here!'

'We thought you were going to die, that's what I'm talking about,' said Jack.

'Been think I vos dyingk?' Joe lumbered to his feet. 'Must ve haf a drink for mine wake, then!' He flung an arm round Jack's shoulder.

Jack shrugged it off. 'Why don't you bugger off back to your alky mates in the Scrub and get smashed with them?' A wounded look came over Joe. The big man's puzzled silence seemed to incense Jack even further. 'That gin of yours'd be happy to share her flagon with you, wouldn't she? She's taken enough of your money off you already!'

Joe stiffened. Allusions to his own shortcomings he was prepared to accept, it seemed; insults to the woman he was currently involved with would not be tolerated. He drew himself to his full, unsteady height. 'Mide as vell I been leafingk now,' he said.

'I'm not standing in your way.' They glared at each other. The thunk of a piece of wood collapsing in the stove's fire-box accentuated the silence. Digger, sensing more strife, jumped up to lick Joe's hand. 'Gedoutofit!' Jack ordered. The dog padded back to his spot on the hearth.

'Mebbe some days,' Joe continued, salvaging what dignity he could from the wreckage of Jack's disparagement. 'Mebbe ven you nod be such a mizzerable bloddy bustard, you vill haf some voomans too. One who will vant to keep liffingk with you. Mebbe she nod runningk away from you this time.' He turned and moved to the door with measured steps. He went out, shutting it behind him with exaggerated courtesy.

I guessed the woman who had 'run away' was Ailsa Hegarty. Mention of her had clearly struck a chord with Jack. He seemed on the point of saying something, then his jaw clamped shut. He turned away to poke more wood into the fire-box, sending sparks flying.

I said, 'Do you think he'll go back to Kerracan?'

'I couldn't give a stuff where he goes. If he wants to mix with that mob of bludgers, that's his look-out.'

I wanted to talk to Jack; about me, about him, about the burning dogs. I sensed I had come close to something that night. But I was worried about Joe, too.' I said, 'He shouldn't be driving.'

'If you want to be his nursemaid, that's up to you,' he said.

He started tidying up the mess left in Joe's wake. The latter's sudden departure had provided him with the perfect opportunity to get rid of me.

I came out into the moonless night, to find Joe trying to disentangle the Falcon's bumper bar from a strand of wire on the fence. He was cursing it in Hungarian. Or so I thought. Then I heard Jack's name mentioned, and I realised the harangue was directed at him. I tried to help him with the bumper bar, but Jack strained his fences tight, and we couldn't budge it. 'Bucker it!' said Joe. 'Ve pull the bloddy thing off!'

Before I could stop him, he was in behind the steering wheel. I slid into the passenger seat beside him. I tried to persuade him to let me drive. He didn't answer. Anger was sobering him up. He pulled the tin of Dr Pat from his shirt pocket. I watched him roll a durry, saw his face light up in the flare of the match and melt into darkness again. He sucked on the fag and broke into a rasping cough. 'Been one day thiz bloddy tobaggo killingk me!' he wheezed.

He sat there in brooding silence, the outline of his face ebbing and flowing in the glow of the fag. He reached for the ignition key and twisted it. The Falcon's motor burbled to life. I was worried about Jack's fence; but more so about the further damage that would be done to their friendship if Joe ripped the thing out of the ground.

I said, 'You can't drive this thing, Joe. The radiator's busted.' That didn't worry him. He reckoned there'd still be water left in it, and if it over-heated on the way to wherever we were going, we could always get out and piss in it.

He reefed down on the gear stick and dropped the clutch. The Falcon lurched into reverse, motor roaring, wheels spinning wildly. It strained against the tension of the fence wire until, with a sudden shock of release, we found ourselves rocketing backwards. I saw the headlight beam glinting off the bumper bar, hanging off the wire. The fence stood stoically intact.

Joe stared at it for a second. Then he said, 'I been take you home now.'

We rattled off along the track to Darby's hut. He asked me how things were going with Jimmy. I told him we had hit a pocket.

'Vot kind off pocket?'

'A good one. We sold up for four grand.'

'Four thousand dollar!' He slammed his foot on the brake. The car slewed off the track and slowed to a halt in its own good time. 'Four thousand, you say?'

He wedged my face between his hands and planted a bristly kiss on my forehead. 'This is beaudiful,' he said solemnly. 'This is vot I vant should happen.' In the green glow of the dash, his eyes glinted with that overwhelming happiness I had seen when he first regained consciousness back in Jack's hut. I was happy that he was happy for me. The heady aroma of Dr Pat and Bundy rum coming off him promised days of beer and sunshine, and the possibility that some of the joy would rub off.

In the next instant he had released my head, reefed the steering wheel down hard right, and pumped the accelerator. 'Been ve go to pup now, for celebratingk!' He swung the Falcon round in a bouncing arc until we were headed in the opposite direction.

'You're barred,' I reminded him. He reckoned Missingham had gone off on a holiday. Whoever was filling in for him wouldn't bother to enforce the ban, even if he knew about it.

As we sped through the dusty night, he warned me, 'Must you nod tellingk effrybody aboud this strike, Neddy. You tell this bustards in pup you hid a pocket, effry man vith his dog is bludgingk you for money!'

To his credit, a good five minutes passed before he put the bite on me for twenty bucks. Maybe he was just illustrating the point. 'Vot you vill do vith all your monies?' he asked, as he tucked the twenty in his pocket.

'I thought I might buy a car.'

'Car, you said? Cheesus bloddy Christ, why you not tellingk this to me already?'

He swung the Falcon off the main road, and we bumped along a track winding through the Scrub. A few minutes later we saw the glow of a camp fire blipping in and out of the trees. The League of Nations, forced to shift camp after Hegarty bought their claim, had moved to a clearing in duffer country at the northern edge of the Scrub Lead. As we drew closer, Joe slammed a foot uselessly on the brake pedal. 'Bloddy brakes!' he shouted, like they should have fixed themselves between now and the last time they had failed.

The Falcon groaned as it juddered into low gear at high speed. There was a bit of a rise just before the camp; Joe cut the motor and we started to slow down. He was leaning out the door shouting to his mates while the car was still rolling. I reefed the handbrake on, but that didn't work either. A second later we crunched into a tree and stopped.

'Hey, you mizzerable bloddy bustards, where you been hide that Bundy?' Joe demanded, banging the door shut behind him. 'Been I'm haf friendt with me, iss one thirsty bustard!'

Gaunt faces, spectral in the half-light, stared at us from out of the flickering glow of the fire. One of them detached itself from the group. I recognised 'Dutch' Harry van der Hoven walking towards us, bottle in hand. He was surprised to see Joe again so soon. 'I thought you was gunna go and see Jack?'

'Been see the bustard,' said Joe. 'Him been in stinking bloddy bad mood.' He snatched the bottle from Harry, took a swig, and passed it on to me. 'Been Ned and me go to pup now.' I took a sip of the Bundy out of politeness, and handed the bottle back to Harry.

Joe got down to business. 'Ned here iss vantingk to loog at your car. Maybe him buy it.'

Someone called Karl lumbered over to retrieve the bottle while Harry lit our way with a torch to the perimeter of the camp, outside the circle of light thrown by the fire. The moon had not yet risen. It wasn't until I got close that I saw the pick-shaped holes all over the bonnet and roof of the car that was for sale. I realised it was the HD wagon I had seen parked in the front yard of the police station.

I drew Harry's attention to the holes. 'How did they get there?' I asked.

He waved them away with a flick of his hand. 'Don't worry about them.' He assured me they didn't affect the running of the car in the slightest; in fact, they helped cool the engine on hot days. The ones in the roof, he said, could be bogged up with Bond-Crete.

'Who did it?' I persisted.

'Ask Sparra Perkins,' he scowled, and went back to extolling the virtues of the car. It ran like a dream, he reckoned.

Joe, who had come over to join us, backed him up. 'Iss bedder as the Falcon!' he said, like I couldn't have asked for a greater recommendation than that.

I beat Harry down to a hundred and fifty bucks. Joe and I drove out in convoy, headed for the pub.

We parked across the other side of the street, to save Gillespie the inconvenience of having to walk past two unregistered vehicles in the one night, if he happened to drop in to the pub for a look around. We came into the bar to find the big-hatted singer had been replaced by a three-piece Country and Western group, currently belting out a Reg Lindsay relic from the '50s. Joe's name was shouted from a far corner of the room.

We joined Sparra and his drinking companion, a man called Tex, distinguished by the black ringer's Stetson he sported. It had silver badges round its crown, its brim curled to a point at the front, like a rodeo rider's. He looked too flabby to have ever done much rodeo riding. I figured he just liked the hat.

'You're the writer bloke,' he said, as we shook hands.

I didn't dispute it. 'What do you do for a crust?' I countered.

'I'm in the butcherin' business.'

Sparra, flipping the top of his lighter back and forth, cut in quickly. 'Whatta you been doin' to yourself, Joe?'

Joe touched his wounded eyebrow gingerly. 'Fence post been yumpingk out off ground, and punchingk mine head,' he complained.

While Joe went off to buy a round of drinks with my money, I took the opportunity to ask Sparra about the holes in the car I had bought. A change of mood came over him. 'How would I know?'

'Dutch Harry said you knew all about it.'

'Harry's fulla shit.'

I was prepared to leave it at that. Tex, smirking, started humming Patsy Cline's *I Fall to Pieces*.

Sparra glowered at him. The top of the Zippo clicked and clacked rapidly. 'Shut the fuck up, Tex.' He downed the rest of his beer, and made to move off.

'Where're you going?' said Tex.

'Home,' said Sparra.

'Come on, mate, it was only a joke.'

'Well, you just keep laughin'. I'm goin' home.'

He walked past Joe, returning with the beers.

'Vere he iss goingk?' he asked.

'Home,' said Tex. 'He got the shits because Ned asked him about the pick holes in the car.'

'Nod a problem, these holes,' said Joe.

'I wasn't complaining,' I said. 'I just wanted to know how they got there.'

Tex was happy to satisfy my curiosity. 'A few months back, Dutch Harry was shacked up with this sheila he met in Clermont when he was up there buying the HD.'

'Joyce,' said Joe. 'Her voss nice lady.'

'A matter of opinion. Anyway, she comes back down here with Harry, and everything's hunky dory until one night when they're havin' a bit of a session on the Bundy, Sparra gets it in his head that Joyce fancies him. She was a bit of a flirt, right? She's given all of us the come-on at one time or another.'

'Voss nice lady,' Joe persisted.

Tex rolled his eyes. 'They're all nice ladies when they're comin' on to you, mate. Anyway, Sparra's put the hard word on her, and she's ready to come across, when Harry gets wind of it. He pulls Joyce into line, and tells Sparra to bugger off. He was so pissed off with Harry for takin' Joyce away from him, he threatened to blow him up.'

'Him like for blowingk things op,' Joe added, flinging bunched fingers wide with an explosive sound, to illustrate the point.

'But we convinced him it wasn't a good idea to go around killing people. So he decided to blow up his car instead.'

'Bud we tell to him this nod goot idea, also. We say if him blowingk op car, vill loose him licence for usingk gelly.'

I could guess the rest. 'So he settled for getting stuck into it with a miner's pick.'

Tex shrugged. 'It was a better idea than getting stuck into Harry with it.'

It was my turn to shout. I headed for the bar, exchanging greetings as I went with people I had come to know. When I got back to our table, I found we had been joined by a mining couple from Tomahawk Creek. The five of us chewed the fat about shafts and claims and the sharpening of picks and the mending of ladders, and whether or not the new counter-lunch cook with the hairy armpits was a bloke or a sheila. All the important things in a miner's life. Joe seemed to have forgotten about the row with Jack, and was settling in for the next bout of boozing. I was happy to go along for the ride.

Thoughts of Jack, my lost childhood, burning dogs all slid away on a slurry of dry dust and Four X. I laughed and shouted along with the others, sharing the pain and misfortunes of life in that strange backwater of civilised society, where physical wounds and scars were badges of honour; emotional ones, signs of weakness.

I had come to the conclusion there were a lot of fucked-up people on the Anakie gemfields; probably a higher percentage per capita than anywhere else in the country. Here we were, banded together, doing the best we could. Laughing, pissing it up, sharing the pain.

It felt like home. A good enough substitute, anyway, for the one I couldn't remember.

I felt the weight of Joe's arm fall across my shoulder as he recounted my reckless attempt to save Pauly in the flash flood. 'Him yumpingk into riffer, like iss noddingk. Like goingk for swim at bich! Him grap liddle Pauly and swimmingk with one hand only, for pullingk him oud off vater. Him bloddy hero man.' He crushed my shoulder to his breast and shook it till I was breathless. 'Him bloddy Superboy!' In that moment, I believed him, and I was grateful to him for bringing it to everyone's notice. Mine especially.

Joe's arm was resting on my shoulder again when we walked out, this time for support. Halfway across the street, he stopped. 'Neddy,' he slurred, 'mine think maybe nod goot idea for mine drifingk.'

Me driving wasn't a terrific idea, either, but I figured I was marginally the better option. We left the Falcon parked in the street, and I drove us back to Dead Darby's in the HD. Joe slept most of the way. He regained consciousness enough to stumble out of the car, and I helped him into the hut. I made up a bed for him on the floor, with a pile of hessian bags Jess and I had salvaged from the rubbish at the back of the petrol station.

As I got him down onto it, he was seized with a fit of coughing. The coughing turned into an awful gurgling sound from deep inside him. He suddenly gripped my arm, his eyes bulging. 'Konji!' he shouted, then something in Hungarian I couldn't understand… a word sounding like *fooladok*, over and over.

The eyes found mine. There was a glimmer of recognition. The grip on my arm relaxed and his head dropped back on the pillow. He fell into a restless sleep, in some distant alien place.

Tibrogargan

The elation of the big strike had been dulled by what had happened at Jack's that night – the falling out between him and Joe; the recurrence of the Smoking Dog syndrome; the unproveable certainty that Jack knew what I needed to know; his stubborn refusal to admit it. Jess had gone to Kerracan for the weekend. There was no one to talk to about it.

She scored a lift to the gemfields early Monday morning, so she could get to Hegarty's claim in time to start work.

'What's this for?' She frowned at the fistful of twenties I held out for her as she walked through the gate.

I said, 'Jimmy and I hit a pocket.'

'Bullshit.'

'No bullshit.'

She put her arms around me and kissed me. 'Thanks, Neddy. It'll come in handy.' She tucked the money away, and kissed me again, hungry for the time together we had lost.

She acted like she was impressed with my new car. She didn't mention the holes. I started to tell her how they got there, but she already knew. 'Bloody Sparra,' she shook her head in disgust. 'And all over that moll Joyce Wolfitt!'

'Do you know her?'

'Met her once, in the pub. She was givin' all the blokes the come'n'get-me. Couldn't help herself. Harry had to stop takin' her in there, she was such a bloody nightmare.' She shook her head. 'Poor old Sparra. You wouldn't wanna hurt him.'

I remembered the way his gaze had kept drifting to the door, the first time I met him in the Anakie pub. I said, 'Did you? Hurt him?'

'Don't worry, lover boy,' she smirked. 'You know you're the only man in my life.' She looked at me and frowned. 'Are you alright, Neddy? You're not worried about that, are you?'

'Of course not.'

We went inside, and I told her about the row between Jack and Joe. I didn't mention anything about the dog incident, or the strengthening of my conviction that Jack was holding out on me. I had dealt with it on my own for two days. Just having her there made me feel better; I couldn't see the point in spoiling our reunion with shit like that.

I talked Jimmy into spending some of our newfound wealth on a jackhammer. We could knock out twice as much dirt with it, I reasoned. We wouldn't have to worry about sharpening picks.

He was worried. 'It's not that I don't trust them,' he explained. 'It's just whenever I get involved with the mechanical side of things, I seem to pull the short end of the pineapple.' He was willing to have a crack at it, nonetheless.

Somebody told me Rocky Myers was selling up, so I went over to Reward to make an offer on some of his gear. I came back with a Honda generator that hadn't done too many hours, a twenty-five pound Kango in reasonable condition, and instructions from Rocky not to let the bugger get away on me or it'd drag me clear through to China.

The pocket we'd hit held out for two days after we bought the thing, then dried up. Twenty weights of quality blues one day, half a dozen rubbishy parti-colours and a fistful of corundum the next. We had enough to make up a parcel for King Star which, with the remainder of the money from our big strike, would see us through three months or so if we didn't live too fancy.

We pushed on, knocking out a yard a day, burrowing through to the next pocket we knew for sure lay somewhere up ahead. The next rich pocket is the ragged-edged dream that drags a miner through the dark nights of his life, in the hope of brighter mornings.

The other thing Jimmy did to brighten up his life, was get a dog to keep him company. Harvey Braam's old Labrador bitch had dropped a litter of six bitzers. Jimmy was delighted to take one of them off his hands. I wasn't so delighted when it tumbled out of Jimmy's front door one morning when I turned up for work. I wasn't keen to have another dog in my life – one I knew I would be seeing every day from then on. But I had no say in it.

The pup followed him everywhere. It waited for him to get out of bed in the morning, so it could splash around under the water from the tank when Jimmy washed himself. On our way to the claim he would scamper round our feet, tumbling in the dirt when a boot accidentally caught him in the guts, then come galloping back for more.

If he strayed too far, Jimmy would let out one of his electrifying whistles, which spun him around as neatly as if an invisible lasso had dropped round his neck. When Jimmy went down the shaft, he would peer over the edge until he was out of sight, then settle down somewhere in the shade, eyes rarely straying from the top of the ladder, until he came back up.

Once, when we were having smoko, he scrambled up the mullock heap beside the wash tank, hooked his paws over the edge, and somersaulted in. He resurfaced, floundering, scrabbling for a purchase in the weird stuff he couldn't dig his claws into. I jumped to my feet, a familiar dread stirring in the pit of my stomach. I was half expecting him to burst into flames.

Jimmy held me back. 'He should learn how to swim,' he said. 'What if he falls into a cut full of water one day, and there's no one around to pull him out?'

He didn't drown, he didn't catch on fire, and he learned how to swim. As he grew bigger, he would take a running jump at the tank and plunge in, swimming in tight circles, splashing all the water out until Jimmy yelled, 'Don't be so flamin' stupid, Les!' We'd pull him out and he'd shake himself dry and rocket off before one of us could find a stick to whack him with. That was his name, Les. After Les Darcy, the greatest boxer the world had ever seen, according to Jimmy.

Two weeks had gone by with no sign of Joe. Jess and I went out to his camp near Rubyvale. The fridge in his hut had run out of kero, and stank of bad meat. In Kerracan, Becky said she hadn't seen him since the barney three weeks ago. She'd give him a clip over the bloody ear, she said, if the bugger had the cheek to turn up out of the blue, expecting her to be all pally with him.

We assumed he was on a binge with the Scrub Alky mob. But Dutch Harry told us he had spent a week with them, then buggered off one morning without saying goodbye. They hadn't seen him since. We started to get worried. The only person left to ask about him was Jack.

He was rummaging through junk in a fallen-down shed behind his hut when we pulled up in the HD. I hadn't spoken to him since the night Joe crashed into his fence. Not that I hadn't wanted to; I just couldn't think of anything to say that I hadn't already said. What else was I going to do – put my hands around his throat and shake the truth out of him? I guess I'd been waiting, hoping he might come round. So far, he hadn't.

'G'day Jack,' I said. 'How're you going?'

'Plugging along,' he replied, bush etiquette requiring him to add, 'Would you like a cup of tea?'

I got some satisfaction out of refusing his hospitality. 'No, that's alright. We're in a bit of a hurry.' I told him Joe had gone missing. I asked him if he knew where we might find him.

He inclined his head towards Jess. 'If he's not with your mob, he's probably holed up with Dutch Harry and his mates out at the Scrub Alkies' camp.' We told him we had already checked there. He picked up a length of rusting axel rod, and examined it. 'Well,' he said, 'if you're not going to have a cuppa, I'd better get on with it.'

We were about to leave, when Hegarty's Range Rover skidded to a halt outside the gate. Jess shot me a look, as if to say. 'Here's trouble.'

Watching Hegarty striding toward us, arms swinging, I wondered if this was going to be some sort of showdown over the bad blood between him and Jack. He sure wasn't paying a social visit. Jack was watching him too. I remembered his warning to me: *Watch your back with that bastard.*

Digger's hackles bristled. I caught sight of Boofhead, his sad jowls hung over the rear window ledge of the Rover. He spotted

Digger and issued a challenging woof. I tensed. This was a bad situation. A two-dog situation.

Arriving in front of the three of us, Hegarty glanced at me and frowned. I said, 'G'day Sylvester.'

He nodded without replying, and turned his attention to the object of his visit. 'How're you going, Jack?'

'Sylvester.' Jack regarded him coolly.

I was put in mind of two men in a boxing ring, eyeing each other off from their respective corners; their faithful seconds, the dogs, doing the same.

'I won't beat around the bush,' said Hegarty. 'How much do you want for all this?' He jerked his chin in the general direction of the hut and the claim it stood on.

'It's not for sale.'

A burst of brittle laughter. 'Everything's for sale. Would you knock back half a million bucks for it?'

'Is that what you're offering?'

'I'll give you twenty thousand, take it or leave it.'

'I'll leave it, if it's all the same to you.'

Hegarty gave a little snort of contempt. 'You like scratching around in the dirt for a living, do you, Jack?'

'I get enough to keep me going. I'm not interested in burying buckets full of money in the back yard.'

'Wouldn't be any room for it would there, with all the skeletons you've got buried there?' He turned to me. 'You should ask him one day. He's got a few stories to tell, the old Trapper.' Jack's eyes flicked in my direction. He turned without a word, and started walking to the hut. 'You could tell him about your glory days in the League of Nations,' Hegarty called after him. 'What was it, the president or something you must've been, were you?'

Jack kept walking, but his dog hung back. Its attention was focused on Hegarty's bloodhound, who had chosen that moment to lunge through the open window of the Range Rover. He landed on the ground awkwardly, a front leg crumpling under him. Digger rushed in. I'm sure he had never seen a more inviting target than those great flapping ears. He latched onto one of them, and shook it until his feet came off the ground. Boofhead, baying in mournful outrage, swung his head from side to side in a vain effort to dislodge him.

I could feel my throat constricting.

'Giddout out of it, you mangey bloody animal!' Hegarty had a boot raised, ready to kick. I was aware of Jack coming out of nowhere, to slam his hands against the bigger man's chest, causing him to stumble back a pace. 'Touch that dog, and I'll knock your block off!'

I was focused on the dogs. Boofhead's moaning howl had become a storm of crackling pain in my head. Digger's coat was smouldering. I braced myself for what I knew would follow. But the familiar symptoms were tempered this time with something new — anger, pity, passion — whatever it was, it drove me to action. I had to stop the pain. Instead of sinking to my knees, I threw myself on top of Jack's dog. I wrapped my arms around his wiry body, and hauled him off his feet. He wouldn't let go of the ear.

The coarse hair of his coat rasped my cheek; my hands pressed into the softness of his guts. I realised I had hold of a real dog, not some smoking creature from hell. Nothing to fear. I reefed upwards again, straining against the combined weight of both dogs – then found myself staggering backwards with the sudden release of tension as Digger let go. Or so I thought.

I heard said Jess say, 'Shit, he's torn the bugger's ear off.'

I still had him in a bear hug, his head so close to mine I could feel the heat of his breath on my neck. A fleshy, dun-coloured wafer flecked with crimson was clenched between his teeth. He struggled and growled. The severed ear plopped in the dirt at my feet.

'Put him down,' said Jack. I put the dog on the ground. 'Git inside.' Digger slunk off in the direction of Jack's pointing finger.

I saw Hegarty crouch down beside Boofhead. The unbearable howling had reduced to a whimper. 'Jesus Christ,' he muttered, as he brushed dirt off the bloodied flap of torn ear. I saw him wrap his arms around a gangling tangle of legs and get to his feet, unsteady under the weight of the great hulking thing cradled in his arms. Blood from the ripped ear dripped in the dust.

He was glaring at Jack. 'You'd better keep that mongrel thing of yours away from my claim.'

'Don't worry,' said Jack. 'He's choosy about the company he keeps.'

Their voices came from a distance. All I could see was Boofhead, bleeding and miserable. I was seized with the injustice of it all. I picked up the flap of ear and took it over to Hegarty. It seemed to quiver with a life of its own. I said, 'You might be able to stitch it back on.'

'Thanks.' He held the dog out from him, so I could tuck the thing in the pocket of his shirt. It struck me that it was a poor return for the twenty-dollar notes he'd been stuffing in mine.

'Have you finished?' Jack had taken a step towards us. 'Now, you can get off my claim.' He shifted his gaze from Hegarty to me. 'The lot of you.'

The bastard was lumping me in with his mortal enemy! Because I had dared to lay hands on his dog, I presumed. I couldn't think of any other sin I'd committed. I felt like smacking him one.

'Leave it, Neddy.' Jess had hold of my arm. I let her steer me towards the HD.

'That fucking arsehole.'

'Another time,' she said.

'That *fucking* arsehole. I'm sick of this shit.'

I was still shaking when we drove off.

Jess said, 'Are you alright? You had one of them turns, eh.'

'Yeah.'

'You looked shit-scared.'

'I was.'

'How come you grabbed hold of the dog, then?'

'I don't know.' I was too angry to want to think about it. 'What skeletons in the back yard? What the fuck was that all about?'

'Jack foolin' around with Ailsa, I suppose. Him bein' a drunk, and all that.'

'Everybody knows that. He meant something else.'

'I don't think so, Neddy. He was pissed off with Jack, that's all. He just wanted to hurt him.' I swerved to avoid a bog-rut in the track. She said, 'You sure you're alright?'

'I'm fine. They give me the shits, the both of them. Everything's giving me the shits. I came up here to learn something, and I wind up being the meat in the sandwich in some stupid fucking squabble between those two arseholes.'

She steered the conversation back to our original mission. 'Why don't we go and see Uncle Bob? He might know where Joe is.'

I'd never met her uncle. He had a reputation as a bit of a hermit. Black Bob, people called him; the only Aboriginal resident of the gemfields. Jess had told me once that he and Jack had worked for Hegarty as ringers, on Upson Downs.

'Is he a mate of Joe's?' I said.

'When Joe's off the grog, yeah. Bob don't touch the drink. They get together now and again for a bit of a yak.'

I was intrigued. 'What d'you think they see in each other?'

'Search me. Maybe they like each other's stories. That's usually why people like each other, isn't it?'

She pointed to a track running off the main road, a mile or so out of Sapphire. It circled round the back of Little Bessy. Duffer country. As we got closer to Bob's place, you could just make out the grassed-over, circular depressions on either side of the track where dud shafts had been sunk fifty years earlier. Nobody in their right mind would peg a claim behind the Bessies. A perfect place to set up camp, as far as Bob was concerned.

He was washing clothes in a tin tub as we walked down the slope towards him. A dripping shirt dangled from his hands. Jess introduced us. He shook suds off his fingers and wiped them on his trousers to shake my hand. His eyes drew me in. A shock of drifting white hair threw the rugged terrain of nose, cheekbone and brow into relief. It was a familiar profile, but I couldn't nail it. He offered us the obligatory cup of tea. We accepted, and he went into his hut to get the makings.

I sussed a movement in the bush up the slope behind the hut. Through a tangle of brigalow scrub a black horse, barely visible, was grazing on what grass it could find.

'That's old Elvis,' said Jess. 'From Bob's ringin' days.'

Bob's tin cave reminded me of my first shelter on the gemfields. Sheets of fire-blackened galvanised iron banged onto a bush-timber frame. Flattened cardboard cartons or sugar bags to fill the gaps. There was an absence of rubbish around it, unlike places like Jimmy's or Jack's where the backyard doubled as a junk dump. A strand of fencing wire did for a clothesline, the clothes he had just washed hanging pegless over it. Beside the fireplace was a dead tree stump with a flat top, all that remained of a stringybark felled long ago.

He chucked a handful of tea leaves into a billy bubbling over a fire inside a ring of rocks. He hooked the billy out of the flames and led the way with a rolling limp through the door of the hut.

It was cool inside from the shade of the surrounding ironbarks. There were no windows. The grass underfoot had become bare earth floor, swept clean, with tufts still growing near the walls. There was a cast iron bed-frame up one end, a horsehair mattress and a wooden fruit crate for a table beside it. A few personal belongings on the crate... shaving mirror and brush, a transistor radio. A stockman's pocket-knife, its bone handle worn smooth. Propped against the crate was a cracked saddle, in need of re-stitching. There were books that didn't look anything like Jimmy's Marshall Grovers or Carter Browns. They had hard covers.

Bob poured tea from the billy into two tin mugs. He found an empty jam jar for himself. Jess and I sat on the edge of the bed while he took the only seat available, the ubiquitous oil drum stool. He hadn't seen Joe.

'Did you try Dutch Harry's camp?' We told him we had.

He sipped tea from the jam jar, holding it between finger and thumb near the top where it was cooler.

I could see Jess was nervous. 'Ned was the bloke that tried to save Pauly,' she said.

'I know.' He blew on his tea.

'He's a writer.'

'Is that right? That must be interesting.'

I nodded towards the books. 'What are you reading?'

'A bloke called Henry Reynolds.'

'Uncle Bob's a big reader,' said Jess. And to her uncle, 'So's Ned. He went to university.'

He nodded.

'What's it about?' I asked, to fill the silence.

'It's about what happened to the Aborigines, after the White invasion.' He sipped his tea. 'Did they teach you anything about that at university?'

I said, 'They called it "white settlement".' I smiled, hoping he would share the joke.

He had the eyes of an old croc, submerged near the bank of a creek. He said, 'What would you call it?'

Jess wrapped a strand of hair round her finger. 'Ned doesn't want to get into all of that, Uncle Bob.'

'Isn't that what you're supposed to do at university? Ask questions, investigate?'

'He was a student, not a friggin' professor.'

'That doesn't stop a man askin' questions. And you watch your mouth with me, girl.'

'Sorry.' She looked at me through the tops of her eyes, and fell silent.

I said, 'Your uncle's right. I probably didn't ask enough questions.'

'It's never too late to start,' said Bob. The old croc moving in. 'You could start now.'

Jess made a move to get up. 'We might have to go, Uncle Bob. We're worried about Joe.'

He didn't hear her. He had come up out of the water and pounced. Challenging me to dismiss him.

I said, 'What happened around these parts, when the white fellas came?'

'It was open war,' he said. 'Like everywhere else.'

'I knew there were massacres. I never heard about wars.'

'What's the difference between a war and a massacre?' He drained the last of the tea from the jar, and flicked the dregs out the door.

Of course I had heard of the massacres. Who hadn't? They were in the distant past. Regrettable, but in the past. Sitting in that tiny enclosure with someone who still felt the pain, they were suddenly closer. Their aftermath lingered in the iron walls around us, creaking under the weight of afternoon shadows falling off the surrounding scrub.

He fell silent. I was sweating. Trapped in a tin shed with an old croc of a Murri ready to roll me under because of what my ancestors had done to his, was the last thing I needed. I fought down the impulse to get up and leave.

I said, 'Jess mentioned you went south after you left Upson Downs.'

He seemed happy enough to change the topic. 'That's right, thought I'd try my luck across the border. New England area.'

I told him I went to school in Armidale. I asked him if he knew the Quinlans.

He said, 'Their mob come up from Kempsey way. I didn't know 'em well, I was only there a coupla years.'

I told him about Ray at St Andrews; what good friends we were. 'I tried to get in touch with him a few months ago, but I couldn't find him.'

Maybe he was pleased to learn I had a Koori friend. He said, 'I was plannin' on goin' back down there for a visit soon. I'll see what I can find out about him, if you like.'

He broke off, his attention caught by something outside the hut. I turned to see a crow had landed on the tree stump beside the fire. I looked at Bob looking at the crow, and I knew where I had seen him before. He was Tibrogargan, the Glasshouse leviathan, in life-sized miniature; a saddened old man gazing eternally into the ocean of his past. It was as if, in searching for my own life, I had wandered into the remnant history of a whole culture. I felt alone and vulnerable. I remembered the contempt in Val Harmon's eyes, that day in the Railway Hotel; my own misgivings about getting involved with Jess.

I looked across at her. Her eyes were shut as she combed dreamy fingers through her hair. For a paranoid split second, she became part of the conspiracy to lure me to this place. Paranoia that had taken the shape of burning dogs, swelled up now to engulf everything.

Bob returned to his primary interest. 'They killed 'em off, and they took their land away from them. But that ain't the worst thing they done. Worse than all the murders, all the stealing of the land, was they destroyed our history. All we've got left is the people who remembered, to tell that story to us. Soon there'll be none of them left.' He fell silent again.

Jess was looking at me. She knew I was in trouble.

'Have you got a story to tell?' Bob was saying.

'Yes.' All I wanted was to get out of there.

'If you've got a story to tell, and you don't write it down, it'll be gone forever.' His eyes shifted. Behind me, satin wings flapped off into the bush. He snapped his fingers. 'Just like that.' He frowned. 'Are you alright?'

They helped me outside.

'It's so bloody hot in there,' said Jess. 'I don't know why you don't put some windas in.'

'I will, one day. How're you feelin'?'

I said, 'I'm alright.'

'You looked like you seen a ghost.'

'I'm okay now. I'm sorry.'

'You don't have to be sorry.'

In the open air I was starting to feel better. I'd been away for a long time. I bent down and put my head between my knees, giving the familiar world time to come back.

'He gets these turns,' I heard Jess say.

Midnight Butcher

It was dark when we got back to Darby's. Jess brought beer out of the fridge. Can't beat a stubby of the old home brew when you're losing your fucking mind.

'Big day, Neddy.'

'Big day.'

'I shouldn't have taken you there. Mad old bugger.'

'It wasn't him.'

'It was him on top of all that shit with Jack, eh.'

'I suppose.' I didn't want to think about it.

'Is it gettin' worse?'

'It was different.'

That's the way the conversation went. Jess doing what she could to get me to talk about it. Me monosyllabic. I wasn't holding out on her, I just didn't know what the fuck was going on.

She said, 'One good thing, eh.'

'What's that?'

'You grabbed onto that dog.'

'Is that good?'

'Whatever it was, you didn't run away from it. You grabbed hold of the bugger.'

'I suppose.' She giggled. 'What?'

'You were huggin' that friggin' dog like it was the last thing you had left in the world.'

'It was.' I started to laugh. We both rolled about. I said, 'I felt *great*, hugging that dog.'

I couldn't work that one out. We cracked another stubby.

Joe was big enough and ugly enough to look after himself, Jess reckoned. She wasn't going to lose sleep over him. I couldn't think of anywhere else to look for him. I had bigger problems.

Easy enough to forget Joe. Not so easy, Jess's uncle. 'Write it down,' he said. But all he was thinking about was the annihilation of a whole race of people. I was wrestling with life itself. *My* life. I had to get to that early place, and a part of me was terrified of what I might find. It was guarded by burning dogs.

I was fast asleep when I became aware of a tentative knocking at the door of the hut. It was a moonless night; I scrabbled in the dark to find a torch. I looked at my watch. Five o'clock. 'Are you there, Ned?' came a muffled voice. 'It's Tex.'

I opened the door and blinked. I hadn't seen him since the night in the pub after I bought the wagon off Dutch Harry. His hook-nosed face under the black ringer's Stetson with the silver badges was thrown into dramatic relief in the torch beam. 'D'you want some meat?' he said.

'How much is it?' I stalled.

'I'm not sellin' it,' he said impatiently. 'Do you want it or not?'

I reckoned I did. He beckoned with a finger and I followed him outside. A Valiant ute was parked at the gate, motor idling throatily. He reached in the back of the tray, pulled out a heavy-looking sugar bag and thrust it at me. 'Gotta get goin',' he apologised. 'Got a few more deliveries to make.' He hopped back in the driver's seat.

I leaned in at the window, the bag dangling from my hand. I saw a .22 rifle lying along the back of the seat; two boxes of bullets on the passenger seat.

I said, 'Thanks, mate.'

'Don't mention it. Sparra said you knew how to keep your mouth shut. Know what I mean?'

He chucked the ute into a reverse U-ey. It lurched into first gear and burbled off down the track.

Jess came out in a T-shirt and bare feet, squinting sleep out of her eyes. 'Who was that?'

'Bloke with some meat for us.'

'I hope it's fresh,' she said.

I reached into the sugar bag and pulled out a hindquarter of yearling, skin and hoof attached. It was steaming. I said, 'If it was any fresher, you'd be chasing it round the paddock.'

I headed for the woodheap. The sky was brightening, the first kookaburra cackling as I hacked away at the hoof with the axe I used for chopping wood. Jess brought a knife out and held the shank steady while I slid its point along the selvage.

The hide dangled from my hand. 'What am I going to do with this?'

'Bury it,' said Jess. 'And if he comes around again, tell him to bugger off.'

'Why?'

She took the hide from me and held it up to the dawning light. 'Open your bloody eyes will ya?'

The sun's first rays lit up the brand burnt into the hairy pelt: a capital 'H' enclosed in a circle. I saw Hegarty jabbing the iron at me as he told me how his grandfather had a reputation for branding everything he owned, including the men who worked for him.

'Who gave it to you?' said Jess.

'I met him in the pub one night. His name's Tex.'

She rolled her eyes. 'Tex Holgate.'

'D'you know him?'

'Hegarty forfeited a claim on him a couple of years back when he was doin' time in Muddrington Road.'

I knew that if a claim remained unworked for a period longer than two months, it could be forfeited by whoever cared to nail a notice to one of its corner pegs. There was an unwritten code amongst the miners that you didn't jump someone's claim if it was known they were sick. Or in gaol. Hegarty didn't care about codes, written or otherwise.

'There was nothin' he could do about it. But when he got out of Muddrington, he went into the butcherin' business. He usually gives you the first lot free.'

I dug a hole fifty yards up the hill from the hut behind the dam, just inside the homestead lease's boundary fence. I buried the hide, taking care to rake gravel and grass over it so it would never be found.

I wasn't there when Jimmy's accident happened. I went up in the afternoon to deliver some carbide he had asked me to collect for him from Jackson's Hardware. I would usually find him pottering around outside, mending mining equipment or scratching through the pile of junk out the back for something he needed. He was nowhere to be seen.

'There, Jim?' I called.

I let myself in the front door. Les snarled at me, hackles up. I went through to the room at the back. Jimmy was laid out on his bed. He tried to sit up. 'Jack!' he said. 'Come and sit down.'

It was no surprise he didn't recognise me. His right cheek was swollen like a fist, the dark-blue colour of a plum. Blood gleamed angrily in the slit of his left eye. The open one was glassy. This was more than Joe's measly little cut over the eyebrow. And there was no one to help me this time.

I said, 'It's me, Ned.'

'Ah, Ned. Time to strike a blow for the wicked, is it?'

'You won't be striking any blows for anybody, mate. What happened?'

He lay back down. 'Les…' he broke off and winced, careful not to touch the eye as he cupped a hand around it.

'Les did this to you?'

'The friggin' windlass,' he croaked. He struggled to remember how it had happened. '…sending some jack-picks down the shaft… went to jump in the bucket… let it go to grab him. Blessed handle jumped up and whacked me. I'm a bit the worse for the wear of it, I'm afraid.' His head wandered like his neck was made of rubber.

I managed to get him into the car while he could still walk. I hoped to Christ he was going to last out till we got to Emerald.

A range of purple cloud had been building in the east, blotting out the last of the sun as the HD bounced along the track to the main road. Big drops splatted on the windscreen. Thunder rumbled a distant threat; a blaze of sheet lightning threw the windmill into relief as we neared Sapphire. Jimmy, barely conscious, slid across the seat, making it difficult for me to steer. I had done a bad job of bogging up the holes in the roof. One of them leaked onto the steering wheel making it even harder to hang on to.

We got to the highway. The HD nearly came off the bitumen onto the treacherous black-soil shoulders half a dozen times on the way in. At the hospital, they brought a stretcher out and got him into casualty where they whacked some morphine into him. An intern promised me they would take care of him.

I collected Jess from Kerracan. The backpack she carried her clothes in was heavier than usual. 'Books,' she said. For her Uncle Bob, I presumed.

We called in to check on Jimmy on the way back through Emerald. He was asleep; the duty nurse told us they'd be able to give us a better prognosis the next day. It was still raining.

We got to Dead Darby's in the early hours of the morning, and put the kettle on. We sat on the floor in front of a crackling fire, sipping mugs of hot coffee, listening to the rain pounding. I wondered what I was going to do next. With Jimmy out of action, I was short of a mining partner. I would've approached Joe, if he had been available. I knew Jack wouldn't be interested. Sparra was too unreliable, and too fond of gelignite.

Hegarty's fifteen hundred bucks was looking pretty good. Could I rationalise that I was really doing Jimmy a favour, by talking him into selling up? No. That was the kind of thing Hegarty might've done. It wasn't fitting for a bloke judged by Jimmy to be 'the genuine sixpence'. I would do the best I could on my own on Bessy, putting some of what I earnt aside for when its owner got back.

Jess had suggested helping out at the shaft, winding up buckets. She had been offered a job packing deliveries at a shop in Emerald. It would mean she would only get out to the gemfields on those weekends when her father was back from the railways. She needed the money. We decided she should take the job.

I was going to miss our nights together. In the few months she had been living there, Dead Darby's had become a proper home.

Jess said she was going to miss me too. 'I suppose you'll wind up in the pub every night.'

'I doubt it. I'd have to dig twice as hard, to pay for booze.'

'Well,' she said, 'looks like you're going to have some time up your sleeve.'

She unzipped the backpack and pulled out some clothes. She dug deeper with both hands, and hauled out something else. She put it on the floor in front of me.

It was beautiful. It was sleek, it was elegant, it was bright orange. It was an Olivetti Lettera, series 52 portable, brand new, its amphitheatre of keys as yet unstained by the gallons of ink that would clog them in the years to come. It set my senses tingling with a mixture of excitement and dread.

'Where did you get it?'

'Ordered it from a shop in Rocky,' she said. 'Gordon Archibald brought it out for me.'

I said, 'You're mad. You can't afford this.'

'Bullshit I can't. Some crazy bugger give me a whole swag of money a while back. Said I could do what I liked with it.' There was a note of triumph in her voice as she added, 'No excuses now, Neddy.'

A nerve jinked somewhere deep. The day in Bob's hut had struck a chord that echoed from deeper down in the territory of my childhood than anything to do with the tragedy of his race. Somehow the two had become intermingled. I could taste the same fear that had paralysed me every time my fucked brain conjured up a burning dog. *No excuses now* was the verbal equivalent of being dragged to the edge of that territory, and told to walk in alone. I would do anything to avoid taking that first petrifying step.

All the joy of seeing Jess, hearing her laugh, the gift of the typewriter, vanished. Panic took over. Rationality went out the door.

I said, 'We can't go on.'

Jess said nothing. I couldn't look at her. I heard her say, 'What d'you mean?'

'I'm no good to you like this.'

'What're you talking about?'

'Me. My fucked-up head. Everything about me.'

I must've looked mad. She leaned back, as if to get a better look at me. She said, 'I know you're crazy. I told you that doesn't worry me, I've known lots of crazy people.' She laughed. 'It's no worse than havin' cancer or something.'

Val's taunting, malicious voice came ringing out of nowhere, just as it had at Bob's place. The old man's reptilian eyes blinked. I fought down the notion of Jess being part of their conspiracy. I kept my voice calm. 'I just don't think we're right for each other.'

'What?' Anger replaced disbelief. 'Are you tryin' to get rid of me?' I couldn't answer. 'Not right for each other, is that what you said? So what's been goin' on for the last few months? You keepin' me hangin' around for a souvenir or something, is that it? You wanna take some pictures of me to show your friends back in Sydney? The little gin you picked up in the bush?'

'You know that's not true.'

'Isn't it?'

The callousness of what I was doing didn't come into it. As I saw it, I was simply doing what had to be done. I saw her face dissolve into a portrait of hate and hurt. My heart dropped like a lead weight.

She drew her head back like she was ready to strike. 'What is it with you? You can jump in a river to save a kid you've never met, but you haven't got the guts to be honest with me.'

'I am being honest…'

'No you're not. You're ashamed to be seen with me because I'm a boong. Say it, why don't you, instead of carryin' on with all this 'not right for each other' shit.'

'That isn't it.'

'Well what is it, then? You just got tired of fuckin' me, is that it? Did you find somethin' better?'

'No!'

'Jesus Ned.'

'There's nobody else, I swear.'

'I'll go home in the morning,' she said.

The space where I was supposed to say something mushroomed. The crushing weight of the night filled the silence. The dreadful prospect of being alone hit me. 'I don't want you to go. This is our home, here.' I was struggling to get back in the door I had shut.

'Not for me it isn't, Neddy. Not when you pull shit like this.'

'I'm sorry. I'm really sorry I said what I did. I'm fucking confused.'

'You and me both.'

'I'm afraid.'

Saffron licks from the fire danced along the profile of her face, blazed in her eyes, and blurred. A log dropped in the fire, a kaleidoscope of unidentifiable fragments, the pathetic weight of my existence slipping with it.

I felt the smooth heat of her hand on mine. 'What're you frightened of?'

'Me.'

'You're Neddy Sheridan, aren't you? That's nothin' to be afraid of.'

'This whole fucking place. It's out to get me.'

I thought she smiled. 'Don't take any notice of all that shit old Bob spouts. It's nothin' to do with you. He's just an angry old man, that's all.'

'When I first met you, I never gave any thought to… where you came from.'

'I come from Kerracan City. Does that bother you?'

'No.'

'You had to think about it. Is that what you meant when you said we're not right for each other?'

'No, it really wasn't that. I was scared of losing you, because I'm so fucked up.'

'So you thought you'd get in first.'

'Something like that. I was scared shitless that day with Bob.'

She squeezed my hand. 'There's nothin' to be scared of out there. It's just the bush. Same as it always was.'

'I don't want you to leave me.'

'I won't. As long as you want me.'

'I want you more than anything else.'

'You're still a prick.'

'I know. But I love you more than any other prick you'll ever know.'

She kissed my cheek. She whispered in my ear, 'If I ever catch you with anybody else, I'll cut your balls off and feed 'em to the dogs.'

She took the coffee cup from my hand. We went down to the hard floor, cloaked in the warmth of the fire.

Apricot Yellow

I had resigned myself to getting nothing out of Jack; if there was anything to get. Since the incident with the dogs, it had become impossible to approach him. Even if I had been able to talk to him, what else was there to say? He had turned into a lumpen, malignant frustration. I was feeling more fucked up than when I'd left Sydney. I would've cut my losses and left the gemfields, if it hadn't been for Jess.

Wherever else I went, I wouldn't have her. She couldn't leave her family. I couldn't bear the thought of not having her with me, even if it was only for the weekends. I had become closer to her than I had ever been to anyone, Cathie included. She accepted me for who I was; I loved her for that, and for who she was. It was the closest I was going to get to happiness anywhere.

We visited Jimmy as often as we could. A doctor told us that under normal circumstances he would have been allowed to leave in a couple of days, but the concussion had aggravated a pre-existing condition caused by the belting his brain had copped over all those years in the ring. They wanted to do more tests. I would be unwise to bank on having him back as a mining partner for some time.

The days were getting hotter. Tough blue skies streaked with mares-tails. The thunderstorms had stopped; the air sticky with the promise of their return. Prices held steady with King Star and the other buyers. More and more itinerants were drifting in from the depressed markets of Lightning Ridge and Andamooka and Coober Pedy, keen to give sapphires a go where opal had failed them. Friday nights at the pub got more and more crowded. Without Jess there, I was enjoying them less and less.

I met up with a couple of hippies who had come up from the Ridge. I took them back to Darby's after closing time. We got stuck into the home-brew and some fierce dope the hippies had brought with them, and I was too sick the next morning to dig. I took the weekend off, and went down the shaft again on Monday. I felt guilty for the two days digging I had lost. I felt like I was being punished for having a good time.

The lack of colour in the wash was compounded by how little of it I could process, working alone. The mining business was giving me the shits. The snake would have been the last straw, if its appearance hadn't coincided with Joe's return.

I was knocking down with the jackhammer, shutting my mind to its relentless, nagging clatter. Through it, faintly wafting down the shaft, came the gentler putt-putt of the generator. The wave-beats of both sounds mingled in a syncopated, hypnotic rhythm. I imagined I could hear my name being called. The motor missed a couple of beats, surged briefly, and coughed to a halt. The hammer stopped rattling. I was sure I had filled the gennie's tank before I began. 'Fuck it!' It had to be a fuel blockage, which might take hours to fix.

A familiar voice came booming from the top of the shaft. 'Whad for you nod bloddy answer me when I'm been call you, you bloddy bustard?'

'Joe,' I yelled. 'I'll be right with you.'

'Take your time.'

'I've got plenty of that.'

'You nod understand,' he persisted. 'Iss bedder you moof slowly.' I stiffened. 'Been ven I am commingk here, a bloddy snake. One black bustard.'

'Okay, I'm coming up.'

'You nod listening. Ven him run from me, him fallingk down bloddy shaft.'

'Where is it now?'

'Nod for worryingk, Ned. Him grap onto rope on way down.'

Nod worry, my arse! In my panic, I had convinced myself that if the thing suddenly dropped it would go straight for me, attracted by the heat of my blood. I knew nothing about snakes. It seemed logical.

I inched my way to the bottom of the shaft. I craned my neck. Maybe Joe was pulling my leg. I looked up. He wasn't. It was a black bastard alright. A big one, wrapped around the windlass rope, winding itself up, tail braced against the wall. With each upwards movement, it shifted its tail, pushing itself up an inch at a time. It slipped back...

'Where is it I now?' I shouted, from the far side of the ballroom.

'Him still on rope.' Then a second later, 'Him drop now.' A coiled tentacle thudded onto the empty bucket hooked to the rope and hung there, draped over the handle like black tinsel.

'What am I supposed to fucking do now?'

'Leaf everythingk to me.' He was laughing.

'What the fuck d'you think you're going to do?'

'I mean I vill drop piss of paper and pen for you been makingk vill. Leaf everythingk to me!' He thought it was the best joke he had ever made. His laughter echoed down the shaft, which must have upset the snake, because it started uncoiling. I braced myself to jump over the thing if it headed in my direction. I had no intention of letting it corner me, to strike and jab and puncture me until I turned blue with its poison. I saw it slither towards the entrance to an old drive to the left of the shaft. I scuttled to the ladder and shot up it in record time.

Joe was still laughing. 'I'm been hearingk some liddle girl down this hole.' He mimicked my shrill plea, '"Vot I supposed to do now?"' He doubled up, until the laughter wheezed to a stop in a fit of coughing.

He had lost weight. He was clean shaven, but there was a grey pallor to his face at odds with the sunburnt ruggedness I remembered. He gripped my arms with his big hands. I thought he was shaking me, until I realised his body was possessed by a constant trembling. 'How youm been goingk?' he said.

'I'm real good. Got a jackhammer!'

'Some bustard been tell me Jimmy bashingk himself around. Some horse kickingk his head, or somezing.'

'Windlass handle,' I said, pointing to my cheek bone. 'Lucky it didn't knock his eye out. So how've you been?'

'Nod bloddy good, madder of fact. Been I am liffingk vith boys in Scrub for some time. Do nothingk all day bud dringk, dringk, dringk, those buckers! Nod eatingk. Been bloddy bad for health.' He coughed again, as if to prove the point. He pulled the tin of Dr Pat from his pocket to roll a durry. 'I'm been leafingk this pipple now. Been for last two veeks I am liff at Dip Crick by mine selluf, for dryingk oud.'

'Deep Creek?'

'Ya. Spent nilly all mine bloddy money for Bundy,' he lamented. 'No lazy bustard of Scrub boys vant to dig for more.' He spat a shred of tobacco on the ground, and picked up a pebble to chuck at a scurrying lizard. 'Been I am vonderingk if maybe you vill like somebody for vork vith you. Till Jimmy commingk back from ospidal.'

I shrugged. 'Why not?' That was our contract, signed and delivered.

I jerked a thumb in the direction of the shaft. 'What are we going to do about the snake?'

Joe tapped the side of his nose with the confident air of someone who had been down this road before. 'Leafingk to me,' he said.

That afternoon we lured the thing into a bucket with some live mice in a cage that Joe got from Fred Coogan, whose little boy kept them as pets. He had rigged up a contraption out of a garbage bin lid with cut up sugar bags hanging from its circumference. We positioned it over the top of the bucket, lowered it to the bottom of the shaft on the windlass, and sat down to wait.

Half an hour later I heard frantic squeaking. We shone a torch down the shaft and saw glossy black coils in the bucket; the dull scarlet of the snake's belly. Joe pulled a string attached to the contraption. The garbage bin lid dropped and the sugar bags flopped over the sides of the bucket.

'Wind op!' Joe shouted.

I pumped the windlass handle until the bucket appeared, wrapped in its sugar bag shroud. A black head poked from under it, weaving from side to side. I stretched back as far as I could without letting go of the handle. The snake was less than three feet away, its glistening eyes focused on me. 'Doan let go!' Joe ordered.

He had banged a six-inch nail, bent over to form a hook, into the end of a long stick, which he now used to jag the bucket over the edge of the shaft. I let go of the handle and the bucket hit the ground. As I stumbled back, my foot caught on a rock. I crashed to the ground on my arse. I watched in horror as the snake slithered out from under the sugar bags.

From a corner of my eye I saw Joe snatch up a shovel. He drew his arm back like a javelin thrower… and launched. The snake, all fluid velocity one instant, was a writhing puzzle of corkscrew loops the next. From ground level I could see it contort in ever tightening coils, powerless to control its own death throes. Its head hung from the rest of its body by a sliver of gristle. Joe jabbed at it with the shovel and it came away, jaws agape, globules of venom dripping uselessly from its fangs. Death spent in death.

I stared at the snake. Joe, pale as a ghost, was staring at me. He hurried over to me, greatly agitated. 'You been okay? Him nod bidingk you? You okay, Konji?'

I said, 'I'm fine. But I'm not Konji.'

Back at Darby's, Joe sat clutching a stubby of brew, staring at the floor. He had hardly spoken a word since we got back.

I said, 'How're you feeling?'

'Been see him again,' he said, without looking up. I waited, giving him time. 'Mine brother. Him allus afraid for snakes.'

'Your brother in Hungary?'

'Vas youngker as me. Him name Konrad. Call him Konji.' He sipped from the stubby. 'Him bin die vile I am holdingk him.' He sucked in a trembling breath. 'Vas eighdeen years olud. Him study for been law man. Him more cleffer as me, Konji.'

'How did he die?'

'Been ven Russkies bring tanks into Budapest. I'm been vorkingk in fagtory. Somebody tellingk me iss big crowd in Parliament Square… tanks are coming there. Konji and him freindts vant for sendingk them back. Alvays I haf tell Konji, "Nod for geddingk mixud up in this things. Iss too dancherous!" I leaf fagtory and I run to this place.'

I waited while he sucked on the stubby.

'Russkie tanks are there. Shootingk start. Effrybody runningk... pipples fallingk. Bloddy bullets...' he imitated bullets whistling past his ears. 'I'm been lookingk effryvere for Konji. Then somebody tellingk me some boy hit vith bullet, him callingk for Josef...'

He trailed off, voice failing. 'Vas Konji. Him been hit here.' He pointed to his chest. 'Him laugh ven I say him nod die yet, him nod old bucker like me. Only snake can kill tough guy like him!' He threw back the rest of his stubby and belched. 'Then him die.'

The day was going. A sheet of iron, cooling, cracked like a gun shot. Joe wrapped both hands round the stubby like he was warming them. 'Been if I am leaf fagtory more soon, him mide be cleffer law man now.' He brushed his cheek with the back of a hammy fist. 'Been I am fightingk in street after this. Then, ven Russkies bringingk more tanks, and pipples from Reffolution been take back to Russia, must I leaf Hungary, or...' He drew a finger across his neck to demonstrate the folly of running the risk of transportation to the Gulags.

I had always assumed Joe had left Hungary voluntarily, in search of a better life; had come to the gemfields with dreams of making his fortune. I realised now, his dreams were of a homeland to which he might never return; a family he would never see; a brother dead before his time. My resemblance to the latter was a last thread connecting Joe to a life that could never be recovered. I was glad to be able to give him that much.

He sucked on the stubby and discovered it was empty. He got to his feet. 'Vere been my bloddy beer, you mizzerable bustard? Iss vorse here as geddingk a dringk off thad mizzerable bloddy Missingham!'

Joe laughed when I showed him the Kango. It was a toy beside the thirty-pounders they used when he worked for the Main Roads.

He picked the thing up in a beefy paw, like it was a water pistol, jammed the pick into the face and squeezed the trigger. A chunk of wash the size of a watermelon crashed to the floor. He raked it back with his free hand and leant in to knock out some more, never letting go of the trigger. I had to shovel like buggery to keep up with him.

I was sorting through the heavy wash at the end of the third week, when an odd-looking stone turned up. A yellowy-orange looking thing that should have been a zircon. You just didn't see sapphires that colour. But I knew it wasn't a zircon. Joe was just as mystified as me. We took a run out to the Willows on the Sunday, to show it to Wally Ingerson, the cutter.

'Whad you thingk is thiz bloddy thing?' Joe asked him.

Wally, eyes bugged in the glass of his magnifying lenses, turned it this way and that between oxide-blackened fingers. He pushed the glasses back on his forehead. 'It's a bloody good sapphire,' he pronounced. 'Cut it on the table, it'd go four carats… maybe four-twenty. It'd be criminal to go for size on the cross, a thing like that. What would you call it… sort of an apricot-yellow?'

'Peach, you said, Ned.'

'Yeah,' Wally agreed. 'Apricot.'

He had seen all the famous stones: Donovan's Yellow, Clifton-Parr's Golden Flower, the Black Star of Queensland - above all else it was their extraordinary size that distinguished these legendary beauties. But he had never seen anything to match the peculiar colour of the stone he was holding between his fingers.

He handed it back to me. 'Do you want me to cut it?'

'Been we doan know who own bloddy thing, yet,' said Joe.

We had agreed from the beginning that we would split all the stone we mined two ways, and make our own arrangements to sell. The way it worked was, one of us would separate the stone into two piles, as equal as he could make it, taking into account all the variables - colour, cross-table, weight, shape, silk, visible flaws, etc. The other one got to choose which pile he wanted. Jimmy would get a percentage from any sales, as rent for the claim.

After we left Wally's we went back to Dead Darby's to divvy up. It was Joe's turn to do the dividing. I left him to it while I went to the fridge to dig out some brew. The process usually took about ten minutes. By the time I got back with the beers, he had finished. On the table in front of him was a pile consisting of all the blue stone we had dug that week. Beside it, on its own, was the apricot-yellow sapphire. I said, 'This pile's worth five times as much as that bloody thing!'

Joe shrugged. 'Then you ged youselluf a good deal, iss it?' He leant back with his hands behind his head, and yawned. In the fading light of day the stone showed the faintest tinge of its rarest colour. It represented everything that was different, every possibility for things I had never dreamed might happen.

My fingers closed round it.

Later, when he saw me putting it in a matchbox for safe keeping, Joe wagged a reproving finger. 'Nod kipping thiz bloddy stone in madgebox,' he admonished. 'Onless you vant iss loosing it foreffer.'

He told me how he had lost a three and a half-carat cut stone a couple of years back. A female acquaintance, thinking she was doing him a favour, decided to clean his hut. Coming across a matchbox lying on the table near an ashtray full of butts, she picked it up and shook it. Hearing no rattle of matches she assumed it was empty, opened the firebox of the stove, and chucked it in.

I said, 'Do they burn?' Sapphire, I knew, was the second hardest mineral after diamond.

'Nod burn.' Joe shook his head. He spread-eagled his fingers and made a crackling noise in his throat. 'Yust shadder. Iss goot if you are vanting a lod of liddle stones.'

I tucked the matchbox in my pocket, making a mental note never to leave it lying around near a stove.

'Been ven I am finish this tin off tobaggo,' he promised, 'I vill gif to you for kipping this stone in. This vay, vill neffer burn.'

Deep Creek

Gem Prince gave Joe a hundred bucks for his parcel of stone. The first thing you did with a hundred bucks, according to Joe's philosophy, was invest a fair-sized chunk of it in booze. He proclaimed the next day a public holiday, so we could all go fishing.

Sparra got wind of it, which meant the whole League of Nations did too. They decided they were due for a holiday as well. Reg was home from the fettlers' gang for a six-day break. Joe would pick him and Jess and Becky up, and whoever else wanted to come. We were to meet up at Beryl Carmody's shop.

It was a stinking hot day at the end of November, the landscape immersed in an endless cobalt sky you could drown in. Not a wisp of cloud from horizon to horizon. The sun beat down like a hammer, pounding the back of your throat when you breathed. 'Bit warm out there,' said Beryl, and you knew it really was hot. She loved the heat, but that day you could see it dragging her down.

We bought bread in the shop, cans of soft drink for the kids, and a few dozen sausages in case we didn't catch any fish. Or in case the water hole had dried up, as gloomily predicted by Sparra. Beryl chucked in half a dozen Paddle Pops for the kids. She reckoned the freezer was going to pack it in if the temperature didn't drop, and she'd lose the lot anyway.

I was walking to the door, when she pulled an envelope from the 'S' slot and handed it to me. 'Jack gave me this to give to you, before he left.'

I said, 'Where's he gone?'

'Search me. Said he won't be back for a few weeks.'

My name was written on the envelope in a script too delicate, I thought, for Jack's callused fingers. Then I recalled the delicacy with which those same fingers rolled a cigarette. I remembered the only book I had ever seen in his hut, an impressive looking thing, hard covered – the words *Gods* and *Graves* in its title. There was much about Jack I didn't know; might never know, I thought, as I took a folded note out of the envelope. It was written in that same effeminate hand.

Dear Ned, it said. *I'm going away for a little while. Not sure when I'll be back. Keep an eye on the hut for me, would you? I don't want anyone camping in it. Don't worry about the poddies, Beryl's looking after them.*
All the best,
Jack

It seemed weird that he would fall back on me, of all people, as caretaker. *What are you really saying here, Jack?* I wondered. *I might never come back at all, so don't bother hanging around trying to dig more information out of me?* I thought, *You're running away from me, you bastard.*

Becky helped Joe carry the stuff to the Falcon, where Reg was waiting with the kids. Val hadn't come. 'She's a bit crook,' he said.

The Paddle Pops were half melted by the time we got to the cars. Glen and Bobby and little Wayne wolfed them down and sucked at the juice left in the bottom of the wrappers. Jess and I were in the HD, Bobby and Wayne in the back. Glen went with Joe. Joyce had tired of Dutch Harry by that time, and had latched onto Angus McLaren. They climbed in the cabin of a cranky old Chevrolet flat-bed truck. Sparra and the rest of the League lay or sat on its tray, like greasy leftovers from the boozing of the night before, frying in the sun. We set off in ragged convoy.

We followed Joe's Falcon west along the road to Alpha and took a side track about ten miles out. The HD bounced through swathes of brown spear grass, scaring up flocks of rosellas flashing in the sun. A bronze-wing pigeon skimmed through the underbrush like a plump bullet. Above the gurgle of the wagon's rusted-out muffler, the throb of cicadas floated in waves on the heat.

The HD's steering wheel jerked to the pull of the rutted track. Brown dust seeped through the pick-holes in its doors. Wayne and Bobby scuffled and laughed in the back seat, until the laughter turned to tears and Jess swung round to yell at them to behave. She rolled her eyes at me as she turned back, her bare brown arm brushing against mine.

I took a hand off the steering wheel to rest it on top of her thigh. 'Cheeky bugger,' she said, teeth flashing in a grin as she brushed my hand away. I put it back and she shoved it away again and we pushed and shoved each other hard, Jess laughing, me steering with one hand trying to keep the car on the road while we rocked back and forth and then Wayne and Bobby joined in, yelling at us to 'bloody behave!' just like she'd done to them, and wrapped their arms round our necks and tickled us until we were all a tangle of dusty limbs and cackles of laughter and the HD ploughed into a rotten wilga stump, and came to a halt with a crunch.

Angus stopped the Chevy and leaned out the window. 'Whadda ya think you're doin', ya mad bastards?' Neither of us could answer for laughing. Angus and Joyce exchanged pitying looks. They waited until I backed off the stump and made sure we were still mobile, and we set off again. I had never felt happier. I didn't care how long it was going to last.

The track converged on a gully that ran into a deeper watercourse skirting the base of a massive granite outcrop. We followed it for twenty minutes, until it petered out in a clearing surrounded by casuarinas. The Falcon stopped. Angus and I slowed our vehicles to a halt behind it.

We all piled out. The kids shouted and laughed and yanked at each other's arms as they chased each other into the bush. I looked up at the towering she-oaks, their whispering voices silenced by the still heat. I could smell water.

Angus hauled himself out of the Chev, followed by Joyce. The others shambled off the back. Jess and I helped Joe and Becky get the food and fishing lines out of the boot of the Falcon. With Joe leading the way, we headed along the track to the creek. We came through the she-oaks, to Deep Creek fishing hole.

The sandy creek bed we had been following butted against a pile of rocks crumbling off the ridge. In the Wet, I imagined, water would tumble over them in a boiling torrent to splash into a broad lagoon below. Now they lay baked dry, glinting quartz sparks in the sun. The recent pre-Wet storms had been enough to send a trickle of water into a deep muddy hole a hundred feet long, feeding the she-oaks clinging to its banks. Water beetles jetted across its surface. Dragonflies hovered, cicadas droned.

Joe doled out fishing lines to those who hadn't brought their own. Becky showed me how to dig for mullygrubs beneath the rotting bark of a fallen tree, and soon we had a jam tin full. We threaded them onto hooks. Jess shouted at the kids bursting out of the scrub across the other side of the hole not to jump in yet or they'd scare the fish away and she'd belt the arse off the first one that did. Their shrill voices trailed behind them as they skittered into the bush, crackling through the brittle undergrowth like a tribe of larrikin goannas.

Joe and Becky found a spot on a rock. Angus and Joyce plonked themselves under a tree away from the rest of the Scrub mob. Reg moved to the downstream end of the hole. He didn't want to be near a rowdy mob like us, he said, making enough racket to scare the fish into next bloody week. He walked slowly along the bank, eyes scanning the waterline for the places yellow-belly liked to feed. Jess and I scrambled over the rocks and settled in the shade of a tall ironbark on the opposite bank.

The sun rode high, pulsing to the beat of the bush. From across the other side of the waterhole came a murmur of voices as the Scrub boys distributed booze, Sparra's petulant complaints rising above the others. Becky's high-pitched giggle erupted as she punched Joe in the ribs for something cheeky he had done to her. Presumably she had already delivered the promised clip over the ear, and was happy for him to be 'all pally' with her again. Yips of laughter pinpointed the position of the kids, scattered through the densely-timbered halls of stringybark and black box.

Reg found his spot, and hunkered down to prepare a line. The Scrub boys stopped arguing. A butcher bird piped two crystal notes. The cicadas, as if conducted by some unseen hand, fell silent at a beat. It was that time of day when the bush falls into a eucalyptic stupor. We might have been an ancient tribe gathered round some primeval billabong, all thought bent to one purpose, fingers busy baiting the hooks that would feed us. The mullygrubs plopped into the water, one by one.

I weighted my line down with a rock, and propped my back against the sheltering tree. Squatted on her haunches in front of me, Jess was concentrating on the point where her line, jerking to faint movements of her finger, vanished in concentric circles on the surface of the water. In my shirt pocket lay the apricot-yellow sapphire. I decided then, that when it was cut and polished I would give it to her. The stone had come to symbolise all the good that could come out of a shitty situation. Jess was my sparkling gem of hope. It had to be hers. I closed my eyes, and dozed off.

I was woken by the shouts of the kids returning from their foray into the bush. Jess had gone back to the other side of the creek, evidently to fetch something she had left in the car. She was coming from that direction, along the path through the trees. I saw her stop as Sparra appeared out of nowhere, blocking her path. Unsteady on his feet, something in the movement of his shoulders suggestive of insistent entreaty. Jess was shaking her head, laughing to conceal annoyance. She tried to step around him. I got to my feet as he made a clumsy grab at her arm, but she was too quick for him.

'What was that all about?' I asked, when she got back to me.

She dismissed it with a wave of her hand. 'You know what Sparra's like when he gets lit up.'

'That's no excuse.'

'I can handle Sparra.' She kissed my cheek. 'You're the one I gotta watch, eh.'

A triumphant shout of 'Gotcha!' rang out. Everybody jumped to their feet to watch Reg hauling a flapping yellow-belly from the water.

'You little beauty!' yelled Becky, picking her way nimbly over the rocks to help him land it. Jess and I stayed where we were, watching them bring it onto the bank.

Glen and Bobby burst from the scrub, attracted by the shouting, racing each other to be first to see the catch. Becky slapped at their groping fingers. 'Gid out of it you kids! Where's Wayne? I told youse to look after him!' Little Wayne came stumbling along behind them, bawling. Becky picked him up. She hugged him and tickled him until the tears became giggles.

I became aware of Sparra standing on the opposite bank, looking in my direction. Our eyes met. He turned away. I thought, *I'm going to have to watch you, mate.*

Reg came with Jess and me on the drive back. The yellow-belly wasn't big enough to share amongst the lot of us. We had decided he should keep it. 'I'll cook it up for you,' said Jess. 'The way Mum used to when we was little.'

'That'd be good,' said Reg.

Mention of Val took the gloss off his good humour. Jess told me she had been on a week-long bender when he'd got back from the fettlers' camp. We lapsed into silence. It stayed that way until we reached Sapphire.

While we swapped cars, Jess told me she wanted to go home with her father. They would call in on Jimmy at the hospital on their way back to Kerracan. I leaned in at the window to kiss her goodbye. The happiness that had consumed me earlier on, persisted. I wanted to drag her out of the car and hold her and tell her how much I loved her. I said, 'Look after yourself.'

'You too. I'll try and get out at the end of the week.' I watched the Falcon rattle across the bridge till there was only a floating veil of dust to show where it had been.

Driving past Jack's on the way back to Darby's, I was reminded of the note he had left me. I wondered if I would ever see him again. I tried to imagine what was going through his head, wherever he was, but it was impossible. He had given me nothing to work on; I knew as little about him now, as when I first met him. I had to reconcile myself to the fact that, however I dealt with my problems from now on, it would have to be without Jack's help. It was small consolation that he had never given any, so I wasn't missing out on much.

Getting closer to Darby's, I noticed a strange car parked outside the gate. An older model Hillman, it wore an apron of road dirt from bonnet to boot, indicating a long distance travelled over unsuitable roads. I pulled up behind it and got out. As I walked towards it the door opened and the driver got out.

She studied me guardedly, like a wary animal ready to bolt at the first sign of danger. She looked tired and dusty. The jeans she was wearing made no attempt to disguise the soft new bulge of her belly.

'Hullo, Ned,' she said.

I said, 'Hi, Cathie. Fancy seeing you here.'

The dying sun spread a warm glow through the hut. Cigarette smoke streamed through the circle of her unpainted lips.

'How did you find me?' I asked, knowing the only possible answer.

'Terry gave me your forwarding address.' She leaned forward. 'He made me promise not to tell you he gave it to me. You won't let him know I did, will you?'

'Of course not.' I made a mental note to kick him in the cods next time I saw him.

Her left knee jigged, belying the nonchalance with which she dragged on the cigarette. She said, 'I could do with something to drink.'

Jess and I had managed to get a batch down a few weeks earlier. I brought two stubbies of brew from the fridge, with glasses. She arched an eyebrow as she watched the cloudy concoction rise to a head.

Perched on my best oil drum chair, she crossed her legs with greater effort than usual, and surveyed her surroundings. 'So' she said brightly, 'Maison Sheridan!' If she intended the remark and the smirk to be amiable, both came across as patronising. 'I didn't believe it when he told me you were living on an opal field.'

'Sapphires.'

'Shows how much I know.'

I said, 'Why are you here, Cathie?'

'I was in the neighbourhood. Thought I'd drop in and say hullo.' When I didn't smile she said, 'I was worried about you.' She held her glass up to examine the brew in the failing light. 'What is this stuff?'

'It's a bit young,' I said. 'Hasn't had time to settle.' She took a sip. 'You haven't answered the question.'

She frowned. 'Why do you think I'm here?'

I said, 'Well, one thing I know for sure, you didn't travel twelve hundred miles just to see if I was okay. There's got to be something in it for you.'

'Such as?'

'I'm not going back,' I said, 'if that's what you've got in mind.'

'I'm not asking you to.'

I saw what she was driving at. I laughed. 'You wouldn't last two days in this place!'

She looked at me directly, gaining confidence. 'I'd last for as long as it took, Ned. Like you said, I didn't come all this way for nothing.' The sun had vanished. The orange glow of dusk soaked into the darkening bush. Her voice became soft. She said, 'So. Do you want to give it another try?'

'What the fuck are you talking about? In case it slipped your memory, you were the one who climbed into bed with our mutual best friend and rooted the arse off him!'

She looked at me without remorse, and I felt guilty for shouting at her. She had got the upper hand. I said, 'It's getting dark.'

She watched while I put lumps of carbide in the lamp and topped it up with water. I put a match to the nozzle and the acetylene flared. It hissed softly, its incandescent blue light wiping out the gentle contours the half-dark had lent her face.

I imagined it amused her to see me drinking home-brew, lighting a primitive lamp, driving a car that looked like a mobile sieve. I was angry, but it wasn't her I was angry with. This was a new kind of anger, rising up to protect something I had found that had nothing to do with her. Something I feared, though I embraced it; coveted, though I feared it. For all that, it was a part of my life that was mine and mine only, that I didn't want anyone else to touch.

Neither of us spoke. When she finally broke the silence, there was an echo of the fragile centre of her I had briefly glimpsed on that rain-lashed day on Edgecliff Road. She said, 'I'm truly sorry, Ned. I never wanted to hurt you, I would never have dreamed of doing that.' She told me she had been worried sick about me after I left. 'You'd been acting a bit weird those last few months, Ned. I don't know if you realise.'

'I know. I'm feeling a lot better now.'

'Terry said you came here looking for someone.'

'Terry had no business saying anything about anything.'

She waited for more, but I wasn't about to give her a recap on all that had happened to me on the gemfields. The mere fact of her presence had stirred up a whole lot of shit I was managing to keep under control. I wasn't going to give her the satisfaction of seeing a reversion to the old Ned; the paranoid, fucked-up Ned who needed her cool head and guiding hand. The only good thing about her being there, was that it coincided with Jess's absence. I could be thankful for that.

Her eyes widened as she caught sight of the Olivetti lying on the floor near the end of the bed; the untidy pile of typed up A4-sheets beside it. 'Are you writing?' she asked.

'Yes, I am.'

'That's terrific. That is really good, Ned.'

I could tell she meant it. My antagonism waned. She had come a fuck of a long way, and there was still the matter of the confession I never got to make after my return from Armidale. I owed her that much, at least. I said, 'I wasn't doing much, when I was with you.'

'You were doing fuck all,' she said wryly.

'Why didn't you say something?'

'I knew you had bigger things to deal with.'

It came as no surprise that she knew there was weird shit happening for me, back then. I was so self-involved at the time, I'd never tried to think about it from her point of view. She told me that when she finally badgered Terry into telling her where I was, she had dropped everything and driven straight through to Emerald, hardly stopping. Spent the night in a motel there, and came out to the gemfields the next day. She stopped talking, and lowered her head. I could see she was crying. I didn't dare move towards her.

Eventually she said, 'You're right. I do want you to come home.'

I said, 'This is home.'

One of Jack's poddy calves was bawling its head off down on the flat. Cathie tugged a handkerchief from her jeans pocket. While she blew her nose, she cast an eye round the corrugated-iron walls, the wattle-and-daub fireplace, the bush timber rafters. She said, 'It's good. I can see why you like it.' And a second or two later, 'I'm pregnant, I guess you noticed.'

'Yeah, I noticed.'

She told me she wasn't seeing Steve any more. She had left her job at the ad agency. She felt confused about everything.

There was another silence, during which it occurred to me she had nowhere to sleep that night. It was a long drive back to Emerald. I said, 'You can stay here tonight if you like.'

'Thanks.'

'I'll sleep in the kitchen.'

She glanced at the mattress on the floor. 'I don't mind sharing. You don't have to fuck me,' she added, as she tucked the handkerchief back in her pocket. 'I'm assuming if you're kicking me out in the morning, you haven't got the hots for me.'

'It isn't that,' I said. 'I can't.' She frowned. Then it dawned on her. I said, 'Her name's Jessica.'

A gecko, sucker-padded to a roof-beam above us, whirred and clucked. The soft hiss of the lamp drowned out all other sound.

She pushed her glass forward, back in control. 'That stuff's quite good.'

'Are you supposed to be drinking?'

'No. But I've been very good, so don't rouse on me. I've earned a bloody drink.'

She followed me to the kitchen, watching me root in the fridge for the beers. 'What's she like?'

'Jess?' I opened the bottles and handed her one. 'You'd like her. She's honest.'

'Unlike me.'

'More than you.'

'Gorgeous, of course.'

'Of course. Like you.'

She smiled wryly. 'Haven't lost any of the old charm, have you Ned?' As we moved back to the other room, she asked, 'Is she a country girl, or a blow-in?'

'What's it to you?'

'I'm just curious. Might as well do a bit of fact-finding while I'm here.'

I said, 'Her people have been in the area a long time.'

'Early settlers.'

'Longer than that.'

She looked at me sharply. 'You're kidding.' It must have popped out before she could stop herself.

I said, 'She's more than gorgeous. She's a really beautiful person.'

'I'm sorry, I didn't mean…'

'It's alright.'

'Jesus, I… that's amazing. I'm proud of you.'

'For what… doing my bit for cultural reconciliation?'

'Christ, Ned. This is a bit hard for me to get my head around, you know?'

I said, 'You don't have to get your head around it, Cathie. It's nothing to do with you.'

She couldn't argue against that. We prattled on for another half hour about everything in general and nothing in particular, and went to bed.

Time Please!

The crunch of tyres on gravel woke me. I struggled into a pair of jeans, squinting against the morning light, aching in one shoulder from a cramped sleep on a pile of blankets on the kitchen floor. Cathie was snoring.

The red Range Rover was parked on the other side of the fence. Boofhead tried to follow Hegarty through the gate. I noticed the ridged welt, hatched with stitch-holes across the bottom of its left ear. The lower portion had a grey tinge to it. Hegarty put a hand down to steer him away. 'Back you go, Boof,' he said. 'You can't come in here.' He dropped the wire loop over the gate-post and turned to me.

I said, 'Morning, Sylvester. What can I do for you?'

'I did a spot muster last week. Looks like I've lost half a dozen yearlings.'

My guts went cold. 'What happened to them?'

'They got knocked off. What d'you think, they went on a holiday to the fuckin' Bahamas?'

I figured he must've made the discovery recently. Fresh rage caused his cheeks to quiver.

I said, 'Are you sure?'

'Sure of what?'

'I don't know. Don't sheep and cattle just... die?'

'They died alright... of a bullet between the fuckin' eyes. One of my ringers found a head buried under some rocks in a gulley up the back of Poverty Hill.'

'I'm sorry,' I said lamely.

'Not half as sorry as the cunt that dodged 'em's gunna be when I catch up with him.' I waited, not sure whether or not he was implying I was involved. 'I hear you've been mixing with the Scrub Alkies. It's odds on it's one of those useless pricks been knocking my calves off. I want you to keep an ear to the ground for me, alright?'

I was about to respond when, over his shoulder, I caught sight of Boofhead, up the slope near the dam. He was scratching around the bottom of the boundary fence opposite a patch of freshly-turned earth tantalisingly beyond reach of his paws, but not out of range of his super-sensitive nose.

I said, 'I'll let you know if I hear anything.'

'Too fuckin' right you will. If I find out who it was before you do, I'll see to it Trevor Gillespie runs you out of town.'

'For doing what!'

'For being a pain in the arse.' He took a step closer to me. 'What you've got to realise, son, is you're living on borrowed time. I don't give a rat's arse that you talked Jimmy out of selling me that claim. I'll get it one way or another. But I do object to those maggots helping themselves to my livestock.' Then, for no apparent reason other than the fact that he'd let off a head of steam, the aggression evaporated. He heaved a sigh. 'How's the book coming along?'

The book? I hadn't spoken to him since the dog fight at Jack's place. His coming to see me, asking for help in his own quaint way, suggested that he now saw me as an ally. I had intervened on behalf of poor old Boofhead, after all; we had been chucked off Jack's claim together. Just the same, I couldn't believe he was still on about the fucking book. I had assumed it was no longer an issue.

'Slowly,' I said. 'Mining keeps you busy.'

'Mining.' He hawked up a gob of phlegm and spat. He shifted his stance uncomfortably, trying to find the words. 'Look Ned, there's something I like about you. You're a useless poor bastard, I suppose all writers are. But at least you've got the guts to stick up for what you believe in. I admire that in a man. I'm giving you the opportunity here to do some good for yourself, for Christ's sake!'

Everything about his manner confirmed what I had suspected from the day Jess told me about his wife leaving him. It wasn't the book he was interested in, it was me. I was a surrogate for the son he had lost. I represented what he might have become, ten years down the track. I got the strange feeling that, in offering me the opportunity to enter into a conspiracy with him, he was patting me on the head; steering me clear of danger, trying to mitigate the pain of my stumbling attempts to write.

I said, 'I don't know what sort of a spy I'd make!'

But he wasn't listening. He was looking beyond me. An eyebrow shot up. 'Fuck me roan.'

I turned to see Cathie leaning against the door of the hut, a hand on one hip. One of my T-shirts hung loosely off her shoulder to a point at the top of her thighs, leaving the rest of her long legs to speak for themselves.

They spoke volumes to Hegarty. 'Done alright for yourself there, son!' He winked at me knowingly, proud of me.

I didn't feel like explaining and, as it turned out, I didn't have to. His attention had once again been diverted, this time by Boofhead's excited whining.

'What's that friggin' mutt up to now?' The dog was clawing frantically at the bottom of the netting fence. Hegarty marched up the hill towards it. 'Boofhead! Git back down here you silly bloody animal!' He dragged it away by the collar, taking care to avoid the mutilated ear.

He helped him into the back of the Range Rover, and banged the door shut. Then came over to me. 'You give me a name, and I'll slip you the readies so you can sit down for six months and write that book without having to worry about all this mining bullshit. Alright?' He winked again. 'Go on then, you'd better get back to work.' He got in the Range Rover and drove off.

Cathie came over to where I was standing, watching the vehicle grow smaller in the distance. 'Who was that?'

'Sylvester Hegarty. Local patron of the arts.'

Cathie asked me if she could stay another day before she set out on the long haul back to Sydney. I was worried about her driving all that way, given her condition. It made sense for her to be well-rested before she set off again. I said, 'Okay.'

I knew she was pissed off, and I could understand why. She'd come a long way for nothing. Jess and I had visited Jimmy in hospital during the week, and he'd asked me to check on his hut. I asked Cathie if she would like to come with me, to see where I was working.

We got to Big Bessy. She leaned cautiously over the edge of the shaft and peered into the gloom. She had no wish to see anything underground at first hand; we decided ladders, in her condition, probably weren't a good idea anyway. I gave her scraps of information about the mining process; a bit of the history of the place. Told her about Joe and Jimmy, and their ongoing battle with Hegarty.

Her appetite whetted for the exotic inhabitants of the gemfields, she hinted at some sort of social activity for her last night there. Could I take her to the pub I had mentioned?

I wanted to show the place off to her. I was proud of it; I wanted her to see how I was fitting in. I could see no harm in taking her to the pub for an hour or two. I knew Jess was tied up with her family, so there was no chance of a clash of females. With Missingham back from his holiday, Joe's ban had come into effect again, so the likelihood of the bar being destroyed around us while we drank, was reduced. The odds against both of these assumptions being shattered on the one night, were slim. Or so I thought.

Saturday night at the pub was a rowdy turn at the best of times. I was prepared for that. What I hadn't allowed for, was Sparra Perkins choosing the moment I arrived with Cathie, to start getting stroppy with Misso for not letting him put a bottle of Bundy on tick. As we walked through the door, Misso was running off a long list of inconveniences he had suffered at the hands of Sparra and his drunken mates: broken items of furniture, toilet cubicles splattered with vomit, smashed glasses etc., etc.

The band had plugged in, the musos tuning up. We found a table just big enough for the two of us, as far away from them as possible. A singer called Bronco, sporting a dusty Akubra turned down at the front, got stuck into a spirited version of *When the Rain Tumbles Down in July*.

We found a table as far away from them as possible, and I went to order drinks. I could hear Sparra, digging in, ticking off the reasons why Missingham should give him credit. There was the piddling sum involved, the amount of money he and his friends had spent in the place over the years, the unblemished record of Sparra himself, as far as behaviour in the pub was concerned. He guaranteed the money would be paid the minute he sold his next parcel of stone.

As I turned to bring the drinks back, Missingham was saying, 'And when might that be? Next month? Next year? I might as well give it to you!'

'Sounds fair enough to me,' said Sparra, without a glimmer of irony. The publican opened his mouth to respond, then thought better of it. He turned his back and walked away in disgust.

'Miserable bastard,' Sparra muttered, as I passed him.

Missingham swung back. 'Miserable bastard. Is that what you said?'

'No.' Sparra shook his head. 'What I said was, "You're as tight as a fish's arsehole, you miserable bastard".'

All the haughtiness went out of the publican. His eyes popped. 'You're banned from drinking in this hotel,' he croaked.

I caught Cathie's eye as I joined her at the table. Her lips pursed in a silent whistle. A pocket of silence had blossomed like an air bubble around the two men. A banning was a serious business, usually reserved for a big-time offence - like riding a horse into the saloon bar for instance.

'Jesus, Misso,' Sparra protested, 'I didn't break anything! I didn't swear. What've I done?'

'You don't have to do anything!' Missingham spat. 'It sickens me to look at you. Go and crawl back into the burrow you came out of, and tell your alcoholic friends they're not welcome here anymore either. This is a hotel, not a refuge for worthless trash like you lot.' He turned and walked away, the embarrassed silence spreading in his wake.

A redness crept up Sparra's flower-stalk neck. He looked down at his bony frame, as if checking to see if Missingham had seen some deficiency in him he had been overlooking all his life. Misso would have laughed if anybody had told him he had wounded the man's dignity; in his view, someone like Sparra couldn't have possessed such a thing. He was wrong.

Sparra made his way to the door. As he drew level, I said, 'Do you want a lift home?'

'No thanks, I got things to do,' he said, and walked out.

Cathie was lapping it up. This would all be recounted one Friday night in the Four in Hand, as an exotic report from the outer reaches of the colony. There was no way she would've been able to see it as part of anybody's real life. My life. I knew I shouldn't have taken her there.

I asked her if she wanted to go home. She pretended not to hear. She squinted at the scene around us, heavily fugged-up with smoke and sweat. I could see her mind working, and I knew what it was about. She said, 'Am I going to meet her?'

'No.'

She was encroaching on my territory. My fingers strayed to the matchbox in my shirt pocket; the apricot-yellow cocooned in its bed of cotton wool. Joe hadn't given me the fire-proof tobacco tin he had promised. I had planned on taking the stone out to Wally Ingerson the next day. In the meantime it travelled with me wherever I went.

'Where do her parents live?'

I thought, *What difference does it make to you? You're never going to meet her. And if you did, you'd treat her like a museum exhibit.* I said, 'Just outside Emerald. Her Dad works on the railway.'

'Is that right?' She gave a passable impression of genuine interest in an Aboriginal employee of Queensland Rail. 'What about her Mum?'

'Household duties.'

She smirked at the irony. 'I'm being nosey, aren't I?'

I said, 'I'm sorry you didn't get to meet her.'

She knew that was bullshit. Her eyes did a tour of the room. 'Who would've thought?' she mused.

'Thought what?'

'Who would've thought Ned Sheridan would find happiness out here in...' She broke off, sensing my irritation at her veiled sarcasm; a Cathie specialty I had been happy to leave behind.

'The backblocks?' I suggested.

'It is rather remote.'

'You mean like hillbilly remote. Backwoods, that sort of thing.'

'Jesus Ned, are we having a conversation here, or a bar-room brawl?'

'You're wasting your time trying to poison my mind against her.'

'Why would I want to do that?'

'Because you want a father for the kid you're carrying, to replace the one that dumped you.'

The sharp report of flesh on flesh caused a hiatus in the conversations around us. I caught a glimpse of Missingham's head shooting up from behind the bar. My fingers involuntarily found their way to the spot on my cheek where the slap had landed, a stinging memory of the last time I had touched on Cathie's sex-life. She knocked her empty glass over as she leaned across the table to hiss, 'Do you seriously believe I need you more than you need me?'

I said, 'I don't need rescuing, Cathie.'

I didn't want to look at her. Bronco was cranking up Slim's *Big Rig* with fierce, clumsy chords. I concentrated on the puddle of beer that had spilled from the knocked over glass. It became a wall of brown sludge, rising up. In it I saw Pauly's pink lips; the white of a terrified horse's eye; a crow's wing flapping.

A part of me wanted to tell her everything that had happened: the flash-flood, Hegarty and Tex the midnight butcher, the fishing trip, our strike on Big Bessy, the importance of the apricot-yellow; Jimmy, Jack and Joe; Jess's family out at Kerracan City. Tell her how much I had changed since I arrived in this place; how much I loved Jess. So she would know I had discovered a life for myself, and she didn't have a hope in hell of taking me away from it.

Another part of me feared that in telling it, I would discover it was a lie. That the living wasn't any easier here than it had been at any other point in my life. That I had found no answers, and in failing to do so had failed Jess; I remained as much a mystery to myself as I was to her. It was that same fear Cathie had recognised in me from the beginning, and protected me against. I had clung to that protection then; it had been the basis of our relationship. Despite my efforts to block it, a voice in my head whispered that I might need it again; that Jess might not be capable of giving it.

I stared at the pool of beer. I felt Cathie's hand come to rest on mine. 'The trouble with you, Ned, is you think everybody's as good as the next person. It's what's lovely about you, but you can't go through life like that. You've got to learn to discriminate.' I couldn't tell if she was being patronising, or it just sounded like that. I refused to look at her. She pushed on, trying to get back in. 'I'm jealous of her, okay? I'm only human for Christ's sake.'

I was flattered by her jealousy. I said, 'I owe you a lot, Cathie. I haven't been fair to you.'

'But you're not coming back.'

'No.'

'I don't suppose it'd help if I belted you again.'

'You could give it a go.'

The grip on my hand tightened, then released. I sensed more love in that simple gesture than I had at any time in our whole relationship. It was heartfelt and unconditional. She was setting me free to stumble on alone.

She said, 'I do love you. Fuck knows why.' She leant across the table to kiss me. 'Good luck, Ned. I hope you find whatever it is you're looking for.'

I gave her hand a squeeze as I returned the kiss. We might have been any young couple in love, snatching a second or two of intimacy in a rowdy public place. I guess that's how it would have looked to anyone coming through the door at that moment.

Cathie frowned. 'What's the matter?'

She realised I was focused on something behind her. She turned. Jess was standing just inside the door, looking straight at us. I raised a hand to signal to her to come over. She turned and walked back out.

'Shit,' I said. I got to my feet.

'Go on,' said Cathie, 'I'll be alright.'

In my haste to get to the door I tripped against the leg of a chair and used up valuable seconds apologising to the person sitting on it. I hurried towards the door, one hand reaching instinctively for the matchbox in my pocket, my fingers closing tightly around it. I had a half-formed idea in my head that when I caught up with her, I might be able to use it as some kind of emotional weapon to cancel out the very bad fuck up that had just happened.

Nearing the double front doors, I was surprised to see Sparra there, in the process of bolting them shut. He raised a hand, like a traffic cop, blocking the exit of a woman in front of me who was trying to leave.

'I want to get out!' she objected.

'Not yet,' said Sparra, a note of urgency in his voice.

'What're you talking about?' she laughed. 'We wanna go home!'

'Not just yet, alright?' he repeated.

The woman's husband had come up behind her. 'What's goin' on, Sparra?'

I made a move to push past them…

What happened next must have passed in a matter of seconds. Details imprinted themselves indelibly: the woman's husband trying to force his way past Sparra; Sparra, hands hard against the man's chest, shouting, 'I told you to bloody wait!' The man stumbling back into me, the startled look on his face; my arm jerking upwards at precisely the moment the door behind Sparra burst open like a giant fist had punched through it.

A deafening blast blew the racket of the bar to nothingness. Lips continued moving noiselessly, and froze. A stubby of Four X drifted to the floor and smashed in silence. Falling back, arm upflung, I saw stars through a gap that had opened between the door lintel and the ceiling; heard timbers splinter in delayed reverb before the deafening roar of the explosion crashed in around us.

As I fell I saw glasses slide off the sloping deck of a table to spill their contents into a sea of stumbling legs and feet; caught a glimpse of doors sagging on their hinges, one falling slowly outwards to reveal the shattered remains of the pub's verandah. Sparra, upside down, drifted into my field of vision.

'Time please, ladies and gentlemen!' he announced triumphantly.

The publican's face, its expression of outrage weirdly converted, by inversion, to one of delight, floated into view an instant before my head hit the floor and the lights went out.

Seconds or years later, Cathie, pale-faced, was helping me to my feet. The place was in uproar. 'I think we should go home,' she was saying. A reasonable request, under the circumstances.

I managed to stand. I swayed. Missingham was hurrying back to the bar. I saw him pick up the phone. Sparra had disappeared. I became aware of my right hand, clenched in a fist by my side. I raised it and opened my fingers. I knew what I would see there. Nothing.

Circle H

That night and the next morning, while Missingham sifted through the wreckage, I searched the floor of the bar with a fine-tooth comb. I explored every crack and crevice. I interrogated anybody I could find who had been there at the time, but there was no trace of the apricot-yellow in its matchbox.

When I told Joe how Sparra had destroyed the pub's verandah with two sticks of gelignite, he couldn't stop laughing. He stopped when I told him I had lost the stone. 'I even went through the garbage cans,' I said, 'in case it was swept up and got dumped in a bin.'

'More likely has god dumped in some bukker's pocket,' he reckoned. I knew he was right. I had to face the fact that I had lost it forever. There were two things I had lost that night. Both were rare; both were irreplaceable. One of them I couldn't live without. I had to get Jess back.

First, I had to deal with Cathie. The trauma of her night out at the Anakie pub had left her short of breath, with a tingling sensation in one ear that affected her sense of balance. I was worried about her, of course. I felt responsible for having taken her to the place that might have killed her. I was also pissed off with her. If she hadn't been with me when Jess walked through the door, I wouldn't be in danger of losing the one person who had brought some sanity back to my life.

Back at Darby's, I made her as comfortable as I could. To her credit, she cut me all the slack she could. 'I'll be fine,' she said. 'Go and find your woman.'

'You should see a doctor.'

'I will, when I get to Emerald.' She knew it wasn't only her health I was worried about. 'Don't worry, I'll be gone when you get back.'

I said, 'I'm sorry it worked out like this, Cath.'

'Don't worry about it, it's been interesting. I've never been blown up in a pub before.'

She touched my cheek with the tips of her fingers, like she had that day in Edgecliff Road with the jacaranda tree spread out below, ready to catch us if we fell. It had been a gesture of reassurance then; this time it was like she was taking a bit of me away as a souvenir.

She said, 'Take care, Ned. I'll always worry about you.'

I drove straight out to Kerracan City. I parked the HD at the top of the slope, and walked down to Reg and Val's.

Reg came out to meet me. He said, 'She doesn't wanta see you, Ned.'

'She has to.'

'I can't make her do what she doesn't want to.'

'I've got to talk to her.'

I tried to step around him, but he was too quick for me. 'She's a bit upset. Give her a bit of time, alright?' He steered me away from the house. 'What happened? She reckons she sprung you in the pub with another bird. Was it the sheila from Sydney?'

'I had no idea she was coming. I got home after the fishing trip, and she was… just there. She came out of nowhere.'

'They've got a habit of doin' that, eh.'

'Jesus Reg, do you think I'd organise something like that behind her back?' My voice had risen. People from surrounding houses were taking an interest.

'Of course not,' said Reg. He hooked his thumbs through the belt of his trousers and looked at the ground. 'She thought the world of you, Neddy, you know that.'

'What d'you mean, *thought*?' He looked up at me. His eyes were those of the father of a drowned child. Only now it was him saying, *She's gone, Neddy. I'm sorry, she's gone.*

'I've got to talk to her.'

He grabbed hold of my wrist as I walked past him. 'Let her cool down a bit. You know what she's like. Once she gets an idea in her head, that's it.'

'It's the wrong fucking idea.'

'She's told me she doesn't wanta see you, and I've gotta respect that, she's my daughter. I can't let you go in there.'

The only way I was going to get past him was to hit him. I was prepared to do it, if it came to that, ridiculous though it would've been.

I said, 'At least tell me what she thinks was going on. Did she say?'

His grip on my wrist relaxed. 'She said... she reckons the two of youse had a bit of a dust-up a while back. Reckons you were worried about her bein' a Murri.'

'What?'

'That's what she said. Then, when she seen you with this other bird...' He shrugged.

'Do you think I'm worried about that? I think less of *you* because you're Aboriginal, is that what you think?'

'I don't think nothin', Ned, it's none of my business. But I know it's something you've gotta give her time to think about. You go bargin' in there now, you've got Buckley's of gettin' her back.'

It wasn't just his physical presence I was up against. What he said made sense.

'Will you tell her I came looking for her?'

'Of course.'

He walked with me up the road to where the car was parked.

'She said to tell you she'll come out and pick up her stuff during the week.' He patted me on the arm. 'It'll work out okay, mate. Give her time, alright?'

True to her word, Cathie had left by the time I got back to Darby's. I walked into the hut, feeling cowed by its emptiness. Everything I looked at or touched bore the imprint of Jess. The Olivetti sat squat and accusing on the floor beside the bed, the stack of laboured typescript beside it reduced in my heart to a pile of meaningless crap.

The overwhelming silence of the surrounding bush, that had seemed comforting and protective on that first walk up on Bower

Bird Hill, pressed in as a threat. The past couple of months, that had become a life self-contained, was exposed as a blind for the reason I had come to the gemfields; the empty hut an echo of the closed door to my childhood that I had failed to open. I caught a whiff of the stench of burning dog.

Over the days that followed I went through the motions of meaningful existence. Sleeping, eating, digging, sleeping again. Wondering how long I could bear to wait for Jess to make the next move.

Joe drove us in the Falcon to the hospital the next day to bring Jimmy home. He was a bit wobbly on his pins. No wonder, after weeks without so much as a stubby to wash away the cobwebs before he went to sleep at night. I had stocked up his fridge with brew, and he was soon looking perky. I brought Les back from the people at Reward who'd been looking after him. The skinny little pup had grown into a shaggy-faced young dog overnight. He might have been getting older, but his energy level hadn't dropped. He nearly knocked Jimmy off his feet when we came into the hut, and Joe had to put him outside. He whined and scraped at the door, before he tired of that and hared off into the scrub to terrorise the wildlife.

We filled Jimmy in on the latest gossip. He was shocked at what Sparra had done to the pub; and relieved that no one was hurt. Joe knocked the scabs off a third round of stubbies, while I brought up the business of mining. I'd been wondering what was going to happen to our partnership when Jimmy came back. For Joe it wasn't a problem. It was time for him to step out of the picture, he said. Simple as that.

'What are you going to do?' I asked him.

His laughter boomed round the hut. 'Whad you think I been doingk you crasey bustard? I kip on liffingk! You thingk I vill starvingk myselluf?' I told him I was worried about how he was going to survive. 'Ned,' he leaned forward, elbows on knees, durry dangling from nicotine-stained fingers, 'any bukker starfs in thiz country, nod deserf for liffingk. Vod is callingk thiz place, some pipples? "Lugky Country". Here a man be his own boss. Here can liff from findingk food from land. Slippingk under stars, and no bustard tellingk him to moof on. Nod you vurry aboud how I survife.'

He was sick of mining. He wanted to get back to Deep Creek to catch the big brother of that yellow-belly Reg had caught. Might camp out there on his own for a bit. He was sick of Sparra and Dutch Harry and the whole League of Nations palaver. He wanted to be on his own.

I would have offered to go out to Deep Creek with him, but I didn't want to be too far away from Jimmy, until he was fully recovered. More importantly, I had made up my mind to go back out to Kerracan the next day. I couldn't wait any longer. I had to know one way or another whether there was any chance of getting Jess back.

I watched Joe and Jimmy working their way through the stock of brew. I could see they wouldn't be happy until they had emptied the fridge, but my heart wasn't in it. I told Jimmy it was good to have him back home, and left them to it.

I walked up the track to Dead Darby's in the half-light of dusk, wondering what Jess was doing at that moment. Listening to Charlie Pride, on her own? Thinking about me? No, trying to keep the kids under control, while her mother drank herself to oblivion, more likely. I was so preoccupied with these thoughts, it wasn't until I was fifty yards from the front gate of the hut that I noticed the two vehicles parked beside the HD. The red Range Rover, and Trevor Gillespie's police car.

The gate was wide open. Gillespie and Hegarty were walking back down the hill from the direction of the dam. Boofhead was loping beside his master, who was patting his head and calling him 'Good dog.' He must have done something to please him. I had a pretty good idea what it was. They had seen me. I had no option but to keep walking.

'Want to tell me how this came to be buried on your property, Ned?' Gillespie dumped the yearling's hindquarter hide on the ground at my feet. Even in the failing light, the Circle-H brand was still visible through the dirt-caked hair.

I said nothing. Hegarty batted lazily at a persistent fly. The sympathy I had detected in him the last time we met, had been replaced by dull disinterest. 'Well, Mr Sheridan,' he said, 'you turned out to be a major disappointment, didn't you?'

In the lock-up at the Anakie police station I told Gillespie I wasn't the one who had knocked off the yearling. He believed me. He knew I didn't own a gun, for starters. But he needed to know who did it. I suppose he was hoping that by keeping me locked up for a few days I would eventually crack and give him a name. It would look better for me in court, he reasoned. He would put in a word with the magistrate, tell him I was a law-abiding citizen led astray by a notorious poddy dodger who had been at it for years. I would get off with a caution.

'So who gave it to you, Ned?' he persisted.

'I don't know where it came from,' I repeated. 'It was left in a sugar bag outside my door.'

'So why did you go to all the trouble of hiding the evidence?'

'I saw the brand. I knew it was Hegarty's, I thought I'd get blamed for stealing it.'

He sighed. 'I thought I'd seen it all till I came to this place.' He shot me a look out of the corner of his eye. 'I gave you credit for having a bit more sense than the rest of 'em.'

There was a silence. To break it, I asked him how the gem cutting was coming along. He launched into an account of the parti-colour he had cut recently for a bloke out at the Willows, with a detailed explanation of his reasons for deciding to cut it as a baguette, rather than a brilliant, due to a flaw below the girdle. The talk of cutting reminded him of something else. 'I was talking to Wally Ingerson the other day. You and Joe found a funny-coloured stone, he reckoned.'

I told him how I had lost the apricot-yellow the night Sparra blew the pub. He was sincerely regretful. 'Why didn't you come and tell me?'

I laughed. 'You think somebody was going to hand it in after they'd gone to all the trouble of stealing it?'

'I suppose you're right.' He looked wistful. 'An apricot-yellow, eh? I'd like to've seen that.' He stood abruptly. 'Well, if you remember anything that might help us locate the fairy godmother who dumped that meat on your doorstep, you know where to find me.'

I called to him as he headed for the door. 'How did Hegarty find out where the hide was buried?'

'Boofhead got off his chain and went for a wander,' he replied. 'Hegarty found him in your place, diggin' the thing up.' He shook his head ruefully. 'Bloody dogs! You can't trust 'em.' He went out and I heard the key turn in the lock.

I remembered Hegarty boasting about the minefield of baits he had planted to ward off marauding dogs. I wondered how Boofhead had managed to dodge through them to get to the hut.

I was caught between a rock and hard place. If I gave Tex up, there was no way I could have stayed on at the gemfields. It was an unwritten law that you didn't dob your mates in to the cops. Not if you wanted to be treated like some form of life higher up the food-chain than a centipede. The problem was, by not giving him up I was running the risk of leaving the place sooner than I had anticipated, whether I wanted to or not. Justice Alexander McCarthy SM was due to sit in the Emerald District Court in five days' time. It was unlikely that I would do time, as a first offender, for such a minor crime, I reasoned. I stuck to my guns.

In the end, Gillespie spoke up for me anyway, but he could have saved his breath. McCarthy was used to dealing with riff-raff from the gemfields. He found me guilty of receiving stolen goods. I got five months, with a month parole for good behaviour. They moved me to the Emerald lock-up, pending transfer to Brisbane.

Joe came to see me. He sat at the table in the visiting room and took a squiz at our sparse surroundings. 'This been nod a bad liddle place for liffingk,' was his first comment. 'Maybe iff you leavingk here soon, I vill be moofingk in!'

I was grateful for the attempt to cheer me up. He went quiet. I expected him to pull the tin of Dr Pat from his pocket, but his mind was on deeper things. He said, 'Ned, you vant to know vot I been thinkingk?'

'What?'

'Been thinkingk this been stinkingk big mess, this whole bloddy bissness!'

'You're telling me!' He couldn't know how scared I was.

'Nod thiss!' He waved a hand around airily. 'This is liddle bid off trupple only. Been I am talkingk aboud *effrythingk*.'

'You mean like, life.'

'Ya.' He nodded. 'Life.' He had pushed the chair back from the table. His arms were resting on his legs, the fingers of his hands interlocked like a puzzle. He studied the ball of digits like he believed the secret of 'effrythingk' was trapped inside them, but he lacked the courage to open them up and look it in the eye. He bit his lower lip. 'Konji...' he began, and faltered. His head sank slowly until I could see only the top of it. He stayed like that for a long time. After a while he looked up at me, unashamed of his tears. I imagined he could hear his dying brother sigh his last breath on the bleeding streets of Budapest.

He unclasped his hands and balled them into fists. 'Ve vill leaf this place!' he exclaimed. 'Ven you are oud off chail, ve go! Ve traffel to the nord. Op the Cape off fuggingk York! Ve fish! Ve liffingk off the land, like iss 'Lugky Country' vot dis bustards tell aboud!' He gripped my hands in his. 'You commingk vith me, ya?'

Compared to the reality of my situation, the absolute freedom of Cape York with its boundless wilds and emerald beaches, with Joe for companion and protector, was a glorious proposition.

'What about Jimmy?' I said. 'We can't leave him on his own.'

'Ve take him vith us! Meantime, I dig vith him for liddle bit. Maybe him come to mine camp at Dip Crick. Ve fish. Till you commingk home from this liddle bissness here. Then ve bucker off for the Cape. Vot you reckon?'

'Sounds good to me,' I said.

His grip on my hands tightened. 'Effrythingk be good now, Neddy, ya?'

Jess came to see me on the second day. The duty constable ushered her into the room. He reminded her it was a no-contact visit, then went back out and closed the door. She sat facing me across the unpainted wooden table. It was the first time I had seen her since Sparra did the job on the pub.

She said, 'How you goin' Neddy?'

'Not bad, considering.'

'What a bastard, eh.'

'Yeah, what a bastard.' It wasn't the sweet reunion I'd been dreaming of. I said, 'I came out to see you at Kerracan.'

'I know. Dad told me.'

'You never gave me a chance to explain about Cathie.'

'She's your old girlfriend. You were holdin' hands with her in the pub. What's there to explain?'

'I had no idea she was coming. What was I supposed to do?'

'Tell her to bugger off.'

'She drove twelve hundred miles to see me!'

'She musta been real keen, eh.'

'Jesus, Jess, she was pregnant! I couldn't tell her to just turn around and go back home.'

She looked at me with the expression she got when she knew she'd been right about something. Even if she wasn't. She said, 'I don't suppose you could.'

A fly circled above us, writing the monumental collapse of all hope of reconciliation in the dead air of the room.

I said, 'I'm not the father.'

'You're sure of that, are you?'

'Yes.'

'So she came all that way for, what? A bit of a chat, did she?'

Nothing I could say was going to make any difference to the certainty Jess had created in her mind. *'Once she gets an idea in her head, that's it,'* her father had said. The idea had been there since she saw me with Cathie. Now it had been reinforced with the knowledge that she was pregnant.

I said, 'I love you Jess.'

'When you need me, you do.'

'I need you all the time.'

I caught a glimpse of the cop's face through a glass panel in the door. I could've sworn he was smirking.

'Look.' Her voice softened. 'When I saw the two of you in the pub, you looked like you belonged together. Know what I mean?'

'No. I don't.'

'I reckon it's time you and me called it quits.'

'Is that what you came here to tell me?'

'You remember that day after we called in on Uncle Bob? You said, "We're not right for each other."'

'I was freaking out…'

'You were right. Only not the way I thought. I thought you were ashamed of being with me, and I was wrong. You're a good bloke, Ned. I've never met anyone like you. But there's another difference between us, that'll never go away. It's nothin' to do with skin colour or good or bad, or right or wrong. It's…' She spread her hands, trying to trap the words.

'Cultural?'

'Yeah, cultural. See? I don't use words like that. I want to be with someone I can talk to like we come from the same place.'

'Same place, or same race?'

'Don't pull that clever shit on me, Ned. I don't want us to be bad friends.'

'I'm sorry.' I really was. I was falling away inside, but I knew it was nothing to do with her. She was doing the best thing for both of us and she knew it.

She said, 'I didn't want you sittin' down there in that shit-hole for five months, expectin' me to be here for you when you come home.' I said nothing. 'I'll come and visit you, if I can get away.'

'I don't want you to.'

She nodded. 'If that's the way you want it.'

The glass in the panel quivered. The door opened.

'Time's up,' said the cop.

He was dead right.

Gillespie came to see me the morning I was being transferred, with some paper work he hadn't got around to before they moved me from Anakie. He shook water off his hat. There had been a crash of thunder an hour earlier, now there was a steady drumming on the roof. He regretted what had happened, he said, but made no apologies. The law was the law, even in a bastard of a place like this. I said, 'Yeah, I understand.'

We finished the paper work and he stood up, ready to go. 'Wanna show you something,' he said, with an air of mystery. He thrust a hand in his pocket and pulled out a matchbox. He rested it on the palm of the other hand, like a magician producing an object from some astonishing place. I prepared myself for a facet-by-facet description of his latest gem-cutting triumph.

'Feast your eyes on this little beauty.' He pushed the drawer of the matchbox open. Nestled on a bed of cotton wool was a cut stone. In the dull light of the cell, spikes of fire flashed off its facets. The colour was unmistakable.

I stared at it dumbly for seconds, before I found my voice. 'Where did you find it?'

'Somebody brought it in, said he wanted it cut. Said he bought it off a miner out at Tomahawk Creek. I knew that was bullshit. The only thing you get out at Tomahawk is those horrible bloody blues with the green cross-table. I took it out to Reward and showed it to Wally. He recognised it right off. He says, "That's the bloody thing Hungry Joe and the young bloke showed me a month ago. I'd know it anywhere."' A sheepish look came over him. He said, 'I hope you don't mind that I cut it. It's just, I thought, well, he's lucky to get the bloody thing back anyway! So I went ahead and did it.'

I told him I didn't mind at all, he'd done a beautiful job. He agreed. He turned the box slowly. The stone glittered in response to the movement. 'What a little beauty,' he breathed.

He closed the matchbox, and became business-like again. 'So what do you want me to do with it?'

I said, 'Give it to Jess Harmon, would you?'

'You want her to look after it for you?'

'I want her to have it.'

He must have been shocked that I could so easily part with something he revered like a devout Christian might worship a splinter of the Cross. His expression revealed nothing. 'I'll give it to her next time I see her,' he promised.

He patted me on the arm, and wished me luck. 'Keep your nose clean in there, Ned. You'll be back home before you know it.'

I called to him as he reached the door, 'What do I owe you for the cutting?'

He thought about it. 'You can give me a copy of that book you're writing. You'll have a bit of time up your sleeve for the next few months, won't you?'

Taipan

Muddrington Road Gaol was filled with armed robbers, rapists and murderers as well as the usual contingent of petty thieves, pimps, fraudsters and tax evaders you got in any metropolitan gaol. Plus one receiver of stolen goods from the sapphire fields out west, first offender. In the reception block near the gatehouse, I toed a white line with ten other new arrivals.

Twenty minutes earlier we'd been crammed together in the back of a cage-windowed paddy wagon, barrelling up Gympie Road from Brisbane Central, where the cops from Emerald had dropped me. The other lags had been picked up from various stations along the way.

No one had talked. With every stop, with each new body bundled in amongst us, the air in the back of the wagon became increasingly fetid; the invasion of personal privacy more offensive. It might have been ten degrees cooler on the coast, but the humidity was a killer. We sat on two bench seats running the length of the van, staring at our feet, or the roof, or the criss-crossed square of sky in the rear door, stewing in each other's vaporised sweat.

An hour after we left the city centre, the vehicle went over a speed hump and slowed to a halt. A voice up ahead shouted something unintelligible. The van moved forward. Light filtering through the meshed window in the rear cut out suddenly, as if someone had thrown a switch. We stopped again. I heard the doors on either side of the cabin open, then slam shut. More voices, trading instructions; low muttering; a burst of raucous laughter.

A key turned in a lock, and the back door swung open. A man in a blue short-sleeved shirt and navy trousers filled half the space the door had once occupied. There was a badge on the sleeve of the shirt. In his right hand he held a black truncheon. 'Out!' he grunted.

The screws in reception chatted amongst themselves like Coles employees taking delivery of a consignment of fresh vegetables. They spread us out along the white line. When it came my turn, I gave them my full name, age, date of birth. The pock-faced screw who had let us out of the wagon read out the warrant for my imprisonment. So everyone would know my crime. I would later learn this was deliberate; and, in my case, a good thing. If I had killed a kid, or raped a young girl, things would have turned out a whole lot different for me over the next four months.

After establishing none of us were suicidal – 'Not gunna top yourself, are you maggot?' - they gave us a short-back-and-sides and a de-lousing shower. Our clothes were taken away. While I was drying off, one of the screws shoved a bundle at me. He said, 'Shirt, socks and trousers. Three of each. Look after 'em, you don't get any more if you lose 'em. Understood?'

'Understood, Boss.' I had quickly learned that 'Boss' was the preferred form of address for all screws. It wasn't obligatory to use it, but you risked being branded as a surly smart-arse if you didn't.

I got dressed in one set of the regulation green clothes the screw had given me – fully designed and manufactured by the 'working' inmates at Muddro, he told me. I believed him. He marched me out of the shower block. We went through a quadrangle flanked by verandahed red-brick buildings. Ahead of us was a ten-foot-high Cyclone wire fence; beyond that, a three-storeyed, gabled brick building with an iron roof. B block.

We went through a Cyclone wire gate. The sun was setting as we crossed the deserted exercise yard. The darkening sky pressed down, squeezing an orange glow off the top of a twenty-foot-high perimeter wall to the left of the block. I imagined there was a hot-golden sunset on the other side. The screw unlocked a heavy wooden door and hauled it open. He stepped aside and nodded his head towards the dark hole where the door had been. I went through. I felt like I was leaving my life behind.

Rows of identical doors were set into each of the walls running along either side of an enormous gallery, dimly lit by the day's fading light streaming palely through an arched window set in the far wall, high up near the ceiling. Two flights of iron stairs led to the upper levels. Gantries bolted to the walls, with grated floors and wire mesh barriers gave access to the second and third floor cells.

Dying shadows of voices floated off the gantries, up into the darkness above.

The screw jabbed his baton in the direction of the stairs. He followed me up the first flight. 'Turn right!' We got to the third door along, and he told me to stop. He unlocked the door, and stepped back. I went in.

There was an iron bedstead with a thin mattress; a two-drawer locker against the back wall; a naked light globe dangling on a cord from the ceiling. The screw pointed to a bucket with a wooden lid, on the floor in one corner. 'Shit bucket,' he said. 'Leave it outside the door when you come out in the morning.' The door banged shut, I heard the key turn in the lock.

I sat on the edge of the bed. I looked at the bare concrete floor. I looked at the shit bucket. I looked at my hands. I clamped them to my knees to stop them shaking. If someone had come in at that moment and said, 'Tell us who knocked off that yearling, and we'll let you go,' Tex would have been out of luck.

I worked through the logic. If I really couldn't handle it, I could always top myself. And if I couldn't bring myself to do that, it could only mean it hadn't turned out to be as bad as I had thought it was going to be; that I believed there was something worth living for. Slender, convoluted threads of reason, vital for survival.

The lights went out. I listened to a ghostly murmur of voices, the rasping cough of a heavy smoker, snatches of muffled Country and Western music from a hidden radio. The distant thump of my heart. The second-worst thing about your first time in gaol is the loneliness. I longed for somebody - Jess, Joe, Jack, Cathie, anyone - to talk to. I pulled up an image of Ray Quinlan, Dorm 2 at St Andrews, having a conversation with an imaginary being hiding in the sleeve of his dressing gown. Acko and I couldn't breathe for laughing. I often wished for an hour or two with Ray, through the long nights at Muddro. I would later learn he might have been closer than I thought.

'Ever been fucked up the arse?' The question was put to me as I took a seat in the canteen a week after my arrival. Bluey Thompson's short-cropped carroty hair sprouted in all directions, like it was trying to get away from him. His high-pitched voice gave every word he spoke a sinister edge. He was in for stealing cars.

I said, 'Not that I can remember.'

Bluey laughed. He liked a sense of humour. 'It's just that Snowy Carroll's on the prowl for fresh meat, that's all. I thought I should warn you.' He had a vindictive streak, too.

The first worst thing about being in gaol, was the fear of rape. Bluey knew that. He took the trouble to let me know Carroll had a name as one of the hardest of the hard men in Muddro. He buggered one new arrival so brutally and over such a prolonged period of time, Bluey said, the kid committed suicide by stuffing his own underpants down his throat and gaffer-taping his head so he suffocated. Snowy told one of his mates he was sorry he hadn't found the body himself - he could've given his little buddy a farewell poke for old time's sake.

Bluey had latched onto Snowy, in much the same way a remora will attach itself to a shark, eating the predator's leftovers in return for devouring its parasites. Proximity to Snowy gave Bluey security from anybody who had it in for him. He paid for the privilege by being Snowy's dogsbody; and pointing him in the direction of fresh meat. I could feel the heat of Snowy's long distance gaze from the far side of the canteen, while Bluey and I chatted.

I put stuff like that out of my mind as best I could. On the positive side, the necessity of dealing with matters relating to mere survival took my mind off the Big Problem - the missing chunk of my life. What I had to contend with in gaol, in the present, was far more urgent. *Stick it for four months,* I kept telling myself. *Then you're out of here.*

As the days wore on, I stayed away from the other inmates as far as possible, and kept myself busy any way I could. The main thing I did was read. The visiting librarian (once a fortnight) was glad of the opportunity to deal with someone whose tastes ran beyond Harold Robbins and Alex Hayley. He was happy to track down anything I ordered. I chewed them up as fast as they came in.

Two weeks after I arrived at Muddro, another sanity-saver arrived. At mail-up after the breakfast muster, my name was called. I wasn't expecting mail from anyone. Nobody I knew from the gemfields was big on letter-writing; no one in Sydney knew I was in gaol.

The screw behind the hatch handed me a weighty cardboard box, crudely re-wrapped after a routine inspection. I could see through the rips and re-ties that it was addressed to 'Neddy Sheridan'. It was the first hint I had that Jess was thinking about me, and it cheered me up. *No excuses now, Neddy*, I could hear her saying. And Gillespie: *You'll have a bit of time up your sleeve, won't you?* If doing time in Muddro meant I got a proper start on The Book That Had to be Written, I told myself, something good would have come out of the whole shitty exercise.

I found a screw and got permission to go back to my slot. His heavy feet clumped a pace me behind all the way across the yard to B block; up the grey iron stairs; along the gantry to my cell. He stood at the door and watched me while I pulled the Olivetti out of the box.

'What the fuck are you going to do with that?' he grunted.

It goes without saying that all the screws at Muddro were hated by all the prisoners. They saw us as thieving, raping, depraved 'maggots'; we saw them as vicious, insensitive, lying cunts. This one was a bull-necked brick shithouse called 'Taipan' Truscott, the most hated one of the lot.

I said, 'I write a lot of letters, Boss.'

I waited for the mucussy snort that usually came out of him, indicating derision or disgust. It didn't come. His eyes narrowed, a sure sign he thought you were being a smart arse. The muscles in my neck tightened. I wouldn't have put it past him to smash the typewriter on the floor. *'Oops, sorry Sheridan, it slipped.'* What the fuck was I supposed to do then?

I could jump in quick and thump a fist into his fat fucking face, I thought – make a better job of it than the ringer I swatted in Anakie. I'd need to make it count, because it'd be the only blow I landed. Taipan would then proceed to beat the living shit out of me with a rubber baton designed to inflict the maximum amount of pain, short of hospitalisation. He was trained in its use. Bluey Thompson had been kind enough to supply me with graphic detail.

They went for the fleshy part of the arms, legs and buttocks, he explained, steering clear of the head and breakable bones. I would learn later on there had been a riot a few months back. Stuff had been coming out in the press about the brutal regime at Muddrington. The guv'nors didn't want any 'incidents' that might be newsworthy. They certainly didn't want any dead prisoners.

'Come on,' said Taipan, 'put it away and get back to the yard. I haven't got all fuckin' day.'

Staring at the concrete ceiling above me that night, I composed a letter to Jess, thanking her for the typewriter. I told her how much I loved her, and missed her. She was the first person I had ever met who treated me as I was, not what they wanted me to be. I loved the way she told me what was on her mind, not what she thought I wanted to hear. She was achingly beautiful. I wanted her there with me, right then. To touch, to talk to, to love.

I called up her voice, from the last time we had talked. It said, *'I reckon it's time you and me called it quits. Don't expect me to be here for you when you come home,'* and I remembered how much I hated her. I cried that night, for the first time in a long time. I never wrote the letter.

I knew Sparra had been sent to Muddro for blowing the verandah off the pub. I asked around, and found out he was on work-release with the Forestry Department. Then, one lunch time in early February, I spotted him in the canteen. They had just wheeled in the hot-box. He was standing in the queue, nursing his tin plate to his chest, knife and fork sprouting from his hand like a bunch of nickel-plated flowers.

While we waited for them to light the burners under the box, I came up behind him and tapped him on the shoulder. He spun round like an animal ready to bolt. He saw it was me. 'What the fuck are you doin' here?'

He had put on weight. Even allowing for the crap food they fed us, for the past couple of months Sparra would've been eating better than he ever had. And drinking a lot less. For all that, there was something about him that made me uneasy. His eyes peered out of some painful place, as if afraid to focus on what was going on, in case it produced even more pain. I wondered what had happened to him while he'd been inside, but I didn't ask.

In answer to his question, I said, 'Sweating on getting out, like everybody else.'

Bluey Thompson was in the queue ahead of us. 'What's on the menu today, squire?' I heard him ask Pete, the lag dishing up the food.

'Same old slops,' came the reply.

Bluey made a show of thinking about it. He said, 'I think I'll have some of the slops, if I may.'

Pete ladled watery looking stew onto the tin plate. The other kitchen lag, someone I didn't know, dug a big serving spoon into the canister beside him. 'You want spuds with your slops?'

'Why not?' said Bluey.

A dollop of mash splashed onto the stew. 'Much obliged,' said Bluey, and swung round to walk away. Sparra stepped forward at the same time. Bluey's elbow came into contact with him, and gravy from the stew splashed onto his shirt. 'What the fuck!' Bluey spluttered.

'Sorry, mate.'

The apology was all the encouragement Bluey needed to up the aggression level. Good manners got you nowhere in Muddro. 'Sorry! What the fuck good's that gunna do, ya clumsy cunt?' He brushed at the spilt gravy with his free hand. 'You must be as stupid as you fuckin' look, are ya?'

The redness began to creep up Sparra's neck, just as it had the night Missingham insulted him. I could feel him seizing up inside; the hurt was palpable. I had to say something. 'He said he was sorry. What more can he do?'

Bluey was happy to turn his aggression on me. 'He can stop bein' a clumsy cunt. Not that it's any a your fuckin' business.'

'It is my business. He's a friend of mine.'

Sparra put a hand on my arm. 'It's alright, Ned.'

Bluey was on a roll. 'It's alright, Ned,' he mimicked. 'It'll be alright when I catch up with you later, in the yard,' he smirked.

The last thing I wanted was a fight. For the twenty or so prisoners milling round, it would have been a welcome relief from the boredom of routine. They would have egged us on, and I couldn't be sure whose side they would take. But my instincts told me if I didn't tackle Bluey there and then, he would do everything he could to make our lives more miserable than they already were. The adrenaline hit I got out of smacking the ringer in the head at Anakie came surging through.

I said, 'Tell you what, Bluey. Why don't we all meet up in the yard? Why don't we make it a little threesome?'

I saw fear in his eye. I felt the adrenaline pump. He sniggered, trying to joke his way out. 'Sorry aunty, you're on your own. I don't take it up the arse like you two shirt-lifters.'

The plate jumped out of his hand like a bunger had gone off under it. Gravy and vegetables sprayed over the front of his shirt. His lips formed an 'O' of astonishment. I put my right foot behind his ankle and lunged into his chest, shoulder first. We crashed to the ground, me on top. I heard the crack of skull-bone against concrete. The side of my face squished into the meat and gravy on his chest; the smell of it mingled with the stink of his breath. I heard voices shouting: 'Smash the cunt!'; 'Belt his fuckin' face in!'; the muffled clatter of feet running across the floor. I pushed myself up and smacked a fist into his mouth. I heard his teeth crack. I pulled my fist back to whack him again, but he got his knee up in my stomach and I tumbled sideways.

There was more shouting, this time from the screws; the thud of their boots coming fast. I got to my knees, ready to launch myself at Bluey, who was scrambling to his feet. Someone grabbed my arm. Hands were pulling at my shirt; its collar was choking me. A voice I recognised said, 'Alright, that's enough now. I said that's *enough*!'

Taipan's grip on the neck of my shirt tightened so I couldn't breathe. I saw a second screw come up behind Bluey and get him in a head-lock. 'Lemme at the cunt!' Bluey was screaming. Blood dripped off his chin.

'Shut - your - fucking - cakehole!' the screw yelled in his ear. He tightened his stranglehold, and Bluey gurgled to silence.

Taipan's mouth was up against my ear. I could feel the tip of his baton digging into my kidneys. 'You gunna quieten down now, Sunshine?' I nodded. He eased his grip on my shirt, so I could breathe again.

The babble of excited chatter from the prisoners who had swarmed in to the fight, grew louder. 'Let 'em sort it out themselves,' someone called out.

Taipan, my shirt still bunched in his fist, swung round to roar at them, 'The rest of you maggots, line up for your slops, or get locked down for the rest of the day. Take your pick.'

Cheated of their fun, they straggled back into a ragged queue, muttering their disappointment. Sparra hung back, looking anxiously in my direction. 'That goes for you too,' Taipan growled, and he turned and joined the queue.

The screw holding Bluey released the hold on his neck. 'Get back in the line-up,' he barked. He shoved him forward and he stumbled off.

Taipan relaxed his grip on my shirt. He inclined his pumpkin shaped head and lowered his voice, like he was drawing me into a conspiracy. 'As for you, Sherman…'

'Sheridan.'

'Whatever your fuckin' name is. Next time you want to hammer a douche-bag like Thompson, do it in the yard, you hear me? Look at the fuckin' mess you've made here!' I looked. There was an Antarctica-shaped patch of gravy and mash and meat splattered over the floor beside us. Bluey's blood smeared the concrete at the edges of it. 'Now go and get a mop and bucket from the store room, and clean it up,' Taipan growled. 'And if I catch you bluein' in here again, I'll clean it up myself and I'll use your head for a fuckin' mop. Got the fuckin' message?'

'Got the message, Boss.'

He went over to the other screw, and they left together. Sparra caught my eye as I passed him on my way to the store room. He was scared, but he needn't have been. I knew Bluey would think twice about causing any more trouble.

We found each other in the yard later that day. Sparra listened closely while I told him how I came to be in Muddrington Road. He shook his head in disbelief. 'I can't believe they'd send you to gaol just for receiving. You didn't knock the fuckin' thing off. It's Tex who should be in here, not you!'

I said, 'I could hardly dob him in. I was happy enough to take his meat for nothing.'

'Still…'

He shook his head again, deeply worried. 'Fuckin' Boofhead,' he said, eventually. 'Somebody should put a bullet in that thing's fuckin' head.'

Sparra

The next time I saw Taipan was after a visit to the librarian. I was walking across the yard carrying two books. He had come through the gate to attend to some matter, and was on his way out. He fell in step beside me. 'What've you got there?' he demanded, jutting his chin in the direction of the books. We stopped walking and I handed them to him.

'What's this shit?'

I told him what I knew about *A Farewell to Arms*. He said 'I didn't want a lecture on the fuckin' thing. What's it about?'

'I haven't read it yet, Boss.'

'What about this one?'

'*Under the Volcano*? I haven't read it either.' He flicked through its pages. I thought he was waiting for me to say something. I said, 'It's a classic. I thought I should read it.'

'Why don't you read what you want to read?'

'I do want to read it.'

'Why?'

'Because it's a classic.' He stared at me wordlessly. My eyes were drawn to the olive-green tattoo of a snake, jaws agape, writhing from under the sleeve of his shirt. I thought of the red-bellied black shooting towards me at the top of the shaft on Big Bessy. All I could think to do was keep talking, even if I was digging a deeper hole for myself. I said, 'I'm interested in writing.'

'Interested. You mean like, writing letters?' A disparaging sneer in his voice.

Nothing he said could have stabbed deeper at my pride. I didn't have a lot to cling to. The possibility that I might become a great writer, someone the world would look up to, treat with respect, was the topmost fantasy keeping me going. I looked straight into his mud pool eyes. I said, 'I'm writing a novel.'

The eyes didn't shift. I could hear the tapping of the baton in the palm of his hand. His head jerked round as a screw called to him from the other side of the yard. 'Neville, got a minute?'

He handed the books back to me. 'Hemingway,' he grunted. He slouched off to join his colleague.

From that moment on I sensed him watching me everywhere I went; the canteen, the laundry, the yard. Sizing me up. I wondered how long it would be before he found fault with something I said or did, as an excuse to belt my snotty-nosed reading habits out of me.

Bluey Thompson approached me two days after the fight, and we shook hands. We were officially friends again; but the malicious streak hadn't left him. Whenever we were forced into close proximity at musters or in food queues, he took the opportunity to feed me snippets of information about Snowy Carroll. He was a serial smash-and-grab merchant who had jumped bail in New South Wales, he told me, and carried on business as usual in Brisbane. Snowy's MO was to crash his Holden ute through a showroom display window around two or three in the morning, load up its tray with as many tellies and hi-fi's as he could grab in ten minutes, and flog them around the pubs the next night.

His luck had run out when he was reversing out of an electrical goods shop in the Valley. Six of Queensland's finest cornered him in an alley behind a fish-and-chips shop. He picked up a lump of wood from a building skip and belted one of the coppers across the kneecap. By the time they overpowered him, three of them were candidates for the casualty ward in the Mater.

The moment I had dreaded most came one morning in the shower block. Laughter and gentle curses mingled with the hiss of water jetting from rust-pitted shower roses. Clouds of steam broiled off the concrete floor. I had drifted into a fog of tangled memory and desire, regret and fear, watching the sluice of suds course down my legs, across the floor; mesmerised by the vortex of sudsy water oozing through the drain-hole, wishing I could go down with it and get flushed back out to the world I had come from.

I became aware that the drone of voices had faded away. Bluey, the last one to leave, nudged me with his elbow on his way out. 'Relax and enjoy it,' he grinned.

I looked up. Snowy Carroll was standing in the doorway. He stepped aside to let Bluey through. A prison-issue towel billowed ludicrously over his beer-barrel gut, like a spinnaker on a tug-boat.

'Lookin' after you alright are they?'

I said, 'Yeah, I'm doing okay.'

'Bluey tells me you were feelin' a bit lonely.'

'I think Bluey got it wrong.'

I went to move around him. He stepped sideways to block me. He said, 'You look lonely to me.'

The cold threat coming off him hit me like an ice axe to the guts. I said, 'I'm fine, really.'

'No,' he insisted, 'I definitely think you're in need of comfort.' He unfurled the towel and let it drop. 'Get down.'

Stupidity was my last line of defence. I said, 'What do you mean?'

'I mean get down on your fuckin' hands and knees with your arse in the air,' he bellowed. 'What'd you think I meant, can I have the next fuckin' dance?'

He put his hands on my shoulders and spun me round. I swung my elbow into his guts with all the strength I could muster. He grunted. 'What'sa matter, sweetheart, don't you fancy me?' I skipped sideways, but he stuck a foot out and I went sprawling. His knee crunched into my back and the breath rushed out of me. He hooked an arm under my guts and reefed me up on my knees. I felt his hands grip the cheeks of my arse.

I wished I had the courage, and the muscle, to defend myself. I wished Joe was there to smash this fucker the way he had the ringers outside the Anakie pub. I wished for anybody.

I had given up the struggle when I heard a strangled grunt issue from Snowy, accompanied by a sudden absence of the weight of his body. I heard a familiar voice. 'I think that'll be all for now, Mr. Carroll, whadda you reckon?'

I fell to the floor and rolled onto my side. Snowy's grub-white body loomed over me, back arched like a bow, his erect penis aimed at the ceiling. His eyes bugged, his tongue lolled out the side of his mouth like a thirsty dog.

'I asked you a question, maggot!' Taipan shouted in his ear. 'Whadda you reckon?' The baton across his windpipe jerked back another inch. Snowy gurgled something that must have sounded like 'Yes', because Taipan eased the pressure. He drew him all the way to his feet, lifting him by his chin with the baton. Two other screws came over and pinned his arms behind him. 'Take him to the Peter,' Taipan growled, and they marched him out.

'Black Peter' was the notorious isolation unit that had become the focus of media attention over the past months. It was a stone cell dug out of the ground, that you got to through a tunnel. It had no ventilation and hardly any light. I might have felt sorry for Snowy spending time in it, if he hadn't recently attempted to ream my arse.

Taipan gave a sniff of contempt as he watched the screws march him off. 'Fuckin' Mexicans,' he muttered. 'They should put a dingo fence along the border, to keep vermin like that outa Queensland.' He tapped the baton against the side of his leg, as I got to my feet. 'You'd better get back to your slot.' He pulled a towel off a hook, and chucked it to me.

'Thanks.' I was trembling so violently I nearly dropped it while I wrapped it round me.

'You won't have to worry about that shit-heap any more. He's being transferred to Grafton in the morning.' He picked up a shirt and a pair of trousers off the bench. 'These yours?'

'Yes, thank you.'

He passed them to me and waited while I got dressed. He said abruptly, 'Frederick Forsyth. Is he as good as this Hemingway, d'you reckon?'

What? 'No, I don't think so.'

He obviously saw me as some kind of authority on literary matters. I read Hemingway. I owned a typewriter.

But it was more than that. He sucked in a breath and said, 'So, writing a novel, eh?'

I said, 'I'm trying to, Boss.'

He moved closer to me. He shot a look in the direction of the door, to make sure we were alone. He said, 'I've been doing a spot of writing myself.'

Taipan took to visiting my slot whenever he could take time off from throwing his weight around the rest of the block. He would sit on the edge of the bunk, thick forearms resting on his knees, baton swinging back and forth between his legs like a pendulum while we discussed the relative merits of Forsyth and Richard Condon; Robert Ludlum and Ken Follett. Forsyth's sprawling international intrigues were his favourites, but he was always on the lookout for a challenge. Hemingway was his first foray outside the genre. He had made a start on *A Farewell to Arms*, but found it lacked the pace and descriptive power of *Day of the Jackal*.

These prolonged visits wouldn't have gone unnoticed by the other prisoners, but I doubt it did my standing in the pecking order any harm. If they thought I was bending over for Taipan Truscott, they couldn't give a fuck. The more time he spent with me, the less there was to make their lives miserable.

My time spent with Taipan, however, taught me that none of us had a mortgage on misery. During our talks, bits of his past were revealed until eventually I got a complete picture. A depressing saga of oppression and violence in the slum district of Inala, an inner Brisbane suburb; of rebellion against a sadistic father who beat his children to submission; their mother to the verge of insanity. He belted her so hard one time, Taipan recalled with a shudder, she lost an eye.

Taipan (Neville, in those days) ran away from this domestic hell-hole at the age of fifteen, aided by an uncle in the police force who had tried unsuccessfully to get the father prosecuted. He got work as a railway-sleeper cutter in the rainforests of Paluma, north of Townsville. It must have been back-breaking, soul-destroying work; I got the impression he revelled in it, because it took his mind off things that didn't bear thinking about.

Due to the rigours of axe work, his joints began to stiffen prematurely. He was forced to look for something easier. He saw an ad in the *Courier Mail* calling for recruits for the Corrective Services Department. He struggled, without help, through the intricacies of the official departmental application form and, on the third attempt, scraped through.

It was the triumph of this first literary effort - Question 26(b) in particular (he remembered the exact number), calling for a brief account of his academic background and his reasons for wanting to become a prison officer - that whetted his appetite for creative writing.

Taipan reckoned he had a story to tell. All he needed was someone to give him the good oil on how to get started, and it would all come pouring out of him like molasses through chicken-wire. He had picked me as the kick-starter. Mention was made of special privileges that would come my way if I could provide the magic ingredient.

He began showing me what he had written, smuggling the hand-written pages into my cell, tucked inside his shirt. He would produce them furtively, like they were contraband; watch me closely, gauging my reaction, while I read. I came to realise that, for all his lumbering aggression, his baton-wielding violence, there was a vulnerable centre to Taipan; like the soft white flesh beneath the uncrackable shell of a crab.

Writing didn't come easy to him. He wrestled with words like they were the enemy, choking them off before they had a chance to say what they wanted; flattening them into a bruised and bloodied slab of mangled verbiage that bore no resemblance to any form of human dialogue.

'Write it like you'd say it if you were talking,' I suggested one day.

'I did!' he insisted. He read out aloud what he had written, word by laborious word, dragging each one into the open by the scruff of the neck and shaking it hard. 'See?' he said proudly.

I couldn't, but I said I did.

From then on, life at Muddrington Road became more bearable. Normally, moving back and forth between the yard and your slot wasn't allowed. On Taipan's shift, he would escort me back to my cell after breakfast, or a visit from the librarian. All I had to do was give him the nod. I had the freedom to read, and write, whenever I wanted.

I had to use the typewriter sitting on the bed. Taipan apologised for not being able to organise a table for me. It would've set a precedent, he said. If the other prisoners found out I had one, they would all demand the same; if they didn't get what they wanted, there'd be another bloody riot. I was a lousy typist anyway, so it didn't matter. I was happy enough that I had found a new patron.

After the incident with Bluey Thompson, Sparra kept a low profile. We sat together at meal times, picking a spot up the end of one of the wooden bench seats running the length of the tables. He would concentrate on his eating, avoiding looking at anything or anybody, pausing only to bat at bush flies swarming around us if it was a hot meal. The screws had taken his Zippo from him when he came in. His right hand seemed lost without something to flick back and forth. He hardly spoke; his mind was clearly elsewhere. I gave up trying to draw him out. I figured he had his own reasons for not wanting to talk.

If it was Bluey he was worried about, he needn't have. With Snowy Carroll on lock-down in Black Peter, Bluey had become suddenly vulnerable to all those he had given a hard time while under Snowy's protection. He was keeping a low profile himself.

Sparra was in D-block, which had its own yard separated from B by a high wire fence. We could talk to each other through the fence; but I hardly ever saw him. I got the feeling he was avoiding all contact with his fellow prisoners, including me. I couldn't help thinking about the wild look in his eye when he turned and saw me that first day he got back from the Forestry detail; his palpable fear when Bluey challenged him. I had heard of prisoners so traumatised they retreated into their cells and stayed there, shrinking back into themselves, swimming against the tide like they were trying to crawl back up the birth canal.

There was a period when I didn't see him for days on end. Then I found out he had a job in the laundry, which would explain why he wasn't in the yard for most of the day. I reckoned this might have been a form of protection on the part of the screws. For just as it was in their interests to segregate prisoners who might cause friction in each other's company, it also made sense to keep the more vulnerable inmates out of reach of the hardheads. Taipan had hinted to me that Sparra had been identified as a potential victim for any muscle-jock looking to prove how tough he was. He was safer in the laundry than in the yard.

If the screws were concerned for him, I was even more so. He had become so reclusive, I was worried he might be losing his mind. One grey day at the end of February, when I finally got to have a proper conversation with him, my suspicions were strengthened. The nights, by then, were stinking hot and breathless. All you wanted to do when they let you out of your slot was suck in fresh air. There was plenty of that in the yard, but you paid for it with the searing heat of the sun.

In the mornings, shade was restricted to a strip along the brick wall of the block. As the sun rose higher, its shadow diminished. By noon it was gone. In the afternoon, the wall that had been a refuge from the heat, became its accomplice, soaking up the sun so the bricks became too hot to touch. After that there was a twenty square-foot shelter in the middle of the yard, with a four-sided sloping iron roof. There was a table there and some seats. Not enough to go around. Next best was to hunker down somewhere, moving as little as possible, until three or four o'clock, when the shadow of the gatehouse began to creep across the asphalt from the west. A cloudy day was a relief.

On this one, I decided to do a tour of the perimeter, rather than squat in a corner somewhere with a book. A group of four or five of the fitter-looking prisoners were shooting baskets where a hoop had been bolted to the brick wall. On a bench set up near the fence separating the two yards, Frankie Stavros, in for a corner-shop heist that netted him seventy-five dollars (he'd picked the wrong day, one way and another) was pressing weights. He grunted with each pump, noisily sucking oxygen as the bar came to rest on his glistening pecs. 'Your mate was lookin' for you,' he rasped, at the end of a press. He inclined his head in the direction of D yard, and jerked the bar up again.

I saw Sparra walking towards me, his lanky frame criss-crossed by the Cyclone mesh dividing us. There was a spring in his gait at odds with the dark, fearful depression I had sensed in him recently. As he drew closer, I saw a glint in his eye that had nothing to do with fear; more like exhilaration.

He got to the fence and I said, 'I haven't seen you for a while. Thought you might've gone on holidays.'

'I've been busy,' he said. No time for joking. 'Can I have a little word?' He flicked his eyes, indicating we should move further along the fence. When we had reached a point out of earshot of Frank, he took a quick shufti over his shoulder to make sure no one was nearby. He said, 'Pack your bags, sport. In six days' time we're outa this joint.'

I laughed. 'I wish you were right. I've still got a month to go.'

He lowered his voice to little more than a whisper, as if afraid the guard in the observation tower at the far corner of the quad might be listening in. 'We're bustin' out,' he hissed.

I listened while he told me how he had met a bloke on the outside, Herb Gardner, while he was on the Forestry job. Herb had just come down from the Quilpie opal fields. As well as their common interest in mining, Herb happened to share Sparra's passion for explosives.

Sparra, I began to realise, was smarter than I had given him credit for. He had landed the job in the laundry, not, as I had thought, out of the largesse of the authorities, but through his own lobbying. The laundry was where most of the prison's contraband – drugs, weapons, radios, alcohol etc. - came in; it was where Sparra and

Herb contrived to have six sticks of gelignite delivered, buried in a pallet of soap powder.

I said, 'What the fuck are you going to do with six sticks of gelly?'

He looked at me like it was a really stupid question. 'Make a bomb,' he said. 'How the fuck else do you think we're going to get out of here?'

For the past three weeks, while I'd been fretting about his withdrawal into insanity, he had been beavering away, scrounging the bits and pieces he needed to make his bomb. He'd gone nuts alright, but differently to the way I had thought. I risked another stupid question. 'How exactly are you going to use this bomb?'

He had it all worked out. There was a blind spot in the perimeter fence, that couldn't be seen from either of the watchtowers on the western wall. He had wire cutters. This would allow access to the 'sterile zone', a twelve-foot strip of empty space between the fence and the main wall. The bomb would be planted at the base of the wall. When it blew, we would be on our way home.

I said, 'Mate, you're due for release in three weeks.'

He said, 'That's not the point.'

'What is the point?'

He was looking directly at me. His face sagged. I hoped it meant he had suddenly returned to his normal, melancholy self. But that wasn't it. There was the same anxiety there, intense, that I had felt when he turned and saw me that day in the canteen. He said, 'I ain't done nothin' wrong.'

I got the feeling he wanted something from me. I felt like a priest in a confessional. I was grateful when he blurted out, 'That arsehole Missingham got what he bloody deserved!'

I said, 'Jesus, Sparra, if you start letting bombs off in gaol, they're going to throw away the fucking key!'

'The bastard spat on me,' he said stubbornly.

In Sparra's mind, the breakout had assumed epic proportions. He was grateful to Missingham, he said, for giving him this opportunity. He would go down in history as the man who blew his way out of Muddrington Road. Nobody could ever take that away from him. I could see his heart was set on it.

It was towards the end of the day, the encroaching darkness made even darker by a black-hearted southerly-buster rumbling in. A jag of lightning sizzled and cracked over our heads. The first big drops of rain plopped as we arranged to meet the following day.

As I dashed through the rain for the shelter of the shed in the middle of the yard, I wondered how the hell I was going to talk him out of this bullshit.

Tex came to see me. We faced each other across a plastic table in the contact visit room. He thanked me for not dobbing him in; it was one he owed me, he said.

I told him about Sparra's escape plan. He laughed. 'Don't worry about it. It'll never happen.'

'You don't think he'll go through with it?'

'It's not that. It's just Sparra's one of those people nothin' ever goes right for. Look at that bloody hole he's been diggin' in on the Scrub Lead. There's no bloody stone down there! I've helped him wash up. There's hardly any ironstone in it, let alone sapphires!' He shook his head. 'Somethin'll happen to fuck up this escape bullshit, you wait.' He lit up a fag and flicked the match out. 'Got a job out at the dam,' he said.

Fairbairn Dam was being built across the Nogoa River, south of Emerald. Miners were taking jobs on the main wall or the irrigation channels, to make ends meet between patches of stone. 'Drivin' a scraper. Should see the size of the bastard. It's like ridin' a fuckin' elephant over a paddock full of soccer balls!' He grew pensive. 'Still, it's tucker money, eh.'

I asked him if the new job meant he would be going out of the butchering business. 'Don't be silly!' he said. 'When the dust from all this shit's settled, I'll get out there amongst 'em again.' He promised me I would never have to worry about fresh meat for the rest of my life. He owed it to me. I had a vision of Boofhead going berserk digging up the remains of Hegarty's missing yearlings in my backyard.

This reminded me of something else that had been nagging at me. I told Tex that Hegarty had bragged to me about the baits he had spread around the fields, to keep other people's dogs away. I said, 'There's no way that mongrel thing of his could've got through them to get to my place, is there?'

'No way,' said Tex. 'That's why he keeps all his dogs chained up. Boofhead included.' He could shed no further light on the mystery. If I was short of cash when I got out, he told me, he would get me work on the dam. Give up his own job for me, if it came to that! He would never forget the debt he owed me for taking the rap for him.

The warden signalled time-up. We both stood. Tex came round to my side of the table, positioning himself between me and the screw. He grabbed hold of my arm and brought it forward to shake my hand. He winked. 'Bloke workin' on the channels give it to me. Never use the fuckin' stuff meself, I'm silly enough as it is.' He withdrew his hand and left me holding a plastic bag full of dope. I shoved it in my pocket and shot a look at the screw.

I said, 'Thanks Tex.' I thought, *if you do me any more favours, I could wind up in this fucking place for life.*

Bombs Away

'I've been thinking,' Taipan began. He had dropped in to see me after lock-down, to return *A Farewell to Arms*. He put the book on top of my locker and parked himself on the edge of the bunk. He licked his lips. His brow creased as he wrestled with the thing that had been tormenting him. It came out in a rush. 'I've been thinking maybe I should give it up altogether.'

He had seemed edgy lately. So this was why, I thought. He had always had confidence in his writing ability. Something must have happened to cause self-doubt to rear up out of the creative abyss. It was eating him up.

'You can't give up now!' I said.

If Taipan gave up writing, all my perks would get flushed down the brascoe along with his tortured prose. If another Snowy Carroll turned up, my arse was history. It would be just my luck to get porked in the last few weeks of my sentence.

'What's happened? It's not because of this, is it?' I pointed to the book on the locker. 'You can't expect to be as good as Hemingway, right from the start!'

He sniffed contemptuously. 'I'm not worried about him.' He took an envelope from his hip pocket and shoved it at me. 'Take a squiz.'

I extracted a folded sheet of paper from the envelope. It was a typewritten note on the letterhead of a major publishing house. 'Dear Sir,' it read, 'Thank you for submitting the manuscript for your novel, *Mongrel Days*. Our editors felt that while it contained a high degree of excitement and energy, its overall philosophy may prove difficult for our readers to grasp. For this reason, it is with regret that I have to tell you we are unable to make an offer for publication. I wish you the very best for your future writing endeavours, etc., etc.'

I handed the letter back to him. 'You didn't tell me you were sending it out.'

'You told me it'd improved out of sight.'

'I also said we were going to have to do a bit of work on it.'

'I did! I did everything you said. I made it sound like talking. I took out the bit about the dead croc in the swimming pool.' He heaved a volcanic sigh. 'I thought it was ready to go.'

'Maybe it is,' I said. 'But not by this particular publisher. We can try another one. After we've done a bit of work on it.'

'You think it's a pile of shit, don't you?'

'No. I don't think that at all. I think it's got…' I struggled to find words other than 'excitement' and 'energy'. 'It's got heart,' I said. 'It's got more heart than just about any book I've ever read.'

He looked at me hard. 'You wouldn't bullshit me, would you? You're not saying that just to keep me on side?'

I met his gaze unflinchingly. I said, 'There are some things in life you don't do. You don't scab on your mates. You don't go around topping people for kicks. And you don't bullshit a fellow writer about his work.'

I wasn't, either. His book might have been badly written, but it came from deep inside him. Taipan desperately wanted to prove he was something better than a deadshit prison screw, hated by all, respected by none. He was no different to the rest of us. At the end of the day he wanted to be loved. By someone, anyone, for something.

He fell silent, staring at the floor. 'What I don't understand,' he said at last, 'is why they'd go for something like this,' he dispatched Hemingway to the floor with a flick of his baton, 'and knock back *Mongrel Days*. You've read that bloody thing. The bloke's an A grade arsehole! He deserts from the army, knocks up this beautiful sheila who thinks the sun shines out of him. She dies having his baby and he wanders off down the street feeling sorry for himself! What sort of a hero is that?'

I agreed that Frederic Henry may have lacked the moral fibre of *Mongrel*'s central character who, I guessed, was modelled on Taipan's idea of himself. I would have suggested that Frederic being less than perfect was part of his appeal, but I could see Taipan wasn't in the mood. 'I'm wasting my bloody time,' he muttered darkly. 'I might as well chuck it in.'

I knew I had to go in hard. I said, 'Don't do that. It's your duty to get it down on paper. You owe it to your readers.'

His bull-terrier eyes bored into mine. 'You think I'll make it as a writer?' It was a prayer, more than a question.

I said, 'You are a writer.'

He pursed his lips and nodded, like a huge weight had been lifted. He exhaled noisily. He hauled himself to his feet. 'Get some sleep,' he ordered. He gave my arm a comradely nudge with the baton and let himself out of the cell.

Sparra was waiting for me at the fence when I came into the yard the next morning. He told me the bomb was nearly ready. He was waiting for an opportunity to get into the kitchen, so he could pinch some aluminium foil – something to do with the detonator. I wasn't really listening to the details.

I said, 'Sparra, this is a seriously crazy idea.'

'I know,' he grinned. 'That's the beauty of it. They wouldn't expect anything like it in a million years.' His fingers were curled tightly through the squares of mesh separating us, like a kid at the zoo. I had never seen him happier. 'Just think,' he said, 'in four days' time we'll be outa this shit-hole.'

I said, 'I won't be going with you.'

He forced the grin wider. 'What're you talking about? It's all arranged, you can't back out now.'

I said, 'I was never in. It's the craziest thing I ever heard in my life.'

A little tic had set off in his left eye. 'You have to go,' he insisted. 'I owe you.'

'You don't owe me anything. If it's Bluey Thompson you're talking about, forget it. I would've belted him sooner or later anyway. He's been on my case from the minute I set foot in the place.'

'It's more than that.'

I waited for him to tell me what the 'more' was, but he didn't. 'Sparra,' I said. 'I'm going to do you a favour. Listen to me, and do what I say. Go back to your slot. Put all that bomb shit in a box and dump it in the garbage before someone finds it. Then forget all this crazy stuff about breaking out of gaol, before you get us both killed.'

But he wasn't looking for advice. 'Have it your way,' he said. 'We could've gone down in history together. The Muddro Bombers.'

'Get rid of it now, alright?'

I walked away from him across the yard.

As predicted by Tex, it all went horribly wrong. We heard on the news that night, that a mysterious explosion in the back of a waste disposal compactor on its way to the Mulgrave Hill rubbish tip had wrecked the truck, and left the garbos in need of counselling. Sparra told me about it in the canteen next morning. The screws had been ramping cells randomly over the past week, ostensibly searching for drugs. It was more likely part of a general campaign to piss us off, as a reprisal for the riots earlier in the year. A tip-up, at best, left your slot looking like a truck had driven through it. If you did happen to have drugs (or a bomb) stashed under your bed, you were fucked. When Sparra conned his way into the kitchen, planning on snitching the roll of aluminium foil he needed to complete the detonator, he had the bomb with him. He figured it was safer than leaving it in the cell.

A screw came along unexpectedly while he had the thing out, checking the wiring. He dumped it in a slops bin. The garbage truck arrived a minute later. With the screw standing right beside him, Sparra could only watch helplessly as the bin, and the bomb, were carted off.

He pushed food around on his plate with a fork. There was no time for him to start from scratch and build another bomb. The purpose had gone out of his life. 'Never mind,' I said. 'You'll be home soon. You can go back to blowing up billies!'

He shook his head. This had been a once-in-a-lifetime opportunity. Now he would simply be released from gaol like any other prisoner, with his belongings in a carryall and a rail pass to

Anakie. His one big shot at lasting fame had been snatched from him; yet another disappointment in a lifetime filled with them.

I thought about Sparra in the dark heat of the slot that night. Mad as he was, there was something I envied about his determination to blast his way through the billy-boulder problems of his life. He was a doer. It was bad luck he happened to be a fucker-upper as well. But at least he made decisions.

I started making plans for when I got out. I made up my mind that if I couldn't patch things up with Jess; if Jack couldn't or wouldn't tell me anything about the Great Unknown of my childhood, I would leave the gemfields. Maybe not knowing where I came from wasn't such a big deal after all. Maybe the dogs would follow me where I went, maybe they wouldn't. If I could train myself to stop worrying about whatever it was they were guarding, they might leave me alone.

I would take Joe up on his offer, I decided. We would head north to the Cape. I had read once that in the early days of the White invasion (I hadn't forgotten what Bob had taught me), escaped convicts would stumble half-starved through uncharted bush in the belief that eventually they would reach China. That's what Joe, Jimmy and I would do. Head for China. At least it was a decision. An objective. A mission.

'*Effrythingk be good op there, Neddy,*' Joe had promised. I kept telling myself he was right; that the Cape was where I had been heading all along. I would recognise it as my fated destination the minute I saw it. The rest of it - Edgecliff Road, the Anakie gemfields, this shitty fucking gaol - had been mere stop-overs along the highway to my future. It was that belief that kept me going for the rest of my stay in Muddro.

One wet morning towards the end of March, I got taken down to reception to put in a request for a warrant check. If none existed for outstanding offences, in three days' time I would be released. Taipan was in the corridor when I came out of the guv'nor's office.

'Where the fuck d'you think you're goin'?' he said.

I said, 'I'm checking out. Got a train to catch, Boss.'

'Aren't you forgetting something?'

I knew what he was talking about. He'd been badgering me to show him what I had written. I didn't want to, but I could hardly refuse. I said, 'Do you want to come up to the slot? I can give it to you now.'

We splashed across the deserted yard, hunched against the rain. He followed me up the stairs and along the gantry to the slot. He brushed the rain off his shirtsleeves with his baton, while I hauled a cardboard box out from under the bed. I extracted a stack of A4 pages with a rubber band around them, and handed it to him. I said, 'It's not finished yet.'

'What the fuck've you been doing in here for the last three months?'

I shrugged. 'Soaking up the atmosphere.'

I realised I had never seen him smile before. He riffled the pages with his thumb. 'I hope it's better'n that fuckin' Hemingway.'

Sparra came into the TV room that afternoon, something he rarely did while he'd been busy with the bomb. I said goodbye to him, in case we didn't see each other before I was released. While we were talking, a message came over the PA that I had a visitor. I shook hands with Sparra, and made my way past the lags sprawled on stackable chairs watching a *Honeymooners* re-run, over to the security door leading to the contact visit area. The electronic lock buzzed. A screw opened the door to let me through.

Friends and relatives of half a dozen other prisoners had braved the weather. Standing beside a table near the far wall, hat in hand, hair plastered to his scalp, was Jack. He turned as I walked towards him. Neither of us smiled.

We shook hands and sat opposite each other at the table. He told me he'd bumped into Tex one day in Emerald. Tex had told him I was in prison. He'd made enquiries and found out my release date.

I said, 'I hope you didn't drive all this way to give me a lift home. They give us a rail pass.' He mumbled something about wanting to pick up some gear from a hardware shop in the Valley. 'You must've needed it pretty bad. It's been raining for five days; all the creeks must be up.'

He nodded. 'I only just made it. The Comet was four foot over the road at Rolleston. Had to wait three hours for it to drop low enough for a truck to tow me through. We'll be lucky to make it back.' His eyes met mine briefly. 'If you want to come with me, that is.'

I was angry. About everything that had happened since I set foot on the gemfields. I had achieved nothing by going there. I had fallen in love with someone who had ditched me unfairly. I had wound up in gaol, protecting some guy I hardly knew from a bar of soap. I was convinced Jack had buggered off from Sapphire, to avoid being badgered by me about something he didn't want to confront. I wouldn't have bothered going back to the place, if Joe and Jimmy hadn't been there.

I said, 'That's okay, I'll use the rail pass. Pity to waste it.'

It was a shitty thing to say, given the trouble he'd gone to to get to me. *Fuck him*, I thought, *he deserves it*.

He fed the brim of his hat through his fingers, as if checking it for flaws. 'I got some bad news. I wanted to be the one to tell you. You were his partner, I thought you should know the real story, before you heard some bullshit version of it from that mob of piss pots in the Scrub.'

The hat kept turning. 'Jimmy?' I said.

'No, Joe. He's dead. Drowned.'

Prisoners and their friends and loved ones moved around us in the cramped space, slowly filling with the smog of a dozen cigarettes. Jack lit one up. I watched the smoke curling off the end of it. I said, 'How did it happen?'

'They were out at Deep Creek. Slipped in, tryin' to pull out a fish, as far as I could tell. I couldn't get much sense out of Jimmy.' He ground the cigarette out in an ashtray after a couple of puffs. 'You could've bet London to a brick on, the big ugly bastard never learned how to swim.'

I struggled to picture it. The sheer drop off the bank, the exposed roots of the she-oak clinging to it, the opaque muddy water. I said, 'Couldn't Jimmy've done something?'

'He was asleep. He heard him yell out. Got there in time to see him go under. He grabbed a stick and poked around with it for a bit, but he never came up. Walked five miles to Dick Prescott's property, and they came back with a tractor. Dragged a chain along the bottom of the hole till it hooked his belt, and they snigged him out.'

I could feel my hands wrapped up in Joe's while he drew the map of our future, living off the riches of the 'Lugky Country', up on the Cape; heard his booming scrub-bull voice, *'You commingk vith me, ya?'*

'Who is this bastard?' said Taipan. He jerked a thumb at the A4 pages stacked between us on the bed. With the news of Joe's death burning a hole in me, the last thing I needed was an editorial discussion with a thick-headed screw who knew nothing about writing. But, as Sparra might've said, I owed him. 'Who is he?' he repeated, tapping the pile of paper with a saveloy sized finger. 'This… what's his name?'

'Daniel.'

'Daniel.' He said it like most people would say 'paedophile' or 'dog shit', and went on to supply the answer to his own question. 'He's a weak arsehole, with no morals, wandering around waiting for something to happen that's goin' to solve all his fuckin' problems!'

I said, 'That's the whole point. He doesn't know what's going on. He's lost. He doesn't know what his life is about. He's floundering, looking for answers…'

'Boring the fuckin' tits off us.'

I knew he was right, but I didn't want to admit it to someone like Taipan. I was in no condition to argue with anyone about anything. I was about to be released from gaol, and I felt like shit.

I said, 'That's your opinion.'

'It's the fuckin' truth. Listen,' he lowered his voice the way he did when he wanted to scare the shit out of you, 'you gotta toughen this bastard up. You gotta grab him by the scruff of the neck, and shake him till his eyes rattle. You gotta kick his arse till his nose bleeds.' He leant in closer. 'Because that's what I feel like doing to him.' The pupils of his eyes stabbed the space between us. I thought he was going to give me a practical demonstration of all the things I should be doing to the character in my book. Then he leant back and fixed me with a look of triumph, evidently satisfied he had made his point. 'Nobody wants to read about some miserable dickhead wandering around the country trying to find out who he really is. Your hero's gotta *make* things happen. Or what's the point?'

'Thanks, Boss. I'll keep it in mind.'

'You fuckin' better.' He stood up. I did too.

I said, 'Good luck with *Mongrel Days*. I wish we'd had more time to work on it.'

'Bullshit. The minute you're outa here, you'll never give it another thought. Why would you?' He was right, we both knew it. He fell silent, his arms hanging loosely. 'Don't worry about me,' he said suddenly. 'Get that fuckin' thing of yours written, okay?'

'I will.'

He looked around the cell like it was the first time he'd been there. 'I suppose you're gunna miss this place.'

I said, 'I can always go out and shoot a poddy calf or two, if I want to come back.' I thought I might get another smile out of him.

I saw the baton rise too late to move; heard it thud into my upper arm; felt the jolt of pain shoot along my shoulder to the bottom of my neck. His face was inches from mine; his voice little more than a whisper. 'I don't want to see you again as long as I live. Got that?'

'Yes,' I gasped, clutching my arm.

'That's a flea bite compared to what we gave Snowy Carroll in the Peter.' He jabbed the point of the baton in my chest. 'Don't forget it.'

He walked to the door and went out. I heard the lock clack home. I never saw him again.

Jack was waiting for me when I came through the gates. The rain had eased. The Comet had dropped by the time we got to Rolleston. We drove straight through to Anakie without stopping, and got back just in time for the funeral.

Eight inches of rain had fallen in twelve hours. Dug out the day before, the grave had filled steadily overnight. The water was six inches from the top by the time we slid Joe off the back of Angus McClaren's truck. We looked on, embarrassed, as the coffin refused to sink. The billies we put on top had slipped off and got wedged between it and the wall of the grave.

A curtain of water streamed from the brim of Jack's hat. Reg and Bob had their arms around Becky. The relentless drumming of rain on the lid of the coffin all but drowned out the sound of her wailing.

Jack stepped forward, then me and Tex and a couple of the others. We wrestled the billies up onto the squelching mud on either side of the grave. I caught myself wishing Joe was there. He would have hauled them out like they were so many oversized potatoes. I wondered if he hadn't shrugged them off his own coffin with a twitch of his massive shoulders, just for a laugh.

The coffin bobbed free. Becky wailed louder. She was shaking.

'Get her over to the car, will you Bob?' said Reg. 'She'll freeze to bloody death.' Bob helped her over to the Monaro parked near the cemetery gate.

Jack shouted above the beat of the rain, 'Has anybody got a brace-and-bit?'

Tex went to fetch one. There was nothing to do but stand there, shivering, waiting for him to come back. The League of Nations was there in force. Karl Krontzke produced a flask of Bond 7 from the pocket of his overcoat. He took a swig and passed it to Dutch Harry, who took a swig and passed it to Jimmy.

The little man's face was grey, rivulets of rain eroding its creased flesh. Nobody had been able to convince him he wasn't responsible for Joe's death. If he had been awake, he believed, he would have been able to fling himself into the water to drag his whale-sized carcass to safety. By his own account, he was out like a light. Sleeping like a troubadour.

Harry went to the truck and broke open the slab of Four X he had brought for the wake. He handed out stubbies. He offered one to Jack. Jack shook his head and pulled his coat tighter about himself. 'Perfect day for a bloody funeral,' he muttered.

Bob came back over, and Harry offered him a stubby. He shook his head. We stood in silence, a mournful pack of human strays bewildered by a loss we couldn't comprehend. The man floating in the box belonged to none of us. His past streamed behind him to a country where I imagined death came often to friend and family alike. Had some message shot through the ether to tell them their old comrade, their vanished kinsman, was as surely dead as if a sniper's bullet had stopped him on Parliament Square on that dark day of the Uprising? Were they weeping for his memory now? Thunder rumbled, the downpour increased in intensity. In that distant graveyard, his birth and death separated by exile in a land that shunned tears, the heavens gushed buckets for Joe Kovach.

'To Joe!' Harry thrust his stubby out at arm's length in a spontaneous display of emotion and we all followed suit.

'To Joe!'

Tex came back with the brace-and-bit. Nobody else seemed willing, so Jack took it and knelt beside the coffin. He felt with his fingers below the water line, put the tip of the bit close to the bottom of the box and started winding. It was soft pine; soon he had drilled four holes, two in each side.

We watched as four streams of bubbles broke the surface like tiny volcanic eruptions. Bob brought Becky back over. The coffin tilted as one end filled, then righted itself as the seeping water found its level. Lower and lower it went, until wavelets lapped the surface of the lid and it sank from sight.

Jack laid the brace-and-bit on the ground at the foot of the grave, like a crucifix, and stood erect. He took his hat off, and we waited. 'Well, Joe,' he said, 'I'm sorry it's such a horrible bloody day, but you can't pick the weather. I'm sorry I never got a chance to talk to you again, after you smashed into the gate that night. I would've said…' The rain came harder. He wiped a hand over his face, and spoke louder. 'I would've said "Don't worry about it". You were a silly bastard sometimes, but you never did anybody any harm.'

He looked like he might have been about to say more. He wedged the hat back on his head and took a step back. Karl and Harry went over to the truck, while Bob helped Becky send the first shovelful of dirt splashing into the hole. We took it in turns then, working against the slippery handle.

Karl and Harry came back with a cross they had made out of a couple of lengths of four-by-two; an inscription burnt into it with a piece of red-hot fencing wire: 'Joe Kovach – Died 1975 – A Miner and a Gentleman.' They planted it at the head of the grave.

The rain stopped abruptly, as if a giant tap had been turned off. A rainbow squadron of lorikeets screeched through the dripping bush, dodging the trees with split-second precision.

Reg tapped my arm as we straggled out of the graveyard. 'Good to have you back, Neddy.' He told me Jess had taken Val down to Rockhampton, to try and get her on the wagon. She had wanted to come back for the funeral, but he told her she'd be better off keeping an eye on Val.

'Drop in and see us some time. We'll have a beer for Joe.' I wanted to know more about Jess, but I didn't ask him. I was afraid he'd tell me she had found somebody else.

He moved on ahead with Becky, and Bob fell in beside me.
'We'll miss old Joe.'
'We will.'

'He thought you were the ducks guts, you know.'

I said, 'He liked you too.'

We walked in silence for a bit. I said, 'What was it you liked about him?'

'We had something in common.'

'What was that?'

'We both lost our country to invaders.' *They liked each other's stories*, Jess had said.

A hole in the clouds opened up, sending light scything through the long grass on either side of the road leading to the cemetery. Reg called out from over at the car. 'You comin' with us, Bob?'

'I'd better get movin',' he said. A crocodile eye winked. 'You look after yourself, eh.'

'I will.'

He ambled over to where Reg was waiting for him. Jack and I got in the HD. The green ute had dropped a tie-rod an hour after we got back from Brisbane. I was driving him round till he could scrounge the part from a wrecker. We set off for the Anakie pub, to say goodbye to Joe.

Our clothes were drying out; the booze warming us inside. From behind the bar Missingham kept a nervous eye on a convicted receiver of stolen goods and a bunch of professional drunks mourning the death of the man who had wrecked his saloon bar by riding a horse into it. He could hardly refuse to serve us. It was a wake, after all.

Jack drank bottles of Clayton's Tonic, in place of our Four X stubbies. He matched us story for story. 'I bought a sheep off Rex Horrigan once,' he recalled. 'Joe was going to help me kill it. So I've cut its throat and it's layin' there and I'm just about to hook it up by the shanks, and Joe says "Wod you bloddy doin'?", and I said "I'm goin' to hang the bloody thing up and skin it, whadda you think I'm gunna do?". And he says "Here, I'm been skin bucker for you!" So he puts his foot on its neck and grabs hold of the skin and he's gruntin' like a bloody great grizzly bear, and he peels it off like he's skinnin' a bloody rabbit! I've never seen anything like it!' He shook his head. 'Like you'd skin a bloody rabbit…'

'Ooh he was strong, alright. I couldn't dispense with that!' All eyes turned to Jimmy. The colour was returning to his cheeks. 'When Sparra Perkins was my partner in crime, I remember one such day there, we were weighing up the long and the short of how to get those blessed billy boulders onto my roof, and Joe dropped out of the blue. "Can I give youse a hand there, boys?" he says, or words of that inflection. So with much ado about nothing, he picks one up,' he encompassed an imaginary boulder in his arms, 'and plonks it on the roof! He put every blessed one of those billies up there without a drop of insistence from another immortal soul!'

As the sun sank lower, the stories grew taller. The taller they grew, the more we drank. The more I drank, the further I slid into a cone of morbid reflection, listening to Jack and Jimmy and Harry bearing Joe to the Land of the Heroes, like they were just beginning to learn who he really was. It put me in mind of the title of Jack's only book – something about *Gods* and *Graves*. I wondered where I would be carted off to when it came my time; how much time I had left. I wondered what was the point of *effrythingk*.

I thought of Joe's little brother bleeding to death on the cobblestones in a land I would probably never see; Joe's tears and the venom on a dead snake's fangs. Joe, twice drowned, sightless eyes swimming beneath coffined lids, his booming voice stilled by the dark.

Jimmy and I would never get to the Cape without him. Joe *was* the Cape. The track had petered out in duffer country and I was digging alone. I closed my eyes. I saw Jess coming out of the scrub under a cloudless sky; her sleek arms, her dust-brown breasts. A shadow flapped across the sun…

I thought about Reg and Val and the kids and the fishing trip; the smell of family in their home. I thought about little Pauly's bloodless lips; how my big Heroic Act had made no difference to anything. Thought about Bob and Tibrogargan and the Kairi warriors hunted to extinction in the boulder-strewn ravines of the Carnarvons. *Effrythingk*, I realised, was a shit fight for everyone.

I was too pissed to drive. Jack took me and Jimmy home in the HD. He dropped Jimmy at his place, then drove me over to Darby's. He would walk home from there. I sobered up on the drive back. I got to brooding over Jack's refusal to talk to me. He'd had plenty to say in the pub, about someone he would never see again. Someone he hadn't been all that keen on talking to when he was alive. Is that what he would do after I was gone – go around telling everyone what a terrific bloke I was, and how much he liked me?

We stepped out of the wagon, under a blanket of stars. The Southern Cross hung over the eastern horizon, so close you could touch it. Jack stood gazing at the vast blazing acres of the universe. 'Get a go at that, will you?' Like a prayer. It didn't make me any less pissed off with him. I was too drunk and aggressive to be impressed with any spiritual epiphany he might be experiencing.

I was about to go through the gate, when he fished in his pocket, and handed me something. 'Jimmy found it in the water hole,' he said. 'It must've floated out of his pocket when he fell in.' I could dimly make out the shape of a tobacco tin. 'I thought you might like it to remember him by. It's about all he ever owned in the world.'

It lay on my hand in the light of the stars. I saw it float from his pocket as he rose spluttering to the surface; heard him curse in Hungarian. Saw him lunge, flounder, sink, the last of his breath boiling above him. All that was left of a life lived larger than life - the titanic chest, the booming laugh, the steak-sized hands, the rib-tickled women. A lousy tin of tobacco.

I could see it cupped in his big paw while he rolled a durry. Saw his face light up in the flare of the match. Smelt it burning. I heard him as clearly as if he were standing in front of me: '*Been one day thiz bloddy tobaggo killingk me!*'

Beneath Stars

'Well, if it isn't the welcome stranger!' He got to his feet too quickly, and sat down again. He made it on the second attempt, and put out a hand to greet me. 'Come on in, Ned,' said Jimmy. 'I'll get you something to settle the cobwebs.' He hobbled to the fridge to fetch two stubbies. He held them in the crook of his left arm to knock the tops off; handed me one and raised the other in a salute. 'To the best of us!'

Les came gangling in from outside, crashing through a pile of empty cans on his way to jump up and lick his master's face with a lolloping tongue. 'Get away, Les!' he spluttered, pushing him away. 'You're a pain in the exterior!' The dog dashed back out the door and Jimmy shook his head. 'I sometimes wonder what impressed me to bring him home in the first place!'

I told him I was thinking of leaving the gemfields. Nothing more; there was nothing more to tell. I didn't know where I was going. I had to get out of the place was all I knew. I asked him who he might find for a partner, if I went. He told me not to worry about that, he was confident of finding someone who would jump at the chance of becoming part of a thriving Soovenear Tubes business. He gripped my arm with the wire-tight fingers of a once punishing fist, his rheumy eyes intensely focused. 'You go and do what you have to do,' he said. 'You're the genuine sixpence, Ned. I knew it the minute I laid eyes on you.'

I finished my stubby and we stood. He asked me if I would mind checking the shaft for him on my way home. He and Joe had covered it with tin when the rain set in. He was worried it might have shifted.

I scanned the ground as I made my way along the path through the scrub to the shaft, in case the storms had uncovered something I could sell before I left. I specked a couple of green chips and a ratty looking parti-colour. As I stooped to pick up a possible, something under a nearby bush caught my eye. I hooked it out with a stick. The wishbone ribs of a snake's skeleton, picked clean by ants, hung in ranks off its spine. They ended abruptly where the head had once been. I scouted round and found the skull. I looked at it lying in the palm of my hand, fangs eternally poised to strike. I put it in the pocket of my jeans and moved on.

A sheet of iron had shifted in a gust of wind, despite the weight of the billies holding it down. I repositioned it, and added more rocks for good measure. The windlass was in good shape. So was the willoughby, its tank brimful with rainwater. I heard wash rattling down a screen over on Little Bessy – some eager beaver taking advantage of the break in the weather. I remembered the blaze of blue stone across the bottom of the sieve the day Jimmy and I struck it rich. I felt a pang of guilt for running out on him; until I reminded myself that he still owned the lease on the claim, which represented more than the sum total of everything I owned.

I took a short cut through the scrub to Dead Darby's. A bearded dragon skittered through the undergrowth and shot up the nearest stringybark. Ten foot off the ground it threw its head back, the frill round its neck fanning and collapsing to the rhythm of its breathing; the colour and texture of its scaly hide blending with the bark of the tree. It belonged to the bush; I was an intruder. Just as I was an imposter in the gemfields community. A blow-in with no credentials. A soft-bellied kid from the city who had tried to mix it with the men and women of the outback, and was found wanting. The sooner I got out of the place, the better.

I came to the peg marking the north-west corner of Jimmy's claim. There was a sheet of paper wrapped round it, in a plastic sleeve. When I got closer, I saw the letterhead insignia of the Queensland Department of Minerals and Energy. It was a forfeit notice, stating Jimmy's claim had remained unworked for a period of four weeks. There was a signature at the bottom. Below it, in brackets, the printed name of the claimant: Sylvester J Hegarty.

Judging by its condition, Jack agreed, the notice had been put up in the last day or so. It was four weeks and a day since Jimmy had got crook; four weeks and a day since he had been working the mine. Hegarty had been counting.

'The guy's been in hospital, for Christ's sake. They can't just take his claim off him!'

'They can do what they bloody like,' said Jack. 'He could've applied for an exemption. It's a bit bloody late to think of that now.'

I said, 'I want to make sure there's nothing we can do about it.'

'You'd have to go to the Mines Department in Clermont for that. I'd come with you,' he added, 'only I know you'll be wasting your time.'

'It wouldn't be the first thing I've wasted my time on in this place.'

He raked fingers through his hair, without replying. I couldn't see his eyes.

I drove the sixty miles to Clermont the next day. At the Department of Minerals and Energy a bony-faced kid in khaki shorts and long white socks took five-and-a-half minutes to prove Jack's prediction right. 'I'm afraid your friend has forfeited the right to mine this particular lot,' he intoned.

An ordnance survey map was spread on the counter between us, showing the townships of Sapphire and Rubyvale plus the various mining areas, reduced to wavy green contours on an expanse of gridded paper. Long Socks had helped me locate Jimmy's claim on Big Bessy.

'Are you sure there's nothing he can do to reverse it?' I persisted. 'I can get a doctor's certificate to prove he was in hospital.'

'Too late for that. An application for temporary suspension of mining activity should have been lodged within the specified period of...'

'Yes, you've told me all that. What I'm trying to say is, this claim represents everything he owns in the world. There must be something, extenuating circumstances, something...'

'I'm afraid not. The regulations are quite specific. They clearly state that if mining activity on a 24B lease is suspended for a period of more than…'

'I'm not interested in all that bureaucratic bullshit!'

There was a silence. 'Is there anything else I can help you with?'

Something had caught my eye. I jabbed a finger at the map. 'What are these here?'

'They're three-hundred-foot mining leases. Like the one your friend used to own.' He made no attempt to conceal the smugness in his voice.

I said, 'It's all duffer country there.' It was where Bob was camped, around the back of the Bessies behind Jimmy's claim.

'I'm sorry?'

'There's no wash where these claims are. If there's no wash, there can't be any sapphires. Why would anybody want to peg a claim there?'

'You'd have to ask Mr Hegarty that. The Department doesn't advise on the prospects for a successful outcome on the land it leases.'

'Hegarty? The same Hegarty that forfeited Mr Ryan's claim?'

'I believe so. Will that be all? There are people waiting.'

Jack shrugged. 'You wouldn't know what the bastard might be up to.' He had his back to me as he grilled chops and tomatoes on the stove.'

'If he was new to the place, I could understand. But everybody knows it's duffer country north of the Bessies.'

Jack agreed. 'That's why Bob set up camp there.' He brought the frying pan to the table and scraped the food onto a tin plate.

I said, 'What's going to happen to Jimmy?'

'He'll be right. He's gone through worse than this.' He sat down and banged tomato sauce from a bottle onto the chops.

I said, 'Have you seen him lately? It'll kill him if he has to move out of that hut.'

He started eating. Through the fatty tail of a chop he said, 'This ringer dragged me off to a boxing match in a tent out the back of McGuire's pub in Barcaldine once. Never had much time for that sort of thing, but he insisted. Jimmy was fighting this bloke twice his size. Every ringer and cocky from a hundred mile round was there, cheering 'em on. Jimmy got knocked down, but he bounced straight back up. For the rest of the fight he ducked and weaved and bobbed around so much the other bloke couldn't lay a glove on him.'

'Jimmy the Duck.'

'That's right.' He paused to tear at the meat on the chop with his teeth. He chucked the bone to Digger, who snapped it out of the air and started crunching. 'The other bloke got tired after a while, swingin' away at nothing. Jimmy caught him one under the chin and laid him out cold as a maggot.'

'What are you trying to tell me?'

'He's a survivor.'

'He's a sick old man.'

'He's made himself sick. He stayed in the ring half a dozen fights too many. Then he hit the piss.'

'So we just sit back and watch a shit-head like Hegarty walk all over him. And Bob. He'll have to go too, you realise that.'

'Don't worry about Bob. He'll be alright.'

'Fuck you, Jack.' He stopped chewing to look at me, eyebrows looped in surprise. I said, 'Hegarty wants to rip the guts out of these fields so there's nothing left for people like you and me to make a living on. One man, one greedy prick, chewing up enough dirt in a month to keep a dozen decent people alive for five years! What's *alright* about that?'

He sighed. 'Ned, I'm just an old bastard who's spent most of his life trying to keep himself to himself. It's not that hard once you get the hang of it.'

'I'm sticking my nose in where it doesn't belong, is that what you're saying?'

'You're doing what you think is right. But your idea of right and wrong, and mine are never going to be the same.'

'You think what Hegarty's doing is right?'

'I think he's got a right to do it. Jimmy knew what the rules were; he knew Hegarty had his sights set on that claim. He should've been more careful.'

'He never thought anyone'd be a big enough cunt to jump it when he was sick. He put his trust in human nature.'

'Bullshit. He lost his claim because he was so pissed he forgot to fill in the exemption form.'

Probably true, but I wasn't going to let it lie. I said, 'Jesus, Jack, aren't we all in this thing together?'

'What *thing*?'

'All this!' I waved a hand around. 'We're a community here, aren't we?'

He smiled. If I was a dog he would have patted me on the head. 'What community? A mob of layabouts and hippies and refugees from the law! A few old bastards like me who just want to be left alone till they die. Community of bloody no-hopers, that's about all.'

'If we stuck together, maybe we'd stand a chance against someone like Hegarty.'

'Shit floats,' said Jack. 'Bastards like Hegarty always come out on top, Ned. It's in their nature.'

I dropped in on Bob the next day, to warn him Hegarty had pegged the ground he was camped on. Then I went to see Jimmy. He showed no anger, no regret, when I told him what Hegarty had done. 'Well, Ned,' he said, after he'd thought about it, 'I suppose you could say I'm just the prawn in the sandwich.'

Les, for once subdued, lay quietly in the darkest corner of the hut. It was raining, though not as heavily as the past weeks. The Wet was tailing off. In a few days' time the small miners would begin working their claims again. Shafts would be uncovered, water siphoned out of cuts, jackhammers and generators greased and cleaned, willoughby sieves patched, jack-picks sharpened.

Over on the machinery lots, mountains of wash stockpiled in the Dry were already being devoured by front-end loaders. Thirty-foot deep open cuts which had become dams, would be pumped out to feed thirsty pulsators. Dozers would carve great gashes in the earth. Dozens of extra labourers would be hired by Hegarty and the other machinery miners to build up parcels of stone in anticipation of the return of the Thai buyers. The Thais would re-appear in their makeshift tin-shed offices, with their attaché cases full of money, and leave with them bulging with stone. The gemfields would be back in business.

But there would be no back to business for Jimmy Ryan. No 'Soovenear Tubes' for the terrorists on McCafferty's Outback Tours. Joe was dead. I would soon be gone. When Hegarty's D9 dozer rumbled onto Jimmy's claim it would bring the machinery men one step closer to taking over what was left of the fields.

I mentioned the two useless lots Hegarty had registered, but Jimmy could shed no light on the matter. Why he would want to peg claims in duffer country was as much a mystery to him as it was to me and Jack.

The rain fell heavier. A sheet of iron not properly weighed down by the billies on the roof flapped in a gust of wind. 'I was going to nail the blessed thing down,' Jimmy said. He looked around him. 'But that's not the point of the issue any more, is it?'

I told him I could stick around for a few weeks till he got back on his feet. He laughed. 'Why would you want to do a thing like that? I'm not on the last of my legs yet!' He was opening the fridge to get more stubbies. His weight shifted to his weaker right side and he swung out with the door. I saw his teeth grit stubbornly as he struggled to correct the downward motion of his body. He crashed to the floor on his back, taking the orange-box shelves of *Britannica* with him, the twenty-four volumes spilling over him onto the dirt floor.

Even as I leapt up to help him, he had rolled over and scrambled to his knees. He swayed. I imagined he could hear the raucous shouts of the fight fans ringing in the dark, the ref counting him out. Les shambled over to lick his face. Jimmy nudged him away with his shoulder. He closed his eyes, and hauled himself slowly to his feet. Ready to box on. Jimmy the Duck.

I couldn't leave Jimmy, Hegarty might come down any day to kick him off the claim. I visited him every day. I kept him supplied with brew, made sure he had enough to eat. I talked to him about lodging an objection to the Mines Department about the forfeiture. At least it would buy him time. 'Time for what?' he asked.

Good question. We both knew his mining days were over. He had no interest in doing battle with Hegarty in court, and no money to fund such a battle. By the time anything was resolved, he could be dead. There was a lot of it going round.

It was looking like I might have to stick around longer than I really wanted to. The last batch of brew was running low, so I put another one down. I tried to blot out the memory of me and Jess squirting each other as we siphoned it into bottles.

Tex paid a visit on his way home from Fairbairn Dam. He dumped a weighty sugar bag on the kitchen table. He hadn't forgotten his promise to keep me supplied with meat for the rest of my life. He had taken the back road from the dam, through Upson Downs, and was lucky enough to come across a mob of Hegarty's Herefords.

'Christ those cattle are in good nick after the rain!' He might have been the boss cocky himself, proud of the way the station hands were running his stock.

The sun was shining, we sat under the porch roof with stubbies of brew and chewed the fat. I asked him how the work on the dam was going. He shrugged. 'Might as well take it while you can.' He had never gone in for mining. 'Too much like hard yakka, mate!' Driving a scraper was a cushier job than labouring, he reckoned. There was all the overtime you could ever want; danger money on top of that. 'You earn it but, haulin' one of those fuckin' things around all day.' I had never seen one, but Tex had given me a description.

A voracious dirt-eating caterpillar on wheels, one of these things could shift earth three times faster than the biggest dozer. I wondered aloud why Hegarty had never used one. 'Not enough room to turn the bastard around, mate. Fuckin' thing's fifty-foot long. You'd need three times the length of a machinery claim to operate it.'

Things were starting to gel. 'What you'd need,' I said, 'is three claims, end-to-end.'

'That'd do it.' He took a swig from his stubby. 'Funny you should mention Hegarty. I saw him yesterday out at the dam. Fuck knows what he'd be prowlin' around out there for.'

'You said it was nearly finished.'

'Now the rain's eased off, they'll concrete the spillway. Flood the coffer dam. That'll be it.'

'What are they going to do with all that heavy machinery?'

He shrugged. 'Take it on to the next job, I suppose.'

'Or sell it.'

'Could do.'

'Hegarty's forfeited Jimmy's claim,' I said. 'He's pegged two more on duffer country right alongside it.'

'Is that right?' Tex sucked on the stubby and wiped the back of his hand across his mouth. He looked down the track towards Jimmy's place. 'With a scraper the bastard'll have the guts ripped out of it before you can blink. All you'll see there in a month's time'll be a dirty great hole in the fuckin' ground.'

Two days later, Hegarty put his D9 through Bob's camp behind the Bessies. I heard about it from Beryl Carmody. 'They must've done it while he was in here, buying tea and sugar,' she said. She was sorting through a goods delivery, her voice sharp, movements choppy.

I said, 'How did you find out?'

'Brindley was in here – his dozer driver. The bastard was laughing about it!' She threw packets of potato crisps into a tin and banged the lid shut. 'He's one of the decentest people on the gemfields, Black Bob. It's a bloody disgrace.'

I asked her how long ago it had happened. She told me the driver had left twenty minutes ago. It couldn't have been long before that.

By the time I got to his camp, Bob had saddled up Elvis. What was left of his hut was spread over an area the size of a tennis court. The trees his clothes line had been attached to were uprooted and sprawled on the ground, the rocks around the campfire scattered. He was strapping a bedroll and other belongings he had salvaged, behind the saddle. He turned as I walked down the slope from where I had parked the car; saw it was me, and went back to what he was doing.

The saddle was in worse condition than when I had last seen it. Tufts of wool padding poked through cracks in the leather. The stitching in one of the flaps was torn, so it hung at an angle. I guessed he had arrived back from the shop too late to drag it out before Brindley put the dozer through.

'Can I do anything?' I said.

'No, I'll be right. Thanks.'

'Are you going to report this to Gillespie?'

'Report what?'

'What Hegarty's done to you!'

'It's his claim, he can do what he likes with it.'

I was thinking beyond that. I was thinking of how he had tried to bully Jimmy and Jack into selling up; then, when that failed, tried to buy my loyalty by chucking handfuls of money on the ground for me to pick up. Not to mention sticking me in Muddrington Road gaol for four months.

I said, 'He always does what he likes. We should stand up to the bastard!'

His mouth twisted in a grin. 'Don't get all political on me, eh.'

'It's nothing to do with politics. It's human decency.'

'If you expect decency from someone like Sylvester Hegarty, you're gunna get disappointed. You should know that.'

I said, 'He's an evil bastard.'

'Sylvester hasn't got the guts to be evil.' He checked the surcingle on the saddle to make sure it was tight. 'His father would've been ashamed of him.'

'Did you know him?'

'I wouldn't have learned how to read and write, if it wasn't for Percy Hegarty. He sent me to school. He was a tough old bastard, but he knew the difference between right and wrong.' He was about to mount up. 'I meant to tell you at Joe's funeral, you remember you asked me about the Quinlans, in Armidale? I went back down there last month.'

I had hardly thought of Ray Quinlan since my return to the gemfields. I felt a twinge of guilt. I had summoned him up when I needed him in Muddrington Road, and abandoned him when I had no further need for him. The mere mention of his name now cheered me up. For all that St Andrew's was a refuge for a whole lot of damaged kids, we had made our own life there. A life that had nothing to do with funerals or gaols or dogs or greedy bastards like Sylvester Hegarty; an innocent time, when the only thing that mattered was waking and sleeping and packing as much fun as you could into the spaces between. Ray was my last connection to it.

I said, 'Did you see them?'

'I did. They've got a house just out of town. Nice people.' He brushed at a fly buzzing his ear. 'Shame about young Darren.'

'What happened to him?'

'He's lame. Got polio when he was little. Good lookin' kid, too.' Like a cherry falling into place in a poker machine window, something clicked.

I said, 'Does he wear a brace for it?'

'Yeah. He'll have to for the rest of his life, they reckon.'

'Did you see Ray?'

'No. He passed away.'

Somehow, I was expecting it. 'What happened to him?' I prepared myself for the car accident, the cranial aneurism, the pedestrian fatality - whatever it was that had snuffed out the life of someone whose lingering memory had helped give me the strength to deal with the shit I had been going through over the past months.

'Committed suicide,' said Bob. 'Hung himself. I told 'em what you said about him being very popular at the school you went to. They said they remembered him talking about Ned Sheridan.'

'When did it happen?'

'Towards the end of last year. He'd moved to Sydney. They couldn't afford to bring him home, they had to go down there for the funeral.'

'On the Daylight Express.'

Bob crooked an eyebrow. I couldn't see the point in explaining how I had seen the family on their way to the funeral; how I had spoken to Ray's father when he rescued me from a burning dog.

'Pity you never got to meet 'em,' said Bob. Elvis's wiry tail switched at a fly as he grazed a clump of grass, the mashing of his teeth amplified by the still heat of noon. 'Well,' he bent down to retrieve the bridle reins dragging behind the horse's shuffling snout, 'I'd better get moving.' He gathered the reins in his hand, put a foot in a stirrup and eased himself into the saddle.

I said, 'Where will you go?'

'I'll find some place. It was gettin' a bit busy around here, anyhow. People droppin' in outa the blue, askin' a lot of questions.' His teeth flashed in a grin. 'Write that bloody book, eh.'

I reached up to shake his hand. I said, 'I will. Take care, Bob.'

'You can count on that, brother.'

Nobody had called me 'brother' since the night Joe and I rescued Jess from the ringers. *'You alright, brother?'* she had said. Half a lifetime ago.

Bob nudged Elvis's flank with his heel. I watched them move off into the bush.

I felt like shit. Through all the time in Muddrington Road, I had kept myself going with the belief that things would get back to some kind of normal when I returned to the gemfields. The place had become a home. I belonged to its community. With Joe dead, Jess and Bob gone, Jimmy on the way out, it was all falling apart. And now Ray Quinlan. The thought of Ray, the kid who could make us laugh just by walking like Mr Atchison, or mimicking Buddy Holly singing Peggy Sue - the thought of him topping himself was the saddest thing I had ever felt.

I went into Emerald to pick up the tie-rod for Jack's ute. The wreckers didn't have one; a new one was being sent up from Rockhampton. It hadn't arrived yet, so I took the run out to Kerracan to say hullo to Reg. Becky, he had told me at the funeral, was helping him look after the kids while the women were away, when he was working on the railways. I was hoping he could tell me something about Jess.

'She's real good,' he said, as we sat at the kitchen table.

'She's got a job in Rocky, in the supermarket,' said Becky.

The really good news though, was that Val had gone on the wagon, and seemed to be sticking to it. I told Reg what had happened to Bob. He'd already heard.

'That mongrel Hegarty,' he said. 'Somebody should drop him in one o'them dozer cuts of his, and back-fill it.'

We comforted ourselves swapping stories about what a bastard Hegarty was. We had no way of knowing that while we were talking, he was taking up the option on Jimmy's claim in his trade-mark fashion.

I stayed an extra day at Kerracan, to help Reg fix up some things around the house that would never get done once he went back to work. I drove in to Jackson's hardware, to find the part for Jack's ute still hadn't arrived. I had to wait for the four o'clock train. It was late afternoon by the time I set off for Sapphire.

I decided to drop in on Jimmy on my way home. I by-passed Dead Darby's, and drove up the track to Big Bessy. It was dusk. It didn't register at first that something was missing from the landscape. My first thought was that some irresponsible bastard had dumped a truckload of rubbish beside the track. When I got closer, I saw it was all that was left of Jimmy's hut.

I recognised bits of his valuable junk scattered around - rolls of rusted wire-netting, a kerosene tin, some steel posts, a rusted engine block. One of the billy boulders that had been on the roof had rolled out onto the road. The sheets of corrugated iron he had been so careful not to spoil with nail-holes were pushed into a heap of twisted metal.

I half expected to see Jimmy rise from the wreckage, Les prancing around him while he steadied himself. Ready to box on. There was no sign of either of them. I felt sick in the guts. *Things can't get worse than this*, I thought. I should've known better.

When I got to Darby's, I saw a vehicle I had never seen before parked outside the gate. It was a later model Ford sedan, nicely polished, not a dent in its gleaming chrome and duco bodywork. There was no way it belonged to anyone I knew.

I stopped the HD and got out. A movement caught my eye, and I spotted a kid up on the hill, head down, hands behind his back, moving slowly over the mullock heap behind the dam. Speckers, I thought. They would come up from the city on the weekends, expecting to make a fortune from a couple of hours scratching around on a fifty-year-old mullock heap. They rarely showed respect for other people's property.

I caught another movement from the direction of the hut. Someone had come out the front door. A stocky man, balding, in shorts and sandals. As I came through the gate, he walked over to meet me. 'Can I help you?' he asked.

'Help me?'

'I'm new here,' he said awkwardly. 'If you're lost, I'm afraid I won't be much good with directions.'

'You're the one who's lost, mate!' I jabbed a finger in his chest. 'What the fuck are you doing in my house?'

Behind him a woman appeared in the doorway. Mousy hair, floral print dress, a dreary face to match. 'Who is it, John?' she called.

'It's alright dear,' John called back.

I caught sight of a covered pile of stuff under the porch roof. There was enough showing beneath the bottom edge of the tarp to indicate my belongings were stacked under it.

'Like fuck it's alright! Who the hell are you?' I moved in on him, ready to punch his lights out.

He stood his ground. 'I'm John Millwall. I own this property.'

'What the fuck are you talking about?'

'I bought it last week, from a lady in Townsville. Her name was…' He trailed off.

'Prentice,' the woman called helpfully.

'Yes, that's it, Angela Prentice. Her father used to own the place.' I stared at him, wordless. 'I'm sorry,' he said. 'She didn't tell us anyone was staying here. We didn't know how to find you.'

Miserable Bastards

Jack was waiting to meet me. He knew why I was there. Les, behind him, jumped up and raked claws down his bare legs. 'Giddout of it,' he growled, flicking him out of the way with his boot.

I followed him into the hut. There were two other people sitting at the table. 'Well, if it isn't the welcome stranger!' one of them said. The other one acknowledged me with a blink of his crocodile eyes.

It didn't surprise me that Jack had taken Jimmy in after Hegarty dozed his house down. I hadn't expected him to do the same for Bob. He brought the billy from the stove and poured four mugs of tea. Jimmy raised his in a toast, holding it in his left hand. The right one was useless. 'Nice to have you back with the quick and the dead, Neddy,' he said.

Jack sat down with his tea. 'I thought you were going to tell that lawyer in Emerald to get in touch with Darby's daughter about buying his hut. What happened to that idea?'

I said, 'I never got around to it. I couldn't see the point.'

He gave a little grimace of disgust. We all fell silent. It occurred to me that I hadn't seen Digger since I arrived. I asked where he was. 'He went off a couple of days ago,' said Jack. 'He was always a wanderer. He'll be back.'

I knew what Bob and Jimmy were thinking, and what Jack didn't want to: that the dog might have wandered too close to Hegarty's claim, and taken a bait.

Jack excused himself and went outside, leaving his untouched mug of tea on the table. We could hear him moments later at the forge, hammer clanging on the anvil as he sharpened his picks.

'At least Jack's still got a roof over his head,' said Bob. Jimmy and I agreed it was a good thing. It was a mongrel of a position the three of us were in. No home, no money: no prospects of finding one or making any. Sitting hunched in the fading light, swathed in the smoke of Jack's burning cow dung, we were the original pack of miserable bastards.

'Young Ned here'll be alright,' said Jimmy suddenly. 'At least he's got youth by his side!'

He was right, I did. Jimmy didn't. Neither did Bob. At least I was physically capable of slinking off somewhere with my tail between my legs, if that's all there was left to do. Back to the city, south to Lightning Ridge, across the Atlantic to Tierra-del-fucking-Fuego if the fancy took me. I was still treading the treadmill.

But the wheel had almost squeaked to a halt for Jimmy. Bob would scrounge another saddle from somewhere and poke on to the next lonely campsite, then the next, until he eventually found one to die in. Like ghosts ahead of their time, they seemed in danger of vanishing into the dung-scented gloom of Jack's kitchen.

Jimmy flexed his shoulders, and I recalled the first time I met him, the fearless, square set of him, the spring in his bony little shanks, the grin that wouldn't leave you alone. I could hear Joe, voice booming from the barrel-drum of his chest: *'I'm been come to say goot eveningk vith you, you mizzerable bustards!'*; saw his yellow-stained fingers pluck strands of tobacco from the end of a rolly. I saw Sparra, crimping a det for his gelly. And Tex, a hefty sugar bag slung over his shoulder; Becky and Reg, hauling a flapping yellow-belly from the muddy water; Jess, laughing. Soon they would be in the past, hundreds of miles away that might as well be millions.

'You'll be right, Jimmy,' I said.

The beat of Jack's hammer rang away to an empty echo.

There was a ramshackle shed out the back, originally built by someone more ambitious than Jack to house heavy machinery - tractors, winches, loaders etc. Over the years, a corner post, eaten-out by white ants, had collapsed, taking the roof with it so it formed a giant lean-to. Jimmy and Bob had salvaged all they could carry from the wreckage of their homes, so at least they had a mattress each. Jack found an old horsehair one for me. We laid a tarp down for a groundsheet.

Bob, Jimmy and I chipped in all the money we had. Jack added ten bucks to the kitty and sent me off to buy tea, bread and sugar. It was Saturday morning, Tex would be coming home for the weekend. I was hoping I might bump into him at the shop.

He arrived there as I was leaving. I told him what had happened. 'I'll bring you some meat as soon as I can,' he promised. As far as work was concerned, I was out of luck. They were putting labourers and drivers off every day at the dam. The main wall was finished. Men retrenched from the construction company were lining up for work on the irrigation channels. 'Sorry, mate, I don't know the foreman on the new site, or I could've done something.' I would have to join the queue, like everyone else.

There was more bad news. Hegarty had pegged a claim where the League of Nations was camped. He had paid Angus and the boys a visit. He told them they had two days to pack up and leave before the dozer moved in.

I had nowhere to live, no way of making money. I might have been able to find a patch of ground to work, but I couldn't have hacked mining on my own for the next six months. Jimmy had moved the genny and jackhammer to safety before Hegarty's dozer went through the hut; I would sell them, and we would split the proceeds. That would give me enough to get to Brisbane and live on for a few weeks. Bob reckoned he'd be moving on as well.

I was helping Jack sharpen picks, when the monster arrived. As I wound the handle of the forge, the surrounding trees and mullock heaps danced in the heat rising off red-hot charcoal.

'What's going to happen to Jimmy?' I said.

Jack pulled a pick-head out of the coals with a pair of tongs, laid its molten point on the head of the anvil, and attacked it with the hammer. The blows rang through the heat and bounced off the wall of the hut. 'Jimmy'll be right,' he said.

She'll be right, no fuckin' worries, I thought. I shoved another pick in the forge and wound the handle, cranking the gears till they whined a shrill protest. Nothing was 'right'. I knew it, and I knew Jack knew it. I saw him stop hammering. He cocked an ear. I stopped cranking, to listen. It was a motor. A big one. We downed tools to go and investigate.

Roaring towards us was Hegarty's scraper. Its driver had evidently taken the back road from the dam, joining up with the track through the Bessies. Its mud-spattered grille looked like the snout of some giant black-wheeled centipede. Its exhaust stack spewed black diesel. Its massive wheels, higher than a man, rolled along either side of the track, crushing everything in its path. The roar of the motor grew louder until we had to shout to be heard.

'Get a go at that bloody thing, will you?' It took a lot to impress Jack, but he was impressed.

I caught a glimpse of Hegarty's dozer driver, Brindley, perched high up in the machine's cabin, hunched over the steering wheel, eyes glued to the road ahead as he struggled to maintain control of the roaring juggernaut entrusted to his care. *Tex was right*, I thought. *You'd want danger money just to get behind the wheel of the bloody thing.*

Through the dust cloud billowing behind Hegarty's latest acquisition, a familiar vehicle appeared. The Range Rover jerked to a halt and Hegarty got out. He walked to the rear of the Rover, turned his back to us and unzipped his fly. When he had finished pissing, he came over to where we were standing, and stopped in front of Jack. 'You given any thought to my offer?'

'Not a dicky bird.'

'I'll give you twenty-five thousand, cash in hand.'

'I'm still not thinking about it.'

Hegarty was looking beyond us. Bob and Jimmy had come out of the hut.

'You've got your grubby mitts on Jimmy's claim,' said Jack. 'Why can't you be satisfied with that?'

'I made Jimmy a generous offer, he threw it back in my face. I can't be held responsible for what happened after that.'

'What about dozing Bob's home into the ground,' I said. 'Is that something you're responsible for?'

His gaze shifted to me. 'Well, if it isn't Mr Sheridan. Haven't seen you around for a while. How's the book coming along?' His hand came up to bat a fly away. There was no fly. It was me he was flapping away.

Jack said, 'If that's the business end of things done and dusted, Sylvester, why don't you toddle off and do something useful?'

Bob's voice came from behind us. 'Yeah, go home and count your money.' He chuckled, pleased with his joke.

'Hullo, Bob,' said Hegarty, like he'd only just then noticed him. 'What've you been up to lately? Still going to change the world are you, reading all those important books? You should get the genius here to write one for you. If he's got time in between knocking off my livestock.'

I said, 'I didn't kill that calf, and you know it.'

'You were happy enough to eat it though, weren't you? And protect the bastard that did knock it off. So don't get up on your moral fucking high-horse with me.' He returned his attention to Jack. 'Twenty-five thousand. Come on Jack, you know if I want something I'll get it, one way or the other. With that much money, you can piss off out of the place, and make everybody happy.'

'You're not going to start telling me how to make people happy, are you, Sylvester?'

The cords in Hegarty's neck stiffened. 'I wouldn't dream of it. You're the expert in that department. Are you going to take this offer or not?'

Jack took the packet of ready-rubbed from his pocket. He stuck a paper to his bottom lip and spread a line of tobacco on the palm of one hand. 'I'll give you a word of advice,' he said. 'If you want to do business with me, don't start off by pissing in front of me.' He rolled the tobacco into the paper, and ran his tongue along it. 'Dogs do that.' He struck a match and cupped his hands to light up. He flicked the dead matchstick to the ground. 'You don't add up to much, Sylvester, but I would've given you credit for having better manners than a dog.'

Hegarty stood stock still, as if the failure of his mission had paralysed him. The vein in his neck pulsed. He turned abruptly and walked to the Range Rover, unlocked the rear door and swung it open. He pulled out a bulging hessian bag and came back with it.

He stopped in front of Jack and dumped the bag at his feet. 'Funny you should mention dogs,' he said.

He went back to the vehicle, climbed in and banged the door shut. The Range Rover lurched into gear and roared off down the track.

We looked at the bag lying on the ground. I could see a white-tipped paw protruding from the open end of it. The bag was smouldering, the stench coming off it so strong I couldn't breathe. I heard Bob say, 'I'll bury him for you Jack.' Jack saying, 'No, I'll do it.'

Through a descending veil of darkness I was aware of him squatting in front of the bag. Saw him scoop it up and walk off with it cradled, smoking, in his arms...

Gravel dug into my cheek. An ant loomed. I was breathing again. Someone was shaking my shoulder.

'You alright Ned?' Bob was kneeling beside me. I could see Jimmy's frayed sandshoes. They helped me to a sitting position. 'You musta had one o'them turns,' said Bob.

'How long was I out?'

'Only a minute or two. You dropped like someone took your legs out from under you. You'd better stay where you are for a bit.'

I looked to where I had last seen Jack. He was nowhere to be seen. I had survived another burning dog. My first thought was, *I've gotta get out of this place, before it kills me.* My second thought was, *The only place that's killing you, is the place in your head.* My third thought was, *We've gotta hit back at that fucking arsehole Hegarty.*

As far as possible, considering there were four of us living together, I kept to myself over the next two days. I was so strung out, the simple act of talking to anybody was an effort. I felt like I was going crazy; on top of which I was in the grip of an overriding anxiety about *appearing* to be crazy. It was the same sort of compulsion I had felt when I left Cathie to go to Armidale, looking for Jack. Now it was compounded by the fact that I had found him, possibly, and nothing had been resolved. There was nowhere else to go looking.

At that stage of my life, Hegarty, you could say, was my salvation. The desire to get even with him had become an obsession that took my mind off all the other shit. It was my new mission in life. It was around that time, too, that I learned something about Jack that would soften my attitude towards him.

I had gone to the shop to buy groceries. I was on my way out when I caught sight of a stack of recently-delivered newspapers near the door.

I said, 'I might as well take Jack's *Courier Mail*.'

'That's alright,' said Beryl. 'He'll be down for it later. He likes to pick it up himself.'

'It'll save him a trip. He can read it over breakfast.'

She smiled. 'When did you last see him doing that?'

I realised I had never actually seen him reading the paper. It was more of a prop, something to swat flies with, or start a fire.

Beryl shifted position to take a squiz out the door, as if worried she might be overheard. 'I always read the headlines for him... any articles that might interest him. He makes sure he comes in when there's no one around.'

'He can't read?'

'Or write. I've been his secretary for years.' I remembered the feminine look about the hand that had written the note he left me when he went away. She said, 'You won't say anything, will you? He's a proud man.'

We sat in the kitchen, eating the chops and mashed potato Jack had cooked. I watched him pick up a bone he had chewed the meat off. For a second it looked like he was going to chuck it on the hearth, for Digger. Then he put it back on his plate. I caught Bob's eye. We continued eating in silence.

Bob had rolled his belongings into a blanket tied with rope. He had done what he could to stitch up his saddle, and dressed it with some oil he found in the shed. All that was left to do was throw it on Elvis, sling his bluey on behind, and ride off down the track. Two days later he was still there. He told me he didn't feel good about leaving Jack on his own. He never talked about it, but we knew the loss of Digger had hit him hard.

Jack wasn't my favourite person in the world, and I had big enough problems of my own, but I felt sorry for him. My anxiety had subsided. I felt like I was getting back to 'normal', whatever that was. I agreed with Bob that we should keep an eye on him for a while. I didn't tell him I had another, more pressing reason for sticking around.

I put a 'For Sale' notice for the jackhammer and genny in Beryl's shop. I got a response the following day. Stumpy Pavlu, a deeply religious man from the Rice Bowl, was another victim of the big machinery miners' greed. Hegarty had stopped him using water from a claim he had recently acquired; water Stumpy had been reliant on for years. With no way of processing his wash, he was going out backwards. He didn't have enough money to buy my equipment outright. I let him put down a deposit.

Tex told me Sparra was back on the gemfields. I was surprised he hadn't bothered to look me up. He'd got straight back to work, Tex said. 'You wouldn't believe it, he's diggin' in that useless bloody shaft in the Scrub Lead. The one I told you about when I saw you in Muddro. I keep tellin' him there's nothin' down there, but he won't listen.'

I said, 'Maybe he just wants to take his mind off things.'

I had never felt like talking about my time in gaol; I had no doubt Sparra felt the same way. On top of which, I knew he would've been nursing resentment at being robbed of the chance to blast his way out of Muddrington Road. Tex gave me instructions where to find his camp. There was something I wanted to talk to him about.

I found him easily enough, following Tex's directions. He had served out the rest of his time in Muddro uneventfully, he told me, and come out to Anakie on the train. I didn't ask him why he hadn't looked anybody up; I figured that was his business.

I got straight to the point. I said, 'I want you to teach me how to use gelignite.'

'You're kidding,' he laughed. 'I thought you were one of them silly buggers'd hack away for weeks with a pick and shovel, rather than use a stick of gelly. That's what Jimmy told me.'

'I'm not talking about mining.' He frowned. 'I want to blow that cunt Hegarty into the next century.' If I was going to leave the place without having achieved what I had come there for; without making it up with the woman I had fallen in love with, the least I could do was exact revenge on the fucker who had made life miserable for me and a lot of people I had grown to like and respect.

In the short time I had spent on the gemfields, there was a lot I had come to like about the place. Nobody asked questions about who you where or where you came from or what you believed in. For all the rowdy social behaviour on display, quiet acceptance of an individual's beliefs and interests was the rule. As long as you didn't impinge on anybody else's, you could do what you liked. It pissed me off that a prick like Hegarty thought he could trample on people who stuck to those principles, and get away with it.

Sparra feigned interest, but I could see he was worried. 'When you say "Hegarty", d'you mean, like, *him*, or...'

I said, 'Don't worry, I don't want to kill him. I just want to bring that poxy fucking office of his down to ground level. With its shitload of stone in his poxy fucking safe, and its pictures of his prize fucking cattle, and everything in it that's geared to fucking us over. People like you and me. You know what I mean?'

'You want to blow Hegarty's office up.'

'Yes.'

'They'll lock us up for fucking ever.'

I patted him on the shoulder. 'Mate, I'm not asking you to get involved. All you have to do is show me how to set the dets, I'll do the rest, okay?'

He said, 'When I wanted to blow us out of Muddrington Road, you said I was crazy. Now you're asking me to help you do something that's even crazier!'

'Why?'

'Because Hegarty's the one who sent you to gaol. You're the first person they'll come looking for.'

He was right. Four weeks ago I'd been trying to talk Sparra down from a lunatic bombing mission; here he was now, doing the same for me. It crossed my mind that I was crazier now than Sparra had ever been.

I said, 'Maybe. But I don't give a fuck.'

He looked at me hard, like he was giving deep thought to something. He said, 'I was going to come and see you about this, but I might as well let you in on it now.'

'In on what?'

He crooked a finger. 'Come with me.'

I followed him through the scrub along a path only he could see, to a spot a hundred yards off the track leading to the camp. In a clearing surrounded by tall timber, he scraped bark and leaves away from two rusting sheets of iron. He pulled them aside to reveal the entrance to a shaft. He climbed onto the ladder. He called out to me when he got to the bottom.

The sides of the shaft were ragged, a legacy of Sparra's preferred method of mining. Shattered chunks of rock hung loose where he had blasted through a layer of basalt. At the foot of the shaft, thirty foot down, there was still no sign of wash. With no wash to follow, there was no ballroom. Instead, a narrow drive struck off directly opposite the ladder.

Sparra lit a carbide lamp he had left down there, and headed off along the drive. I scurried along, crouched low, in the wake of his silhouette showing stark against the acetylene flare of the lamp. Of the two of us, he moved with the greater ease, even though he had the lamp to carry. He knew every dip and bump. He called over his shoulder now and again, to warn of a jagged rock protruding from the wall, or a pothole where one had been torn from the floor. I lost sight of him altogether as the drive changed direction sharply and I had only the faint glow of the lamp to follow.

When I caught up to him, I became aware that light from the lamp no longer splashed the walls on either side of us. We had arrived at another drive. The old-timers didn't mess around following skinny little bands of wash. They plundered the richest veins, leaving the rest for future generations to pick over. Modern mining was often a matter of reworking those old diggings, following up the narrower bands of wash that had been overlooked, hauling stow to the surface, sifting old mullock heaps.

Sparra, by design or otherwise, had broken into one of those old drives. We could stand up straight in it; stretch our arms wide without touching the walls on either side. 'They reckon this wash was so rich,' he said, 'you could pull stone out of it with your fingers. Like pickin' raisins out of a Christmas cake.'

We set off to the left along the drive. 'Watch out for the tracks,' he warned. Too late. My foot caught the edge of something rigid and I stumbled. Lamplight glinted on metal. I could make out the parallel shafts of rail tracks, vanishing into the darkness. We came to a skip squatting on the tracks where it had been abandoned fifty years earlier.

The sound of our breathing became magnified in the stillness of air that had remained unchanged for half a century. I imagined whole gangs of miners swarming over the fields, tearing away at the faces of a hundred drives. Knocking down thousands of yards of wash at a furious pace, hauling it to the surface without pause from morning till night. I could hear their picks ringing, the echo of their voices railing and cursing.

The drive curved to the right in a sweeping arc into an underground forest of dead, barkless tree trunks the size of young brigalows, evenly spaced about twenty-foot apart, holding up the roof high above our heads. We had entered an immense ballroom, the extremities of which were so distant they fell into darkness before the light could reach them. In all the stories I had heard about the exploits of the old diggers, I had never heard of anything like this.

'Wash here musta been ten-foot deep!' Sparra marvelled. He held the lamp high and swung it in an arc, the splayed shadows of the toms swaying to the rhythm of its movement. We made our way through the forest of toms. As we drew closer to the wall ahead of us, I saw that it was actually a massive column, twelve-foot in diameter, in the centre of the ballroom. He stopped in front of it and reached out to rake his fingers across its face. A shower of pebbles fell to the floor. He stooped to pick one up, the size of a marble, glistening oily black in the palm of his hand. I took it and held it against the flame of the lamp, releasing its azure brilliance.

The acetylene gleamed in his eyes. 'This is the bugger I've been looking for,' he said.

Sparra wasn't as stupid as Tex had thought. All that time we had imagined him sweating his guts out down holes that were never going to make him tucker money, he had been burrowing around looking for the rich pickings the old-timers had left behind. Finally, he had hit the jackpot.

His plan was simple: remove the pillar of wash and help ourselves to the stone in it. He guaranteed it would be ten times richer than anything I had ever heard of.

I remembered something Jimmy had told me, the first time he took me down his mine. I said, 'Aren't you forgetting something?'

'What's that?'

'Wasn't this pillar left here for a reason?'

'Of course. To stop the fuckin' roof falling in.'

'So…'

'So as we take the pillar out, we put toms in to replace it. As many as we can fit, the strongest we can find. You can't be too careful with that fuckin' slippery-back.'

Slippery-back. Jimmy had mentioned it that first day on Bessy. It sounded dangerous and, as I later learned, it was. He was hazy on the geological details; so was everybody else I asked about it. It was enough to know that if you were tunnelling through the stuff, there was an increased danger of the roof of the drive collapsing on you. My mind shied from trying to calculate the tonnage of earth and rock lying above us.

Sparra knew what was going through my mind. He laughed. 'If the fuckin' thing wanted to drop, d'you think it would've waited all this time? Nah,' he scoffed, 'slippery-back's nothin' to be frightened of! You gotta respect it, that's all. Mind you,' he added regretfully, 'it means gelly's out of the question.' For that I was grateful.

He beckoned to me to follow him, and we headed back the way we had come. Five minutes later we arrived at the point where he had broken into the old drive. Instead of turning right, he kept going straight ahead. We eventually came to another ballroom, smaller than the first. He pointed to the other side of it. 'That's where they sank the first shaft,' he said. 'Now I'll show you something interesting.'

I followed him over to the shaft and looked up. A chink of light crept between sheets of iron covering the top of the hole, twenty-foot above my head. There was a ladder, most of whose rungs were broken. 'It doesn't look much, but you can get up it,' Sparra assured me.

'Why would you want to?'

'You'll see.'

I watched as he inched his way up, avoiding the broken rungs, until he reached the top. A shower of gravel rained down as he slid the sheets of iron across, and a pool of light flooded the bottom of the shaft. His voice came floating down. 'Step on the outside of the rungs. Some of 'em are a bit dodgy.'

He was wrong, they were all dodgy. Five minutes later, I crawled out into the open like a cicada emerging from its hole in the ground. I blinked in the glare of the sun. A diesel motor grumbled somewhere in the distance. Sparra was watching me closely. 'Bet ya didn't expect this, eh?'

He was right. I had imagined we would come out into mullock heaps and old tailings, but all I could see was blackberry bush. We were surrounded by it. Now the rains had stopped, the fruit had matured and was hanging off the canes in knobbly black clusters. We were smack in the middle of a huge thicket that had grown right over the hole. Sparra had hacked and trampled enough of it to allow some movement.

'Have a squiz,' he invited, pointing to a tunnel that had been slashed through the thicket. I was reminded of the time in Muddro when he had proudly unveiled his plans for the bomb. He had that same wild look in his eye.

I said, 'You want me to crawl through that?'

'You won't have to go far.'

I got down on my hands and knees and started crawling. The blackberry tore at my arms and snagged my clothes. Inches from my head, a flock of scrubwrens tittered. The diesel motor I had heard was now labouring under full throttle. I could hear it coming closer. I reached the end of the tunnel and thrust my head and shoulders out.

I fell back an instant later, heart pounding, as the bellowing roar of the diesel reached a crescendo and Hegarty's scraper thundered past, one massive wheel rolling by a yard from where my head had been. Through a vignette of blackberry thorns I saw a ton of rocks and dirt trail from its guts. Its hind wheel spat up a dead branch hidden in the grass, hurling it into the berries beside me like an amputated limb.

I watched the monster clank off into the distance, past the limits of one claim and onto the next; saw it turn in a sweeping arc to make another run through the cut, scooping up another load of overburden, to regurgitate on the heap nearby.

Beyond the cut, ringed by the few remaining trees in the wasteland surrounding it, a two-storeyed corrugated-iron structure squatted, its ridged iron walls glowing orange in the rays of the morning sun. A sandy-haired figure was walking towards it, tracked by the snarling and snapping of dogs. Hegarty, returning to his office after feeding his pack of piggers.

'It's smack under the bastard's plant!' Sparra said, as I rejoined him at the top of the shaft. 'The pulsator, the machinery shed, his office, they're all sittin' on top of the ballroom. That's why he's never got around to puttin' a dozer through it. And he's got no idea what's down there!' He gripped my arm. 'You can't back out on this one, Neddy.'

'Back out on what?'

'I want you to help me take that pillar down. It'll hurt the bastard more than blowin' his plant up. And we'll have enough money to piss off outa this place forever. Whadda you reckon?'

I thought of the pile of twisted iron sheets that had been Jimmy's home; and what had happened to Bob. I thought of a white-tipped paw protruding from the hessian bag at Jack's feet; the time I had spent in Muddrington Road gaol. Sylvester Hegarty had become a symbol for all that was wrong in the world, and everything that had gone wrong in my life.

I said, 'What are we waiting for?'

Partners in Crime

It was standard practice with the machinery boys to strip every square foot of their claims until all that was left was the patch the plant was sitting on. The plant would then be shifted, and the last cut put in. On 'Eureka', that day was drawing near. We would have to move fast.

The problem was, how to get the wash to the surface without Hegarty getting wind of what we were up to. The shaft in the blackberries, only a few hundred yards from his office, was out of the question. On the other hand, hauling it all the way back to the one Sparra had sunk, was a mammoth task. It would've slowed things down so much, Hegarty might have dozed his way to the ballroom before we had time to clean it out.

We settled on a third option. We would sink a fresh shaft into Sparra's new drive, closer to the ballroom than his original shaft, but well clear of 'Eureka'. We chose a spot hidden away in the bush. We planned on making use of the rail system that had been waiting down there all those years. Even though it would mean dead time lifting and re-laying the tracks, it would pay dividends in the labour saved by not having to shovel wash in shifts back to the shaft.

Sparra insisted we keep it a two-man operation. I argued for cutting Jack and Jimmy and Bob in. 'We'll work a helluva lot quicker. What if Hegarty starts shifting the plant quicker than we thought? I know splitting it five ways means we'll make less than if it was just the two of us, but it might turn out better for all of us in the long run.'

'No. This is just for you and me,' he insisted. 'I owe you.'

I said, 'You don't owe me anything, Sparra. I told you before, I wasn't protecting *you* when I took Bluey Thompson out. I did it for me.'

He said, 'It isn't just that.'

That's what he had said in Muddro. 'What else, then? Tell me.'

Again, he wouldn't elaborate. 'Nothin',' he said, and changed the subject. 'Promise me you won't breathe a word of this to the others, or the deal's off.'

I said, 'I promise.'

To explain my long absences during the day, I told the others I was doing a bit of dry-sieving out at the Willows. I felt guilty about lying to them, but I knew the only way to ensure secrecy about anything on the gemfields was to keep your mouth shut. Like Jimmy had once told me: 'What the goose doesn't know, the ducks won't know either.' I resolved to split my share of the profits with the three of them, when it was all over. If they were a tenth as big as Sparra predicted, I could afford to.

Sparra was the happiest I had seen him since the night he blew the verandah off the Anakie pub. Disappointment from the fact that our current project didn't involve blowing anything up was more than offset by the fortune he figured on making out of it.

'Like taking candy off a baby!' he said, as he helped me lift the genny out of the wagon.

I felt less confident. Before we took any candy, we had to find the baby. That meant working out where to start digging in order to drop in on his new drive. In changing direction so often, he had made the task difficult.

Sparra had the solution. 'We'll dig up!' he announced. 'From the drive. That way, we won't have to worry about finding the bugger!'

Clearly, he had never used a jackhammer. The thought of holding its twenty-pound load over my head, getting dumped on by bucket-loads of rocks and earth didn't appeal. 'No,' I said, 'we won't be digging up.'

'We could blast,' he said hopefully.

'Too noisy. We don't want to attract attention.' Most of all, I didn't want to attract attention to two corpses buried under several tons of slippery-back.

In the end, using a ball of twine, a broken tape-measure scrounged from the junk in Jack's shed, and a ton-and-a-half of educated guesswork, we calculated where to dig. We brought the windlass over from Jimmy's old claim, and got started. We got to the forty-foot mark after two days. After that we were on a short cut to China. We'd missed the drive.

We had to decide which direction to strike out from the bottom of the shaft, in the hope of breaking into the drive. Even then, there was the risk of tunnelling over or under it. Every day wasted was a day closer to Hegarty breaking into the ballroom with his scraper. We tossed a coin. We went south.

'Thought you might like to know Stumpy should be able to pay off that money he owes you for the jackhammer before long,' said Beryl. I was in the shop, stocking up for the next few days. 'He's got a job. You'll never guess who with.' I was helping myself to eggs, loose in a basket. 'Hegarty.'

'After he stopped him pumping water from his claim?'

She shrugged. 'I suppose he needs the money.'

'What sort of work?'

'Pulling down his plant. He starts next week.' I dropped an egg. 'Don't worry about it,' said Beryl. 'The dog'll clean it up.'

Sparra's jaw set as he tried to convince himself. 'It'll take the bastard a fortnight to pull everything down and set it up again.'

'The way we're going,' I said, 'it could take us that long to find the bloody drive! He'll have the guts ripped out of that ballroom in a day once he gets the scraper into it.' I took a breath. I knew he wasn't going to like it. I said, 'We're going to need help.'

He didn't like it at all. I told him it was better to have a smaller share of the take, than a bigger share of nothing. He could see the sense, though he tried to draw the line at Jimmy. 'I've got nothin' against the poor old bugger, but Christ he can hardly walk, let alone swing a shovel!'

I told him if Jimmy was out, so was I.

'You're talking about ratting another man's wash,' said Jack stubbornly.

'Not just any man, for Christ's sake!' The last thing I expected, was to have to talk him into it. 'This is Hegarty we're talking about. He's cheated Jimmy out of his claim. He's bulldozed Bob's house into the ground. He's killed your dog. The man's a cunt.'

'That doesn't mean I have to stoop to his level.'

'Maybe Jack's right,' Sparra chimed in. 'I mean, if he doesn't feel right about it...' He was mentally calculating his share of the spoils, divided by four rather than five. But I knew we needed Jack's muscle and mining expertise to give us our best shot.

Jack's chops were like leather, I was feeling like crap. I let rip. 'Jesus Christ, Jack, we're talking about a man who tortures pigs for sport! He's a racist arsehole! He thinks nothing of running a bulldozer through a man's home, so he can gouge more stone out of the ground, so he can make more money to buy a bigger bulldozer. This man has spent his whole life walking over other people, climbing up to his air-conditioned tin shed so he can piss on them from a great height. This man isn't just a cunt, he's the king of all cunts!'

It was the longest speech any of them had heard me make. Jimmy's mouth froze in a little 'O' of surprise. Bob's eyes widened, like he was hoping there might be more to come. I thought I detected new respect in the way Jack looked at me.

I was wrong. He said, 'You should've been a politician.' Coming from him it was an insult, not a compliment.

Something came back to me. I said, 'You weren't so worried about where that big yellow stone came from.' He looked at me sharply. 'The one Hegarty's son specked, remember? The one you lied about, so Ailsa could have it.'

Nobody said a word. They all knew the story of how Jack had helped Ailsa Hegarty leave her husband, taking their son with her.

'Spoken like a true politician,' was all he said.

Jimmy shook his head. 'I know what Jack's saying. It's the moral principality of the thing I'm dubious about.'

I said, 'People like Hegarty don't know about morals! They make them up as they go along.'

There was a drawn-out silence. The door opened a crack and Les squeezed through. 'Outside, Les!' Jimmy shouted. The dog lolloped over to each of us in turn, tongue flapping, ignoring his master's repeated commands to clear off out of it. Jimmy got painfully to his feet.

Jack waved him back down. 'Leave him,' he said.

Les had squatted on his haunches in front of him, eyeing the chop bone in his fingers. His tongue flopped over his teeth, flanks pumping like bellows to the rhythm of his panting. Jack reached down to tug at his ears. After a while he said, 'If you haven't even located that drive yet, we'd better get cracking.'

He chucked the bone to Les. Two rows of teeth snapped it out of the air with a crunch.

Jimmy might not have been able to swing a shovel, but he saved us days of wasted labour in another way. He had salvaged the set of *Britannica* from his hut, and brought them down to Jack's. As soon as he learned about the problem of locating Sparra's drive, he started flicking through them until he found the trigonometrical diagrams the Professor from Adelaide had shown him, when he was helping him peg the boundaries of his claim.

He paced out the distance from Sparra's original shaft to the blackberry thicket. He went down the hole with the ball of string and the tape measure, and came back up twenty minutes later with figures scribbled on a page torn out of an exercise book. He found a piece of milled timber in Jack's shed and marked off feet and inches on it. He told Bob to hold the makeshift chain-staff in a particular spot, and squinted along a piece of string stretched taut across the top of a 44-gallon petrol drum. He scribbled more figures. He told Bob to move the stick three feet to the left.

'This is all bullshit,' Sparra grumbled.

Jimmy scribbled again. He told Bob to move the stick a foot to the right, squinted across the top of the drum again, and scribbled some more. Eventually he walked to a spot ten feet south of the shaft

Sparra and I had sunk, and dug his heel in the dirt. 'Unless I'm outspoken,' he pronounced, 'this is where the drive is.'

'That's nowhere bloody near it!' Sparra scoffed.

Jimmy screwed his heel deeper into the dirt. 'This is where you'll find it, or I'm a double Dutchman.'

The rest of us watched the two of them facing off. The drone of Hegarty's scraper carried through to us on the still air.

Jack pointed to where Jimmy's heel spiked the dirt. 'Jimmy reckons it's there,' he said, 'Where d'you reckon it is, Bob?'

Bob shrugged. 'Wouldn't have the foggiest.'

'Ned?'

'Search me.'

'What about you, Sparra?'

Sparra looked embarrassed. 'I wasn't sayin' I knew,' he mumbled.

'Then let's get started,' said Jack. 'You can bet Hegarty isn't sitting on his arse waiting for us to make up our minds about where to dig a hole in the ground.'

Sparra and I went down the shaft we had sunk. They lowered us the jackhammer. From the top, Jack lined me up with a steel post banged in the ground where Jimmy had planted his heel. I started driving off the shaft in that direction. Sparra filled buckets. Jack and Bob took turns winding up. Just after smoko the next day we broke into Sparra's drive.

Four of us worked below, barring up tracks from the floor of the old drive. Jimmy held the fort up top, refuelling the genny and topping it up with oil, driving into the shop for supplies, keeping the billy boiled for smoko and lunch. By the light of a 32-volt globe on a cable plugged into the genny, we laboured on into the night and the early hours of the following morning, working in shifts. One by one we re-laid the lengths of track in a line from the ballroom to the bottom of the shaft.

Jimmy came down on the third day. While the rest of us knocked down a corner on a dog-leg in the drive, he went to work on the old skip with a tin of axle grease. Forty-eight hours after we had broken into the drive, and as many years after it last saw service, the old wagon rolled along the track on its inaugural run through Sparra's new drive.

We had bought up all the cable they had in Jackson's Hardware, enough to reach from the top of the shaft to the working face on the pillar a quarter of a mile away. It ran like a monstrous orange tape worm from the genny, over the lip of the shaft and down, along Sparra's drive to the old one, on up to the ballroom.

Jack had always been distrustful of the jackhammer. His doubts were soon justified. Jimmy started up the genny. The message was relayed to me in the ballroom. I lifted the jack-pick into position against the column of wash and squeezed the trigger. The motor whirred feebly. It hadn't occurred to any of us that the current wouldn't travel the distance.

The way I saw it, we had two options: sink a new shaft closer to the ballroom, or run the genny underground. The first would mean more precious time wasted, plus the increased danger of discovery. The second would have killed the lot of us with carbon monoxide poisoning. Jack looked on in disgust as we argued about it. He dropped a couple of hand picks in the windlass bucket, plus half a dozen heads he had sharpened in anticipation of a mechanical breakdown.

'Are you blokes going to sit there yackin' all day, or can we get on with it?' he grunted. He was down the hole before we could answer.

Jack and I got stuck into the face of the pillar with the picks. Bob and Sparra shovelled the knocked-down wash into the skip. When it was full, they trundled it along the track to the bottom of the shaft. Jimmy manned the windlass. We were worried about how he would hold up, but he insisted on 'pulling his weight for his keep'. It was something he could do with one-and-a-half good hands. When he wasn't winding up, he screened wash. He worked the same hours we did. The idea of getting even with Hegarty was a tonic for his condition. It was the thing that was driving all of us.

Using picks instead of the jackhammer, double-handling the wash, the distance from the face to the shaft - all combined to make it a backbreaking process. But it was the only way it could be done, and nobody complained. We carted the willoughby over from Jimmy's old claim and filled the tank with water. After three days digging there were a couple of yards of screened wash piled beside it.

Jack operated the jig while Sparra shovelled wash into the sieve. We watched a slurry of clay and muddy sand rise to the top as it bounced up and down in the water. I scraped it off and Sparra shovelled in more. We did it three more times. Ironstone was building up quick - a good sign. On the fourth rake-off I noticed it had changed colour. I realised it wasn't ironstone any more. Sparra realised it too. 'Jesus Christ!' He sucked in a breath.

I said, 'Lock it off Jack.'

Jack slipped the pole in its cleat, and came over to the tank. Jimmy and Bob dropped what they were doing and moved in. I raked the top layer of ironstone off with my hand. We breathed out, as one, like we were trying to blow out a fire. Spreading out from the centre of the sieve to all its corners was a mosaic of glistening black-indigo, so liquid at its core that it pulsed. We must've looked like seekers of the Grail at the end of their quest, our faces radiant in its glow.

'Jesus...' Sparra repeated, whispered, like a prayer.

'Pwhoooo...,' breathed Bob.

'Get a go at that will you?' said Jack.

Jimmy, a catch in his voice, spoke for all of us. 'Wouldn't that take the apple clean out of your blessed eye!'

We worked like navvies over the next two days, knocking down and winding up; Jimmy screening, the pile of wash mounting. We didn't bother to wash up again for fear of wasted time. Bob and Jack cut down rosewood saplings. We sawed them into lengths and lowered them down the shaft and railed them to the ballroom. As the pillar of wash shrank in diameter, we put in toms to replace it, ever aware of the menace of the slippery-back above us.

Hegarty, meanwhile, had started working the ground where his plant used to be. The ground trembled to the muffled roar of the scraper as it made run after run along a cut separated from us by a wall of earth barely twenty-foot thick. The next cut would break through to the ballroom.

Bob spelled Jack at the face while he took the blunt pick-heads to the forge. Wash tumbled from the face. The skip rumbled back and forth on its track. The windlass rattled to the drop of the empty bucket, and groaned with it full. The pillar grew smaller; the heap of wash higher and higher.

We stared at the mound in the flickering light of the campfire, sipping billy tea after a slap-up meal of sausages and boiled potatoes, each of us lost in his own world of thought. We slept beside the pile of wash. Our mountain of dreams.

Towards the end of the third day, Jack and I were working together, levering a billy out of the face when we heard the sound.

I said, 'Did you hear that?

We stopped to listen. All we could hear was the rumble of the empty skip returning along the drive. It came into view a few seconds later, Sparra and Bob behind it. One look at their faces told us they had heard it too. 'Sounded like a fuckin' dog!' said Sparra.

'Not like any dog I ever heard,' Bob muttered.

It came again. A drawn out, mournful howl, floating down the drive. It bounced dismally round the walls of the ballroom, and died away to nothing, leaving the soft rush of our breathing. Then came another, harsher sound. The laboured panting of an animal, the soft crunch of its pads on loose dirt. Sparra held the lamp high.

Boofhead emerged from the dark throat of the drive, limping on three legs, a raised forepaw hanging uselessly in front of him.

'It's that mongrel fuckin' thing of Hegarty's!' said Sparra.

On seeing us, Boofhead flopped back on his haunches, pointed his nose to the ceiling and howled.

'How the hell did it get here?' Bob shouted above the racket.

Sparra rolled his eyes. 'How d'you think it got here? The fuckin' thing's gone and fallen down the old shaft!'

In my mind's eye I could see the animal's slobbery snout snuffling through the tunnel in the blackberries on the trail of a familiar scent; right up to the top of the shaft, onto the sheets of iron covering it. I could hear its yelp of fright as they gave way beneath him, the frantic scrabbling of claws on iron, the diminishing howl as he plunged into the abyss.

'You can bet your balls Hegarty won't be far behind,' said Jack grimly.

He was right. Boofhead was never let off his leash unless he was in his master's presence. He was still baying. Sparra walked up and gave him a cuff over the ear to shut him up.

We heard a new sound then, a metallic scraping echoing faintly along the drive from the direction of the shaft. A familiar voice drifted down. 'Boofhead! Are y'alright fella?'

We looked at each other, eyes bright in the acetylene punctured gloom, none of us daring to utter a sound. Then Hegarty's voice again, 'I'm coming down, alright?' followed an instant later by a brittle snapping sound, a shout of alarm. A series of snaps in rapid succession. A dull, bone-crunching thud. Then silence.

Sparra shook his head. 'Shoulda fixed that ladder.'

Hegarty's voice came faintly. 'Fuck me dead. A man could get killed...'

'The bastard's still alive,' Sparra muttered.

'Looks like the party's over, fellas,' said Bob.

Jimmy wound the picks up in a bucket and we came up the ladder one by one. We told him what had happened. It was a pity we had to leave the last bit of the pillar. We got satisfaction, though, at the thought of Hegarty groping around in the dark looking for Boofhead; the two of them freezing their bollocks off till morning.

We knew we didn't have to worry until then. It was a hundred-to-one against Hegarty finding his way through the labyrinth of drives to our shaft, in the dark. It was doubtful he would be able to get back up the way he had come down. He and Boofhead could keep each other warm overnight, we decided. In the morning we would trailer the wash to a safe place, to process at our leisure. By the time he found his way out and sussed what had been going on, we would be long gone.

We hunkered around the fire, warming our hands with mugs of tea, basking in the glory of our achievement. We looked forward to the wash-up and made guesses at how much saleable stone would come out of it. Guesses made not in penny-weights or ounces, but pounds. King Star's car would be down to its axles with the weight of it. He would have to make special arrangements with the bank to withdraw the money to pay us. He would have to charter a Hercules fucking transport to fly it back to Thailand! We would take nothing but cash. If we realised a twentieth of the meanest of our fanciful estimates, it would be years before any of us would have to work for a living again.

As I lay in the back of the HD that night, staring at the bogged-up holes in its roof, I believed there was some justice in the world. We had got the better of Hegarty. I was financially secure for some time to come. I rolled over on my side and something in my pocket dug into my leg – Joe's tobacco tin. In a rush of sentimentality, I was seized with the urge for a whiff of the Dr Pat that was so much a part of my memory of him. I pulled the tin out of my pocket, and twisted the top. Rusted tight after the dunking it had received, it refused to budge. I returned it to my pocket, shifted it to a more comfortable position, and dozed off into a half-waking dream of Joe and Jess; wishing Joe could've been with me to share in this last great adventure – *Effrythingk vill be good now, Joe* – wondering if Jess thought of me when she looked at the apricot-yellow – was there another one waiting in that mountain of wash...?

I came out of slumber to a howling nightmare, a shriek of twisting metal mingled with the roar of a diesel engine filling my ears. The world was shifting, rolling from under me. The HD was crabbing sideways, metal against metal screeching in protest. Water sloshed through one of the windows.

I rolled out under the rear hatch, hitting the earth shoulder first, barely managing to stumble out of the path of the bulldozer's clanking tracks. From the ground I watched it thrust forward inch by crunching inch, its steel blade crushing the HD against the willoughby tank. Water bursting from its split seams sparkled dully. The wagon's windscreen splintered and popped.

I scrambled to my feet. An angry shout from Jack rode over the confused cries and yells from the others. Puppet-like figures staggered, arms waving angrily, as the dozer cranked on, belching diesel dust to the night sky. Behind it loomed an even bigger monster, trundling along the freshly blazed trail, blotting out the moon with its bulk. Its massive wheels crushed everything in its path as it rolled towards where the wash-tank had been. I saw Sparra running towards us, his flailing arms strobing the air. 'The fuckin' wash!' he screamed.

The timber struts of the wash-screen splintered and spat in all directions, trailing strands of chicken-wire. The scraper's giant wheels straddled the mound of earth next to where it had been. The blade dropped from its hopper like a ravenous tongue.

Sparra stopped running. We watched, transfixed, as our fabulous mountain of wash was scooped up like so much gravelly nougat shovelled into the mouth of a gluttonous child. The scraper rolled on in the wake of the dozer. Sparra raced after it, lurching and tripping in the dark. Bob and Jimmy and I watched as he drew closer to the back of the dozer. We saw the silhouette of a hatted figure detach itself from the darker shape of the lumbering machine; the glint of moonlight on a rifle barrel.

There was a sharp crack. A jet of orange flame spat skywards. The barrel came down to point at Sparra. He stopped running. The twin monsters clanked and rattled off into the pinking dawn. Sparra's shoulders slumped.

I became aware of a figure standing beside me. 'Shit floats,' Jack muttered.

Payback

'I knew we shoulda pulled that fuckin' ladder up!'

Sparra banged his fist on the table. The rest of us, huddled in Jack's kitchen as dawn approached, barely reacted. Jimmy had the shakes bad. Bob, hunched over like a man who had just spent a month in the saddle, stared into the hot coals of the stove Jack had stoked up.

Jack, rolling a durry with one hand, thrust a kindling stick into the coals with the other until it burst into flame. He lit the cigarette with it, and his eyes crinkled in the smoke. 'Bastard must've crawled on his hands and knees in the dark for hours.'

'Well, it's no use crying over troubled waters,' Jimmy lamented.

Sparra jumped to his feet. 'We've gotta report the bastard to Gillespie!'

Jack spat a loose strand of tobacco onto the hearth. 'What're you going to tell him? That he stole the wash we stole off him, and now we want it back?'

'He's wrecked Ned's fuckin' car! We can't let him get away with that!'

'Forget the car,' said Jack. 'Have you thought of a good excuse yet for why you were burrowing through his wash like a randy rabbit? He'd have the lot of us in court before you could bat an eyelid! He might do it anyway.'

'D'you think he would?' I said.

'I'm not going to stick around to find out.' I thought of the twenty-five thousand bucks Hegarty had offered him for his claim. As if reading my mind, Jack added, 'This place doesn't owe me anything. I always knew I'd walk off it sooner or later.'

'So the bastard'll get your claim for nothin' as well,' said Sparra. 'He's shafted us again!'

A sullen silence descended. Les had curled up on the cool end of the hearth. His sorrowful eyes met Jack's... and looked away again. Jack made a little snapping motion with his fingers. The dog pushed himself to his feet and trotted over to lie beside his new meal ticket, chin resting on his paws, as if infected with our despair.

A wave of depression hit me without warning. I was used to it by then, but this time it was magnified by comparison with the elation of the past few days. Hours ago, I had been sleeping secure in the knowledge that we had outwitted the bastard who had treated us with contempt; riches I had never dreamed of were within my grasp. Even if a big chunk of my past was still missing, I had a future to look forward to. Now all that had gone. I saw Jack's free hand drop to the soft petal of Les's ear, fondling it until the dog grew drowsy... fingers working away...

...I see Digger, panting in the heat, dreaming under his master's touch. Ash drops from Jack's cigarette and hits the hearth... a tiny smoking log... Digger's paw protrudes from a hessian sugar bag, stiff, fuming...

...the stench hits, filling my nostrils, stinging my eyes. Everything around me – walls, floor, Jack, stove - dissolve into vague, translucent forms; the only thing in focus Jack's hand, dirt-ingrained and leathery one instant; in the next, the hand of a little boy. Stroking, clutching; singed tufts of brindled hair sprouting between sticks of fingers...

'Bad dog!'

I'm not sure if I have uttered the cry, or merely heard it. It comes from deep in the past, somewhere so far down the pain of dragging it to the surface is unbearable. The hand is mine, burning. The dog refuses to budge.

'Bad dog!'

A bigger hand reaches down to take hold of the boy's skinny wrist. He fights it off. He throws his arms around the hairy-ribbed warmth of the dog, still not moving. He clings, not to what remains, but to what has gone; not wanting to make the connection between the burnt stillness he embraces, and the rifle barrel hanging alongside the trouser leg with the brown-red stains...

The mocking cackle of a kookaburra jolted me back. I was staring at a lump of cigarette ash on Jack's hearth. Sparra's Volley OC sandshoes came into my range of vision. His hand fell on my shoulder, I heard his voice, 'Are you alright, Ned?'

I didn't answer. I couldn't have, if I'd tried. I took each breath slowly, coming back. I let my eyes rove, absorbing every atom of that corner of the universe I had strayed into - those men I had come to know – as if it were the last chance I had to commit it to memory. I stored details carefully - each inflection, each nuance of expression, every blink, every tic – against what I knew and remembered. I saw Jimmy stagger defiantly to his feet out of the wreckage of his spilled *Britannicas*. Sparra, face aglow with the explosive triumph of his battle against Missingham's tyranny, plotting his next act of vengeance. Jack's eyes never leaving Hegarty, while the fingers of one hand rolled the perfect durry.

I saw Joe's splayed hand slap the broad acreage of Becky's arse; those same sausage-sized fingers, bunched in a fist, smack into a ringer's nose in the name of respect for a true and trusting friend; felt the weight of his arm on my shoulders, smelt his tobacco and his sweat, heard his smoke-throat voice: *'You commingk vith me, ya?'*

I heard Reg and Val weep for their lost son, while his brothers and sisters ran chattering and laughing through the bush where a red gum sapling soared into a hot blue sky; kids who would one day listen to the ghosts of their ancestors, through the dying words of an old ringer resting his head on a cracked and bleeding saddle, somewhere west of the Drummonds.

I saw Jess. Walking towards me, bare legs gleaming in the setting sun, the laughter and love of the days and nights we had shared reflected in the graceful swing of her hips. Felt the heat of fire smouldering behind her soft eyes. I remembered the first time we were together, and how she had stepped out of the darkened bush to guide me through the night.

I wondered what it meant that I had strayed by chance into the orbit of their lives, all these people; what influence, if any, I might have had on them. I thought of how the lives of all of us affect those of others. I thought about things I might have done that would have meant something to them, and to myself. Time was running out. Soon it would all be blemished memory.

The present came into focus. I tried to think practically about the situation I was in. *This is fucked*, was the first thing I thought. I had arrived at a point where a whole lot of fucked-up things had come together in one intense fuck-up. Everything - Cathie, Jess, Joe, little Pauly, Muddrington Road, Bob, the apricot-yellow, Digger, burning dogs – all seemed conjoined in some malicious chain of events designed to drive me down to dark nothingness. The old paranoia was back. With a difference.

This time it had a focus. Sylvester Hegarty was the malignant factor common to these fuck-ups. The overwhelming need to humiliate him, that had caused me to seek out Sparra to give me a crash course in the use of gelly, had never gone away. It rose again inside me, stronger than ever. That's what he had done to Jack, to Jimmy, Bob and me; dozens of others for all I knew. Humiliated us. He had stolen our livelihoods and our homes, killed Jack's dog and put me in gaol. And laughed about it. When we thought we'd got the better of him, he had turned our triumph into defeat. He would be laughing about it now.

'Are you alright, mate?' Sparra repeated.

As I raised my head I saw Jimmy pull a handkerchief from his pocket - a laborious process. Tremors ran through his limbs, like they were full of lizards. The right side of his face sagged. The man who could once make a shovel sing, could hardly blow his own nose. He had no home, no 'soovenear tubes' business left to sell.

I sat up straight. 'Thanks, Sparra. I'm okay.'

They had all been watching me with great concern, and seemed relieved to see me coming back. They must've been grateful that I hadn't passed out this time. All the talk about Hegarty had been momentarily forgotten. Not by me. I said, 'What are you going to do next, Jimmy?'

The question, coming out of nowhere, seemed to distress him. His head danced. 'Well, you know, I thought I might get back in the fight game. Not on the boxing side of the matter,' he added hastily.

'I thought I might go into management.' There were some promising young blokes out around Winton way, that he'd had his eye on. He was confident they would welcome the chance to benefit from his years of experience 'on the canvas'.

I said, 'Doesn't it worry you, what Hegarty's done to you?'

His enthusiasm faded. 'I should've taken his offer, is that what you're implicating?'

'No. I'm saying you had the right to refuse it, without forfeiting your whole life.'

I turned to Bob. I said, 'What're you going to do?'

He shrugged. 'Thought I might push on out to Cunnamulla. Got a cousin there lives near the showground. He'll put me up until I find a place to camp. Might even find myself a proper house! In town,' he added after a pause. 'One no bugger can kick me out of.'

I couldn't see Bob in a house. It would be like planting a tree in a broom cupboard. The bush was his home – an endless tall-columned house without walls or doors, the sky for a roof.

'What about you?' he countered. 'You gunna write that book?'

'Yes. I'm going to write the book.' I heard a familiar two-toned clicking sound, *Phlick, clunk, phlick, clunk*. The cap on Sparra's lighter flapped back and forth to the rhythm of his anger. 'But I've got a job to do first. We've all got a job to do.' They were looking at me, expectant. I said, 'How many sticks of gelly can you get hold of, Sparra?'

I told them what I had in mind. Nobody was against it.

Jack and I were waiting for Stumpy Pavlu at his camp in the Rice Bowl when he got home from work. We told him what I had in mind. He shook his head. He couldn't possibly do what we were asking, it was against his religion. Jack shook his head in disgust. 'What kind of religion is it that turns a blind eye to the things an evil bastard like Hegarty does to his fellow man?'

I said, 'You know who we're talking about here, don't you Stumpy? This is a man who thinks nothing of destroying another man's home, depriving him of his livelihood, killing his animals…'

'Man, woman or child, they mean nothing to him,' Jack continued. 'This bastard is the devil in disguise. Think of what we're doing as a message from God. A message saying he can't get away with treating people like rubbish for the rest of his life.'

'I know. I know all that!' Stumpy blurted out. 'I want to help you.'

'So what's your problem?'

'It's a Sunday. I couldn't do it on a Sunday.'

Jack's eyes rolled. I told Stumpy it had to be a Sunday, when the sorters and the other dogsbodies on Hegarty's payroll wouldn't be around. We couldn't run the risk of somebody getting hurt.

In the end, we promised to donate five hundred dollars to the Save the Children Foundation if he helped us. He settled on six hundred. Cash. Business was business, it seemed, even with God as your bookkeeper.

We called in at Beryl's shop on the way back. I waited in the ute while Jack went in. He came back out with a load of groceries, and a copy of the *Courier Mail* tucked under his arm. He was smiling. *Beryl must've read something to you that tickled your fancy*, I thought. I waited, but he didn't elaborate.

Next morning, sausages and bacon were frying when Jimmy, Bob and I came into Jack's kitchen. The juicy smoke stung our eyes, steam rose off a bubbling billy. Greetings were gruff and cursory, filled with the tension of great expectancy held in check.

Tea spoons clanked as they stirred. Words were few, laughter soft. Les sat quietly in a corner, ears pricked, watching. When the last mouthful of toast had been swilled down with the last gulp of tea, we stood. Jack closed off all the rings on top of the stove and damped the flue. He knocked a lump of wood down in the firebox, and closed its door for the last time. Nobody spoke. Bob and Jimmy and I went out to collect our stuff, leaving him alone inside.

Bob had Elvis saddled up. Jimmy and I dumped our things in the back of the ute. After a while Jack came out, carrying a Globite suitcase with rusty locks. In his other hand was the leather strap with the big buckle that I had seen hanging on the wall the day I first met him. The copy of the *Mail* was stuffed in his hip pocket. He pulled the door shut behind him and walked down the path without looking back.

He dumped the suitcase in the back of the ute. Bob, hauling himself into the saddle, noticed the bull-strap in his other hand. 'Gettin' a bit long in the tooth for that caper aren't you Jack?'

Jack chucked the strap to him and he caught it. 'You're the bugger never knew when to call it quits,' he grunted.

He went around to the driver's side and got in. We winced as Jimmy put his fingers between his teeth and whistled. Les came hurtling around a corner to jump in the back and I piled in after him.

Squatting in the tray of the ute, an arm draped over Les panting in the glassy morning heat, I watched Jack's hut, and Dead Darby's up behind it, grow smaller and smaller. We rounded a bend in the track and they were gone.

We called in at the League of Nations to pick up Sparra. He chucked a canvas duffel bag and a coil of knotted rope in the back and climbed in after them.

When we arrived at the shaft where he'd been busy the day before, he handed Jimmy the rope. 'Make you sure you tie it tight,' he said.

'You can bank your life on it,' said Jimmy.

Sparra jumped to the ground with the duffel bag over his shoulder, and strode towards the shaft.

Jack leaned out the window. 'When Jimmy whistles, right? Not before.'

We dropped Jimmy about five hundred yards from the turn-off to 'Eureka', at a point where he could cut through to the blackberry thicket. There was a spring in his step. The shakes had almost gone, as though the mission we were embarked on had rejuvenated him. He scurried into the scrub on his nuggety legs, the coil of rope slung over his shoulder. I replaced him in the seat up front with Jack. A minute later we swung off the road onto the track leading to Hegarty's plant.

We threaded our way in and out of cuts and mullock heaps until, cresting a ridge, we saw Hegarty's claim below. Jack stopped the ute. He nodded, satisfied. Stumpy had done his job well.

In the end, it had been simple enough. There was some welding still to do on the roof-ribs of the new shed Stumpy was building. He had told Hegarty he wanted to work on Sunday to make up for lost time. Only trouble was, the earthmovers were being temporarily housed there overnight; they would have to be moved out of the way. Hegarty told him he could tell Brindley to put them wherever he wanted.

And there they were, the twin monsters who had ambushed us in the night, sitting exposed in the sunlight like two gargantuan, vulnerable termites.

'Isn't that a pretty sight?' said Jack.

What we knew, but couldn't see, was even prettier. Directly below the earthmovers, separated from them by twenty-foot of slippery-back, Sparra was busy inserting the dets in twelve sticks of gelly taped to strategically-selected toms supporting the roof of the biggest ballroom ever carved out in the history of the Anakie gemfields. He would be the last person to see it.

Jack put the ute in reverse.

'Wait!' Jack looked to where I was pointing. Hegarty was walking down the stairs from his office. 'What the fuck's he doing here on a Sunday!'

'Counting his money,' Jack muttered. 'Who knows? Let's get out of here before he sees us.'

'Too late,' I said.

Hegarty had paused halfway down the stairs. He was looking right at us.

'We'd better pay our respects,' said Jack. He put the ute in gear, and we rolled forward.

By the time Hegarty had reached the bottom of the stairs, we were slowing to a stop fifty yards away. We got out of the ute. Hegarty was striding towards us, Boofhead limping behind him on his three good legs. As he passed the pig dogs, they lumbered to their feet to set up a chorus of sullen barking. A familiar sense of panic stirred in me.

We met Hegarty halfway between the ute and the relocated office shed. He stopped in front of us, arms folded across his puffed-out chest. The stance of supreme commander. For all that I hated him, I felt intimidated. Back in Jack's lightless hut, pumped with outrage at the injustices he had inflicted on us, it had seemed rational enough to want to blow his plant to smithereens. Now, with the man himself standing in front of us, knowing we had already committed one crime against him, the idea of compounding it was revealed for what it was: an act of madness.

'What are you two stone ratters doing here?' he said.

It was a reasonable question. I couldn't think of an uncompromising answer, so I let Jack make the running. What he said next came as much of a surprise to me as it must have to Hegarty.

'I was wondering if you were still interested in buying that claim of mine.'

'Is that right?' Hegarty's lips cracked in a smile.

'I'm prepared to negotiate,' said Jack.

Hegarty started laughing. When he had settled enough to continue talking, he said, 'I don't think you're in a position to negotiate anything right at the moment, do you Jack?'

As he said it, his gaze shifted to a point behind us. I turned to see what had caught his attention. Over on the far side of the claim, Bob was easing Elvis to a halt beside the blackberry thicket.

Hegarty shifted his feet to a more strategic position, and dropped all pretence of joviality. 'What the fuck's going on here?'

'I already told you,' said Jack. 'Are you interested in buying, or not?'

Hegarty shot a look at Bob on his horse. He came back to me and Jack. He looked at the earthmovers. 'You wouldn't have sabotage on your mind, would you Jack? Handful of sugar in the fuel tank, that sort of thing? Tell me you're not that fuckin' stupid.'

Jack said, 'Give me credit for a bit more imagination than that, Sylvester. I'll take fifteen thousand, and that's the last you'll see of us.'

'Get the fuck off my claim.'

'Make it twenty, if you like.'

'Keep pushing it, Jack. I can have Trevor Gillespie down here in half an hour, if that's how you want to play it. So far, I've turned a blind eye to you and your mates ratting my wash, but there's a limit to my patience.'

'Rich little pocket was it?'

'What?'

'The pillar we dug out for you. Plus what's still down there. What's it worth, d'you reckon? Two? Three? Four hundred thousand?'

Hegarty laughed again. 'Break your bloody heart, wouldn't it?'

'How much of that are you going to declare to the taxation department?'

Over near the office, the pig dogs had ramped up their howling. Les, from the safety of the ute, barked at them fearlessly. A figure appeared at the top of the stairs leading to the office. Even at that distance, Brindley's stooped posture was unmistakeable. He was holding a rifle in one hand. I couldn't make out what it was he had in the other.

'How much tax I pay is between me and my accountant,' Hegarty was saying. 'Don't try and fuck me over in that department, Jack. You're out of your depth.'

'I don't doubt that for a minute. All I'm saying is, it might be a lot simpler all round if you at least paid Jimmy what you offered him for his claim. I'll throw mine in as a bonus.'

I had to hand it to Jack, it was an inspired stroke of improvisation. From Hegarty's point of view, it made sense for him to get us out of his hair by paying half what he had been prepared to pay for both the claims. We would let him have his earthmovers. Sparra would be disappointed at losing another opportunity to blow something up, but we'd all be happy to walk away with a few thousand bucks in our kick. If Hegarty dug his heels in, we could go back to Plan A.

Hegarty hadn't taken his eyes off Jack. I imagined he was trying to work out how dangerous he might be if he had gone seriously mad. Out of the corner of my eye I saw Brindley walking towards the dogs. I still couldn't make out what he had in the hand not holding the rifle.

Whatever conclusion Hegarty might have reached never had a chance to formulate. The piggers, enraged by Les's constant yapping, were going ballistic. Les, evidently sussing they could travel no farther than the length of their chains, had leapt from the back of the ute and was racing towards them, barking a challenge he knew could not be answered. For the moment.

Hegarty saw what was happening, turned, and gave Brindley the nod. Brindley lifted the wire-cutters he was holding in his left hand… a second later the piggers were slipping off the snipped end of their line one by one, chains trailing like death rattles, hell bent on tearing the little cattle-dog to ribbons. Boofhead tried to join in, stumbled, and drove his nose into the dirt after three crippled steps.

Les, realising there was no mileage in making a stand, pirouetted like a Viennese dancing horse and bolted. Straight towards the scraper and the dozer.

'Les, you brainless bloody animal!' Jack shouted. 'Get back here!'

Les wasn't stupid. He had a lead on his pursuers and his legs were young. He knew his best chance was to keep running. By the time he had reached the other side of the patch the machines were parked on, the piggers had barely started across it. Accustomed to the evasive tactics of feral pigs, they fanned out in anticipation of a change of direction by Les. It was the last strategic manoeuvre any of them would make.

Jimmy had emerged from the blackberries at the sound of Jack's shout. Peering anxiously in our direction, he saw what was happening. The piggers, spurred by bloodlust, were gaining ground on their quarry. I saw Jimmy put his fingers between his teeth.

Jack saw it too. His eyes closed. 'Not yet Jimmy, for Christ's sake!'

A shrill whistle split the air.

'Get back!' Jack shouted. He lunged at Hegarty, shoving him back so hard, they crashed to the ground together. The big man's head hit the hard earth with a dull thunk.

Beneath the ferocious barking of the piggers, came another sound. A deep-gutted rumbling from the bowels of the earth. The ground beneath us wobbled like jelly. A cobweb pattern of dust-puffing fissures spread out like nuclear static from a centre near the earthmovers. One of the scraper's massive wheels slumped like a foot snapped off at the ankle.

The dozer began to sink. It bucked once before subsiding rear-end first, blade angled skywards as if gasping for air. A great gout of dust erupted around it as the subterranean rumble exploded in a bilious roar, spewing up earth and rock.

As the leading dog drew level with it, a section of the mosaic of cracks yawned beneath his flailing legs and he vanished from the face of the earth. The scraper groaned, its articulated joints buckled. A fit of violent trembling seized my body... an invisible cord tightened round my throat...

...I choke on the stench of scorched hair. The rest of the pack, coats ablaze, pitches into the abyss, entangled in a network of hydraulic tubes whipping and writhing like dying nerve-ends. One of the dogs detaches from the pack and slides towards me... a wall of fire blazing behind it. Through a gap in the flames, a door... a window. Curtains flap... an arm, waving. My legs give out, but I can't fall, only watch, feel, smell. Remember...

...a toy tin truck, reluctant wheels grinding through the dirt... the pressure of my tiny hand guiding it. A dog's wet tongue slaps across my eye... Poidy, first friend. A dress with big flowers, its hem scything too-white legs at the calf. Shirts, socks, underwear hanging breathless in the time-stilled heat... my bindi-eye prickled bare feet... the smell of starch. Other legs, trousered, stride to the gate at the end of the path. Sometimes the rifle. Shots, later, from the unknown distant world. The cooling sheets

of hot summer nights… hypnotic croon of cicadas in endless, sun-drenched days… the sheltering, gum-scented bush around. The known universe.

Out of the gate, one day, Poidy lolloping ahead, I pad barefoot over the rise, beyond the silenced shed, to the empty shearers' quarters. Rows of wet pink skins on hoops… bundles of rusted traps slung over a wire… stink of discarded carcasses. The trapper. Visitor from the outside world, delivering its mysteries in language familiar but new… voice like the deep hum of a bee swarm high in an apple-gum… dirt-grey fingers working the stock-knife's blade around the neck, the joints above the paws… peeling off the pelt.

Early magic… a boiled egg standing upright, not in a cup! A spoon for me too, with a sprinkle of salt. And smoke from the white tube in his mouth… streaming from his nostrils like a dragon! And the little grey log left after it burns… soft… vanishes under my finger. Once he holds me very tight. His eyes are wet. Another home. Another friend…

Early brutality… in the first home. Kitchen table… knives and forks… red-hot coals in the firebox… oven door swung wide… mutton roast, spuds and pumpkin… louvre windows… buzz of blowflies. Their shouting brings me running… arrive to see spuds and roast smash against the Cane-ite wall, dripping gravy. Shouts louder, move inside the house. Shouting, shouting… a shot! Run to the hallway. The flowered dress lying on the floor… one red flower, growing bigger across the chest, below the seriously tucked in chin. Trousered legs behind her… terror drives me towards them… greater terror halts me… rising to look at me, the barrel of the rifle. Looking, too, the eyes of someone I don't know, blazing out of a face I have known my entire short life. I turn back… stumble into Poidy coming in, barking, racing to protect me. Run, calling to the dog… out the back door. Another shot! Run, run, run, run! Down the path, out the gate, up the hill… over the rise.

The trapper's hut squats lead-red in the bush-fly buzz of mid-afternoon… see him hunched over his rabbits… race downhill, almost hurtling headfirst into the dirt… screaming my terror. He folds the stock-knife shut… crouches in front of me… grips my shoulders with his bloodied hands. 'Settle down now,' the bee-swarm voice urges. 'Tell me what's happened.'

He strides out fast... rifle gripped in one hand. My little feet struggle to keep up, going up the hill... smoke rising from behind it. He reaches the crest... stops. 'Jesus!' I catch up to him... see what he sees. A black pall billows from the roof... scarlet tongues lick at the cracking windowpanes. I stumble down the hill after him...

...through the gate, up the path. 'Wait here!' he tells me, like he does to the dog. He goes closer... another shot! From inside. I see him then... my friend, lying on the ground in front of the trapper. He looks tired... blood drips off the end of his panting tongue. His coat is black. 'Poidy!' I shout, starting forward. Trapper's rifle dips. Another shot...

I feel his wiry hair between my fingers... his warm body wrapped in my arms... not moving. Strong hands grasp my wrists... pulling me away. I try to scream, but it chokes in my throat... a blast of heat from the blazing house hits... the dog is moving away, I can't free myself from the grip of the hands, taking me further and further. He's burning... burning... dog burning...

I wrap my arms round the closest thing to hold... face buried in the coarse cloth of the trousers, the fresh-skinned smell of dried blood. The hands peel my arms loose... he's crouched in front of me. His tobacco breath puffs in my face. 'It's alright...' he says.

Those arms, wrapped tight around me, the only thing stopping me from falling to the ground; or flying apart from the tremors racking my body, preventing speech, blocking breath. 'It's alright,' Jack kept saying, over and over. 'Everything's going to be alright.'

Curling grey filaments came into focus – the hairs on his neck. The plump grub of an ear lobe, folds of wrinkled skin; frayed shirt collar embedded with grime; the sweaty odour of him, as if it had always been there, a living part of me. I clung tighter, afraid I would lose it. 'It's alright,' he said, until the trembling died away, and I could breathe.

Over his shoulder I could see a smoking crater of jumbled earth; a disinterred grave showing the steel bones of exposed monsters. A stocky, sandy-haired figure lying on the ground a short distance from the edge of the crater. *Fucking madness*, I thought. I saw Les, sitting on his haunches on the far side of the crater, head cocked, looking for the pack that had been baying for his blood. I started laughing.

Jack pushed me away, so he could see me better. 'Are you alright?'

I stopped. I said, 'It was you, wasn't it? You shot my dog.' His blurred form quivered in front of me. 'You shot my fucking dog.'

I saw Bob riding towards us on Elvis. Sparra had come up out of the shaft in the blackberry thicket, and was headed in our direction as well.

Hegarty groaned. He stirred, rolled over and hauled himself to a kneeling position. He stayed there, unable to go further.

Bob had come up behind us on the horse. 'Here,' he said, 'Looks like you might need it after all.'

The bull-strap landed on the ground at Jack's feet. Jack picked it up. He put a heel to Hegarty's arse and rolled him on his back. He strapped two of his arms and a leg together with deft movements born of years of practice on the scrub bulls of central Queensland. Hegarty's eyes opened. He grunted and struggled.

Brindley was moving towards us, holding the rifle uncertainly, like he wasn't sure if he should do something with it or not. A booming explosion, accompanied by a column of dust and dirt spurting twenty-foot in the air, relieved him of any decision. My eardrums popped, as a shower of gravel rained down on us.

Sparra was walking towards Brindley, Jimmy not far behind him. 'That was just a little fella,' he apologised. 'This one,' he held a second stick of gelly aloft, short fuse dangling like an unlit candle wick, 'will blow you clear into next week.' The Zippo in his other hand clicked, and a flame shot out. Brindley stopped walking.

Sparra's face glowed as if he had been anointed by the God of Blowing Things Up. 'Did ya see it blow?' he shouted excitedly, standing like the Statue of Liberty, holding aloft his unlit gelignite torch.

'You could've killed the bloody lot of us,' Jack snapped.

The statue's face fell. 'What're you talking about? Jimmy whistled, I let 'er rip.'

'He was whistling that stupid bloody mutt of his!'

Hegarty, regaining full consciousness, curtailed the post-mortem. Straining against the bull-strap as Boofhead limped over to lick his face, he raged, 'So help me Christ, I'll make you pack of dag-maggots pay for this!'

Jack looked down at him disdainfully. He said, 'We've been doing that for years.'

'What're you talking about?' Hegarty snarled.

Jack knelt beside him, taking his time. He said, 'I'm talking about all those "maggots" you've been pissing on from a great height, all your life. Jimmy and Bob's houses dozed into the ground. Ned's little stint in gaol. And my dog,' he added, almost as an afterthought. 'We've paid you plenty, Hegarty.'

Hegarty's mouth twisted in a sneer. 'Real champion of the low-life, aren't you Jack? Dogs, boongs, and fuckin' Tolstoy here! You should start a fuckin' zoo!'

'Any one of 'em'd buy and sell you,' said Jack, as he stood up. 'Even the dog's got the wood on you, Sylvester.'

A movement in a stringybark high above Bob's shoulder caught my eye. Black wings flapped and folded silently. A yellow eye glinted. The veins swelled in Hegarty's forehead as he renewed his struggles to free himself. I saw something in him then, that I had never seen before. He was afraid.

He hasn't got the guts to be evil, Bob had said. Now I knew what he'd been trying to tell me: that his fear was inherited. It came down from his father and his father's father and Horatio Wills and the hundreds of pioneer settlers who had pushed into the wilderness to make their fortunes in the black man's country. Forging their way blindly through the bush, knowing nothing of its dangers: therefore fearing everything. Attack was the only form of defence they knew.

'You think all this is going to hurt me?' Hegarty scoffed, giving his best impression of a man afraid of nothing. 'You've blown up a couple of machines, that's all. I'll be back in business next week. And

I've got a shitload of stone to sell to King Star on Tuesday, thanks to you blokes!'

'You won't be selling anything to anybody,' said Jack. 'This week, or the week after that.' He pulled the copy of the *Courier Mail* from his hip pocket and dropped it on the ground near Hegarty's head. From where I was standing, I could easily read the banner headline: VIET TROOPS ENTER PHNOM PENH. 'You should read the paper more often, Sylvester, you might learn what's going on in the world.'

He came over to me then. He put an arm round my shoulder. 'Why don't you and I go somewhere a bit more peaceful.'

Last Camp

Deep Creek, with its tiny catchment, was already drying up after the rush of the Wet. There was a bare trickle of water across the quartz outcrop into the fishing hole. In a few weeks it would be nothing but a muddy pond, and you would wonder how anybody could have drowned in it. People had stopped coming to fish it. We decided, in the event that Hegarty decided to come after us, no one would come looking for us there until they had exhausted all the likelier possibilities.

Jack's ute rolled to a stop at the end of the track. I pulled in behind him in the HD, and we piled out. We started setting up a makeshift tent, with a tarp slung between two trees. Bob turned up twenty minutes later, unsaddled Elvis, and tied him on a long halter to a tree. Sparra and Jimmy got a fire going and put the billy on. Jack had cleaned out his pantry. We had enough food to last a couple of days.

I said, 'D'you think Hegarty'll sool the cops onto us?'

'I doubt it. It'd only draw attention to what we did to him, and he'd hate that. He'll be covered by insurance for the machines.' He laughed. He looked more relaxed than I had seen him in months. 'No, I reckon Sylvester's going to be too busy trying to flog off all that stone he's stockpiled, to be bothered with the likes of us.'

'Were you serious when you said King Star wouldn't be back?'

'Deadly. The war in Cambodia's over. The Thais can go back to buying all the stone they want from there, plus Burma. A lot bloody cheaper than coming all the way here for it.'

'He must be able to sell it somewhere.'

'Of course he will. For a fraction of what he was expecting.'

'The bastard's still come out on top then. All we've done is cause him a bit of inconvenience, and turned ourselves into criminals.'

He laughed again. 'Jesus, you were the one who was all gung-ho for it! Are you going to tell me now I shouldn't have listened to you?'

'All I could think to do, was blow those fucking machines to bits. I was going crazy. I've been trying to tell you that, since I got here.'

'Maybe you're not as crazy as you think you are. I've been trying to tell *you* that.'

'What d'you mean?'

'How would you be feeling about yourself now, if you'd done nothing to hit back at the bastard?' He was right. I had become a fugitive from the law, with no money and nowhere to live, and I felt better than I had ever felt in my life. 'What you've got to ask yourself is: Who would you rather be for the rest of your life, Sylvester Hegarty or Ned Sheridan?'

I said, 'I'd have to know more about Ned Sheridan, to answer that question.'

He looked off into the surrounding scrub, and I wondered if he had heard me. He said, 'Fair enough.'

Towards sunset, as the heat went out of the day and the bush started up its crying and chattering, Jack and I went to a spot away from the others, at the edge of the water. I reckoned it must have been near where Joe went down. Directly opposite was the tree I had sat under, watching Jess bait her hook for yellow-belly; listening to the kids crackling through the underbrush. A hundred years ago.

While the sun climbed down to the tops of the trees, and sent their shadows scurrying across open spaces to the waiting night, Jack talked.

'What can you remember?'

'Nothing, until an hour ago. Bits of it are coming back. You worked for my father, right?'

'In a way. I trapped rabbits on his property. It was 1955, myxomatosis was losing its sting. A bloke in Barraba put me onto this sheep station with a big rabbit problem. On the Baker's Creek road, ten miles out of Bundarra.'

'Sentry Box.'

'That's where you grew up. It was a soldier-settlers block. When the war ended, the Government was selling land to demobbed soldiers for sixpence an acre.'

As Jack described the place, each tree, each shed, each paddock; the sheep dip across the other side of the creek, which fell out of the scrubby range rearing up behind the cultivated paddocks; the pump, the windmill, the fenced-in chook run, came into focus like a time-lapse film of a brush painting a watercolour.

'I can remember boulders, on a hill. Bushranger country…'

He smiled. 'The bushrangers had gone by then. There were plenty of boulders, though. Thousands of the bastards.' He grimaced. 'Granite country. Not worth a pinch of shit for sheep. The rabbits were the last straw. Frank told me I could pocket the money from the pelts, in return for keeping them down. Even gave me a place to stay, in the old shearers' quarters. The shed didn't operate any more, the huts weren't being used for anything.'

'I saw you there…'

'You used to come and visit me from time to time. I suppose there wasn't much else for you to do, stuck out there on your own with no playmates.'

'You used to peg the rabbit skins out on wire hoops.'

'Plenty of 'em, too. I made a good living out of it. The rabbits were kept in check. Frank was happy to have me back, year after year.'

'What was he like?'

'Frank Sheridan?' He thought about it. 'He was an angry man. He couldn't make a go of it, and instead of walking off, like a lot of 'em did, he just got more and more bitter.'

I thought of Hegarty, and his fear of the world he inhabited. There must have been thousands like him and my father. I said, 'I can hear him shouting now.'

'That'd be Frank, alright. Your mother copped the brunt of it.'

A breeze sprang up out of nowhere. The whispering of the she-oaks carried a murmur of voices from where the others were cooking up something to eat. The smell of baked beans and burning eucalyptus floated across.

'What was *she* like?'

He took a long time answering. 'Alana was a good woman. She deserved better.'

'They died, in the fire, right? The both of them…'

He nodded. 'I wished you hadn't been there. It wasn't something a kid…' He trailed off, shaking his head.

'How did it start?'

'This is what I mean, see?' His voice had risen. 'You would've been better off leaving all this buried.'

'Is that why you wouldn't talk about it?'

'Of course it bloody was. It's not going change anything, is it, knowing about it?'

I said, 'It already has.' His brow creased. 'You can't bury stuff like that, Jack. It won't leave you alone. If you can't see it, if you don't know what is, it terrorises you. Eventually, it'll drive you crazy. Those fucking dogs were out to get me.'

'What dogs?'

'It doesn't matter. They're gone.'

He heaved a sigh. 'I did what I thought was best.'

'So how did it start? The fire.'

'Frank did it.'

'He was so angry, he burnt the place to the ground?'

'He wouldn't have known what he was doing, by then. In those last few days, he'd gone real strange. I've got no idea what tipped him over the edge. Your mother was frightened. I should've done something…' He stopped. I gave him time to get back to it. The setting sun was behind him, and I couldn't see his eyes. He said, 'He shot her first. It's just as well you weren't there, or he might've had you too.'

'I was there.'

'Jesus.'

'My dog saved me.'

'The red kelpie…'

Rage lying deep over a lifetime bubbled up. 'You shot him. You shot my fucking dog, didn't you?'

He recoiled, as if hit physically. 'Christ, you don't think…? He was as good as dead already. Frank must've put a bullet in him, before he shot himself.' He touched my arm. 'Christ, Ned, I never knew you saw it all. The first I knew anything was up, was when you came running over the hill, screaming your head off. I knew it was something bad. I never would've dreamed... You never said anything.'

My anger evaporated into the settling dark. 'I can't understand how... Did he ever threaten anything? Was he violent, normally?'

'No, not like that. They were always blueing, the two of 'em. But he never hit her. If he had, I would've...'

'Protected her?'

'That's what a bloke's supposed to do, isn't it? Protect the woman?' He shot me a challenging look.

He snapped a twig that his fingers had mindlessly found, and dropped the pieces between his raised knees. He gazed into the distance. I got the feeling he was looking into the past, rather than at our physical surroundings.

'Anyway, when it was all over, and the police had done their business, I told 'em I'd take care of you. There was no family to speak of, on either side.'

'That was a big thing to take on, for somebody else's kid.'

'It's what your mother would've wanted.'

'You got along well with her?'

'Yes, we got along well.'

I said, 'It was you, wasn't it, who took me to St Andrews?'

'Who else was there? Everybody knew about the place, it was where they took all the homeless kids. All the...'

'Orphans.'

The pain in his voice was palpable. 'I couldn't have done it. I was on my own. You needed proper looking after.'

I felt like I should touch him, give some sort of physical sign. In the end, I said, 'I appreciate what you did do.'

'They looked after you alright, did they?'

'They did. I had lots of friends.'

'Did you do well at school?'

'I was good at English.'

'The writer, eh?' He gripped my arm with surprising intensity. 'You turned out alright.' His eyes glistened in the semi-dark. For the briefest moment we were joined by some force stronger than muscle and bone.

The sun had gone down. A wafer of smoke spread out over the surface of the darkening water, giving it the appearance, in the half light, of some thermal spa the bush Gods might have bathed in. What would they have made of Joe, I wondered, barging in on them, tobaccoey breath fuming, *I'm been come to say goot eveningk vith you, you mizzerable bustards!*

Jack, Jimmy and Sparra said they'd stay put for a day or two until the dust settled, then head for Gin Gin where Jack knew people who would put them up. Bob reckoned he'd travel the back country to Cunnamulla, rather than up the drover's route along the main road as he would normally have done. It would take longer, and he would be living rough, but that didn't worry him. 'I've been up and down the old long paddock so many times, it's gettin' a bit boring,' he told me. He was looking forward to a change of scenery.

As for me, I had no idea where I was going. I only knew I had to go. Somewhere. Anywhere. It was as though, having been drawn by mystic forces into a sideshow of my life - a surreal world where horses and fish and raging waters and priceless gems and exotic women and gelignite shaped the future - I was being released back into the mundane world. I was no longer afraid of it, but I hated the thought of it.

Bob was the first to leave. I walked with him to the creek, so he could water Elvis before they set off. The horse trailed behind us on a bridle lead. A kingfisher landed on a dead branch overhanging the bank and perched, still as a sniper, watching for tell-tale ripples on the water.

'Well,' he said, when Elvis had had his fill, 'I'd better get goin'.' He climbed into the saddle and leaned down to shake me by the hand. 'You look after yourself, University Man. Write that book.'

'I will. Take care, Bob.'

He gave Elvis a nudge with his heel and rode off. The creak of saddle leather spoke to me long after he had vanished among the trees, the crackle and hum of the bush folding him in to the dreaming of his ancestors.

Reg turned up in the Monaro. When word reached him about what had happened, he had driven straight out to Deep Creek. For him, it was the most logical place to look for us. He knew the cops would be on the lookout for the HD. He thought I might want a lift with him into Kerracan City, where I could pick up Joe's Falcon. He reckoned I had as much of a right to it as anyone else.

The temperature fell quickly after the sun dropped. Jack chucked a log on the fire and we sat round it, hugging our knees. It seemed like years since that first thunderstorm... the flash-flood, the day I met the Harmons. Joe, Jess, Jack... the Anakie pub, Big Bessie, the apricot-yellow... the Scrub Alkies, Hegarty and his murderous pig dogs... yellow-belly fish and home-brew beer... the whole cast and stage-set of a period in my life that would alter what remained of it immeasurably. We would never be here, together, again.

Sparra, I knew, would leave happy in the knowledge that he would go down in gemfields history as the man who blew Hegarty's machinery plant to smithereens. Nobody could take that away from him. Returning to the camp fire after taking a leak behind a tree, I found him standing in front of me. He was about to turn in for the night. He knew Reg was going to take me to Kerracan early in the morning, while it was still dark.

'I'll say goodbye now, Neddy,' he said. He gripped my hand in both of his and shook it hard. 'You stood up for me. I'll never forget that.'

I said, 'You were worth standing up for. That's what it's all about, isn't it Sparra?'

He shook his head, looking at the ground. 'That's just it. I wasn't worth it.'

'What're you talking about?'

He looked up. 'It was me that dobbed you in to Hegarty.'

The corners of his mouth sagged as if pulled down by the weight of the words that had exposed his guilt. My first impulse was to punch it in. I'd had a bit of practice over the past months, I was getting good at it.

'Why?' was all I could say.

'Jessica told me...' he began, and trailed off. 'That day when we went fishin'. I asked her if she'd, you know, come to the pub with me. For a drink, that's all. I just wanted to... you know, I just wanted company.'

'We were living together for Christ's sake, Sparra! Didn't you notice?'

'I know. But I was a bit tanked, and... I always thought the world of her. I always thought, one day...' He couldn't look at me.

'So what did she say?'

'She told me she couldn't have anything to do with me... because she was with you.'

'You got knocked back by her, so you took it out on me.'

'I didn't think they'd put you in gaol, I swear.'

I remembered the shocked look on his face when he turned to see me in the canteen at Muddro; the number of times since then that he'd said, *'I owe you.'* He'd been desperately trying to atone, ever since.

When my anger abated, it occurred to me that he had already redeemed himself. If I hadn't followed Sparra along that ghost-inhabited drive to a pillar thick with gemstone, I would never have got involved with him and the others in hauling it to the surface. If Hegarty hadn't stumbled on us ratting his wash, and taken it off us, we wouldn't have needed to get even. If we hadn't blown his plant to bits, his doomed dogs wouldn't have provided the catharsis necessary to unlock a buried horror that might have haunted me for the rest of my life. I owed Sparra for that. For giving me back my childhood. I could argue that it cancelled out five months of living hell in Muddrington Road gaol.

I said, 'It was a cunt of a thing to do.'

'I know. I tried to make it up to you. I only wanted to blow the wall at Muddro because of you. And I blew Hegarty's plant up for you, didn't I?'

'Jesus, Sparra, you can't go on blasting your way through life with gelignite!'

'It's what I do best.'

Despite the shitty thing he had done to me, I knew I would never forget him. I would dine out on tales of Sparra for years to come.

I said, 'Do me a favour, will you?'

'What's that?'

'Don't do me any more favours. I don't think I'd survive the next one.'

He smiled, like I'd paid him a huge compliment. He gripped my hand again. 'You're a good bloke,' he said. 'They don't come any better. Look after yourself, Neddy.'

He went over to curl up on the ground a short distance from the fire, and was soon asleep.

Jimmy waited till Sparra was settled-in, before coming over to take his place in front of me. He thrust a hand out to grasp mine. I was pleased to find its grip fighting-hard.

'From the day we first met,' he said, 'I knew you were the genuine sixpence.' The trademark grin was in place, with an added touch of solemnity.

I said, 'That goes double for me, Jimmy.'

Les jumped up between us and I ruffled his ears. Jimmy said, 'He'll miss you, silly blessed animal.' He was wrestling with something, searching for the words. 'I suppose you'll be a far cry from here, before you can whistle "Jack be nimble, Jack be quick"!' he exclaimed. I agreed we would all have to move fast once we got out in the open. 'So our paths might never cross under the same bridge again.'

'You never know,' I said. We both knew he was right.

'Joe...' he began, and stopped. Les jumped up again, and he pushed him away. 'The morning of the day Joe... the last day he...'

'The day he died,' I said.

He gave quick little nods of his head. 'We were having a bit of a chin wag, while he was getting his fishing parafamiliar together, and he mentioned your name in the to and fro of the conversation, and, well... he... he liked you a lot, Ned. He liked you very much.'

I said, 'That cuts both ways, Jimmy. Joe was a good bloke.'

'He was going to give me something, to give to you. He said it was very important that you got it.'

'What was it?'

'That's just it, you see, he never told me what it was. He never got the chance. Because the next thing you know...' He brushed at something bothering his eye. He had that same shrunken look about him I had seen in the graveyard. He shivered although, with the fire blazing, it wasn't cold. I could see the right side of him tightening up. When he spoke again, it sounded like a different person, frail and tormented. 'I should've been awake, Ned. That's the long and the short of it.'

'Christ Jimmy, what difference would it have made?'

'I would've been there sooner.'

'But you couldn't have pulled him out. He weighed a bloody ton, you know that.'

'I would've jumped in and got the blasted thing myself!' he blurted out.

'What thing?'

'The blessed tobacco tin. It floated out of his pocket when he fell in, and he was trying to get it back. That's how he drowned.'

'Jack told me he was trying to pull a fish in.'

He shook his head impatiently. Jack had got it all wrong. 'By the time I got there, he...' He couldn't continue. I imagined he was reliving Joe's last futile, watery struggle.

He was too upset to notice a dawning comprehension registering in me. I said, 'Was it the same tobacco tin you gave Jack?'

'Yes. That was the final straw in the ointment! The blessed thing floated across to the other side, anyway. He didn't have to risk his life for it!'

A log on the fire collapsed, splashing ruby-red coals in the grass at our feet. I said, 'I think I got what he wanted you to give me.'

He frowned in puzzlement. I pulled Joe's tobacco tin out of my pocket. I wrestled with the rusted lid.

'Here,' said Jimmy, 'I can be of insistence there.'

I handed him the tin. He gripped the lid in his wiry paws, and twisted it off with little effort. He held the opened tin out.

Nestled on its bed of cotton wool, where Joe had said it would never burn, was the apricot-yellow sapphire. It was burning then, with a fire of its own, its shimmering facets splintered by the light of the stars.

Kerracan Revisited

'Time to make a move, Neddy.' Reg was shaking my shoulder. It was past midnight.

The fire had died to a midden of orange coals. I hugged my jacket about me as I stamped my feet, trying to draw heat from the earth. Jimmy and Sparra were dead to the world. Reg had loaded up the Monaro.

Jack came over from the ute, his arms loaded. He put the pile of stuff, including my rucksack, on the ground, and rubbed the cold air between his hands. 'Like the middle of bloody winter,' he grumbled.

'Bloody freezing,' I agreed. We avoided looking at each other.

I squatted on my haunches, close to the warming coals. The sound of Jimmy's gentle snoring came from behind us. Jack hunkered beside me. He took something off the pile of things and handed it to me.

'I'd like you to have this.'

It was a book. I knew which one, though I could barely see it in the light from the dying fire.

I said, 'This is the only book you own. Don't you want to hang onto it?'

'What'd I just say?'

I nodded. 'Thanks, Jack.'

'Your mother gave it to me.'

I held it down to the glow of the fire, and opened it to the title page. *Gods, Graves and Scholars*, it said. There was a hand-written inscription under it: *Remember me*. There was no signature. I turned it in my hands, half expecting to feel something of her that I would recognise by touch, trapped in its pages.

He said, 'You'll put it to better use than me.'

He pulled the makings from his shirt pocket, and rolled a smoke. 'Anyway,' he said, 'I needed a new dog. Looks like I've got Jimmy into the bargain.'

'You'll miss the gemfields.'

'You're joking! This place is the arse-end of the earth.'

'You stayed here long enough.'

'There was never any reason to leave.' He struck a match and lit up. 'Till now.'

I said, 'What're you going to do?'

'Same thing I've always done, I suppose. Get on with it. Something'll turn up.'

Beside us, the dying fire pulsed like a heart torn from the earth. The darkened bush around us spoke in whispers. The Monaro's engine rumbled.

'You'd better get cracking,' said Jack.

I picked up the rucksack and walked to the car. I got in and he leaned in at the window. He gripped my arm with the same intensity I had felt when I told him I did well in English. 'Look after yourself,' he said. 'I'm proud of you.' He banged the mudguard with the palm of his hand as a signal to Reg to leave, like he couldn't wait to get rid of us.

I looked back after we had travelled fifty yards. I would have waved, but he was busy poking life into the fire. He didn't look up. The darkness swallowed him up.

We took the back route through Reward, by-passing Rubyvale. As we navigated a maze of two-wheel trails through brigalow scrub and emu bush in the dark, the headlight beams picked out tree stumps and rut-holes and bog detours seconds before we were onto them. We took a wrong turn at Reward, and had to back-track two miles. We crossed a swampy section south of Poverty Hill. The Monaro slid into deep ruts scooped out during the Wet and I thought we had come to the end of the line. Reg planted his foot and powered us out of it.

We came out on the road to the Bessies. Jack's empty hut squatted in the dark, up a track running off to the left. I half-expected someone would be lying in wait there, ready to spring onto the middle of the road and flag us down, handcuffs flashing.

We came up over the crest of the hill at Sapphire, and rolled down past Beryl's store. Soon we would be on the unsealed road to Anakie, then the bitumen to Emerald and through to Kerracan City. We were passing the petrol bowser when twin circles of light materialised in the rear-vision mirror. They flashed twice on high beam.

'Shit!' said Reg. I could see he was about to accelerate.

I said, 'Pull over.' I didn't fancy our chances of outrunning a high-powered police car in the Monaro.

He slowed to a halt and cut the ignition. The other car stopped behind us. We heard a door bang shut. Gillespie's face appeared at the window on my side.

'Ned. Like to hop out for a minute?' He was wearing his official look.

I got out and he steered me by the elbow to a spot about twenty feet away, out of earshot of Reg. He grimaced and exhaled noisily. 'Had a visit from Sylvester Hegarty,' he said. 'Can you guess what he might've wanted to see me about?'

Jack had been wrong, I thought. Hegarty wanted his pound of flesh. I said, 'He wouldn't have been after a miner's right, I suppose.'

'Don't play the smart-arse with me, Ned. He's complaining about the destruction of hundreds of thousands of dollars' worth of mining equipment.' His voice dropped to a menacing level. 'This is a bit more serious than driving an unregistered vehicle into town. Know what I mean?' I nodded, wishing he would cut the preliminaries and get it over and done with.

'Anyway,' he continued, like he was giving a press release to a news reporter, 'I have been instructed to check out the known haunts of two individuals wanted for questioning in connection with this matter. I did that,' he paused to slap at a mosquito buzzing his ear, 'and there was nobody home.'

I thought, *'Now who's playing the smart-arse?'* I couldn't work out what sort of game he was playing.

'I will be in touch with my colleagues in Emerald,' he went on, 'to tell them I have received information to the effect that these people were last seen heading in the direction of Barcaldine. Of course...' he paused, the mosquito still bothering him, 'Of course, if the suspects happened to be travelling in the opposite direction, it would mean they might get clean away.'

I said, 'I guess it might.'

He narrowed his eyes to scrutinise me. I steeled myself for the revelation that this was a sick joke he was playing, toying with his victim like a fox with a wounded bird. He said, 'How's the book coming along?'

I couldn't believe it. I said, 'Not good, now you mention it. I'm a bit stuck.'

'You had plenty of time up your sleeve in Muddrington Road, didn't you? Neville tells me you were at it every bloody day!' I gawped. 'Neville Truscott,' he elaborated. 'He's a prison officer at Muddro.'

'Neville...'

'Got a tattoo of a snake on his arm,' he said impatiently.

'Taipan?'

'Taipan! Is that what they call him?' He repeated the name, with a chuckle. 'Neville's my nephew. He's a good kid. No thanks to that pig of a father of his.'

So this was the uncle in the police force, who had tried unsuccessfully to bring Taipan's father to justice. 'Neville's mother is...'

'...Audrey. My sister. She married the Pig when she was seventeen. For the usual reason. He started layin' into her the minute they got back from the honeymoon.' His brow knitted like he was in pain. 'She went blind in one eye. Can you believe somebody would do that to a woman?' He fell silent, mulling over it. 'That prick Hegarty isn't much better,' he observed. 'I hear he used to slap his missus around, too, before she had the good sense to leave him. I can't abide a man who'd hit a woman. It's the worst sin.'

I was wondering why neither uncle nor nephew had bothered to mention the connection they had with each other, when Gillespie supplied the answer.

'I lost touch with young Neville, when he went off sleeper cutting. Then the other day, there was an article in the *Courier Mail* about an inquiry being set up concerning conditions at Muddrington Road gaol. Some toe-rag from down south filed a complaint about the way he'd been treated there. Said they locked him up in a hole in the ground, knocked him around a bit. Neville's name was mentioned. So I looked him up.'

'And when you told him you'd been posted to the gemfields, he remembered that's where I'd come from.'

'Small world, isn't it? I hope he wasn't too hard on you?'

'Not at all. We got along well. We had a shared interest…'

'He told me. Neville's always fancied himself as a bit of a writer. He said you were helping him out.'

'He's coming along nicely,' I lied.

The cop laughed. 'He's convinced he's Ernest-bloody-Hemingway!'

'I think he's aiming higher than that.'

'Anyway, he asked me to give you a message. He said, "Tell him I hope that miserable bastard…" what was his name…?'

'Daniel?'

'That's it. "Tell him I hope Daniel isn't still wandering around feeling sorry for himself". He said you'd know what he meant.'

I said, 'I do. If you're talking to him, tell him he's okay, he's snapped out of it.'

The sky in the east was brightening. From the flat over near the creek, the shrill cackle of a plover faded into the retreating night.

Gillespie sucked in a breath. 'I never saw you today, alright? I'll deny it if you say I have.'

I nodded. 'Thanks, Trevor. I won't forget what you've done.'

'I'd rather you did. By the way, they're going to be on the lookout for that HD of yours. I described it to 'em… told 'em to look out for a Swiss cheese on wheels.'

'It's out at Deep Creek. Reg'll take care of it.'

'Tell him to leave it for a few weeks. And whatever you're driving, steer clear of Emerald, alright?' He patted me on the shoulder. 'You'd better get mobile, or I might have to arrest you.'

We approached Kerracan City at dawn, as quietly as the Monaro's leaky muffler would allow. A dog started barking. It came up the hill, yapping from a safe distance as we rolled to a halt. We got out and walked down the road to the straggle of huts sleeping below. Remnant threads of ground mist rose off patches of grass between the huts, to mingle with smoke drifting from a tin chimney.

I remembered first walking into the place, that night we brought Jess home from the Anakie pub. I had felt like a visiting alien. Now, it had become something beyond a collection of dilapidated shanties, inhabited by a bunch of people I knew nothing about, and didn't care to know more. Back then, I knew Jess, Reg and Becky because they were part of what was happening in my life at the time. Nothing else mattered. Now, it was as if the place was speaking to me for the first time.

Since the encounter with Gillespie, Reg and I had exchanged hardly a word. We had been too wrapped up in our inner thoughts; too concerned with merely making it safely to our destination. Now that we had made it, he said, 'I rang Val the other night.'

'How is she?'

'Real good. Been dry for a coupla months. Spoke to Jess, too. I told her what happened.' A scrawny bantam hen skittered across the road in front of us, chased by a determined rooster. 'It's a shame you two never got a chance to get together again.'

'She wouldn't want anything to do with a criminal like me, would she?'

His mouth twisted wryly. 'She didn't sound too worried about that.'

Becky had opened the front door of the house before we reached it. She was fully dressed, waiting for us. The kids were still asleep. She made us tea. We filled her in on the incident with Gillespie.

Reg disappeared into the bedroom. He came back a few minutes later and chucked me the keys to the Falcon. He said, 'It's got a new battery.' I gave him the keys to the HD, repeating Gillespie's advice not to pick it up until the dust had settled. I said goodbye to Becky, and she wished me luck.

Reg and I went outside. We shook hands and he said, 'If you're ever up this way, you know where to find us.'

I walked back up the two-wheel track cutting between the shanties that was Kerracan's main street. A fresh jungle of kikuyu crawled through the cavities of the dead Chevy resting on its stumps, brake-drum bones exposed. With its motorless bonnet agape, it looked like a giant abstract of the snake's skull I had found near Jimmy's hut. I had put it in my rucksack, as a memento of Joe.

The rising sun struck gold off a grease-smeared pane of rare glass in someone's kitchen wall. There was the faint sound of a motor, receding. At the top of the rise, where the track merged with the horizon, a dust cloud swirled, and dissipated. Out of it, a figure materialised. I stopped walking.

Same height, same slender shoulders, same flashing black hair. Same easy, confident gait. Same voice, when she drew closer.

'How you goin', Neddy?'

'Not too bad, considering. How are you, Jess?'

'Not bad.'

We stood looking at each other while the new day went on around us, brightening, flexing, rustling.

She said, 'Dad told me you were leavin'.'

'Haven't got much choice. I don't think Sylvester's too happy with me at the moment.'

'He never knew how to take a joke.' She flicked hair from her face the way she always did when she smiled. 'Where're you gunna go?'

'As far away as possible.'

She said, 'That's a long way, eh.' She fell in beside me, and we walked together up the slope. 'Did you get the typewriter?'

'I did. It saved my life.'

'Bob reckons you were all nearly millionaires.'

'Nearly.'

A boy and a girl, skinny brown legs white with dust, followed us at a distance. The girl was hauling a brindle-haired pup by a piece of string tied round its neck.

'I'm sorry I didn't get to Joe's funeral,' Jess was saying. 'We miss him around here, silly bugger.' She sniffed. 'He was hopeless at fishin'. I'm not surprised that's what killed him.' I couldn't see the point in telling her what had really happened.

I said, 'Did you give him the apricot-yellow?'

'Yeah. I couldn't keep it, Neddy, it wouldn't have been right. I told him to give it back to you. Did you get it?'

There was a gentle whoosh of air above our heads and a shadow flicked across her face. To a rustle of black wings, a dark shape dropped onto a branch high up in a stringy-bark.

I said, 'Yeah, I got it.' I pulled the tobacco tin from my pocket and put it in her hand. 'Don't give it to anybody else ever again.'

'Somethin' to remember you by, eh.'

The sadness in her voice had been lingering in the dust-haze above the street from that first day we walked up it. The day she thanked me for trying to save her brother's life. A hot, cloudless day like this out of which had roared an angry tide of water that had swept Pauly out of her life and left me in his place. The muddy waters of Deep Creek had cut Joe short of Cape York. Water, in that arid place, gave life and took it with an equal measure of cold-blooded efficiency.

She said, 'I suppose you'll be goin' back to her, will you?'

'Cathie? No.'

'Why not?'

'We just... I don't know.'

'You don't need her anymore?'

'I didn't say that.'

'You didn't have to.'

'Is it so terrible, to need someone?'

'I didn't want to be needed, Neddy. I wanted to be wanted.'

I said, 'I want you now.'

She flapped at a strand of hair drifting across her face. She said, 'I'd come with you, if it wasn't for Mum and the kids.'

'I know.'

We were acting like the Fates had conspired to keep us apart. I believe we both knew it could never have happened. The Fates were merely confirming the inevitable.

She unscrewed the lid of the tin and looked at the stone.

'There isn't another one in the world like it,' I said. 'There never will be.'

She kissed me on the cheek. She put her arms around me and held me, like she didn't want to let go.

The crack of a rifle shot came from somewhere far off. Breakfast for a hungry dog; another one of Hegarty's yearlings gone missing; some hoons taking pot-shots at a road sign. It didn't matter which any more.

She let go of me, and we continued walking. The crow in the stringy-bark caarked dismally. The kids with the dog started throwing stones at it.

'Cut that out, you two,' Jess shouted. 'Go on, bugger off before I sool your olds onto you.' They retreated sullenly. 'And don't let me catch you chuckin' rocks at a crow again, ever.'

The Falcon's busted headlight had been replaced. The allegedly new battery kicked the starter-motor over, just. The engine burbled to life.

Jess rested an elbow on the window frame. 'We had some good times eh, University Man.'

'None better.'

She leaned in to kiss me goodbye. 'Cheeky bugger,' she whispered.

Heeding Gillespie's advice, I took the road north past Rubyvale to bypass Emerald. I came to the T-junction a mile outside Capella. The road straight ahead would take me to Oaky Creek from where I could cut back along coal-mining access roads onto the Capricorn

Highway at Blackwater. From there to Rockhampton, then south to Brisbane and the border. Back the way I had come.

The Falcon's motor idled as I waited for a semi-trailer to cross the intersection, headed north. As it flashed by, its big diesel roaring a defiant warning to anyone in its path, I caught a glimpse of a young bloke sitting in the passenger seat. His eyes seemed fixed on the road ahead and I wondered if his thoughts were intent on some predetermined destination; or if, driven by the winds of chance, he was rushing anxiously into the unknown.

In the vacuum left by the rush of the truck's passing, a hawk returned to the road-kill breakfast from which it had been disturbed. Behind it, on the other side of the road, a green-and-white DMR sign pointed to Emerald to the right, twenty-five miles away. In the opposite direction lay Charters Towers and all points north. The hawk tugged at a stubborn strand of gristle.

I swung the wheel…

Epilogue

'I thought he would've told you,' she says.

'He was trying to protect me. Isn't that what fathers do?' She frowns. 'Once, when he was talking about my mother, he said, "That's what men do, don't they? Protect the woman". And me, I guess.'

'You shouldn't hold that against him.'

'He was protecting me against what I needed to know.'

She balances stiffly on the edge of the room's only chair, ready for flight. Holds the scratched Duralex glass in both hands like she's afraid it will drop. I top it up with the cheap whisky for which I have already apologised.

'Was there any doubt?' I ask.

'I can only tell you what Jack told me. Frank and Alana were barely talking to each other by the time Jack came along. "A poisonous relationship", was the way he described it.'

'It couldn't have been like that in the beginning.'

'Jack never said as much, but it's my guess Frank couldn't give her children. Maybe that's when the rot set in. We'll never know.' She sips the whisky, and sucks her lips.

'Did he talk about me?'

'He couldn't talk about any of it unless he was plastered.' She settles back in the chair. Her mouth purses in a rueful smile. 'That was the price I paid for getting him off the grog. He went back into himself.'

'What did he say? When he was plastered.'

'He blamed himself for what happened to your parents.'

'Should he have?'

'Of course not. That bastard… excuse me… had a right to do what he liked, to Jack, for having an affair with your mother. He had no right to…' she closes her eyes, and opens them again quickly. 'I'm sorry. To think what it must've done to you…' We fall silent for a bit. 'How did you find out he'd died?' she asks.

'It was in the paper. In my line of business, you check the obituaries.'

I laugh. She says, 'What's funny?'

'I found him in the newspaper. And he died there.'

'He was your father, you should respect that.'

'What respect did he show me? He couldn't even bring himself to tell me… to call me his son!' She looks frightened. 'He walked away from me.'

She's watching, waiting for me to calm down. 'He was a bit crazy himself, then. Try to understand that. He hit the grog, but that only made it worse. He honestly believed you were better off without him.'

'He was my father. You just said it.'

'He had a hideous childhood. He wanted better for you.'

'And he was protecting the woman.'

'He loved your mother, you shouldn't feel bitter about that. He wouldn't have wanted you to think she was doing anything wrong.' She drains the glass, and grimaces. 'You're right,' she says. 'It's rotgut,' and we laugh. I top it up for her.

'For whatever reason,' she says, 'the fact is, Jack could never commit to anything.' She sounds bitter, herself.

'I guess that's why he specialised in married women.' I don't say it to be offensive, and she doesn't seem to take it that way.

She angles her head as if to see me better. 'You're taller than I imagined.'

My shoulders ache from the driving. I lean back on the bed on one elbow, balancing the whisky glass. I shift position, to avoid the glare of the naked globe under the dangling milk-glass light shade. 'Why didn't he go with you, when you left the gemfields?'

'I asked him not to.'

'Why?'

'Because I knew he didn't want to. Jack could never be a father. A lover, a protector, yes. Never a father. You should know that.' She peers at me over the rim of her glass, gauging my reaction. She says, 'You'd like Michael.'

I feel close to her in this moment. Something more than the warmth of the whisky. It's the first time we've talked… it could be the last.

'You never got married?'

'No.'

I'm longing for sweat and a ceiling fan; the erotic charge of danger a wall's width away. Deadline panic. Survival adrenaline. I reach for the cigarette pack in my shirt pocket… and push it back.

'It's alright,' she says. 'I don't mind.'

I light up, and reach for the glass ashtray with the chipped edge. Lying beside it is the flattened toy truck from the ruins of Sentry Box, its paint and perspective reduced to a rust-pocked, abstract profile.

She notices it. 'I went out to the old homestead,' I explain. 'That's all that was left.' I pass it to her, and she turns it in her slender fingers. 'We were ten miles from the nearest neighbours with kids. I used to drive over and see them in that.'

'Jack told me you had a good imagination.'

'That's all I had.'

She probably feels sorry for me. People do, when I tell them of my childhood. What she can't know is, I'm feeling elated; a resurgence of that ecstasy of rebirth that flooded in when two monsters sank beneath the earth, and a burnt, bloodied dog made me whole. Once the horror had been exposed, it lost its hold. My life began again. I embraced the fear that had ruled me, and used it to steer a course through my life. Courting danger, recording horror, moulding it into a lifestyle.

'He would've been proud of you.'

'He was. He told me so.'

'I meant, proud of what you've done with your life since then.'

I'm struck by the quiet. In Timor, the nights are alive with noise. The threat of death. Here, west of the Great Dividing Range, the smallest insect sleeps. Life, beyond the double-hung window with its broken sash cord, has gone to ground.

She says, 'Will you go and see him?'

'Michael? Yes, of course.'

'I'm sorry it's been so long. I had no way of finding you.'

'I have to get back to Timor. I had a visa problem, or I wouldn't even be here…'

'He'll wait. He's very patient.'

'He must've got that from you.'

The sad smile. 'Don't be hard on Jack. It turned out worse for him, than for any of us.'

She's right. He did protect us, one way and another. In the end, there was no one to protect him.

'Tell Michael, when I get back from Timor…'

She nods. She puts the empty glass on the dresser, and stands, suddenly formal. 'It's been lovely meeting you.' She extends a hand. Her grip is firm, and lasts longer than required by convention. She kisses me on the cheek, still holding my hand. She says, 'He was right to be proud of you.'

There's a putty-coloured stone block, not much more than a house brick, up one end of the mound of recently-turned earth, conspicuous amongst the half-acre of flatter, weed-encrusted graves with their sagging headstones; his name etched on a brass plaque bolted to it. Must've had it done before she came. I stand looking at it, not knowing what I'm meant to feel. Beneath the mound lies my father, held at bay from the burrowing coffin flies by a flimsy wooden box. With him lies everything that never happened between us. And all that did. He is all that I am, and ever will be. I owe him.

Valentine Press and Leon Saunders welcome feedback on *The Gaze of Dogs.* You can tell us what you think on the Valentine Press website, under the Readers' Comments tab:
 http://valentinepress.com.au/?page_id=1251

www.ingramcontent.com/pod-product-compliance
Ingram Content Group UK Ltd.
Pitfield, Milton Keynes, MK11 3LW, UK
UKHW041432180426
11947UKWH00007B/392